LOST NATION

LOST NATION

Jeffrey Lent

ATLANTIC MONTHLY PRESS
New York

Published simultaneously in Canada
Printed in the United States of America

FIRST EDITION

Library of Congress Cataloging-in-Publications Data
Lent, Jeffrey.
    Lost Nation / by Jeffrey Lent.
        p. cm.
    ISBN 0-87113-843-3
        1. Men—New Hampshire—Fiction.   2. Marginality, Social—Fiction.   3. Wilderness areas—Fiction.   4. Teenage girls—Fiction.   5. New Hampshire—Fiction.   I. Title.

PS3562.E4934 L46 2002
813'.54—dc21   2001056495

Atlantic Monthly Press
841 Broadway
New York, NY 10003

02   03   04   05   10   9   8   7   6   5   4   3   2   1

for Elisabeth Schmitz

LOST NATION

The Year of Our Lord Eighteen Hundred & Thirty-Eight

One

They went on. The man Blood in hobnailed boots and rotting leather breeches and a stinking linen blouse, lank and greasegrimed hair tied at his nape with a thin leather binding cut from a cowhide, goad in hand, staggering at the canted shoulder of the near ox, the girl behind barefoot in a rough shift of the same linen as Blood's shirt, her fancy skirt and bodice in a tight roll jammed down in the back of the cart atop her button-hook boots furred now with green slime, the girl's hair no cleaner than Blood's but untied and tangled, redblonde, her face swollen from the insect delirium that her free hand swiped against, an unceasing ineffectual bat about her head. Her other wrist cinched by a length of the same stripped cowhide tethering her to the rear of the lurching groaning cart. The huge dog trotting on the off side, directly opposite Blood.

The cart was loaded with twin hogsheads of black Barbados rum, smaller casks of powder sealed against moisture with beeswax, pigs of lead, axeheads, a small brass-strapped eight-pound swivel gun without carriage and bolts of plum and violet cloth—this last acquired through whimsy; the bolts were stolen and unwanted and so pressed upon Blood by their most recent possessor and Blood, who knew no thing was free, could not resist the frivolous drygoods. Thinking they might even prove useful in some as yet unseen way. Blood believed there was no happenstance, that all things served a purpose if a man only knew how to look for it. Otherwise, there was nothing but careful forethought in the contents of the cart, right down to the last ounce-weight of pigged lead to powder. So he added papers of pins and ones of needles. And a sack of pewter thimbles. Blood made no mistakes. He'd long since used up his share.

Thus he chose to go up the east side of the mountains instead of following the easier water route of the Connecticut River to the west. Once north of Fryeburg and the Conway intervale there were few people and fewer settlements, and those that were, were less inclined to interfere with questions of any nature. They had paused some days outside of Conway, camping in the woods, not availing themselves of the tavern in the village but allowing word of their presence to seep around the rough bitter populace; here he sold her service to what few men had hard coin which were not many and he was not interested in barter, not yet wanting to accumulate a thing beyond what he already had. Disgusted at the paucity of the place he pushed on, knowing the worst lay ahead. That fact alone delighted him, now faced with the worst, he had the opportunity to wrest himself from it. There was no other possibility. His delight was grim.

For some weeks they had outraced spring even at ox pace but the weather turned and softened as they halted in Conway and so they traveled then with less speed and comfort even as they climbed into the mountains toward the notch and the land beyond, their destination that vast lost land north of the mountains that might have been American or Canadian but of which no men knew or if they did none it seemed cared. The corduroy road, ill-made anyway now began to fall apart and disappear into the frost-ooze, the dank black mud that sucked at the cart wheels so they screeched in their hubs and there was often no way to know what was road and what bog or beaver marsh or simply muddy meadow surrounded by long-dead drowned trees. Their tree-corpses silver and white in the spring light; shorn of their smaller limbs they seemed to Blood to be giants of longlost men, struck mute and helpless where they mired. And then they would pass out of the muck and back into spruce and hemlock forest or hardwood and the road would be there; often not more than a crushed track pressed through the woods lining. And where the mud had not yet broken through the frost there were boulderbacks with faint scars, the sign of some other, earlier, passage. Reassuring to other men perhaps but for Blood nothing but reminder for vigilance.

And everywhere, over everything, as if boiled out of the mud by the sun, the swarms of gnats and blackflies, no-see-ums, clouds in the open bogs like silver glistening screens, lit by the sun, prismatic. Over all open skin and in ears and nostrils and eyes and mouth. As if the land was not enough but the air must join to fight against their traveling. Blood cut a square of cloth from one of the bolts and folded it into a triangle and tied it over his face, just below his eyes. He offered nothing to the girl.

He had purchased her from a gin-sot bawd in Portland in the small hours of a cold early April night, raining there in Maine, the cobbles wet and slick from offal and garbage, rats rampant off the harbor ships, the alleys littered with glass shards that glistened when chance lamplight struck against them. The rain windblown, salt laden, the shifting and supplications rising off the wharf-fettered ships long groans in the night. This Anna far gone with gin hallucination, having lost her night's earnings to him. Blood sat across from her with his toddy of rum, the cards greasy and blunt edged and he chose his moment well, interrupting her keening over her misfortune and offering the eagles back for the girl over one more hand. Anna gathered the cards and spilled them and shuffled them and spilled again and dealt them out, Blood taking his time studying his own as if unsure of his game and the woman suddenly animate, swift and avaricious, her eyes pouched and ruined in red glare, watching while Blood drew and studied and drew again, all the while Anna holding her first draw and Blood called and turned out a straight and the girl and coin were his. By the time they'd roused the sleeping girl Anna was sobbing, bereft, breathless and beseeching. The girl was her daughter. The girl, dressed, stood mute before the spectacle of her mother and the silent ruffian man. As if this had someway already happened to her. Anna was pleading.

Blood said, "Have gratitude woman. A girl is naught but trouble for a mother. She'll fare as well with me as here with you."

Thinking Anna had already paid twice for the girl, the once unknow-
ingly begetting the child and again now, losing all she had been willing
to stake. He led the girl out by the hand and she walked yet silent beside him, taking no leave of her mother. They went through the dead-
dawn streets to the stable where his cart was already laden and where
by lantern light he cut the tether for the girl and goaded up the oxen
from the dirty litter and yoked them and spoke to the big mastiff/wolf-
hound and together the five of them went out through the port onto
the turnpike road inland, away from the coast, toward the small towns
and the mountains beyond. Still raining and the drizzle held back the
dawn so they were well out into the countryside by the time some indeterminate shadowed light filmed over them and the rain turned to sleet
and the caulked shoes of the oxen chipped against the hard road, the
pods of urine-stained ice and packed bleak snow mired in frozen mud.
So the first day passed and they did not speak. Blood had nothing to say
to the girl and she was frightened by her prospects or of him. Perhaps
she even was dumb—either way it did not matter to him.

At night they camped in a riverside glen of elms away from the road
and fed on cold boiled bacon and ship-biscuit crackers and made their
bed under the cart, the cowhide serving as a groundsheet and damp wool
blankets over them and the cold bore down upon them and the girl
pressed up against him.

"They call me Sally," she said. He could smell and feel her breath,
sour after the long day. "I'll work to please you."

He pushed her away from him. "Sleep then," he commanded.

They traveled through the bleak time when the winter has exhausted
itself but still holds the land for near three weeks when they stopped at
Conway and he first sold her out to whomever had the coin and was
willing to lie with her beneath the cart. Just some feet away in the woods
Blood kept a fire going and drank black tea. After the last night of it
there, when they were going ahead into the first warm day and the road
was softening and Blood's head was lifted to study the mountains still
well west and north of them but inevitable as a fist of god, she spoke
up, calling from where she walked barefoot leashed to the back of the
cart.

"That last one, he used me hard. Where he hadn't ought."

He did not look back although the great beast of a dog paused and cocked its head back at her, one foot arrested up before it turned forward again. After a time Blood said, "Some men will." Still not looking back.

The next day he took her skirt and bodice from her and wrapped them in her woolen shawl and set them along with her boots down into a crevice of the cart and left her in her linen shift and he did not need to tell her that it was to save them. It was warm enough with the rough walking to keep her well. But in the muck and mire of the road her feet turned softer even as they tried to blister and toughen and were stabbed through with the spikes of dead branches buried in the road and bruised on hidden stones so that by the end of the first day they were swollen and raw, punctured gruesome things. After she washed them clean in a snowmelt rill he knelt and portioned her a dab of axle grease from the pot suspended under the cart, which she worked into her feet. And each evening he allowed this. She did not know if this was kindness or prudence on his part and only wished that he'd allow her to re-dress her feet also before the start of each day but he did not offer and she did not ask. So far, he had not touched her and she knew enough to know this meant that if he should it would not be a manner she would want or welcome and so intended to keep it that way.

Anyway it was just her feet and the mud wouldn't last forever or the road either. Although she did not allow herself to think about where the end of the road might be. She still bled when she shat. But that would pass and her feet would toughen. The days warmed more although the nights stayed cool. She did not know if they were less cold or if she was getting used to it. They began to climb into the mountains and afternoons she sweated through her shift; then came the blackflies and midges and she ceased her worries over their destination and more than once found herself thinking kindly of Portland until she caught herself, knowing that if nothing else Blood represented prospects as yet unknown, whereas what lay behind her was all too clearly limned. She believed she could endure anything if there was hope for change and she knew that walking with this brooding quick-paced broadbacked man was the best hope for change that had come her way. If pressed she would not have been able to say what exactly she hoped for. But each step forward was one toward that possible unclear clinging thread. Blackflies after all just blackflies and while she could see how a man might lose his mind attempting to get away from them she knew it was a lesser man than Blood was, or herself for that matter. She had no education but a quick mind and saw already that she had learned something from Blood. She was fifteen years old as best she knew.

They passed through a settlement called Errol, a plankbuilt tavern and store and rough log houses. They did not pause there but Sally watched as a woman in clothing as crude as her own came to a rawtimbered door and studied her with open disdain and she thought Women is the same everywhere if they don't know better. They crossed over the Androscoggin River by rude ferry and then for some miles had decent road, the corduroy of logs with bark yet on them firm atop the ground and that afternoon made good time toward the cleft of mountains before them. At dusk Blood clubbed a partridge that stood motionless studying the approaching apparition as if for the bird such strangeness could only be curious and not danger. It was the first fresh meat since he'd bought lean tough pork in Conway, although each day the dog would disappear into the woods and return hours later with blood on his muzzle and the sweet reek of raw meat about him, a smell that overwhelmed her, filled her mouth with saliva that she swallowed over and over as if to find succor there. And now this partridge. When the dusk was all gone to dark but for pale green light off within the trees they made camp and Blood threw the bird for her to pluck while he gathered wood, dead branches broken off the lower reaches of spruce and tamarack, and for the first time made a fire of consequence and roasted the bird. As if he'd passed an invisible line in his mind, a point where some sense of safety gained upon him. Not quite ease but something she could not name. Anyway, the fire was pleasure enough without parsing Blood. Whatever it was she knew it was more than the simple river crossing of the noontime.

The ship-biscuit crackers were gone but there was a sack of wormy meal that she mixed with water and patted into flat cakes to roast on stones turned against the fire. While above the bird dripped and spat grease and blackened on the thick ramrod spit from his rifle. The smell unbearable.

When they finally ate she burned the roof of her mouth on the first hank of breast torn from her half of the bird. Blood had split the carcass evenly and she considered if this was kindness or if he was simply maintaining his investment. For the moment she was happy to be maintained. The corncakes were dry and hard but also hot and she sat on the ground with her legs curled under her to one side and felt for the first time as if, things turned right, she might sometime prosper.

They woke some time of the night to horrific ascending unending screams seemingly rods away in the woods surround. The fire burned down to nothing, a scant mask of color over heaped dead coals. The oxen stamping, trodden beasts chained in place, low moans from them as if they scented their own death. The dog paced the dim rim of light, its hair hackled in a sharp quilled ridge. Blood spoke a low command to the dog, locking it in place even as the girl rolled over and grappled Blood, against and then over him, pressed tight, her hands locked in hard knots that grasped through his linen blouse to clutch the curls of his chest hair and wrapped both her legs in a hard cramp around one of his, it feeling to Blood like her legs encircled his times beyond counting. He was pinned, constrained, snared all ways. Her teeth grazed his neck, terror all through her, a possession absolute, and through her pants of fear her voice choked, begging to be saved.

"It's a cat, girl." His hands up pushing against her shoulders' writhe. "A catamount is all."

"It's after us idn't it? It smells us idn't that right?"

"It's not after nothing. They scream like that."

"No. It's coming. Screaming to scare us witless is what it's doing."

He paused. He'd heard the screams before and always took them to be because the cats could—they could curdle the night and freeze up all living creatures—but he'd never considered it might be for hunting. It was the first rule—the notion of not alerting your prey in any way. But for a moment he reflected on the child logic laid before him. And Sally took that moment to harden her hold of him and his hands were ineffectual against her and so they grappled and he did not hear the cat cry again. But could suddenly smell himself reflected against the girl and could smell her as well, no fresher than himself but still the deep emission of an other, and could taste also the girl of her, the woman, the bitter salt of her skin and the roasted meat breath and the other, the smell of the ocean sea she was born beside. And then got his free leg up, his knee raised as he pulled his heel up for purchase against the ground and he threw her up and not off him for that was not possible and no longer wanted but over where he followed down on top of her and the breath went out of her as her back struck the earth hard and he raised himself and tore up her shift and unbuttoned his flies and sank back against her and he jerked into her but also into the night, into the very earth itself, and the small sounds that came from her were not her child's voice but some other voice altogether as she locked around him and he pressed harder against her, harder to try and drive away the sound of that voice, to drive it out of her. And could do that no more than he could drive it from his own brain. As she spoke, her voice stretched and drawn, that one word Oh Oh Oh over and over and it might have been, surely was, No No No and he would never know how she knew, how it came from her but it burst through him and ran heat through his spine and the tendons of his legs and arms and a scree of chill over him and he clenched his eyes shut and finished in her, already again just the girl Sally. Already back exactly where he was. By a cold dead fire on a cold spring night in the deep north woods, the mountains with names he did not know, the place he was aiming for and did not know either; all this again before him. He lifted himself from her and stepped away, pulling up his breeches as he went.

He went out into the dark and stood there. The dog came up and sniffed and marked a tree and Blood went around to the oxen and tugged the ring in each nose to settle them and he saw there was faint light in the east and turned back to see the girl up, scraping open the fire with a stick and then feeding wood onto the flaring coals. Her shift was on the ground where they had joined and when she bent over the fire her small breasts stayed high and tight against the bones of her ribcage shown in the firelight as bars of orange and black. Her hair down loose shrouding her face, the slight swell of her hips where she squatted.

Blood's groan inaudible to her.

* * *

Midmorning she walked up beside him, a short dangle of the tether displayed from her wrist, the end gnawed and wet. They were climbing into the notch now and the sliced sides of the mountains overshadowed even the thin wedge of sky, far up the slopes bare of trees where sunlight struck off white quartz. The brook alongside the road was overflowing, snowmelt water jammed in the narrow confines of boulder and ledge. The brook was all they could hear, that and the ever-anguishing creak of the cart.

"See," she said, her wrist held up for inspection. "There idn't no need to tie me like a beast. I'm not going nowhere you ain't anyhow."

He called up the team and the oxen stood blowing, heads dragged earthward. He sighed and took up her hand and studied the strap still around her wrist; then he released her and unrolled the cowhide from the cart and cut a new, longer strip while she stood watching him. He made a loop in one end of the thong and caught up both of her hands and bound them together fast so the leather cut into her skin and tied her again to the rear of the cart. He paused a moment and then took up his knife once more and cut off the remnant of the first strap and pitched it into the shadbush growing between the road and the brook and walked back past the cart and took up the goad leaned against the cart wheel and spoke up the oxen and the mean conveyance lurched and ground forward again.

"Treat me how you will," she sang out. "I'll not forget a bit of it."

"I'd not think so," he called back without turning or breaking stride.

Late afternoon found them stalled three hundred yards from the constricted top of the notch, the road here a jumble of boulders and mud-slick gravel, the cart listing off to one side, one wheel mired, the other up on a boulder. The oxen strained to hold the angled rig in place; Blood had stacked stones behind the lifted wheel to help. Now he sat off to one side in a scanty stand of scraggly spruce. Ravens barked from the ridgeline out of sight. The sun was gone although the light streamed high above them. The freed girl hunched on a nearby stone, her arms wrapped around her chest. There was a whetted wind. The axle was broken.

There was a shadow of bruise on her face where he'd slapped her when the catastrophe first occurred and she had turned striving to hide her laughter—a glee he thought edged with excitement, as if immediately she knew the pendulum had swung ever so little toward her in balance. Now she sat, her face vacant, waiting.

Blood held his head with his hands. He was tired and his head hurt. None of the remedies that occurred appealed. He knew in all likelihood in the open land beyond the head of the notch there would be a farm, perhaps more. Perhaps a forge but even if not, probably someone who could help mend the axle, fashion some sort of replacement, whatever was needed to limp onward to wherever a permanent repair could be made. Although uncertainties they struck him as being not unreasonable. The problem, most simply, was how to get here to there.

Even with his head held he knew she was watching him, knew also that if he did not speak she soon would. And silently pleaded for her own silence. He did not feel up to her.

"It's a pickle." Her voice almost gay, only scarcely guarded.

He said nothing, did not lift his head.

"I don't know what's more trouble, the load or me. But I know this: Even I wasn't here that load would set right where it is, regardless of what you was to do. I don't see how you could just leave it, go off for help. Someone might come along. Of course, there's that—someone might come along, be willing to help we waited long enough."

He looked at her now but remained silent.

"How long," she asked, "you think before that might happen?"

After a time he spoke. Slowly. "The way it works, it'd be just a minute I was to leave it here and go after help. But then, we was to set here, we'd likely eat up both the beeves before we saw a single living soul."

She nodded. He wondered if she really understood this, the full implications of this formula and how it applied to their peculiar circumstance. Then recalled her background and guessed likely she did. She said, "What do you figure to do?"

"I don't like any of it."

She nodded again. "One of us has to stay and one go on for help. That's all there is to it. Question is, which one's the better guard?"

"You got that calculated."

She shrugged. "I'm tougher'n dried cod. You was to leave the dog, if he'd stay, and leave me your rifle, I'd do just fine unless it was a passel of em and then likely it wouldn't matter twas you or me here."

"You could as easy see me top the ridge and strike out back the way we come. I got no idea how far it'd be to find repair even of the roughest kind."

"But if I was the one to go after help you'd have no idea when to expect me back. You'd just be setting here. Either way you got to trust me."

"Mind your tongue girl."

"Listen," she said. "I'll whore for you cause I got no choice in it. But it seems to me, we was to work together just the least bit it might not be such a bad thing. You was to trust me some I'd trust you to watch out for me. That's the plain truth."

"You say that now, cold and brokedown. But you'd skedaddle first occasion you thought might be just a smidgen better."

She studied him, raking fingers through her hair, tugging at knots and tangles, freeing bits of twig and trash. She said, "Whoever you are, you're a fearsome man. And wherever you come from I doubt I even want to know about. But I got no choice but to trust you. And I'll tell you this too—I might be off here in the woods set to whore for you when the chance comes but it's still better than what I'd be up to every day back to Portland. At least this is—"

"What," he asked. "What do you call this?"

"Well," she said. "It's interesting, is what it is."

"Christ girl," he said. "Look at you. Half naked, feet all cut up and swelled all over with the fuckin bugs and bout starved to death and you set there and tell me it's interesting."

She stood and stretched her arms up high over her head and he turned his eyes from her and she came and leaned her hands on her knees and brought her face close to his and said, "It takes a rough patch to get you talking, don't it?"

He stood off the stone and stepped around her and bent once more to survey the busted axle. She squatted down beside him to look also. When he glanced to her, she said, "It don't change much, looking at it. Does it now?"

He pushed up, his hands on his knees. She stayed where she was, her face tilted toward him. He said, "All right then. Get your clothes on, your skirt and such."

She stood. "What for?"

He was too tired to tell her to just do it because he said to. He said, "So, if someone does come along, you look respectable."

She stood then too. Looked at him and nodded. Then said, "Is there a name to call you?"

"Name's Blood."

"I mean one I can get off my tongue."

"Get dressed." He turned from her. "Blood's all the name anyone needs of me."

He worked while she knelt at the brook and washed herself. He packed more rocks around and under the cart and levered it up with a stout pole and wedged more rocks to hold it in place. He used the pole as a mallet to remove the cotters from the wheels and pulled them from the axle and then, lying on his back under the cart cursing, worked free the axle. It was near dark, the long spring twilight. He unhitched the oxen and chained one to a tree and strapped the axle across the back of the other. Then stopped and built a fire and hauled in loads of wood so there was a great pile alongside the cart and last he gave her the rifle and told her to just hold it up steady and aim at whomever she might need to and let the dog do the rest. He did not need to tell her the gun was useless after the one charge it held. The dog was called Luther. Blood bent, grunted and lifted it in his arms and placed it atop one of the rum hogsheads and commanded it to stay. He had no idea how long he'd be gone. He took only a single piece of corncake and a moldy chunk of bacon, hoping his scanty rations would reassure her.

He left as the light went purple, not looking back at where she sat up on the other hogshead in her skirt and bodice and shawl, the rifle gripped before her like a talisman. Her feet dangled bare, too swollen to fit into her shoes. The fire burned sufficient beside the cart, the stack of wood high enough so that for the time being at least she could merely lean to feed it. He yupped the laden ox and they went up toward the last feeble light at the crotch of the mountains just above them. By the time he could see out onto the open vastness beyond he could no longer see the cart or her. Just a pale flicker high up where the firelight struck against the bare quartz rock or the last rotten embedment of ice.

* * *

There was a light far out ahead in the vast black bowl of broad long valley surrounded by the mountaintops now low hills rearing also black against the sky. But what he paid first attention to were the stars coruscating overhead, cut off midway to the horizon by a bank of rolled cloud coming from the north-northwest down upon where he stood. The wind that felt so keen down below had lost some bite so he could not say if he faced rain or snow but either way he and the girl were in for it and he hoped they were both equal to whatever came. With this study he placed himself in the otherwise measureless landscape ahead. He rested a hand on the dingy ox-shoulder beside him and yupped it again and moved forward into the night, onward toward the light. Which was soon lost from sight as they descended the valley and into the growth of hardwood and spruce and tamarack forest which surrounded them. The road underfoot firm with frost and back in the woods the snowpack, a luminescent shadow of the night itself. This land stalled in winter.

He told himself it was April and whatever the weather it would change soon. Even a heavy snow would linger but a handful of days. The girl would be all right. The important thing was the glimpsed light. It would've been so natural for it not to have been there at all. He could not predict this land. It was this fact, most simply, that had brought him here.

She had dragged the cowhide up onto the hogshead and had the luxury of both blankets and so was sleeping curled tight to fit the round space but more comfortably than she had since the man took her from Maine. This after supping on the rich hot black tea that he reserved for himself and great rinds of bacon that she could not slice but washed the worst of the mold in the bitter brook water before roasting so the fat spit and burned her face and what mold was left was burned clear and she ate as much for once as she wanted. Sharing the hide-rind with the dog who sat atop its hogshead watching her as if recording her transgressions with some silent stamp. Still, the dog was happy to eat the offered food. All the time with the wind funneled piercing down through the cleft above. But the fire was high and warm and there were no blackflies and she went to sleep with her belly stretched and her mind slowed and easy. So when the enormous hound woke her with his roaring she was blear-eyed and thick-headed.

She thought at first it was the snow the dog sounded, great platelets the size of saucers in a drafty sweep down through the wavering ovoid of firelight, and was scrambling up to her knees and holding the rifle tight as she reached one hand to try and calm Luther when she saw the wolves. Three of them. She had never seen one before but there was no mistake, the nightbeasts shadowed gray against the black, the yellow rimfire eyes turned hot sideways toward her as they moved, pacing back and forth just at the edge of light, the three forms weaving past one another the way water braids through a cat-tail stand. The lone ox was bellowing now also, heaving its weight against the side of the cart as if it might join the dog and girl atop the load, the cart rocking against its terror.

The wolves still had thick winter pelts and against the new-fallen snow and the light of the burned-down fire they appeared to float. They were silent, making a half circle back and forth where the cart was lodged against the steep cliffside of the road, leaping dainty over the brook to keep as close to the cart as they could or would. The ox was down on that open side of the cart and the wolves would make slight feint as they approached and fall back again as they passed, the dog Luther stretched high and quivering on his stoop, howling, extended as far out as he could over the bulging fearful ox, his four legs bunched together, feet jammed against the cask-rim, his head lowered so that he bayed his awful roar down the side of the stricken ox and the sound flowed out toward the wolves.

Sally had her feet pulled under her and her shawl over the flintlock of the rifle although she guessed the cap was already wet from the snow but did not know enough to know what to do about it. Her hands wet and there seemed no way to check it. With her other hand she reached out and dug a hard hold of the heavy hair and fold of skin at the base of the dog's tail and he turned and snarled at her but she gripped harder and shouted at him and he looked at her again and then turned back to the wolves. She would let the wolves eat the ox before she would let the dog off the cart. He was all she had. She thought a moment of Blood returning with a mended axle and only a single ox for a load that needed a team and wished he was here, that he'd waited until morning to set off and then she realized that if the ox was killed they would have to go through something like this all over again and she began to shout at the wolves. At first just words yelled, Git, Git, Git Out Of Here, and then the delicious fever of release came over her and she began just to scream, the high drawn pitched cry of her soul—and her screaming seemed to enthrall the wolves. One sat on its haunches in the snow and tipped back its head and watched her and the other two slipped back a scant pace and weaved among the trees. The one seated then began to howl, its mouth agape to the night and the long cry coming as if answering her. And she screamed back and the hound and ox roared their wails as well and the night filled with this music against the silent old forbearing earth.

One of the other wolves, made bold by the sound or finding it provoking or just too hungry to wait longer made a dash in toward the ox and the ox turned and slashed with a hindfoot that struck nothing but sent the wolf back toward the dark and it was then, still screaming and not knowing what she was doing, that she raised the rifle and did not aim so much as simply hold the howling wolf with her eyes so it was secured under the barrel of the gun and she hammered back the lock and pulled the trigger and the rifle went off with a tremendous concussion that nearly threw her from the hogshead. A glut of powder-smoke sifted through the air and the falling snow was obscured for a moment. And the music was smothered. The first thing she could hear out of the ringing silence was the trifling spatter of snow against the covered ground.

On the evening of the third day Blood returned with the repaired axle, a hindquarter of young moose and a soft-tanned bearskin slung over the back of the ox, coming through the snow that had fallen that first night and most of the following day but was now shrunk back and melting under warm days and the night interval, the snow rotting from the bottom up and so running streams of water in every declivity and pooling in every hoofprint or smallest depression between stones, and found her, back in her shift with her stream-washed clothing hung to dry over a shadbush with swollen buds and the wolf carcass hanging from a tree where she had drawn it up on a length of rope to keep the dog from attacking it, far enough from the cart so the camped ox was calm but close enough to warn off other wolves.

The fire was still going even with the warmth of the day, piled over with fresh spruce boughs to smudge against the blackflies now out and the stack of wood was even greater than what he'd left her with and he stopped above the camp on the track down from the notch and surveyed all this while she stood silent waiting him. And when he finally looked back at her after this long perusal she saw he understood everything, even likely the liberties she'd taken with their provision.

He goaded the loaded ox down the last length of rock-strewn trail.

She said, "I drank up all but the last of the tea. I figured the bounty on that wolf would pay it back."

Blood nodded. He was unstrapping the axle from the load. His leather breeches were soaked through to mid-thigh. He said, "It's a long ways to anyplace might have tea to sell. Or to collect wolf bounty either one."

"Well," she said, "we'll just have to make do then."

He laid the axle next to the cart and took down the rest of the load, setting the bearskin up on the pile of bedding without speaking of it and passed over to her the weight of moose meat. Then he handed her his belt knife and said, "Cut a pair of thick steaks but take that smudge off before you roast them. Cook em slow while I ready the cart. Don't rush it—I'm starved for fresh meat myself but waited to get back here."

"I ate up most of the bacon."

"Get yourself sick?"

"Not hardly."

"I couldn't stomach any more of it myself. I'll miss the tea though."

"There's a mite left."

He was down on his knees, fussing and adjusting the stone tiers holding the cart aloft. Then turned on his back and pushed under it, dragging the axle with him. She used a stick to clear the smudge from the fire and turned to the meat. She had no idea how to cut it but would not ask him and so ran her fingers over the quarter of meat, letting them learn the muscles and tendons and how the bone lay underneath and trying to gauge how to butcher. Then he came out from under the cart, his back and one side streaked and grimed with mud. He held his hand over his eyes against the sun and looked up at her. He said, "When was it you shot the wolf?"

"That first night. When it snowed."

"You reload the rifle?"

"I don't have the first idea how."

He nodded. Then said, "That was some god-awful snow, wasn't it?"

"It weren't so bad."

"Was it just the one wolf?"

"There was three of em."

He studied her. "What happened to the other two?"

"They left."

"Well by Jesus. I bet they did."

She said, "If you got that axle on we could eat and get along. I'm sick of setting here."

Blood sat looking at her. Then he slid down out of sight again under the cart. He heaved and cursed and writhed against the ground, his heels kicking for leverage as he worked. She cut the meat as best she could and hunkered by the heap of coals with two chunks of moose impaled on peeled branches, positioned where she could watch both the cooking and the repair. After a bit he stood and wiped dirt from his face with the grimed back of his hand. Then sat with his legs splayed before him, his bootsoles showing holes. Blood said, "Time comes to collect that bounty, it's not just the tea and bacon gets deducted. But the cost of the ball and cap as well." Watching her.

"That's fair," she said. "You going to charge for my supper here too?"

He stood and wiped his hands on his breeches. "No. No, I don't believe I will."

"Well then. You ready to eat?"

Both squatting before the fire, holding the slow-cooked meat in both hands and eating, he looked across and asked, "Can you sew?"

She shook her head. Chewed and swallowed. "I can mend. Why?"

"Never mind."

Later he left her with the cowhide as a groundsheet and the bearskin to wrap herself in beside the fire and took the foul blankets and himself off into the underbrush and she lay warm listening to him thrash and groan as he turned for comfort against the muck and hard ground and rocks. "Come in by the fire," she called. "Come warm yourself."

No he called back, the word choked as if the thoughts behind it were some kind of bile or vomit he would force down before spewing.

They had traveled from winter through spring back into winter again in the notch and now they would travel spring once more. In the morning they went that final three hundred yards up to the head of the notch before sunup and descended into the valley, into the boundless unbroken northern woods as the sun cleared the mountains behind them and lit the land, a pale washed lambent glow settling on the red buds of the maples and the pale quaver of spring branches. In daylight there was no light to mark the farm far down the valley where Blood had found repair for the axle and purchased the hide and fresh meat, and although he could see the languid lean smoke-rise from the house of the goodwife there, he did not point it out to the girl and she did not see it, so far away and faint it was in the morning sun. The people there had been accommodating and the man indeed had a forge though little custom. He and his wife were pleasant but reserved and the smith made no offer to accompany Blood with the repaired axle. As if they read correctly Blood wanted nothing more of them than what he bought. They were happy enough for the hard coin currency, having already, Blood was sure, a box stuffed with scribbled promissory. More important, they told Blood of the shortcut road north he'd find not more than a mile from the head of the notch, a road coarse and ill-made, largely untraveled but yet one that could save him a week, perhaps more, than if he followed the main road on west beyond their farmstead to the Connecticut River where he would only then turn northward. They warned against the inferior route but in such a way that Blood was convinced they correctly read his desires. He had no interest in the settled towns and expansive farms along the big river valley. If he could circumvent he would. And so the shortcut road.

The girl said nothing when they turned onto the ragged little track studded even at the junction with small stumps and upthrust rocks not cleared from the road and young alders, no more than waist high and lithe as grasses but clear signs of the conditions ahead. She only paused at the junction, still out in the muck of the main road and peered awhile down where they would not be going, as if trying to divine what she was missing. And he did not speak or call out to her but went on, knowing she would follow. She was no longer tied to the back of the cart.

Loosed from her tether, her tongue was set free also. As if some part of her long damped down was allowed to breathe and flare. She chattered along, her words as unencumbered as the rush of water that ran everywhere, small mountain snowmelt brooks making their own brief courses where they must. She was more child than woman then, even if she spoke as a woman and child oftentimes all at once. Blood knew she was freed not once but twice; the once when he'd assaulted her as some demon of his own mind—that had been Blood's first forced hard look at her as something more than a method for possible gain. The second when she'd shot the wolf and for her this had been clear and easy victory—she could take care of herself. And Blood. There was a tenderness in him that he thought had been gone long since. Determined she would never know it, he now thought of her as something out of providence; perhaps, he thought, nothing more than yet another test of his soul.

And like her words the world was coming alive around them, the roadside birds—the waxwings and red-winged blackbirds, nuthatch and robin and chickadee—the birds of winter and summer mixed as easily as the woman and child bound up in the one body, all these seemed to enjoin her to sing out, to cry full throat the day.

Blood could walk miles without once responding to her. There was no need. Everything she said was addressed to him but she expected nothing in return. She would as easily tell herself to the oxen or the hound Luther. Whom she was trying to make a pet of and who would snarl at her if she got too close, ran her hand too long along his back. But who had taken to bringing back from his afternoon disappearances meat for them all, snowshoe hares still in their winter white pelts or ducks or geese ambushed from some thick reeds, once an inedible muskrat. And Blood saw this and knew the dog's loyalty was not redirected but expanding and this troubled him as some outward sign of his own feeble wavering. If Sally saw any of this she did not speak of it. And Blood was sure she saw at least something of it. And so was impressed again by her. And further disturbed within himself.

Could he resent her springtime?

Did he have a choice?

He was a man self-shorn of choice. But he could not stop her and she knew it. If it was a perverse god who had brought her to him he knew also that he was his own agent, he had someway sought her. If a man acts that does not mean it's condoned. And there she was, a pretty little girl with her feet toughened, in her plain shift with her hair loose down her back skipping along to his steady trudge, her hand batting at the blackflies, her life so unexpected, ingenuous with delight.

She said, "I was figuring to slip on out of there someways, anyhow when you come along, I just didn't know how, and then I didn't have to. I had you pegged for a fearsome kind of man right off when she woke me and you were standing back there in the dark of the hall. I thought if it's got to be one that takes me off it might as well be one that others will be feared of. So much the better for me, is what I'm hoping. I might be wrong but I can't help it—it's how my mind works. These black-flies are a plague, idn't that the truth? I never seen nothing like em. But it beats the nits, I give you that. That house was lousy with nits. She bought that special soap off the barber and we all washed with it but some more regular than others. Without naming no names. But, you laid with her, you might like to check yourself good. Not that there's much you could do. 'Cept to stay away from me. I'm clean as a whistle and know it. I check myself every day. She was a bad one for it. Didn't care. I recall once setting to eat and looking over and seen em working in her eyebrows. Just crawling. She'd buy that soap and then not use it. But she had to have it there. Some men was particular about their parts, wanted to wash before and after. It was the old married ones mostly. The young ones, they'd be too worked up to care. Most of em sea-men anyhow and most of them was the ones brought the nits in the first place. I guess. I always thought they was something about like rats—just always there, a part of things. These blackflies they ain't nothing next to nits. You could lay there and pick em off with the tip of a pin, had to pry em off and then crush em with the head of the pin and you could do that all day long and the next day there would be as many as before. The most terrible wicked itch I ever known. You scratch, scratch, scratch and it just makes it worse.

"You're not married are you? You're the most single man I ever seen. She always claimed she was my mother and I guess maybe she was. I couldn't see myself, looking at her, but that don't mean a thing. If she had a clue who fathered me she never let on. I never had but the one name as far as I know. Just Sally. Come to think of it, you see the need for me to have a second name we should talk about that. I wouldn't care to have two but I'd like some say in what the other might be. Just don't spring one on me, introducing me to someone wherever it is we're going. If you have any mind to do that I mean. Not only cause I'd like some say but also I might go ahead and forget what it was and botch things up somehow. I got no objection to just being Sally. Sally's who I am, always has been. Sally and Blood. It makes for an interesting couple, don't it? That fearsome thing you got about you, it just rolls right off up against me, don't it? It would make people curious. Might be, it could work good for us. Whatever it is you got in mind. Although I guess I know well enough what that is. Leastways for me. But"—she turned where she was ahead of him on the path—"that don't mean I won't take what comes my way."

"Why don't you hush," Blood said. "Doesn't your jaw ever get sore with all that jabber?"

"I like you Mister Blood. You're the first man ever in my life I felt like I could say whatever came to mind without him trying to figure out how to get something out of it for himself."

"Well you could take a pause, couldn't you?"

The track ran along the edge of a widespread openland of beaver marsh and ponds, and meadows of harsh wild hay just beginning to green at the base of the dried clumps of last year's grass and they stopped for a night although it was not yet the usual stopping time of dusk. Blood lifted the yoke from the oxen and ran a length of chain between their nose-rings and turned them loose to forage. Sally was already gathering firewood; it was her job and since the wolves she liked a big fire she could feed throughout the night. Blood took a hook and handline and baits of cubed salt pork and caught a string of orange-bellied spotted trout, all the while watching the network of beaver lodges strung throughout the ponds to see if they'd been trapped out or not. He heard at least a couple of warning tail-slaps and saw one swimming and what he thought were young atop one of the more distant lodges. Not perhaps abundance but they hadn't been wiped clean, at least not yet. Some feller would be in here soon enough. He had no traps himself. Beyond all edges, that's what he thought of the trapper's life. The ones he'd known all went crazy or broke or both. Maybe crazy to start with. There was much wrong with himself, a blunt fact, but he was not crazy. And as pleasing as the prospect might seem, it was not for him to do. It was his job to keep himself right where he was. All the time every inch of every way aware of himself. The way a drunk would struggle to keep his finger in a candleflame for the count. Except there was no end to it. And no free drink at the end either.

Picking trout bones from her lips and flicking them into the fire, her mouth shining with grease, she looked up at him and said, "You had to've been to that house before. For her to play cards with you that way."

Blood had been enjoying the quiet. Had even stopped eating to leave the rest of the trout for her, thinking a full belly might send her to sleep and bring quiet if not peace for himself. Now he frowned at her and did not answer. Then wanted one thing made clear and so spoke.

"It was not my habit. But yes, I'd stopped there a time or two. There was a time when she was a fair hand to the cards."

"That gin's something bad. I'd never let myself get like that."

"Nobody ever knows what lies ahead. But you can try and learn I guess."

She nodded. Then said, "So it's awhile you knowed her."

"Some years yes. Infrequent, like I said."

"How many?"

He made a gesture with his hand. He didn't know, wasn't sure. "I couldn't say."

She was quiet a moment, wiping her hands on her shift. Then looked back at him and said, "I'm either fifteen or sixteen, I ain't sure which."

He looked at her a long while. Then he sighed and said, "It hasn't been half that long ago. I know for certain. Don't even be thinking that way."

She nodded and looked away out into the dark. And he thought she was done with it. Then she looked back at him and said, "I don't care

anyways. But, also, I don't see you as the sort would take his own daughter out to whore."

     She had no chance to stir he moved so fast upon her, dragging her
upright by her hair and his free hand slapping one side of her face and
then the other, gripping so hard her eyes bulged and he continued
backhanding her even as she began to scream and beat her through
her screaming until she was broken to soundless sobs, draped down
limp where he held her up by her hair, her eyes white and rolling and
he dropped her then and went to the meadow and brought in the oxen
and hooked their chain to the side of the cart, still not looking at where
the girl lay on the ground, the dog Luther standing near her, looking
neither at her nor at Blood. Who looked away from her and reached
down into the cart and found the cob-stoppered clay demi-john of
Barbados rum and took that up and went out into the woods away
from her.

     After some of the rum he went back in and took up his rifle and
turned back to the woods, then stopped and looked over at where she
lay by the dying fire. She had turned on her stomach and was flat against
the ground. He leaned the rifle against the cart and went over and
dressed up the fire and laid spruce boughs over it to smudge against the
insects. Then got the bearskin from the cart and spread it over her and
retrieved the rifle and went back to the woods.

     He drank no more of the rum and neither did he sleep. Twice he went
in and built the fire back up and smudged it down. At first light she was
still sleeping, now on her side with her knees pulled up. He went past her
and down into the beaver meadow where he stripped off his clothes and
waded out into the snow-shocked water and slid forward into it and swam
until he could not breathe. Came out and stood dripping and looked upon
the day. A delicate blue dawn. Some few high rose clouds in the west.
There was no air moving. Trails of mist smoked off the beaver ponds.
He dressed and went up to what remained of the fire.

     He would sell the girl for good the first chance he found.

Two silent days later they passed the blazes and posts of a surveyor that
cut in a straight line angled across the road. Blood guessed it was a grant
boundary and not some individual's pitch. The day after that the road

took a sharp turn to the northwest, following a river that if his information was correct was a branch of the Dead Diamond. Or perhaps the main stream itself. His inkling was that the land itself was the only source of truth. Even the farmer-smith in the notch valley had been vague.

He did not regret his actions. And he felt her firm-shut mouth was good for her—the world did not reward gladhearts or levity. But yet he missed her prattle. What little of innocence she owned he'd squelched and while it was inevitable, by someone else if not him, he thought it would have been a meager indulgence to have allowed her that enjoyment for whatever time it might have lived on within her. The two of them alone, traveling thus, he could have endured it. He'd taken nothing from her—she'd earned it well and true. Still, he thought, if this be her sole happy time then too bad it must be so short. But then all things were so. More than any other the farce of happiness.

The following day they came upon a dwelling set amongst the trees with no effort of clearing made, a one-room single story palisade of unskinned logs chinked with a slurry of mud and moss and a lean-to roof of great slabs of elm bark held in place with a crosshatch of unpeeled poles woven together. A daub and stone chimney leaned more than stood against one end of the structure. There was the distinct stench of rotting flesh, given off Blood guessed by the flayed carcasses of animals trapped and skinned over the winter and the ones not edible thrown off into the deep-frozen quietude of winter drifts, now come back to haunt the place. Blood guessed also that the trapper did not smell them, sure that the small hot interior had endured the winter with a like reek of flensed pelts, stretched and salted but pungent nonetheless. He whoaed the oxen and halloed the log house. Whoever dwelt there, if he be home, already knew of their presence. It was quiet awhile but Blood stood where he was in the road. The girl mute with hapless downturned head at the rear of the cart. The only sign of life a crew of ravens that lifted out of the woods behind the house when he first called out.

"Make one step, I'll blow you through." The voice came from behind them, from the deep woods across the road from the log house. Blood thought Of course he heard us coming long before we come into sight. Blood was up by the team, armed only with the goad. The rifle was back in the cart. He couldn't see Luther.

He paused a moment before answering. "I was already stopped, you called out. I'm no harm to you, friend."

A long silence. Blood cursed himself. The man, whoever he was, a trapper certain but how insane there was no way to judge. He could shoot Blood and bury him off in a bog and the cart and all the stores would be his. All for Blood's own lack of caution.

Then he heard the man stepping through the underbrush and Blood turned slowly to face him. To show dearth of fear as much as view what was coming.

The man was in filthy imperfectly tanned leather leggings and tall moccasins and a tunic shirt belted around his waist. His hair was loose, in strings pushed behind his ears. His face the color of old brick, not only from sun but also wind and cold, this coloring clouded by a layer of grease and woodsmoke. His eyes bright and dark as river water were neatly focused on Blood, not roaming the cart or the girl, which Blood took as a good sign. He carried a shotgun which Blood guessed carried a heavy charge of buckshot. What would rip a man in two.

"What's your business?"

"Traveling through is all. Up toward the Indian Stream."

The man peered at the cart and back at Blood. "That's not household goods you're freighting."

"No. It's not. I was thinking to do some trade."

"Trade for what?"

"For what there is. I have yet to learn the country."

"Pelts? Furs?"

"Why yes. Could be."

"Mostly what there is. That's worth anything but to barter anyways. Otherwise it's just grain or meal or potash, some charcoal. Maybe a little linsey-woolsey some of the women work. But it's scanty for hard money. Furs is the closest thing you'll find."

"I thought maybe."

"I've got some pelts."

Blood nodded. "I guessed you might. But most of what I've got is in full lots. I'm not set up yet to piece-trade."

"Tell you what," the trapper said. "You look at my bale, then see what you might have handy. It might work out for both of us. It'd save me a trip, maybe."

Blood didn't like it but there was nothing to do. The man still held his shotgun, loose down at his side like it wasn't even there but Blood knew how fast that scatter-gun could rise. As close as they were the man could shoot one handed from the hip. Blood said, "Won't hurt either of us to take a look."

The man stepped up. Extended his hand. "Name's Gandy. I didn't have any idea what was coming along. You're the first white man I seen on this road cepting the survey party last summer. And they didn't want to have much to do with me." He grinned. Broken black and yellow teeth. "I was on the wrong side of their line for them to have any claim on me. And I wouldn't work for em. Wanted me to guide em through the woods. Last thing I wanted, was anybody else knowing how to get around. I've got trouble enough from the Saint Francis heathen."

Blood took the hand and spoke his own name. Then for the first time Gandy looked at Sally. Who was watching both of them. Gandy said, "Is that your woman there?"

Blood said, "She's with me ain't she."

The furs were a prime lot. Marten, fisher, wolverine, lynx, some mink, more of beaver, some white weasel, two black bear hides, all carefully stretched and salted, supple. In a ruder state than Blood had seen before but they looked good to him. About what he'd hoped for. In a separate stinking roll were uncured pelts of what Gandy said were thirteen wolves. Gandy would not untie them but dug his fingers along the edge of the roll to count.

He said, "For the bounty they don't need to be in any special condition. I tried awful hard to get one more. You can't get em in the summer. I hated to end the season on thirteen. But it looks like that's it. Might be the bad luck is the wolves not mine."

The log house was close, smells layered too thick to break apart into any one source but together making the air a paste of dread and death. A hand-split plank table and bench was the only furniture other than a rope-strung bed built into one corner, a mattress of stinking dried rush with no ticking of any sort and a snarl of soiled blankets.

Blood said, "What do you want for them?"

"You're the trader."

"No. Not yet I'm not. I'm not ready to break into my goods. You seen my cart, it's about a load as it is. I'd be pressed to get that bale up on there. I could pay hard money or you could wait and come up to the Indian Stream and find me there."

"I'd do as well to haul em on a hand-sledge over to the Connecticut."

Blood nodded. "It's a hard haul."

"Or I could float em down the Dead Diamond and over to Maine."

Blood said, "You could. And paddle upstream coming back."

"Either way, either place, I know I could get just what I wanted."

"Sounds like, that's the best for you."

"But you're here right now."

"What I need to do, is get on. I need to get set up. You're not the only one'll be coming out of the woods."

Gandy said, "All I really need is powder and shot. And some of whatever you got in them hogsheads. I need a good bit of that. The way I see it, we could be convenient to each other."

"I can't tap a cask here. I'd be sure to loosen the bung on this rough road. I won't risk it."

Gandy's mouth was moist. "What is it anyhow?"

"Black Indies rum."

"Oh my Christ Mister. I'd certain like some of that. All I had this winter was some of that potato licker them farmers make over along the river."

"I've a demi-john near full. That's all but the hogsheads. I'd risk opening a powder keg for you, you wanted enough of that. You got a mold?"

"Yuht."

"There's pigs of lead too. If you could be happy with the powder and lead and a small bit of rum. I'd let you have the rest in coin and come time you run low it'd be an easy hike with no load up to find me. It'd be worth the trip then. It can't be but about a dozen miles. Ain't that right?"

"Sixteen or so to the Connecticut Lake. But it's big country up there. You could be anywheres at all, I came looking."

"I plan to be right in the center of things. A man wants to trade, it's where he needs to be."

Gandy looked around the room as if seeking some answer there. Then he said, "Show me the rum."

* * *

Outside, with the girl watching at a small distance, Gandy hefted the clay john but made no move toward the cob stopper. He leaned toward Blood and said, "It's a rough country up there. There idn't no law but enough people so there's problems. So mostly they solve their own. There's all kinds but each one's ill-disposed to somebody they don't know. They might be glad to see your goods but that don't mean they'll welcome you."

Blood nodded. "I'm not accustomed to welcome."

Gandy thought about that and then said, "How about the girl? Can I get some of her in the trade? Against what's coming to me?"

Blood said, "No."

"It's an awful mean hard winter alone."

"No."

"I don't mean offense."

"No. Listen, figure what you want. Make a total of it and then we'll go over the stock you can get now and I'll make up the rest in cash money. I can't be all day at this."

"Why now," Gandy said. "I thought you'd stop the night."

"We'll be going on."

Gandy said, "If I was a mind for mischief it would be the easiest to let you go along. The pace of an ox team ain't much to match. And I could slip in on you sleeping. So stay the night."

Without raising his voice Blood said, "Luther." The dog came out of the woods silent as a trout in a stream.

Gandy said, "Good God."

Blood said, "You'd never see him coming. I sleep when and where I want to."

"That's the goddamnedest creature I ever saw."

Blood did not smile. "We going to do business or should I call my girl and get on?"

They went on through the dusk and into the night. There was no moon and Blood got down his candle-lantern for the first time and lighted it and left open the slide so he could see the worst of the stumps and rocks ahead. The girl Sally was up on the cart, half-seated, half-wedged against the hogshead to rock against the bale of furs which were rough-lashed with rawhide strings to the top of the load. The stinking wolf skins jammed down in the back corner on top of the skin from her wolf.

"I'm hungry," she said.

"We're not stopping yet. All we have's what's left of the bacon anyhow. If you're famished eat it cold. But don't come crying it makes you sick."

She spat a thick spume of bile. "It makes me retch just thinking of it."

"Then wait. Cooked, it'll freshen up."

"You afeared that man'll follow us?"

"No."

They went on silent. An owl called off in the woods and from another place a different one echoed back. The calling did not frighten her but seemed to soften the night. As if there was something sweet and unknown out within it. She wondered how owls coupled. If they did it flying. She wondered what that might be like. She guessed one owl would be hard-gripped by the talons of the other. She guessed she knew which would be the one gripped, would bleed from the wounds of the mating.

After a time she said, "That trapper-man back there. When he wanted to take part payment in me. How come you to say no?"

Blood said nothing. Going forward at the head of the oxen, goad in one hand tipped back just before their noses to stop them quick, the candle-lantern held high in the other to shine the light. The cart was rocking over uneven ground and she realized they were climbing now, rising slowly up some height of land. The dog Luther was trailing the cart instead of his usual lead or side post. As if he knew without command where his master wanted him.

She had given up on response, had almost regretted asking. Wondering what it would take for her to learn to leave Blood be. When without turning his voice came back in the night.

"I don't know what to do with you."

She thought about that. Long after a sickle moon lifted over the treetops and long after they stopped and made a small fire and cooked bacon he trimmed with his knife and even after she'd rolled herself into the bearskin and the cold night air settled down and promised frost on the hide in the morning. Long after she heard the steady tortured snoring of Blood and after Luther had come in from the night to not lie but sit upright between the two of them, watching out into the midnight. She was still thinking about it the next morning when he roused her with the sun already up and breaking slantwise among the trees. It was the first thing in her mind. And she said nothing. Was determined for once to be silent and wait. She'd discovered that what she knew of men wasn't near what she thought. Not near what there was to know. But maybe Blood was the man to learn from.

Whatever he was, was a way she would like to be. What it was, she thought, was opportunity.

Also she figured not to give him reason to whale upon her again. But would not stop from speaking up if she had to. The rest of it, what lay between her speaking and his reaction, was up to him.

Midday they came out onto the open height of land they'd been climbing toward and paused to survey what spread before them. A little east of north lay a large lake, only partly visible although he could track the vague outline of it by the treeline and the surrounding low hills. From near the lake rose trails of flimsy smoke and further up one hillside was a lush billow where men were burning slash where they were making a field amongst stumps. With the distance they could hear nothing, could not even smell the woodsmoke but there it was. Between where they halted and the lake were a series of low hills and in places he could see silver stands of dead trees marking bogs and beaver marshes. Beyond the lake the land stretched off toward the north in long low ridges. To the east were larger mountains and looking back, southwest, more mountains stood. The shortcut, he saw, had been a good one.

When they camped at dusk they were all but out of food and Blood took his handline and turned rotted logs for grub-baits and went after trout in the roadside brook. After the other night it was almost the last thing he wanted but the only thing worse was alerting the settlement with gunfire. He wanted to come in unexpected. They were close enough now to smell the woodsmoke from the houses and he told Sally to keep the fire low this night. An unneeded caution as the blackflies and midges were swarming from the nearby marsh and she needed a low fire to hold a good smudge. He wasn't worried over the smell of smoke. There was plenty of that. It was light he wanted to avoid. There was no way to know who might be situated so as to look out over this stretch of land.

They ate by that dulled light. If the trout reminded the girl of anything it was only how hungry she was. He studied her, eating. She stripped the meat from the bones with her fingers, as if combing a loved one's hair. When she finished each trout there was a head and tail connected by the bare spine and most of the ribs intact and she would hold each out in the flat of her hand. Luther would take up the offering with mild courteous mouth and they could hear him chewing the bones and head of the fish. When she was done she took herself out into the bushes and then to the brook where she washed her hands and face. Then returned and dug her skirt and bodice and shawl from the cart and shook them out and draped them over a bush to let the night take the wrinkles from them. She sat again and looked at Blood.

"I'll have to walk in barefoot. My feet's too swelled to get my shoes on."

Blood said, "You won't be the only one barefoot there."

"What sort of place is it?"

He shook his head. "I can't tell you much. What I heard it's rough. As you know, it's a good long ways from anywhere else, so it's whatever the people there have made of it."

She was quiet, clearly considering the implications.

After a moment Blood sighed. He spoke again. "However it is, there's a chance there may be someone who thinks they know me, one maybe who's heard something of me. There's stories told of me. You can believe what you want. Just don't bother me with any of it. I won't dispute a word, truth or no."

Saying this he looked severe upon her but once done turned his gaze off into the darkness. Not daring her to probe but unmistakably ending it.

After another time Sally said, "There was people to know them, there could be plenty stories told of me I guess. True and not true, I'm sure. But it don't change who I am."

Blood looked back at her. He said, "Oh, the true ones change you all right. There's just nothing you can do about em."

*   *   *

There was hard frost on them in the morning and she huddled shivering before the small fire and turned journeycake on stones while the
woods about them filled with mist from the unseen marshes, trailing
through the bare gaunt trees in phantom multitudes and the light when
it came was a hard blue that seemed to come from some far more distant sun than the one they knew. Even Blood was shivering where he
hunched.

"Damn it," she said. "Ain't there ever a spring to last?"

"I don't know. I sure hope so."

"It makes me wonder what winter must be like."

"Don't think about it. We got all spring and summer before worrying about that. No telling what winter will bring. Where it'll find us,
you or me both."

By late morning they were sweated through when they came out into
the opening of the first cleared lands although even here north-facing
hillsides held crumbling remnant snowbanks and all meadow edges ran
overflow brooks and they passed through without seeing a dwelling or
person. The field they were in had not been worked but tatters of last
year's cornstalks flagged among the stumps. They came out the far side
of the field beside a flooded river and onto a real road, one mired thick
with a sandy marl and rutted where the ground was firmer and they
went up that toward where they could see woodsmoke and dwellings,
a house of logs some better than the trapper Gandy's but not much and
across from that a larger two-story house of boards beside a mill that
stood where the lake emptied over a ledge into the river. Sally walked
by the side of the road, pressing through close-packed underbrush of
old broken grass and bracken of brown-rotted ferns where here and
there a gray-green uncurled new fern was pushing up. She had her skirt
lifted to her knees and her feet and ankles were overlaid with layers of
dried mud. She carried her shoes in her hand, not as if she would put
them on but to be seen as a person who owned shoes.

A quarter mile before the mill three men came out of it and stood
watching down the road at them and soon another man came from the
log house and joined the first three. None carried guns of any sort but
one in a heavy smock had a sword in his hand and the man from the
log house had a club of firewood with him. The board house had heavy

shutters over the windows and gun-slits cut in the upper story, a small fortress. As Blood watched the house some unseen hand pushed the open front door closed and even this far away he could hear how solidly it shut into the frame.

Sally said, "I'd feel better I could see a woman."

He looked over at her. "Those fellers don't know it yet but they're going to be some glad to see us, is what I think. Also, you might find the women here not as friendly as the men. I might be wrong but that's my guess."

She looked at him as if gauging his intentions but he already was looking ahead up the road. Then he said, "Get back in the road, behind the cart. Walk there with the dog."

So she waded back into the slurry and wordless lurched after the cart which was pitching and heaving side to side as the wheels found irregular frozen foundation deep within the mud. She stepped up and set her shoes in the cart and then fell back a few paces, trudging slow with the waist-high dog beside her. Luther walking through the mud as if it wasn't there. She wanted to rest a palm on his head but did not want to risk rebuff. It was enough he was beside her.

There were stacks of board lumber up on chocks alongside the mill and in a field opposite were a hundred or more logs. The lake stretched capacious beyond the mill, the water blue near to black and glittering as if strewn with chipped and sharded ice. The lake and sky were bright and clean, while the road was a mean puny thing and the four men out awaiting them seemed to be more of the road than of the land around them. She wished the men weren't there at all, that they might just travel through. To where she could not say. Just on into this good day.

Blood halted the cart fifty or sixty yards down the road from where the men stood waiting and walked forward to meet them, carrying with him the ox goad because he already had it in his hand and it was natural to take it with him and would look otherwise were he to lay it up in the cart. Blood was only of medium height but thick-trunked and wide-shouldered, with heavy arms and thighs and the goad itself was a sinister tool; heavy ash-wood with an iron point on the slender ground end and the thick butt capped with bullhide over a brad of lead. He came to a stop a dozen feet from where they clumped, ample room for the goad should he need it. The men were winter-lean save for the stout miller but Blood had long since learned that heft or the lack of it could be a trivial feature in a man.

"Good morning," he said to all or none of them. "Or is it noontime yet?"

"Still forenoon," said the miller. "You carrying an Eastman deed?"

"I'm carrying no deed at all, Eastman or otherwise. I'm not looking to farm but trade." All the men but the miller leaned to peer down the road at the cart. Blood waited, silent.

"Where'd you come from?" The miller again. This brought the attention of the other men back.

Blood determined to take the question in a local manner. "Come up the road through the puckerbrush from the head of the notch."

The man with the firewood club said, "That so."

"It's some rough road."

"You didn't come up through Coos County then?"

"Not that I know. It's not a place I passed through."

The miller frowned at him. "You didn't come through Lancaster?"

"I busted the axle in the notch and there was a farmer with a forge told me there was a shortcut road."

One of the other men said, "David Brown."

Blood nodded. "I believe that's what he called himself." Then, wanting the rest out of the way, added, "The girl and I brought the load out of Portland down in Maine up through Conway and Errol and then through the notch. Then north to here."

"What's in the cart?" One of the other men.

Blood ignored this as bad manners. "The word I got was that a man could make a start for himself here. If that's what he was looking for."

The miller said, "And you have no deed?"

"I didn't know I needed one."

One of the other men smiled. "Most likely, you're better off not having one."

"What you're talking about is land speculators, idn't that so?"

"Honest men that done the work here don't care a whit what some fool paid for and so thinks they own."

"All I own's my stores. Of course, I'd be looking for someplace to set up shop. Someplace not too far out of the way if I can help it. Maybe some feller who things ain't worked out for the way he'd like. But I'm not looking for anything but one where everybody'd benefit."

The miller now said, "You're not after some place in particular? You don't have some one feller's name in mind?"

Blood said, "I've got no tomfoolery about me."

The miller said, "You've got some years on you. To be starting new in a place like this."

"Older men than me have had to start over."

"Now, that's true."

The man with the club said, "There's plenty this time of year discouraged with the outlook. If it was cash money you was talking about." He grinned.

Blood looked hard at him. "When it's the right man I'll make my arrangements with him. To his satisfaction and mine too."

Club said, "I wasn't prying. Spend the winter and see how you sing then."

The miller said, "Every man's business is his own. But there's too few of us here not to watch out for each other."

"Mostly." One of the other men spoke for the first time.

The miller looked at him and back at Blood. "You'll not get rich here."

Blood said nothing to this.

The miller ran his free hand over his face, thumb and fingers kneading cheek muscles. "There's Sam Potter."

"Why yes." Club interrupted.

The miller went on. "Lost his wife trying with their firstborn this winter. Took the piss right out of him. Sold his cow for potato licker and lived on moosemeat and I don't know what. He's young enough but was tender over that girl. I imagine he'd be happy to hump back downcountry, he had something to show for it."

Blood said, "It never makes me happy, to hear of another's misfortune."

The miller nodded. "Everyone gets their share. Some sooner than later."

"That's right. This Potter place, is it off in the woods or someplace people could get to easy?"

"Why it's right down to the mouth of Perry Stream. Most of the land's north-facing but that wouldn't make a difference for you I guess."

"I'd want pasture meadow for the oxen."

"There's a intervale by the dadewater. It's not much but it would do for winter hay. And there's all the upland you could ask for to summer them on."

"Summer," said Club. "Now what's that?"

"You recall," said one of the others. "That's when the sledding gets bad."

Blood said to the miller, "You think I'd find him to home?" Asking far more than he appeared to.

The miller understood this. "He's not taken to woods-running. Just setting with the mope, mostly. You want, I'd walk down there with you."

Blood studied the lake a moment. Then looked at the miller. "It might be less harmful to his pride, I was alone."

"That's right."

Blood said, "I've got powder and pigs of lead. Other goods as well." He glanced toward the board house. "There's some bolts of cloth might be welcome to your women." Then he extended his hand for the miller and said, "Name's Blood."

The miller took up his hand, a short hard grip. "Mister Blood. I'm Emil Chase. Saw your logs or grind your meal. For cash or shares, either one."

Blood looked at the other men but made no effort at introduction. He turned back to Chase and said, "I've got two hogsheads of good Barbados rum as well. I come to terms with young Potter, come down and have a dram."

Chase nodded, promising nothing. Then he could not help himself. "Have you a Christian name?"

Blood stood stone-still, holding the other's eyes. "Just Blood."

Sam Potter was more boy than man and Blood would not allow himself to consider how it must've been only the year before when he brought his young already pregnant wife into this wild land with his head and eyes full of expectant vision, nor would he consider the events that ruined that twist of hope in the boy. He saw how Potter looked at Sally, his eyes raw with hunger and then self-disgust but Blood did not send her from the house; it was not in his interest to diminish Potter's despair.

The pitch was poor enough with few improvements made—the log house was but a single large room with a loft although Potter had taken the time to build a center standing chimney of well-fitted stone and back-to-back fireplaces, the only true measure of the young man's ambitions. The intervale meadow was greening nicely but the hillside pasture was barely halfway cleared, no more than five acres of stumps with slash piles still heaped, not burned over the winter as they should have been. There was a log barn smaller than the house but snug and well-built. Beside it was a small lot barricaded with a tight fence of upright poles. Inside that was a small log pigpen but there were no swine and Blood guessed this had been built for a future that would never be. With the stream yards away there was no spring dug. All in all it was a gloomy place and even cleared of mourning detritus it was not the spot Blood would have hoped for, if he'd hoped for anything specific which he had not: other than by the road which it was and close enough to the mill to be easily incorporated into the rounds and needs of the people. Potter was willing to lose money and most of that he took in a note and Blood was willing to let him, thinking that however the man looked back on this place it would only be grievous anyway and it was not Blood's job to alleviate that even if he was inclined. Which he was not.

But at the last minute, seated at the year-old table hand-worked to love's smoothness, writing out the note for the balance agreed upon, Blood did pause and offer ten more dollars in coin for direct and immediate occupancy, furnishings intact. And so midafternoon Potter hiked south along the road with a rucksack of clothes and what other few items he held dear. Blood had not remained in the house to watch Potter pack but under pretense inspected the barn.

"It idn't much of a house." She stood barefoot on the rough plank floor, sunlight coming skewed through the open door.

Blood said, "It'll do fine. It's got the center chimney, that's the main thing. I can partition off this downstairs and build a counter in one half to set up a store. The rest of it, we make do for living quarters. For now, we just see how it goes."

"That upstairs's nothing but a loft. I work up there, anybody down below will hear every little thing."

Blood went to the door and stood looking out. Then said, "We'll go slow. Get everything set up right."

"I'm awful hungry."

He turned to her. Then drew out the leather pouch he wore around his neck under his blouse and dug and handed her a silver piece from it. "What you do, is walk back up to the mill. Tell Mister Chase I came to terms with young Potter. Ask if we could buy some meal and meat to get us started. Then, whatever he says, make sure you tell him I'd be happy if he was to come for a dram at his convenience. Be polite. If he's got no provender I can likely walk out and find us something, fish or game. All right?"

She nodded. Stood a moment and then went around him and out the door. He called from the doorway before she was out of the mud yard.

"Sally."

She turned.

"Be modest. Don't be bold with him or no other man might be hanging around the mill. Keep your eyes down. To yourself. And if you should meet his woman don't let her pry. You're an orphan girl here to help Mister Blood with his store. My ward. That's all. Do you understand?"

"I ain't in no hurry to whore."

Blood said, "I need to take measure of this country. Cipher the people here. Learn who's who. That's how it works, a new place."

"I'm ignorant," she said. "But I ain't stupid Mister Blood. Long as you keep telling me what you want of me, best as I can, that's what I'll do."

"Sally," he said.

The entire journey lay heavy on him as he stood looking down at her. Not just the cart trek. But along with everything else were the two hogsheads of rum that word was already spreading of and that he needed to get inside before night came down. It was late afternoon and they would come off the cart hard and harder up into the house. If the goddamn door was wide enough for them. Which, one way or another, it would be.

"What is it," she asked.

"Nothing," he said. Then added, "Take the dog with you. I believe he'll serve to discourage anybody gets rude with you."

"I can take care of myself."

"No," he said. "Take the dog. And wear your shawl."

"It ain't cold out."

Blood sighed. "It could be, the time you head back."

She went to the cart setting askew in the yard and dug out her shawl and notwithstanding the afternoon warmth spread it over her shoulders and closed the ends over her breasts. She looked back at Blood. "Is that better?"

Tired, he spoke without thinking. "You're too goddamn pretty for this place."

She tilted her head and looked at him. "I thought that was the idea."

He scowled and shook his head. "Go on. Get us some food if you can."

She walked out to the road, Luther beside her as if he'd heard and understood everything said. At the road edge where it was driest she turned and tramped up toward the mill. For a long moment, Blood stood and watched her go.

He had to knock both door jambs out to get the hogsheads through and then he got the rest of his stores off the cart and piled everything in one far corner and holding an axehead in his hand he used it to hammer the jambs back into place. It was a rough job but would hold the door. There was a twig broom and he used it to sweep the ceilings and walls and then the floor. What he really wanted was to heat water and scrub everything with lye soap and he would've done it if he'd had a brush or lye soap either one. He wanted to rid the house of its mourning, to wash out the young wife and dead infant, the months of the young man's grief, the long winter nights of whiskey-tears and the short days of interminable hours. All the remorse and what-ifs that clung to the place like shipwrecks at the bottom of a harbor, unseen but there certain as the tidewater washed over them. And it would happen, Blood knew. Not this afternoon or evening but over the days, with building the place into a store and letting it fill with new humanity, all the complexions and tonalities of the living. For a house was nothing but the structure its inhabitants erected within the walls. Everything came before passed away. Except in the minds of the living. Those certain rooms remained forever.

The man Blood sat waiting the girl Sally and what she might bring for food as dusk came on that first evening, landed where he hoped to remain as long as fortune turned whatever snarled look she had his way, landed in the far deep reaches of the great northern woods, a place he'd not been driven to by any but himself, as the years passing had drawn him in ever-greater outer rings from where he started.

Blood and Sally supped together on a wheaten loaf that he knew was dear and a piece of brined beef that had already been soaked and slow roasted—the miller's own supper he guessed. And was not happy for it implied debt of some sort. But did not complain to the girl, could not lessen her delight in having been so sharp in her trading. He had fires going in both fireplaces and had dropped the bar on the inside of the door and they ate by the firelight that filled the house with blistering orange tongues of light. Running along and over her face as she tore the soft stewed meat apart with her hands and fed herself, chunks of the bread also. The dog Luther lay silent, unmoving, his head on her near foot. One of his eyes tracking every motion of her hand to her mouth.

"I like that Mister Chase," she said. "The miller. He was kind to me. I didn't care for his wife though. That's a hard worn-down woman, she is. Looked right through me. Like I was taking their last bit of loaf. But he says to me, 'Don't worry about it, dearie.' Said, 'You and that man look like you've a rough bit of trek behind you.' Wasn't after anything but a niceness. I know the difference."

"You leave that miller be."

She looked at him, frustration on her face. "Like I told you, I'm leaving everybody be, less you tell me otherwise. It was you sent me up there. I behaved myself."

"I'm sure of it."

"It ain't going to work good between us, you double-guess everything I already been told once about. I never had no father and ain't looking for one. We're in business together is how I see it—even if there was somewhere to go I wouldn't run off on you, you're the sort would hunt me down and cut me up. Or worse I guess. Although this is one piss-ugly place to choose to set up business. I guess that's the idea. You and me, we're going to be the big show here, idn't that right?"

Blood looked at her. Long enough so she looked away from him. The small tilt of her nose in profile. Her chin just raised, not defiant but making clear she was not scared of him. Which of course she was. Then, Blood still studying her, she raised her hand to her mouth and sucked the meat-grease from her fingers. Afraid and hungry. He wondered what caused him to come to such a land at the spring of the year and not think to find room for more than the single sack of wormy meal, most depleted. Even if the land was full of meat it would be winter-lean. So he paused, his eyes still upon her, pondering if that was the only mistake he'd made. This matter of food was such a simple oversight it worried him. As if some warning of what else he might have missed.

He was tired. He said, "You flap your tongue at me all you want and I'll do my best to bear up under it. But otherwise, the rest of these people here, you keep buttoned up for now. We come up from Portland Maine and anything else, you tell whoever's doing the asking to talk to me. I'm serious as can be. I catch you blabbing on I'll work you over so bad you'll wished I killed you. We can make something out of this place, we watch ourselves sharp to start. You hear me?"

She turned and faced him. Her lips in the firelight grease-stained, fresh as new-cut fruit. She said, "It irks me some to hear you. Ain't you listening to me?"

"You're young. Young forget themselves."

"I ain't that young."

"No. I guess not. But not one of us is ever as smart as we think we are."

She said, "You just speak up, you see me going wrong."

"Don't you back-talk me."

"Idn't there no pleasing you?"

He was quiet then. Sat a time. Considered the gallons of rum just feet away and dismissed the notion. Not now. Not for some time. He wanted to be vigilant as he could be. After a bit he turned to face the girl again. Seated across from him over the lovestruck table, her hands cupping her chin, her face waiting for him, her hair spilling down meager with grease and dirt but pretty around her bright face. She was looking at him with something that might have been affection. Or amusement of some kind. Most likely, he thought, just her paying-attention, ready-to-run face. Practiced and for good reason. He sighed.

He said, "You please me as much as I want pleasing. It's just that what's ahead of us is two three weeks of hard work and tight lips. And after that we'll have this place stitched tight as a mean woman's purse. And those that don't like it can frig themselves in the woods for all I care. That's how it'll be, as long as we step careful at first. It's a lesson in life, one you likely know but maybe never put so many words to it: You let the other feller talk enough and you'll know everything you ever want to know about him. Idn't that right, now?"

"I seen that work."

"I imagine you have. It's like that here, except it's more than one feller. It's the whole place. It's got its own ways and they're going to be somewhat different from what either one of us seen before. So we go easy at first. That's all."

"Let me ask you something."

He wanted to rise. Go outside, walk around studying the sky and the clearing of land. See how things felt. Try and divine if there was any danger working immediate or close. He said, "What is it?"

"Are we partners here? Or do you figure you own me? How's that going to work?"

He studied her. So goddamn young. Still thinking she could inform her life. He said, "I guess that part's up to you."

"What's that mean?"

He stood and stretched. The hound rose with him, also stretching, a shudder running along the ridge of his spine. Blood looked up at the rough rafters of the loft and back to Sally. He said, "That's enough. It was a hard trek here and I'm worn to a nubbin. And we're not even started yet. What I'm going to do is go out and scout around, make sure I feel comfortable to get some sleep. I'll take the dog with me. What you do is bar the door after me and then stand by it, ready to let me in when I holler. It's another thing for you to recall: However good things are you can always depend on them to turn against you. You follow me?"

"That's a shitty deal."

"I didn't bring you here to pamper you."

"I'm not asking for nothing like that."

"I've got no intention to be cruel to you either, you don't demand it. You shouldn't trouble me with this sort of thing. I got enough to worry over. And I'm not as young as you. I'm a tired man tonight. I get back in I plan to make up a bed one side of the chimney and let that heat seep into my bones. You can sleep the other side of the chimney or up in the loft, I don't care. Either way will be better than anything either of us has had in a while. But right now I want you to stand by the door. I won't be long, so long's there's nothing to trouble me out there. After that, we can sleep and worry about the rest of it tomorrow. All right?"

She sat a long moment and then rose and came around the table and stood near. She was so small and he felt her shaking so close to him. Not a fear but some other pulse. As if she would give him something. She said, "You're a strange man, Mister Blood."

He said, "You're the most recent in a long line to make that cipher. There's no help for it, none wanted nor needed. I am who I am and that's not a matter for human eyes to see or judge. But you mean a kindness, Sally. You're a good girl."

"That's not something I've been called before."

"Like I told you, you can't expect what life will bring."

She nodded. Did not move away from him. He was sweating. It was the first time he'd been warm in weeks. He didn't want to leave it but needed the sudden sharp clarity of the cold one last time for the night. He paused and ran his hand over his face, squeezing the muscles, to try and let his eyes open a little wider. To see more clearly.

"By Jesus," he said, "I feel like I been trampled by an elephant."

She stepped back. Then reached one finger out, a delicate tenuous impact that touched just the tip of her chipped and chewed nail to his skin where his linen blouse opened down from his throat onto his chest. Took her hand away and held it with her other before her breast. She said, "What's a elephant?"

Two

High summer. Days carved by the heat, explicit, exact, the world as if new each day. Nights so short as to be little more than a single dream, if the day's labor left any dream room to work. Winter altogether vacant from the land save for the short gnarled trees and the bitter bite of spring water, river water, lake water. As if winter slept in the water.

A man called the Deacon lived in a collapsed cabin built by some long-forgotten departed trapper in the bog up on Coon Brook, dwelt there on the meager rations provided by his negligent god, living his days to a calendar unknown to other men and so his Sabbath day fell not by a simple cycle of seven but according to some reckoning of his strident parched soul. This Sabbath not a single day either but a pilgrimage of however many days and nights without stopping it took him to tramp the rough circuit of dwellings of the Indian Stream country, those hundreds of miles surrounding the four Connecticut lakes.

Regardless of the hour of arrival he'd stand outside and hold forth, his harangue particular and directed, as if the log or frame walls themselves gave forth knowledge of the infirmities of the souls within. It was a mystery what he knew for otherwise he did not venture from his miserable den and would not speak of the everyday when encountered on his rounds. More than once he'd been shot at, not yet with any intent to kill but only to drive him off, the gunner wanting his sleep or dinner in peace. Even if the Deacon's words rang a bright shade too close to true he was tolerated as a nuisance child: not imbecilic but touched, and in such a place this gift was not important but neither was it scorned. Only the Papist Saint Francis Indians avoided him. When he would come upon their trapping encampments, regardless if day or pitch night, they would leave him ranting to rouse and pile their gear and goods onto hand sleds and drag them off into the woods, leaving him with his head tilted to the sky, his words trailing after them as if it were nothing to him if they heard him or not; he was speaking for them. He made no effort to follow them. As if this was not necessary for his commission.

The Deacon came to Blood's door one midmorning. Not his first visit there but the first so public. A gang of men gathered inside and out in the shade of the rock maple relaxing after the morning scythe when the sun burned dry the dew that let the blades cut clean. Men lounging in linen shirts black with sweat, some seated upright, backs against the outside wall with legs splayed full out before them, the blithe exhaustion of work well done. The air steady as water in a bucket. Pewter and tin cups of rum. Clay pipes, smoke a blue pleasant blur to the air, fragrant as the spruce from up hillside. Meadowlarks crying from Blood's own uncut meadow.

Blood himself was inside, in the dim cool, seated high on the stool he'd fashioned from the top of a powder keg and three peeled-pole legs. Behind his plank counter, a tally sheet beside him, a quill and well with ink ground and mixed just that morning. So it was the farmer Cole who spied the figure surging up the road raising his own small devil of dust, a scarecrow in rough linsey-woolsey the burnt black of a dead crow, pantlegs and coat-arms too short so his scabrous wrists and ankles were displayed, the boneyard glimpse calling all to view their own future.

Cole in slow motion was sharpening the blade of his scythe, spitting to whet the stone. His pewter noggin secure against his inner thigh. He said, "Bless the day. Here comes something lively."

One of the Canadian habitants, Laberge, said, "One good swipe that throat be stopped for good."

Cole said, "You Papist bastard, it idn't his fault he puts the fear of God to you. Do you good to mind the Deacon."

"Plenty fear in me, plenty God too. But my business, that's mine. Not his."

Cole grinned at his neighbor. "It do make you uneasy don't it? The way he knows what he hadn't ought. It ain't like nobody talks to him."

"The Devil." Laberge spat and rinsed his throat.

"Oh, I don't reckon so. I guess when he's not out spouting he's shut up in that shack listening to voices you and me can't hear. Or maybe just slipping around with his ear pressed up against walls, doing the same thing. It's one or the other I guess. But he's harmless, less you let him get to you. There ain't no hiding from the Deacon."

"Something wrong with that man."

"Why sure there is. But that ain't a reason to cut his throat or we'd all be dead."

"It be a hard travel to find a priest to hear my confession. So maybe only one two times a year I get before a true man of God. The rest of the time surrounded by heathens. So it is. But I got nothing to hide. Pure is me, pure before God."

"Oh Jesus," said Cole. "Ain't we all."

Blood heard this from inside and frowned. It didn't matter that the men made light of the Deacon—he saw the man as bringing trouble. As if the man gave voice to those few who by nature or some garnered sense of the appropriate had aligned themselves against Blood from his arrival. Mostly women but he did not discount the power of women over their men. Even, perhaps especially, those men who flaunted their wives and came to Blood's for what they would anyway. Blood licked clean the quill tip and laid it atop the tally sheet and waited for the first words to issue from that parchment throat. Both hands flat on the counter but he did not realize he was leaning forward until there came the swift urgent cries from the back of the store, from the log room built onto the domicile end of the house with a single door, from the inside. Sally at work with the young pitch-holder Bacon who'd arrived only days after them to start his work, his wife and children left behind this first season down-river at her parents' home in Bath. Blood didn't blame Sally. She knew what took a man over the top, could gauge it in each and every one of them. But he regretted the timing.

So he rose, pushing himself up with his hands, wiped them on his breeches although they were clean enough, went around the plank counter to stand in the shadow of the open door and watched the shabby devout come on toward the group of men, he alone in his ragged black not arrested by the fierce urging of the girl. But ploughing through the road dust, a filament extended out from him.

The Deacon came to a stop before the group as she sang out. One of the men snorted phlegm-choked laughter. A short bark of wet sound. Then all was quiet.

"Whore-master," cried the Deacon. "The rest of you also. I speak to you all. For what one man provides and another embraces, the second man is as guilty as the first. Nay, I say even more so, for in his taking, in his embracing, by his allowing the supplies of evil to flourish, he makes possible the existence of the first man. So. All should heed. But Whore-master. How come you to this wilderness? What brings you here to this spot near barren of every kind thing needed for simple human sustenance? Why would you descend upon these good people, these people come forth onto this hard land to try to make a simple life for themselves and their families. I speak not of the criminals among them—they know who they are and they know I know it also—it's no mystery to any of us why they are here, beyond the reach of law. That is what they believe. But there is a greater law and all men know this in their hearts. So tell us now, Whore-master, why choose this place to defile with your demons of ruin, your drink, your whore? We'll speak not of that child. Not now. That poor little deformed pretty child you pervert to the lust of any man with a bit of the devil's own coin. We'll not speak of her. But of you, Whore-master. Tell us, tell your new neighbors, tell us all where it is you come from and why. Tell us what has brought you among us?"

Blood stood without moving in the doorway. He heard Sally come into the room behind him. He studied the insane unrestrained eyes of the phantasm stalled now before the group in the yard. The farmers silent, unmoving. None looked at Blood and most looked down or away from the Deacon. Blood said, "She is pretty, idn't she?"

One of the farmers sniggered. Another, out at the edge under the maple shade, stepped off and away around the corner of the store. Blood wondered what he didn't want revealed.

The Deacon said, "Look about you good men. Look sharp neighbors. It's not his drink, not his taking your goods in usurious trade, nor even the corruption of your flesh with the bought services of that poor child, no, it is not these things you should tend to. Although they be enough, and not a man among you knows different, to make you tremble for your measly mortal souls, for your immortal perishment within those same souls. But look to this man before you. Walk up close to him and sniff if you so dare. It is the reek of his bedfellow you'll detect. I promise it as the Lord promises the new day. Who is that bedfellow you might ask? Well yes indeed brothers that is the question before you. Who is that bedfellow?"

Blood stepped down into the scabby yard. Did not look away from the derelict but could feel the eyes of his customers upon him. Appraising, no doubt. Some merely waiting the next step. Which Blood was considering.

One of the farmers, Peter Chase, brother of the immaculate and incorruptible miller, spoke up. "Why yes, I can smell him from here. It's that same sweet stink of sulphur water, ain't it now."

"Yes," said Blood. "I am found out. It's the devil himself visits me every night. Although there is no bed-pleasure. I'm no sodomite. It's been one long card game though, I can tell you that. You see boys, he ain't won my soul yet and it just frustrates the bejesus out of him. Wears me right out, I can tell you. Up night after night after a long day doing my business the best I can. But we're even so far fellers. In fact"—and here he paused and looked around the ring of men, taking each one in his eyes for the briefest of tenures—"in fact, right now I'm one lick ahead in the game."

Laughter. Some few lifted their drinks and sipped, as if no longer caring for the figure out before them in the dust. As if they had been awaiting for someone among them to take this game up and play it with the pious lunatic. As if Blood had stilled what trifling doubts any felt before the Deacon.

Who threw back his head and roared at the heavens. "O Lord deliver us. The Stench and the cloven hoof is loosed upon this blighted land."

One of the men interrupted. "We most all got oxen."

The Deacon did not avert his eyes where he gazed direct it seemed into the sun as if daring it to blind him. "Lord," he implored. "Give these men eyes so they can see. O Lord smite this attendant of the devil. Save these men, Lord, save these lost men."

"Shit," said Cole. "I ain't lost. I know exactly where I am."

Another spoke. "What that poor fool needs is a drink. I ain't cheap, I'll stand him one."

This was enough for Blood. As if a weathercock indicated his customers. So he strode forward toward the Deacon and took the man by his decrepit coat-front and shook him until he looked at Blood. His eyes rolled, but there was no way for Blood to know if this was fear or sunstroke. Blood then held him still and without turning his head called out. "Sally."

She came out from the store and through the group of men and stood by Blood's side. Wearing her one skirt and bodice, now worn thin from washing with hard soap. She smelled fresh to Blood, as if her work with young Bacon had not even raised a sweat on her. Blood stepped now to one side of the Deacon, still clamped to one scrawny elbow. So Sally was before them both. Blood lifted his other hand up and covered the back of the Deacon's head, hair thin and meager, as if the skin over the bone was too poor to produce hair of any substance. Held the head thus to direct his gaze.

Blood said, "Sally, take down your bodice."

She looked at him.

The lounging men heard this and rose and closed upon them, a half-circle not too near but all of them there.

After a moment studying him Sally reached up and opened the buttons so her skin showed from the base of her throat in a long white strip down her breastbone and the swell of her navel to the waistband of her skirt. She looked at Blood.

"Take it off your shoulders."

So she lifted each hand and tugged the sleeves down onto her upper arms so her shoulders were bare and the fabric came away and revealed her breasts.

Blood tipped his head so his mouth was close to the Deacon's ear and said, "Now just look at those bubs. Ain't they the sweetest things you ever saw in your life? I tell you what. You're a poor man. It's no secret. It ain't even anything to be ashamed of. So be honest now. Wouldn't you like some of that? Wouldn't you like to just roll with this girl here?

Ain't it what you really came up here after? To look upon her and go back to your puny little shed and work on yourself as if upon her? Idn't that truly what you're about here?"

The men were silent.

Sally did not move.

The Deacon said, "Lord. Lord, Lord."

Blood said, "All you got to do is tell me that's what you want and you can have her this time, free of charge. But after that it's full price."

"O my good Lord. Help me. Help me now."

Blood said, "You're crying out for Him and you don't see Him but brother, He's right here. Look." He took his hand from the Deacon's head but gripped tight the knob of elbow and with his freed hand took up one of Sally's breasts. He said, "If that idn't God Himself right there I don't know what is. It's what starts us all off in the world. As if God Himself meant us to feed and live through this. And then we keep all our lives returning to it. How's that wrong, you tell me? How could any Lord have made this and not wanted us to come back to it again and again? Why man, it's as perfect a thing there is in all creation. Idn't that so? Just look at it. Tell me it's not."

The Deacon moaned, a sound like the whimper of a horse dying in harness. He made no movement, not trying to get away from Blood or draw closer to the girl.

"Look," said Blood. "I'll show you how it's done." And dropped the elbow and bent and took the girl's nipple in his mouth and stroked it with his tongue and then opened his mouth wide and sucked so near her whole breast filled his mouth. Then stepped back. Her nipple was up hard, swollen and her breast was blushed rose and the blue veins seemed to pulse against the skin as if to break free. Blood looked at the Deacon. "See?"

And a sound came forth from the thin cracked lips even more awful than the last, a sound that had nothing of whatever god in it and the man turned in his black clothing and flapped an awkward, knees-out-to-the-side gallop a short distance down the road where he then stopped and with his back to them bent and beat his hands one after the other into his crotch. From behind it looked as if he were being jerked by invisible strings.

Blood would not watch this mortification but turned back to Sally. The circle of men were gazing after the Deacon. Blood reached out and lifted Sally's bodice and her hands came up to fasten it closed although her eyes were severe and hot on his. He faced away.

The men in the group broke. One began laughing and others also. Then whooping.

Blood spoke to Sally. "Get on to the house." Did not watch her go but turned upon the men who were replaying the Deacon's flight and he spoke. This time his voice a clear command, perhaps brusque. "Stop." They looked at him. He glanced around them but not once down the road, not wanting to see if the figure was still there or had journeyed on. He said, "Finish your cups and settle up. I'm closing for noontime."

It had been a good spring once the trappers started coming out of the woods, enough so Blood was gaining confidence, though one inner eye remained tilted askance. Most of his commerce was in rum—he'd expected this; his sales in lead and gunpowder would gain as the settlers ran low on their own supplies and his convenience would be appreciated.

He'd shipped five cartloads of furs south to Bath, that village the most northern navigable reach for river freight, where he contracted with an agent of a fur house in Boston. Blood himself made only the first of those five journeys: alone, not even taking Luther for company or protection, leaving the dog alongside the girl minding the store. Equipping her with his long rifle, after spending an afternoon teaching her; loading and unloading over and over, measuring the charge, placing the patch, setting the cap—all that a dozen times before he let her make the first shot. By the time he was certain of her ability they had drawn a small crowd by the steady rhythm of the practice and he was satisfied with that also. Let them know she was capable. Sat that night before his departure watching her rub grease into the yellow and purple bruise on her shoulder.

So he traveled with only his goad and confidence to protect him, making the trip down to Bath in a week. He stayed at the public house and ate and drank well—knowing it likely that if he should return again someone would have heard something somewhere about him. So he took minor pleasures and returned north with a new load of rum and some lesser personal goods, candles and such, including small twists of paper holding vegetable seeds and a sack of seed potatoes. He thought Sally might make a garden.

The remaining cartloads went to the same agent with the trapper Gandy as teamster—the agent in Bath had been apprised of this and arrangements made. Gandy only entrusted with the load of rum for the return trip. Sometime later a man working for the agent would ride horseback to deliver the balance of cash money due Blood, the cost of that extra trip deducted. It was the best Blood could come up with short of traveling each time himself. There was some small danger in it but Blood doubted Gandy would flee with the furs or the rum. Altogether it struck him as being more provident than leaving his store in the hands of the girl. Shooter or no, hound or no. And Blood without intent to return to Bath, a quiver of doubt paid true when Gandy returned from his initial journey and looked Blood up and down with the nerve of a man who believes he knows something of another.

His voice soft, his eyes keen, Blood said, "So how did you find Bath?"

Gandy studied him a moment more and then looked off and said, "It's too many people for me. But that feller Moore is all right."

Blood said, "He treat you right?"

Gandy nodded. "Bought me a couple of drinks. Plus he give me the money for a bath at the public house and some new cloth breeches."

"I seen em. They look good."

Gandy scratched at where his winter-beard was freshly gone, the skin there a strange pale white, with only the least tinge of color to it. He said, "He likes to talk, that Moore does."

"I don't care who you listen to," Blood said. "Just so long as you re-call who pays your wages."

Gandy was quiet a time and then looked at Blood. "It's not for noth-ing I live off in the woods like I do."

Blood stacked coins on the counter and pushed them across. "It's not a bad place to be. The woods. As long as you don't mind your own company."

Gandy grinned. "You take off whatever strikes you as fair. I want a night with that girl."

Blood said, "I don't think so. It's not a good idea."

"Why ever not?"

"Well. She works for me and so do you. I got a deal going with each of you and I keep those things neat. Separate."

"Good God man. Have pity. She's the only girl in trade up here."

"You should've considered that you was down to Bath. There's pretty girls serving in the tavern there."

"I know it. I seen em. I didn't have the money though. I hadn't been paid yet."

"Well," Blood said. "Next time you should be all set then."

Three more loads after that. He had enough rum, powder and pigs of lead to go through a long winter and cash money for what he couldn't get in trade. Besides the room built off the back of the house for Sally, he also constructed a double-log storeroom behind the tavern-side. It was no one's business how much inventory he possessed. The door was behind the counter and had a bar set in braces and a great iron padlock and chain running between the middle of the bar and a ring and bolt set into the floor. It was only opened when he was alone.

She had squatted on her heels against the warm southern end of the house watching while he dug up a piece of the streamside meadow, the place that got the best light and was well drained. The earth here had never been turned but once the tough deep roots of the wild hay were cut through and lifted the dirt was dark and dense—a handful would crumble even while staining his hand from the moisture in it. There were few rocks. It was topsoil made from centuries of flood. He turned it three times with the spade, his only tool. He planned to carve her a hoe from a fine shaved plank of ash and bind it to a handle of ironwood. When he was done the plot was even and free of clumps of wild grass. He'd bent over and over while digging to lift up and toss away root-clusters and all but the smallest of stones. It was as fine a garden-piece as he'd ever seen. He went up and sat beside her, his hands stained with earth, his face damp from the work and muscles in his back strained in odd places. As close to happy as he thought he might ever be.

He said, "There's English peas and beet-root and parsnips and white winter pease. And the potatoes. Oh I can almost smell one hot and broke open right now."

She was studying her fingers mingled in her lap. She looked at him through the hair spilling over the down-turned side of her face. "I never cared for potatoes."

"What?"

"We ate potatoes most of the winter. Tough little bitter things, bland even with all the salt to spare and like chewing something been sitting in dishwater. I'm just as happy with the meat and bread. I like that just fine."

He looked at her. He said, "Why girl, there's almost nothing better than a fresh dug potato with a little butter on it. Salt's fine but you don't need it. It's about the finest food there is. Except maybe those green peas fresh out of the pod."

"I never ate no butter."

"Is that so?"

"But it's like milk idn't it? I mean from the same creature so I expect so. I never could stand milk neither. Near makes me puke just thinking of it."

He sat a moment, considering a girl who'd never tasted butter. He could imagine what she'd been served and called milk. And could even guess that the shriveled and sprouting seed potatoes in the sack would look better than any she'd seen. He was quiet.

Suddenly, her tone bright as if she'd hurt his feelings someway she said, "But those peas sound good. I like a soup of em. Get a chunk of salt pork in there and that's some good. I know that."

After a time, only because he had to, he said, "You never had a garden before, have you?"

She looked at him, a little alarmed. "Like I said, meat's fine with me. I like those trout too. You'd show me, I'd bet I could catch a plenty of em for us."

Blood shook his head. "I'll mark your rows and show you how to plant. But you have to tend it."

She sat back and stretched, her elbows lifted beside her head. She said, "I don't see why. You got a good start on it. It was your idea. I don't care a thing about it."

"The thing is," he said slowly, "it's not my job."

"Why'd you start it then?"

He stood up. "I only did the hard part for you. It's a woman's job."

She looked up. "I didn't know I was your woman. I thought I was something else."

"Right now, we're the closest each one of us has to a man and a woman. That's all I have to say about that. Now, I'm going down there and start to plant. And you'd better get your little rear down there and watch what I'm doing because the first time you hoe up even the first potato plant or beet sprout will be an unhappy day for you."

He turned from her and bent and picked up the sack of seed potatoes and the bundles of seed-papers and stalked back down to the turned earth. All joy out of the day. He used a stick to dredge up rows and before he was halfway down the first one on his knees, scattering the small hard near invisible pods of beet-seed she was beside him, not yet on her knees but bent close to watch what he was doing. He did not speak again but to announce at the commencement of each row what the seed was. Then when all was planted he walked back along the rows and covered the seed by collapsing the small ridges with his boot-sole and then broke sticks to mark the ends of each row. Finally he waded into the alder thicket by the streamside and with his beltknife cut young trees and stripped the limbs of their new leaves and brought out these slight skeletons to stick upright in the middle of the rows of pease. Saying only, "This is for the plants to vine up on." Then, done, he turned from her and walked up to the bend above the store where the stream held a deep pocket against the bank and stripped and let himself down into the water and washed himself. After a bit he floated downstream just enough so he could see her pacing up and down the rows as if memorizing them. Or cursing them. He swam back against the current and sat in the pale late-day spring sunlight to dry himself. He waited until it was dusk to dress and go back to the house. He was eaten-up with mosquitoes.

Still, the next load of furs that went south, this being the third of the final five, he sent a letter along with Gandy and so a portion of his payment arrived this one time with Gandy and the hogsheads of rum—a young freshened milk cow. A simple churn wedged between the casks on the back of the cart. Gandy had not tended the cow for the journey home and so it was three days before she would let down milk. Blood squatting on his heels morning and night at her side rubbing her bag and stroking her teats. Until the streams finally came. Blood thinking Good Christ I've turned into a farmer on top of everything else.

It was some time before Sally would try the fresh milk or spread the butter that Blood himself churned on their rough bread and days of silence before she would admit she liked it. Even longer before she would churn the butter. Blood did not ask her to take up the milking. Telling himself not to expect too much from one such as her. But he had grown to like those quiet moments he spent that framed each end of the day beside the cow, when he could rest his head against her warm side and think of nothing at all. That was worth everything. In the end it did not matter that he was the only man not living alone who milked his own cow. Whatever people might think he did not care. It was a simple pleasure.

Sally took up the hoe he made her and worked the garden. And he did not have the first complaint. However it happened, she knew weed from seed and the garden was as clean as any he'd seen. She did the work at dawn, while the soil was still soft with the night dew and the weeds came away cleanly. Times during the day when he knew her to be sleeping he would walk down and not enter but stand and look out over the filling rows and the vees marking her slow bare-footed tread down along them. Something in the impressions left by her feet touched him. He believed this was nothing more than her doing what she'd been told.

Her customers paid her as well as Blood. It took him some time to discover this. When the man came almost immediately back into the public room with his complaint Blood did not blink but told him it was the policy of the house. After the fellow had gone Blood went to her room before she'd finished washing herself at her basin. He stood in the door and watched her. She knew he was there but did not look at him until she was clean and dried and back in her clothes.

She said, "It seems fair to me."

"How do you figure that?"

"There'll come a time, one of us is cold, the other still quick. It happens I'm the one still living I want to be able to do whatever I need to do without starting out from scratch flat on my back somewhere."

"It'll take more than you to kill me."

"I never thought I'd be the one."

He stood looking at her. She looked back at him, arms crossed over her breasts, eyes reasonable, not placid. After a time he asked her what she charged. It was exactly half his price. He considered how many men there had been before one spoke out. Then he said, "Is there anything else we need to discuss?"

"There's some men I won't go with. I ain't a animal."

"I don't blame you, the ones you refuse."

"Well. I need a new dress or two. I can't go on wearing the same clothes forever."

"I asked could you sew."

"Well, I can't. But you got that cloth. Seems we could find some woman who could measure and cut and sew."

He shook his head. "I dress you in that cloth I won't sell the next yard of it."

"That don't change the fact I need some new clothes. A new outfit sparks men up, ones that might've thought they'd lost interest in me."

Blood smiled. Then said, "All right. Use the tape and measure yourself and write it down and next time someone goes to Bath or even down to Lancaster we'll send along an order. Pick your colors but nothing like what I've got in the other room. All right?"

"Who pays for them clothes?"

Blood nodded. "I guess we'd split it."

"Thirds."

"What?"

"I'd pay a third, you the other two. It's how it breaks down now."

"But you'd be the one wearing em. And like you said, something happens to me, why I wouldn't be taking em with me, now would I."

She shook her head. "Thirds. I'm more than just the money men put in your hand. There's plenty come not just to drink but to look on me as well. Ones that wouldn't lie with me except in their heads. So I make you more money than we could sum, most likely."

He was quiet some time. Then he said, "You got it all figured out, don't you?"

"You're the man that knows business."

Blood knew he was not being flattered. It might be one of her gifts but she reserved it for success and expediency. He said, "Think hard on your colors. And write down your measurements."

"I can't."

"You can't what?"

"I can't read the numbers. Nor write nothing down."

Blood studied her. "How do you keep track of your money then?"

"I can do money in my head. I learned that much. I wanted to, I could tell you how much I have. But I couldn't write the figure out."

"All right," Blood said. "I see."

So spent a long hour after closing one night measuring her with his tape and writing these measurements down with his terse descriptions of which body parts the numerals referenced. And noted also that she was not as meager or shrunken as she'd been when he first acquired her. She had fleshed up to a good sturdy body that was now all of a piece and her skin was taut and shining, as if the very life of her came near to overwhelming her body's simple bounds. He was careful and steady with the tape and when finished wrote down the colors she'd chosen and indicated which color was for dress, for skirt, for bodice, for shawl. Then folded the paper in half and placed it under the salt cellar on the table.

After she'd gone to bed he let himself back into the store-side and for the first time poured himself a cup of his own rum and sat there drinking it with only the light of the single candle beside the salt on the table coming slantwise through the open door. Pallid, fluttering light. Nothing like the hot bolt of rum in his throat.

One mid-July dawn Blood was halloed from his bed and went out in his breeches to the already warm, sunless day. It had rained during the night and would rain again by noon. It was a good month since the last of the winter furs had been brought out of the woods and he smelled it before he even opened the door. A handsled stacked high and the load roped down. Something odd atop the load, a rotten pumpkin, a ball of hide and hair. The man calling, the sled-puller, was half-naked also, barefooted, shirtless, his knee breeches fretted and tattered by his passage. His chest and arms and legs bore great welts and cuts, some oozing yellow puss. His hair and beard were grown together, a thick black mass that surrounded his head like a crazed halo and covered halfway down his chest. Matted with twigs, leaves, caked dirt, appearing to sleep not upon but within the ground. He stood before the sled, calm and facing Blood but passing the tumpline back and forth from one hand to the next as if the hauling process were ongoing, as if his motion could not be altogether arrested.

Blood remained just outside the door. A host of flies rose and fell around the sled. It seemed to Blood that even the flies were not sure they should land. He said, "What's this?"

The man peered at him, his eyes so red they seemed on the verge of seeping blood. He said, "It's furs. You're the one buys furs ain't you?"

Blood rubbed his face as if to push sleep away. He was wide awake. He said, "I bought some in the spring. When they was fresh. Whatever else that load is, I can smell from here it's gone off."

"It couldn't be helped. I got here quick as I could. There's been problems." He stepped toward Blood, the fetor coming with him. He dropped the tumpline and stretched a hand, "Simon Crane."

Blood did not move or speak. After a moment he said, "Where'd you come from?"

"Up in the bogs southeast of the Third Lake."

"I can't take your furs."

"Oh no Mister. Don't say that. You got to look at em. It's mostly beaver and mink, some otter too. They's prime furs."

"They don't look so prime. They sure don't smell it either. They been out in the heat awhile. You waited too long."

"There wasn't no helping it. I got em here quick as I could. You got to at least look at em."

"There is nothing," Blood said. "That I have to do."

Simon Crane turned back and went to the sled and picked up the tumpline and dragged the sled a little closer to where Blood stood. Then he dropped the braided rawhide line and walked around the load as if studying it all over again. Finally he stopped and seated himself on the load, facing Blood. As if the most natural thing in the world he reached and rested a hand atop the globe strapped to the load. Blood could see now that, whatever it was, it too was strapped in place with rawhide. Strings put on wet so they shrank and melted partway into the globe. That object was going nowhere.

Crane said, "You got no idear man. What it's like up there. Beaver and mink and marten and every last good thing you could think of but the land is like some froze-over spot of hell. Water everywhere. You'd walk out onto what looked like dry land, some hummock with trees growing in it and you'd be up to your ass in water. Right through the snow. Didn't make one good goddamn how cold it got, that water was everywhere. It's why nobody had trapped it. And we only touched it. We only just got it started. We didn't hardly tap it at all. It'll be good like that three four more years, no one else goes in there. And I tell you what." He looked at Blood then, his head tipped sideways, a grin splitting his face. "There ain't no one going in there. I know it. I seen to it. Ain't that right Wilson?" He turned to face the globe that his hand rested on. And Blood saw the hand stroke the top of the globe, near a caress. And saw the globe rock, shudder, a wavery, watery look to it. As if it would come apart if not for the rawhide lashings.

Blood said, "What's that there?"

"This? Why, this here's Wilson."

Blood took a step closer. A man's head, the flesh black and putrefied, the mouth a taut lipless grin, the eyes gone from the sockets, either rotted away and fallen free or eaten out by something or removed some other way. Blood halted and spoke to Simon Crane. "He don't look so good."

Crane said, "He's the best partner a man could ask for. I would have to say that Wilson is the best. And I'd fight a man would say otherwise."

Blood was fascinated. "How's he so good?"

"Well right off I'd have to say he's agreeable. We don't have no arguments, Wilson and me. But the best part, the best part of all is that he's doing what no other partner could do."

"And what's that?"

"Why he's in two places at once. He's right here alongside where I can see everything he's up to. But he's also back to the camp, keeping track of things there. It would be a tough man would go up against Wilson either way, either place. Like I said, You couldn't ask for a better man to work with."

"How come," Blood asked. "How'd he come to be in two places at once?"

"Well it were easy. When it came down to it. But before that, it was some tough I can tell you. Like I said, there's been problems. To tell the truth Mister, it was not a winter I'd care to go through again. The spring either. And the water wasn't the most of it either. Say, there been any Indians come through here?"

"Not that I know."

"I'm not talking about them Saint Francis people all with their nuts cut off. I'm talking honest-to-god savages. Not but two, maybe three of em. It ain't like I've seen em—no they're too clever for that. But they're out there. Been so right along. I don't know what they are. Sometimes I think they're some sort of ghosts. Except Wilson here he done a fair bit of time with em. Could be Mohawks, maybe even Cree. Wilson never did say. For that matter they might be some band I never even heard of. But they're ugly sons-a-bitches I can tell you that. You sure you ain't seen anything like that?"

"Like I said, no. And I'd know it, I did."

Crane shook his head. "It seems like they're behind me all the time. But I ain't stupid. The rate I been traveling they could've caught up anytime they wanted. So I was sort of thinking maybe they was circling around me. It would be like em to do that. So I just wondered if you'd seen em. Or heard anything."

This time Blood just said, "No." Then after a minute he said, "So what was it happened with Wilson? How'd he get so lucky as to be two places at the same time?"

"The luck's all mine Mister." Crane paused and squinted at Blood. "You ain't wintered here yet."

Blood remained silent.

"It's a hard winter. Hard as Satan's anvil. You look like you can stick it. But there ain't no way to tell. Now, come next March or April, whenever it is you think you'd crack your own head open for a new thing to look at, you remember how lucky you is to be here, where there's mankind coming and going. Even if they be the same measly handful of ugly faces. You bear that in mind."

Blood waited.

"The long and short is it weren't that hard. It was Wilson's time is all. It was either his or mine and I'm just as happy with the result. It was between the two of us is what it was. It was some time simmering, I tell you that. Now listen. You want these furs or not? I ain't got all the day to stand jabbering. Them savages is around somewheres close."

"No," said Blood.

"I'd let em go cheap. I ain't going back up to that bog anyways. Leave it to Wilson, is what I think I'll do."

"No."

"They was prime once," Crane said. "There's some good to em yet. I just need some cash money to travel on."

"No."

"I'd take Wilson with me. For Christ sake man, I'm needing some Christian kindness here." Crane stood from the load and came close to Blood. The smell was someway the most solid part of the man. His redshot eyes were wet, close to tears of some kind.

Crane said, "I split him brisket to breadbasket. I didn't have no choice. It was him or me. Even then the only way I could get him to quit that grin was to cut his head off. And them awful eyes. No man should see such a thing. Not even on his own best partner. I need to quit this country. I need some help man."

Again Blood said, "No."

"I heard you was buying furs." As if he could not get past this idea. That had driven him through however many days and nights, and so could not release Blood from this obligation of his own mind.

Gently Blood said, "They're no good. They're shot. You should just haul em off in the woods and leave em. Give up on em."

His voice a scabbed whisper Crane said, "They're all I got."

Blood paused and then said, "That's a sad fact all right. But I can't help you."

Crane kicked one horn-hard foot in the wet sand of the road. Watching his own foot as if it might turn up the missing answer he sought. Then looked up and said, "I'm well and fucked ain't I?"

Blood looked off at the lowering clouds and then back at the creature before him. He said, "Each man-jack of us is, one way or another."

Crane said, "That ain't no help to me right now."

Blood said, "I didn't intend it to be."

Blood went back inside and shut the door but stood and so heard the blunt hard groan as the man took up the tumpline and drove himself forward, the handsled pulling up from where it had settled in the wet sand and man and burden went slowly away, a receding sound of sucking runners no louder than the pant of the man hauling. After a time Blood went back outside. It was still early. The road was empty but for the skewed tracks of the runners. Where it had stood there was a slight stain where the load had seeped its liquids down. The air was moist, inert, fresh with moisture. Blood considered the taint in the road and the churn of footprints to and fro, then looked up at the lowered sky. As he stood with his face tilted up the first of the new rain began to fall. Small spatters at first. Then a gust of air pressed through the trees and the rain came in hard, straight down and then abruptly sideways. Blood stood until he was mostly wet and then went back inside. He built fires in both fireplaces, small fires that he tended to ward the dampness from the rooms. With the rain stalling their harvest or as excuse to avoid other labors men would flow freely in through the day. He wondered if any others had seen the carrion voyage this morning. It was possible some had been about that early. He hoped not. It was not anything he wanted to talk over. Or even listen to.

Two mornings following he awakened early to the smell of tobacco smoke. The night had only begun to slip back, nearby trees mere dim presence, gray shadows. No more than quarter past three. The rain had passed and the weather cleared and so was cool, chill with the dew and mist off the lake this time of day and so he dressed fully and stepped to the door where the hound lay, wide awake and silent, his head tipped up and his hairline raised. Blood knelt and whispered the dog to Stay and opened the door and stepped out, letting the door settle back into the frame but not shut tight.

A pair of Indians sat against the side of the store, hunkered with their knees up before them, their thighs bunched muscles against their ankles. Naked but for loincloths and moosehide moccasins and the straps and pouches of some considerable arsenal. Both had muskets and huge Canadian hunting knives in soft-worn sheaths, and the rest of their accoutrement consisted of supplies for the muskets. One was smoking a short-handled clay pipe and the other sat with a handful of the not-quite-ripe English peas from the garden, slitting the pod with a thumbnail and then running his thumb back up to free the small fruits and tip them into his mouth as a powder off a paper. A pile of empty peapods lay between his feet. Blood had been watching these peas ripen. He stood before the wild men and said nothing. When the pea-eater was done with his handful he rose and spoke to Blood in a tongue Blood did not know.

Blood asked if they spoke English.

They looked at him.

He tried again, this time in French.

They looked at him, faces immutable.

Then he considered and after a moment of recollection asked twice more, first in Latin and then Greek. Not only for the small pleasure of the recall but more to impress; if he did not know their tongue they also did not know the variety he occupied.

They said nothing more to him. The pipe-smoker rose and leaned forward and staggered a short distance down the road, his free arm stretched taut behind him, a rudder for a ship gone aground. Then he turned abruptly and, full upright, slashed his free hand against his throat. Looked at Blood with nothing quizzical in his gaze, as if knowing Blood held the answer he sought.

Blood nodded. Then held up two fingers and passed them in the air in a small circle. Two days. Then pointed down the road.

The pipe-smoker stepped and came close to Blood and stood looking at him. Blood shook his head. The pipe-smoker waited a long beat and then nodded. He started to turn and his companion caught his arm and delayed him. The pea-eater then looked at Blood and raised his hand in a drinking gesture. Blood did not move, did not change expression. Only looked at the man. Then slowly shook his head. The pipe-smoker turned again and again the pea-eater caught his arm. This time Blood spoke. "Luther."

The hound nosed the door and stood looking out at them. The savages looked at the beast and back to Blood. This time Blood smiled a moment before he shook his head once more.

The pipe-smoker bobbed his head once at Blood. Then stepped out of the hold of his fellow and turned and went at a slow lope down the road the way Blood had pointed, his pouches and powder flask bouncing in even motion as he went. The pea-eater watched his partner a moment and then followed, not looking at Blood until he was a hundred feet or so down the road when he flashed his face back once over his shoulder. As if to tell Blood something. Perhaps to warn of possible return.

Blood spoke as if the man were still next to him. "You do it, bastard. But give it another week so what's left of those peas'll be ripe."

Blood's measurements were good ones. The bundle of new clothes arrived and fit Sally well. In this place of drab linsey-woolsey she was an indigo bunting, a scarlet tanager, a bluebird among the sparrows and wrens of the women residing. If this raiment marked her more clearly to those same women she did not care; she had no friends among them and expected none. If they saw her as some broken vision conjured by the worst of what dwelt in their men she saw herself otherwise—as beyond all men, all time, all places or situations. She understood herself to be free of all that bound those women to this place. Even as she herself was bound in other ways to Blood. They were partners was how she saw it. Even if she was not equal to him in their partnership. What woman was? She could pick and choose whom she took into her bed. She might wear what she wanted, as little or much of it as pleased her. She slept in, ate when she wanted of what there was and took pleasure in the late nights of the store which more and more clearly to Blood was becoming a tavern and not a store at all. His bolts of impetuous cloth lay uncut.

Twice a week early morn, though it meant a short night of sleep, she gardened. She found that she enjoyed the mild work, the stretch and strain of her muscles in the cool damp summer dawns, the dig of her toes in the soft crumbling earth, took pleasure in how tending the plants produced fresh sweet food. Was as amazed as Blood had forewarned with the rich steaming broken-open new potato, a taste that she thought of as the earth itself passed through some invisible hands to render it this sweet white flesh. And most simply loved the quiet time of it where her body and mind folded all to one without her ever having to consider the needs or desires of another. And so learned the grace of simple work. And the attendant grace of solitude. A child of a whorehouse, a simple garden was not some chimera of paradise—it was wholly and directly what it was. A place where things grew and she the mistress of this. A garden of food. Among all the other things it allowed her to understand appetite. She who had only known hunger.

She wore her old shift to garden in. The sun would be up when she finished and she would carry whatever she had picked to the kitchen table and then go out again up through the meadow intervale of swale hay to the curve of the stream to bathe, walking back down drying inside her rough smock, going into her small room to dress then for the day. And come out to drink the sweet milk still warm from the cow and eat lightbread spread with the butter she'd finally learned to churn and be seated there, a sight for the men coming in for their early morning tots of rum. To remind them she was there. As if any had forgotten.

She implored Blood until he finally consented and cut her a small window high up in her room. Before this, she would swelter there on summer afternoons and into the long evenings. The window was cut high and narrow, to blunt any attempt at spying upon her, perhaps also to make impossible her taking any illicit trade. She did not complain. It let in air and some light. Lying under the shudder and spasm of one man or another it gave her a tender slice of sky to gaze toward. Alone at the end of the night she could look out upon the stars. A narrow rectangle of moonlight would track over her bed.

The time had arrived to fortify against all unforeseen possibilities—Blood expected and desired no troubles but it had not been whim that caused him to bring the small cannon north with him. And from the first morning when he scanned the miller's house and saw the double shutters and gun slits he'd known his impulse had been correct. It was winter he feared, a hard time in this place and when any number of men might grow mad as the season ground on and their own supplies fell short and lucid thought was replaced with more outlandish schemes or notions.

So he buttressed the loft from below with posts of peeled whole trees and then built in the loft a rude carriage for the swivel gun and mounted it there. He cut a narrow three-foot-long section from the roof that allowed the muzzle of the gun to look out upon the yard of the tavern, end to end. He fashioned a tight shutter to fit the gap, the shutter secured by a double length of gut that ran back taut to a rafter above the gun carriage so it could be cut to fall open. He laid beside the gun a supply of charges. He had no cannonballs and wanted none. Among the supplies was a keg of musket balls and each charge would take a double-handful of them. As badly as he wanted to see how wide a swath one charge would cut in the trampled yard he resisted the urge to testfire. There was no reason to doubt that the damage would be considerable. Beyond that, he counted on the terror such a surprise would provide.

Simon Crane's body was found high up alongside a brook that fed east into Indian Stream by a new settler making his pitch far up the Stream, found when the man was seeking a wandered cow soon to freshen. A crew of ravens alerted him. He feared a wolf-killed newborn calf. He forgot directly the cow and came down to report and seek help—to have other men see what he saw. Blood did not go with the party and they brought no body out with them, burying Crane there deep in the woods but Blood heard plenty about it.

Crane had been bound hand and foot, his arms tight to his sides, and buried up to his neck in a small beaver bog that was boiling with mosquitoes and deerflies. Very precisely his eyelids had been cut away. Not the sort of wounds that would allow a man to lose consciousness. Not anytime soon at least. The load of stinking furs was nearby. No one mentioned another head and Blood did not ask. Whoever had put Crane in the bog had taken Wilson with them.

The men overflowed the room, milling in the yard. When the long twilight deepened they prevailed upon Blood and built a bonfire in the road. Early on, after the initial party had returned, two men had ridden horseback to find the cabin and seek Wilson, to either inform him or see if he had disappeared. Blood let them go. Among his reasons was his curiosity to learn what the rest of Wilson was up to.

The horsemen were back soon after dark to tell of Wilson decomposed but upright in a chair, lashed in place with old rawhide, the lacings ineffectual sutures against the spillage of his insides from being cleaved from his throat to his scrotum. His head was gone. The men had left him there. It would take more than two men to bury him and other than a cart or sled there was no way to bring him in—already he was falling apart like an overcooked chicken.

Blood was behind the counter, leaned forward with his forearms on the rum-run boards to listen. Sally sat up on the stool nearby, mute, unnoticed by the men. Emil Chase arrived, his first time inside the tavern although he'd twice delivered orders of sawn timber daytimes. He came to the center of the room and removed his hat and held it before him as either a vessel or to ward off something of the room and said, "What do we have here." It was not quite a question. He already knew as much as the others.

Cole, one of the riders, said, "Somebody killed them two trappers. Each one different but each one horrible."

Gandy spoke up. "You got to consider that whoever killed Crane was not certain the same as killed Wilson."

"Why?" Chase said.

"Well. First off, I knowed them two. They made a strange pair. They was partners and had been some time but you couldn't say they liked each other. Whenever I seen em they was bickering about one thing or another. Worse than two old women they was. Except, there was a meanness between em. Plus, you got to wonder where Wilson's head is at."

Chase said, "It was not on him?"

Cole said, "It wasn't nowhere that we saw."

John Burt, another of the summer's new pitch holders said, "Someone ought to send down to Lancaster for the Coos high sheriff."

Chase turned to him and said, "You think so."

"Well it's a heinous thing."

Chase said, "I don't know you."

Burt introduced himself.

Chase said, "That doesn't mean anything to me. John Burt. And there's nothing to stop you from being the one to ride to Lancaster and find Sheriff Hutchinson and he'd be plenty pleased to ride up here and poke around. Maybe poke a little further than even you might like, John Burt. Or if not you then maybe some of your neighbors. For that matter, you want to fetch a New Hampshire sheriff in here then you might as well go on over to Saint-Hereford or whatever-it's-called there in Canada and talk to the magistrate they got. We be somewhere between Canada and New Hampshire you know. Just where is pretty much left up to each man every day to decide. Some would have it one way, some the other. Some have good strong reasons for their choice. You might think on that too, John Burt."

Cole said, "We don't need anybody from outside in this. It's trouble enough."

Another man said, "They was just a pair of crusty old sons-a-bitching trappers anyhow, God rest their souls."

Cole said, "It sure wasn't Wilson buried Crane in that bog. Wilson has been right where he is some ripe time, I can tell you that."

Gandy said, "Wilson run with some Indians time to time. True savages from I don't know where. Mohawks from over to York State I think."

Emil Chase turned his hat over and looked in it and looked back at Gandy. "You think they killed Wilson?"

Gandy drank off his rum and set the tin cup on the counter and Blood refilled it. Gandy left it sitting. His expertise was rare. He shoved his hands under the waistband of his breeches and said, "They could of. I'd suspect that type capable of anything. But then you got to wonder two things."

Chase was irritable. He was terse. "What's that?"

"Well, like I said, you got to consider his head ain't there. And if they killed Wilson why'd they lead or track poor Simon Crane all the way to hell and gone before they done him. Now, Wilson, that sort of killing, that could've been done by any simpleton. But the way Crane was killed, there's a talent to that."

Chase said, "So you think Crane killed Wilson and what may or may not have been Indians killed Crane?"

Gandy thought a moment before committing, sensing Chase was near done with him. The circle of men all leaning toward him. He took up his cup and sipped and nodded. "It was Indians all right that killed Crane. And I'm betting it was him that done in Wilson. After all, there was that sled of furs setting not ten feet from where they sank poor Simon into the marshland up to his neck." Then paused and in the lowered voice of the punchline added, "Right where he could keep an eye on em."

The new man John Burt spoke up. "So what do we do? Do we go after em?"

Chase turned to look at Burt. Cole said, "Go after em where? Where do you propose we go looking for em?"

Burt said, "I don't know. You're the ones know this country. Just go track em I guess."

Chase spoke up. "You'd as well track air boy."

Chase's farmer brother Peter was back in the group. One of the men who had gone to recover Simon Crane. He said, "Still it might not be a bad idear to make up some patrols and move around the backcountry a little bit. If those devils are lingering it might persuade em to move along."

Burt said, "We can't just go on about our business with them out there somewhere."

Emil Chase spoke to his brother. "You can disregard your rowen if you want. One excuse is good as another." Then he turned to Burt and said, "Son, they ain't after you."

"What makes you so sure who they might be after next?"

"Well I can't say. But I can tell you twas you they wanted they already would've plucked you."

Men laughed, short uncomfortable snorting. Emil Chase put his hat on his head and turned to face the full group. He said, "Go on and patrol if it makes you feel any better. I'll stay put myself. But tomorrow morning I intend to ride to that cabin and see the man is buried. What remains of him at least. And I want men to go with me but none so rum-soaked as to mistake it for a lark. Don't none of you offer now but whoever's at the mill come six-thirty I'll count on to ride with me."

Cole said, "I'll be there."

"I know it."

Then came a cry from the man standing just inside the door watching both the proceedings and the bonfire as well. He took up his musket and jumped outside the door. There came a warning cry from him, commanding someone to stop. A shot. Then another cry from him, something inchoate then choked off. The men scrambled for their weapons and the room emptied. Only Blood and Emil Chase stood still. There were more cries from outside and then an aggregated sound, a groaning gasp from the group. Blood looked at the miller. Emil Chase had again removed his hat as if knowing there would be no quick departure this evening. Perhaps it was his way of readying himself. Blood took up Gandy's unfinished cup and took a swallow from it, his first of the night. As the men came slow back through the door in a tight clump. Inside they stepped apart, to reveal as well as gain what distance they could.

It was the Deacon. His ankles were hobbled with rawhide, not bound but short enough so he could only shuffle forward, each footstep one that came to a harsh halt and jerked both his knees. He was upright but barely, with clotted blood dried down his face from his lidless rolling eyes and his mouth was sewn shut, a rough job done with an awl and deer sinew. Behind his lips his jaw was clenched tight so the muscles of his cheeks and jawline leaped and twitched and from low in his throat came a sound as a kitten mewling. His elbows were lashed to his sides and his hands were before him. From him came the smell of a keen and utter corruption.

His hands were bound by the wrists to a dense wet ball also wrapped in lacings, tied so his wrists lay either side of the mass. Despite this his fingers gripped hard the thick pelt of hair as if the object were sacred or valuable. As if he had any choice.

What he gripped and offered to the men around him was what was left of the head of Wilson.

Sally began to scream.

Blood cleared the room. He came around the counter and went first to the Deacon and touched the man's forehead and spoke to him, his fingers and words stroking. Gazing into the sightless eyes. Then without taking his eyes from the Deacon spoke in a low voice and ordered all out. The men milled, some drinking hard at their cups. Blood looked around and spoke sharp, "Get to your families." As if released from thrall the men surged and checked their weapons and conferred amongst themselves and left. From beyond the open door Blood could hear them talking where they gathered in the last light of the bonfire and he stepped around the Deacon and went and closed the door and dropped the heavy bar in place. Other than the Deacon the only man left in the room was Emil Chase. Blood ignored him. But neither did he request his departure.

He went to Sally and took her by the arm and when she would not move, still perched on the stool, still keening, he wrapped his arms around her and picked her up and carried her through the other door to the house-side into her own room where he set her on her bed and lighted a candle and stood on tiptoe to close and bolt her window and then turned back to her and told her to stay where she was. When she clutched at his arm and would not free him he did not struggle with her but instead spoke the dog's name and the hound came into the room and stood before the bed gazing upon them. Blood pointed at the bed-covers and said, "Up," and the dog made a graceful leap onto the bed and circled once and settled with his back against the now sobbing girl. In such a way that she might hunch over him and wrap her arms around him and he would be as solid to her as any thing on earth. Blood left them there and went back through the house to the tavern.

The Deacon stood where Blood had left him. Emil Chase had like-wise not moved. Blood glanced at him and Chase looked away.

Blood went behind the counter for an empty powder keg and his whet-ted belt knife. He stood before the Deacon with the powder keg caught between his knees and cut free Wilson's head. Which dropped into the keg with a wet slop. He took the keg and considered it and then placed it up on the counter. The smell was high and he didn't want it in the house but he could not bring himself to just set it outside. Then he went back to the Deacon and knelt and started cutting at the hobbles and worked his way up until all that was left was the fine hard sinew stitching through the man's lips. Here he paused and went and whetted his knife once more and returned. With his free hand gripped hard the man's jaw and tilted the dreadful head back and slid just the point of the blade behind each sinew and sliced them open. He made no effort to pull the cut strings free. Blood dippered water from a bucket and held it up to the man's mouth and let him drink a small amount and then took the water from him, dashing out what was left in the dipper onto the floor. Back to the counter where he filled a cup of rum and came back and again held the man's jaw tilted up and forced the rum down his throat. The Deacon choked and swallowed and choked again and then came his first clear groan, the sound of rock cleaving. Blood set the cup away and took up a clean rag and wet it to wash as best he could the man's face. Just dabbing the crusts of blood-tears. Immediately fresh blood began to ooze from his cut-open eyes. The Deacon lifted his arms and groped for Blood and Blood held him and the man clutched Blood a moment, then sagged and went down onto the floor. Lying rolling, crying out. Blood looked at Emil Chase and again Chase looked away from him. Blood looked down at the Deacon who was now thrashing, his knees drawn up to his chest in pain and his arms wrapped around his head.

Blood said, "We can try to talk to him but he won't be able to tell us anything useful. Likely not even where whoever it was waylaid him. Or how many it was or what they looked like. But we can try."

Chase did not look at Blood but said, "Have mercy on him."

Blood stepped to the woodpile before the fireplace and lifted a club of firewood. He hefted it and passed it one hand to the other and then turned it around for balance until he held it just right. Then crossed back over the room and straddled the Deacon and bent forward and timed the twitching rolling and brought the club down softly square on the back of his head. The Deacon stopped mid-roll and shuddered once, then fell back face up on the floor and did not move. His chest rose and fell but that was all. Blood got a fresh rag soaked in water and laid it still wet across the now-blind eyes. He went behind the counter once more to wash his hands and face and stood a long moment considering the powder keg set on the counter. It had a dire stink. He couldn't see what to do with it just then, so left it where it was. He poured out a cup of rum and went to the bench by the dying fire, sat heavy upon it and drank from the cup. Finally looking at Emil Chase who had watched wordless throughout.

Emil Chase was Blood's age or a few years younger. There were a few older men in the Indian Stream country—some farmers, some trappers—but Chase was the senior man of the community. Not so much from age or his considerable physical condition as from his nature and his enterprise. There was not a man but Blood not indebted to Chase. Chase was practical, thrifty, hard-working, sober—near everything that Blood was but also held the simple belief that he was a whole man. While Blood knew otherwise of himself. Still, each recognized the other as adversary, opponent, as the one man in this place who, save by chance or accident, might destroy the other if either chose. So far they had deferred any confrontation by the neat method of avoidance. What business passed between them had been one-sided and Blood paid in hard cash for those services he required of the mill. So far, then, they were even by virtue of distance.

Chase spoke first. "This is a mess."

"It's not pretty, is it. But the worst of it is this poor feller lying here."

"You discount the Indians?"

"Well I wouldn't know. But the whole thing has a private feel to it. It makes sense that they wasn't the ones killed Wilson, that it was Crane did that. And if the savages was cronies with Wilson it makes sense they went after Crane."

"And the business with this poor soul here?" Chase indicated the Deacon.

"That's the problem. The most likely hope is they was sick of his rant and thought he'd make the ideal courier to send the rest of Wilson."

Chase said, "How would we know em anyhow? It's not like any of us ever laid eyes on em. Except maybe that little bantam trapper that hauls rum for you. But if he had seen em I don't imagine he'd announce it, do you?"

"I can't see what benefit would be for him to do that."

Chase said. "The greater problem I see is there's near a hundred men will be talking about this. Word's bound to spread south. Trappers or no, it'd be just the thing Mose Hutchinson could be waiting for as excuse to come up here."

"That the Coos County sheriff?"

"That's him," Chase said. "Down to Lancaster."

"Frankly, Mister Chase, I don't see the difficulty. It's a clear-cut thing. Some piddly sheriff wants to poke his nose into it, let him, I say."

"You ain't got nothing to hide, do you Mister Blood?"

Blood looked level at Chase. "Not one thing." Then he added, "I gather some do though. It's best if all keep their mouths shut. Now, I think you set that young feller Burt straight and likely others got the message too. Beyond that, what can you do?"

Chase walked to the fireplace and spat in the cold ashes. He turned and said, "I ain't sure." Then he approached Blood, coming close. "What do you intend to do about this feller here?" Again indicating the Deacon who lay in some awful twitching sleep.

Blood said, "Let him spend the night on my floor."

"That's it?"

Blood said, "What else is there? How he's going to live with himself is not for me to scrutinize. I couldn't make the first guess."

Chase nodded. He directed his gaze toward the powder keg and said, "You were to scoop some cold ash from the hearth to cover up that feller's head it wouldn't stench so bad."

Blood said, "He's been through enough. I don't intend to pare any more of his dignity from him by shoveling cold ash over him."

"I can't see it would make any difference to him now."

"It would to me."

"You're a peculiar man."

Blood drank from his cup. Remained silent.

Chase sighed. Then said, "I've heard tales about you."

"That Gandy gets around, doesn't he."

"Seems to me, you'd be craving to be left alone by Mose Hutchinson as any other man."

"I've nothing to fear from any man."

"And your Lord?"

"I'm still living."

"I see."

"Perhaps you do."

"Whatever else, that girl you got here is a minor child."

"That sheriff's got plenty of that in his own backyard I'd bet. He doesn't have to come all the way up here after any of her."

"That was not my point."

"I force her to take no man. Nor any man to go with her."

"Does that make it right?"

"Now, we're not going to talk about what's right."

"Why's that? Whatever you are, you're an educated man. That's plain as the nose on my face. How did you get educated so far beyond right or wrong?"

Blood sighed. "You're plenty curious, yourself."

Chase shook his head. "I don't like what you or her do down here. But there's women who feel even stronger about it."

"There always are."

"It's them could make the trouble for you, is what I'm trying to tell you."

"So it's most always been."

"That's not the way I hear it."

"I was claiming no innocence." Blood drank again and said, "What those women don't understand—those well-intentioned goodwives— is this girl here is living some kind of lovely life compared to where she came from. It may look debased from where they're setting, I can see that. Especially the ones know their own men come down here for perhaps more than a toddy of rum. Even those that don't cavort with the girl surely carry her home in their heads. But what I'm telling you is this—you can keep it to yourself or do your best to explain it to your wife or any other that asks—Sally is happier than she's ever been in her life. Or ever would've been, I hadn't come along."

"How can you be sure of that?"

"There are places in this world where a body just starts out flat and goes lower and lower. There are places that don't have any doors, no ways out. You understand what I'm telling you?"

Chase was hushed a long moment. Then very quiet said, "I guess you'd know."

Blood made a delicate near invisible nod.

They stood silent a time. It was very late. Somewhere up the valley a cock crowed, an hour, perhaps two, ere first light. Blood thought to himself that as long as he had a cow he should get a few chickens. He could eat a fresh egg or two. Yolk with toast. Of a sudden, he was tired. Wearied right through.

When it was clear Blood would say nothing more Chase turned his hat over in his hands and put it on and said, "Well. Tomorrow is a long day."

"Today."

"What?"

"It's already today."

Chase nodded. "I guess that's right. Ain't it always, somehow?"

Blood said, "It's all right with me."

Blood slept a scant time and had been awake less than an hour when Chase and three other men on horseback arrived: his brother Peter Chase and Isaac Cole and young John Burt, who did not look as if he'd slept at all. None of the party were rested, and they had the edgy tempered look of men unhappy but bent on their work. When Blood carried out the powder keg with Wilson's head the horses snorted and thrashed in the road, backing and sidestepping. They tried to rig a sling of ropes to carry the keg slung between two of the horses but one or the other would spook sideways when brought close upon the load. Finally Peter Chase whipped his horse up and raced to the mill and came back towing a hand sled. They lashed the keg to that and the party went up the road finally with the freight some distance behind, the keg a small squat lonely burden centered on the sled. Blood stood out in the road watching them go, recalling that other morning when Wilson's head went the other way atop a similar sled.

It was only when he went back inside that he realized the Deacon had left while Blood slept. There was no sign of him but the wet bloody rag left on the floor. And the cut-away rawhide lacings. Blood built a fire even though it was a warm day already and burned the debris and then heated water in a kettle suspended from the crane and used old sacking to scrub the room. Walls, the plank bar and finally the floor. When he was done he opened the door to let in fresh air to help dry and purify the room. He built the fire high and then let it die. No men came for their morning rum and he expected none, would've turned away any so bold. He went out and dug some potatoes to boil for breakfast and started them cooking.

He was milking the cow when he heard Sally scream. He tipped over the milk bucket getting off the stool and ran for the house. She was sitting upright in bed with the blanket wrapped around her, her head down, rocking back and forth. Her screams had stopped but she was sobbing, her delicate shoulders wracking in hard shudders. The dog Luther lay on the bed against her thigh, his head lifted sideways to gaze upon her, his eyes deep and sad as any creature's could be. Blood knelt on the flimsy mattress and held her by the arms and talked to her until she would look at him. Once she finally lifted her head she turned her ruined eyes full upon him. Her face was bloated, her nose running, her hair wet where she'd sweated before waking. She'd had a bad dream. Her arms locked Blood's neck, her head sank so her cheek was flat against his chest and she would not let him go. He knelt like that holding her, patting her back a long time. One of his feet fell asleep and he felt the needles of pain, waiting for it to cramp but still he held her. There was nothing else he could do. He put his nose against her hair, smelling her. She smelled like someone he knew.

* * *

At midday Emil Chase rode up alone and called Blood out into the yard. There had been no one come by all morning and now with the noon-time upon them Blood had begun to wonder how long this might go on. It was not so much that he was losing money but he understood men fell in and out of habits and he worried now how many might leave this particular habit be, how many might have considered the entire episode to reflect someway upon them personally. So when Chase called him out he did what he would not otherwise have done. He went out to meet him.

The horse was lathered from its morning's work, having glimpsed and smelt things no horse should. Chase sat the saddle a little heavily but command radiated down his arms as if his hands themselves gripped the bit, with the reins mere extensions. He did not attempt to keep the horse stationary but let it pivot and swirl and thus controlled it even as it spent itself.

Chase did not greet Blood but spoke. "The cabin was burnt to flinders when we got there. Still smoking and somewhat of a fire remained but the house was gone. It was the heathens' doing all right—there was an owl wing and three raven feathers bound up together hanging from a nearby tree. Out where you couldn't miss em. We got no idea if they took Wilson's body out of there or burnt him with the rest of it. But the way them fellers described Wilson it's my bet the savages left him right where he was. It's got the men all worked up, those savages around as recent as last night. There's no telling where they are or what they're up to next. If they valued Wilson so much as to do Crane the way they did they might feel they're not done with the rest of us yet. There's men called for a meeting at the mill this afternoon to divide themselves up into patrols and elect officers and such."

"What'd you do with the head?"

Chase looked at him as the horse swung away and rode the horse around in a circle to face Blood again. His hat was jammed on his head, over his ears. Blood guessed he'd had some hard riding.

"His head? I'll tell you what we did with his head. My brother and I stretched it out between us on a pair of ropes and set it down in the middle of what was left of the cabin. We pushed up the rest of the half-burned timbers and threw what remained of their woodpile on and got the whole thing going again. That young John Burt was stalking around with his musket, peering off left and right and swiveling around quick to check his back. Then, when the fire caught and started up good again you could smell that head burning and he threw down his gun and bent over puking. We got him onto his horse and rode out of there. So I'm afraid your keg is gone, Mister Blood."

Blood said, "I wouldn't have wanted it back anyhow." Chase was angered over more than his recounting, the anger seeming to gain as he spoke. It appeared he blamed Blood for all that had occurred. As if Blood's enterprise was seeping over the surrounding countryside and the endeavoring inhabitants, their modest aspirations, perhaps mocking their efforts—Blood's gains the very sweat and festered blisters of their labor. Blood was mildly provoked, but also ambivalent. He had no wish to be drawn into some other's vision of himself.

Then Chase said, "You shouldn't ever have done that poor idiot the way you did. Humiliated him that way. I hold you as much to blame as what those heathens did to him."

Blood stepped close and caught the noseband of the bridle and spoke to the horse in a low tone, soothing chanted monosyllables. Then looked up at Chase and said, "Whatever are you talking about?"

"Just what every other man, woman, and child's been talking about. How you brought that girl out here in the road before a crowd of men and humbled that poor fool, that holy idiot, that man whom nobody knew where he came from or what happened to soften his brain the way it was. But was tolerated because he was all those things, and you knew it too. You had to've known it or you never would've done what you did. In some ways it wouldn't have been as bad if he'd been an eleven-year-old boy. In some ways it was worse."

Blood ran a hand up the horse's head over the crest between the ears and the horse dropped his head so Blood could look square at Chase. "I leave every man to his own opinion. Of myself and my doings. But I won't tolerate being accosted directly. As far as what I did with that fool they call the Deacon it was only what part of him wanted. If it had been any other man saying the things he was I would not have been so thoughtful."

"Are you threatening me, Mister Blood?"

"Why no," Blood said mildly. "I've got no need, that I see."

Chase said, "You're a confident man, Blood. That can be dangerous, taken too far."

"I'm not dangerous to any man," Blood said, "that leaves me be."

Emil Chase spat to the side. He said, "Well the Deacon won't be bothering you no more. We came back from the trapper's cabin and found him floating facedown in the pool below the millrace. So it's two events this afternoon, the mustering and a burial. I don't know which will be first. The burial I expect. He's awful to look at."

"I'm sorry to hear it," Blood said. "But not surprised. He's better off."

"None of em should've died the way they did. But there is no promise as to one's own end. Still, three's a lot of men in gruesome death, such a short time."

Blood said nothing.

Chase said, "Release the horse. I've things to attend. I don't expect we'll see you for the burial or the mustering, either one."

Blood held onto the bridle. He said, "I didn't have anything but pity for the feller, regardless of how you see it. I'll surely walk up to see him laid in the ground. But no, you're right—that mustering business just sounds like so much play to me."

"You might feel different, those savages choose to come after you next."

Blood recalled the wild man eating his peas. He let go of the bridle and stepped back, still looking at Chase. He said, "Anybody wants to come after me, I expect I'll be ready for them my own self. I look to no others for help."

Chase said, "That's the right attitude for this country." His voice shivery with contempt.

"Why yes," said Blood. "This and all others. But I'll walk up there and help bury that man. I'll be along as soon as I wash myself."

"Do as you choose," Chase said. "Just leave your whore to home. There's decent women and children will be there."

He jerked back on the reins and brought the horse's head around and let the horse circle hard upon Blood once in the road. Blood did not move. Chase backhanded the reins against the horse's neck and they went furious up the road toward the mill. Blood watched them go, the churn of dust thrown up screening all but a sense of man and beast. Beyond that he could see the waters of the lake, black and shimmering

under the noonday sun. Then he turned and walked to the house for
the bucket and went down to the stream after fresh water. Coming back
he paused by the garden. There remained half a row of English peas.
Pods filling. Near ready. He thought to have them for supper. Better
eat them young and sweet than not at all.

To his surprise she did not argue or question but washed herself and
dressed in her best outfit—that is, skirt and bodice all the same moss
green rather than mixing the colors as she was wont to do—and again
without prompting despite the warmth of the day wrapped her shawl
over her shoulders and upper arms and drew it together before her so it
covered her breasts in the thin bodice. Stood patient as he brushed out
her hair and did not complain when he pulled it back to her nape and
gathered it there with a string. He came before her and pulled the hair
a little loose from the string so it was full around the sides of her face.
She waited while he sat and worked cooking grease into the chapped
and cracked leather of the buttonhook boots she'd not worn since March.
Her feet, although brown and hard-calloused, were no longer swollen
and slid easily into the softened leather. She stood rather than sat while
he put on his one decent shirt and newer breeches.
    They went up the road together. Starting out, she stumbled in the
unaccustomed shoes and grasped to steady herself against him. Once
her balance regained she took her hand away but he retrieved it to tuck
into the crook of his elbow. So together, side by side, they made their
way up to the mill and beyond that to the fresh raw cemetery and the
group gathered there on a small open hillside above the lake. There was
a mound of earth to mark the hole and a roughboard coffin rested on
planks over the hole and they stood not away from the group but off to
one side and back a little, present but not intruding upon their neighbors. All of them thus waited in silence until it was clear that those coming had arrived. The Chase brothers and two other men stepped forward
and lifted ropes either side of the coffin and an appointed boy came forth
and slid the planks away from the hole and they lowered the Deacon
soundless into the earth. Then Emil Chase read briefly from Paul's
Letter to the Corinthians. Blood was surprised at how poorly he read,
without pause or inflection but all the words running together as if any

one word was the same as another. Chase looked to the hole again and
bade farewell to the man whom not one present knew by any true name
and commended his soul to Christ. Again, wordless, the four men took
up spades and began to fill the hole. And the people remained watching a short time before commencing to speak among themselves and so
formed small groups and clumps that soon began to drift, not one alone
but all together down the hill and away from the man who would have
a plain unwrought stone and within a generation would be forgotten
completely, or if recalled at all only for the way he died.

Blood and Sally stood a time longer. Not until the work was done
but until the rest of the people were gone from the hillside. Most but
not all had gathered at the mill to await the men laboring over the grave
and thus get on with the rest of the afternoon, with the martial business
at hand, with the prospect for adventure, the tingle of danger. Halfway
down the hill Blood spoke to Sally without looking at her. "Take my
arm." She did and so linked they passed by the group outside the mill,
mostly men but some women too who would wait by their men until
the meeting started and then repair to the house with the miller's wife
for tea to await the outcome.

Blood and Sally walked by them, Blood looking straight ahead until
he was abreast of the party when he turned and looked the men over
slowly, letting his eye linger here and there as if judging them for abili-
ties yet untested for their undertaking. He raised his hat and bid them
a good afternoon. Replaced his hat and walked with the girl close beside him down the road to where his tavern stood open and untended,
knowing they were watched all the way. He did not pause in the yard
or look back but strode inside with Sally behind him. Shut the door and
barred it. He was not open for any business. Although he knew that late
afternoon, when the sun diminished and evening slid long over the land,
he would open the door and light his fires and hear then all he needed
or desired about the plans made that afternoon. But for now he wanted
only to be alone. He was hungry. There was most of a smoked ham taken
in trade he could cut slabs from. There were potatoes. There were the
rest of the English peas. He decided to pick only half the peas and chance
the rest. He loved peas. Once gone, summer would in some way be over.
He decided they would sup early. Then he might take a nap. He was
tired from it all. He felt as if he'd been standing at attention for hours

and hours, for days. He would've loved a tub and hot water and a bath. A nap would do.

For some days Sally could not sleep and when she did she woke crying out.

She could not differentiate between dream and waking-screaming until Blood came and comforted her, holding her in an odd crabbed kneeling on the bed beside her, his knees prodding her thigh as he bent hard at his waist to hold her shoulders and head against his chest, his body stiff and arched, as if she were dangerous to him, or he dangerous to her. Cradling her head against his heavy laboring chest as if some last piece of solid earth for her to grind her fear against. Talking to her, the same simple words over and over, varying the order but not the words themselves the way one would talk to a child. She did not know this. There had been no other children in the house where she had grown.

He would say, "It's just a dream. A dream is all it is. Only a dream." Over and again.

Most times when her crying stopped Blood would settle her down again in her bed and leave her, stepping from the room wordless. But one time she went from sobbing directly to speaking and he sat and listened to her, as if there was no difference to him between her cries and her words.

She told him, "I wasn't ever happy. When I was just the littlest girl I was always in the way or making noise when I shouldn't so somebody was always cuffing me or slapping my rear and telling me to hush. There was a old woman that I don't know if she was partners with my mother or if maybe she owned the house until she died or what. She might've been my mother's mother but I don't think so, though my mother and all the other women there called her Mother. Mother Holmes. Oh she was a wretched hunched-over old thing with chin whiskers out of a mole and smoked a pipe like a man. She was the worst to hit me but the other girls seen her at it and none of them would hold back if they felt a reason to wallop on me. And all they was doing was passing along what came their way. I don't know if it's just whores but men will be vicious to a woman, they turn their minds to it. I seen my share of black eyes and busted noses and broken arms and such. It's a ugly world is what it is and I never knowed it for a hard fact until you come along and carried me off up here. It was just what I knew. You can't say one thing is worse or better than another if you only know the one thing. I was never one to think Poor me. But I was thinking maybe this wouldn't be so bad. And then that poor man, that idjit. Can you imagine not being able to close your eyes? I can't imagine that. Not being able to close your eyes. I can't imagine a worse thing."

There are worse things, Blood thought but did not say.

"When I was little, maybe four, five, I had a tiny kitten that showed up and I claimed. Scrawny sad little thing. White and orange striped. Well you know how that story ended. Some man coming drunk downstairs at three in the morning and the kitten bolted down the steps ahead of him and he trod on it and slipped and fell and slid down the stairs and come up roaring and got hold of that little cat and swung it by the body and busted its head open on a chairback. I was awake, right there to see it happen. I didn't know nothing about right hours when I was that little. It was only later I learned about what happens at night and what happens during the day for most people. But when I was little time didn't make any difference to me at all. Pussy. That's what I called that cat. I didn't know that some call a cat Puss. I just knew the word, knew it was the best thing a body had in this life, the one thing you had that everybody else wanted. It was the simplest thing in the world to call her Pussy. But I never wanted another cat after that.

"The summer I was either ten or eleven, I already told you I ain't sure just what my age is, never was sure. Nobody around me was and so I wasn't either. Now you'd think my mother would know. That's part of what makes me wonder if she really was my mother or if she just got me someway when I was too little to recall it—there's children left or sold or some even likely stole although I can't imagine her wanting me enough to steal or buy me—I expect if I wasn't hers then I got left there. Maybe some girl working in the house had me and fled or maybe I was just brung there someway. Or maybe she did birth me, the fact she couldn't keep my age straight don't mean much, not with her. But anyways, that summer I was I guess a pretty little girl, growing up although I didn't know it. I didn't have boobies yet and was a couple of years from my monthlies but I guess I was starting to be pretty enough. So there was this man, big old hairy fat thing, at least it's how he looked to me, I overheard him talking to my mother trying to settle on a price for me. She called me in for him to look at me and made me lift my skirt and turn around for him to see me front and back. Then they begun hollering at each other. I guess she wanted more than he wanted to pay. Anyway I'd seen just about everything there was to see by that time and I couldn't begin to imagine his big ugly thing going inside me so I ran right out of there. I doubt they even seen me leave, they was so heated up at each other. But I run right out of the house, right through the kitchen and down the alley and hid myself. And every time after that whenever he come to the house I'd be spying for him and I'd go to hide. It got my mother worked right up, I can tell you. Each time I'd come back she was in a terrible lather and she'd blister my behind. I guess they come to terms over me but it was a long time before he got what he was after. I'd duck out the back and run down the alley and cut across to another place where there was big old barrels all over the place, new ones, what do you call them places?"

"A cooper," said Blood. Looking at her eyes. "A cooperage."

"I'd run down there and find one of them barrels tipped over on its side back behind some others and hide in there until I felt enough time had passed to go home. And there was rats all over that place and one time one climbed into that barrel with me and all I did was suck my breath and punch it right in the nose. It took off out of there I can tell you. Didn't even rear up and snarl like one does when it's cornered."

Then she grew quiet. It had grown light, pale dawn coming through her high window. Blood in his nightshirt, Sally under the blankets pulled up, her knees drawn up and her arms down around them, her back naked, the spindle of her spine raised as her back curved forward. Her hair a tempest. She gazed away from him at the log walls. He waited until, hating it, he knew he had to ask.

"What happened?"

She turned her face sideways so her cheek was on her knee and said, "What do you think? One day he outwaited me and I come back to the house and there he was. It was terrible, I tell you. Any tenderness he might've once had for me was long gone. The funny part about it all was that while it hurt when he done me that wasn't near so bad as the rest of it. I thought I was going to die. I mean I thought he was going to kill me, to smother me with his weight. I couldn't draw a breath. It was a while before I learned that a man should take his weight on his elbows. But what happened was I started to scuffle so bad trying to get him free so I could breathe that it got him going faster than I guess maybe he'd counted on. Or maybe the wait for me done that. Or maybe it was just having this little girl under him. Whatever, I learned something because once I started in thrashing and twisting under him that emptied his sails real quick. And I learned something else that time too. When a man is done with you he is done. He didn't even bother to wash his dick in the basin although I guess he knew there was no need of that."

She raised her head to face Blood squarely and said, "Truth is, I always thought happy meant when you got paid or when there was a morning you could sleep in late or when there was a bad storm and there wasn't any men about. That's what I thought happy was. At least until you come along. I thought maybe this was a good place, that maybe things would work good here. But it's ugly here. There's meanness here. And the way I feel, it could easy get worse. That poor idjit, I can't get him off my mind."

Blood stood off the bed and stretched. He looked away from her, toward the narrow window. He spoke to the bit of sky beyond the window. "It's not such a bad place. I think it'll work out fine. There's good and bad everywhere you go."

"Maybe," she said. "I just only known bad and so thought maybe this would be good."

"No." Blood turned to her. "It's always part and part. Most places have more of one than the other. Myself, I still have hopes for right here. My thinking is all this is just an incident. It'll pass. Things'll settle down."

She studied him a moment and then dropped her blankets and stood naked off the bed and bent for her shift where it lay on the floor. She pulled it over her head and turned to face him, pulling her hair free of the neck opening. She said, "You think?"

Blood milked the cow, carried the warm milk to the house and went to the stream to wash his face with the cold clash of water. Slowly went back toward the house. He could hear her working, going back and forth between hearth and table. He remained outside and sat on the chopping block beside the woodpile and held his chin in his hands. He was trying to understand why he had bought her, what it meant that she had come into his life. He did not believe that he owned her, had never believed that. But now he felt he owed her something. Why he might feel that way was too obvious to him and he did not believe in that sort of reckoning. But he had to ponder what power had delivered her to him. Or him to her. Perhaps, at best, each someway deserved the other. This not a matter of redemption.

For several days she would take no men at all to her bed. This at least in part because she slept much of the day and early evening. Because, as Blood knew, she tried to stay awake through the fearsome quiet dark when the tavern was still and humanity had fled before the night and Sally would lie then fighting sleep and the terrible dreams. Sometimes he would wake in his sorry loft bed beside his crude gun carriage while it was still dark and hear the poked-up crackle of a fire below and her stealthy movements. He would lie there knowing her furtiveness was only meant not to disturb him. He trusted her more than he'd trusted anyone in years.

Then for the next week she seemed to be awake around the clock and would take most any man at all—old men she'd spurned and the few young ones that before she'd flirted with but kept away from for reasons of her own divination and the stinking rabid trappers drinking away their summers and their winter earnings, even the barbarous habitant bachelor settlers who had little or no English and were of a caste separate from even the poorest of the other farmers—all these she took.

Finally she came to Blood. "I got to stop. I don't know what's got into me but it ain't no good I keep up like I am. I got to stop."

Blood nodded. "All right." Then, after a moment he said, "Just how long a holiday you intending?"

"A what?"

"How long you intend to stop for."

"I don't know. A week. Maybe just a few days."

He studied her face. Open, intent, determined. Free of guile. He said, "Keep in mind. Too little can be as bad as too much."

"I know it. I just need a little time. Tell em I got my monthly."

"Again?"

She looked at him. "Men don't keep track."

*   *   *

The men formed a Committee of Safety and drew themselves up in
patrols with elected captains who devised a schedule and were charged
with keeping order. Parties rode or hiked out daily in diverging directions, each footpath, trail or crude road followed only until the last
habitation of even the most unlikely kind had been reached, the squads
of men numbering no less then six or seven and often more since the
younger men found an excitement and purpose in this activity that allowed them to overlook their more homely work. Because not all
places could be reached and returned from in a single day these patrols overlapped so that at times as many as twenty men would be gone
from the farms along the river falling out of the lake. In the evenings
whatever men returned gathered at the tavern to drink and talk of
what they had seen. Or rather what they had not seen for it appeared
the two wild men had left the country and the men held themselves
responsible for their departure.

For Blood, beyond the bothersome repetition of the tales, mostly this
meant the long-awaited increase in sales of powder and lead—not exactly the circumstances he'd have chosen but he was not a judge but a
businessman. Still, there were some few men who requested quantities
beyond good reason. Blood offered the excuse that he was not yet amply
supplied for the winter. Which he was beginning to suspect might be
true. But there was plenty of summer left and he would only slowly
increase his stores. Prudence was all that was.

So he told no one when the last of his English peas were taken one
night. Nothing else was touched. Luther had sounded no alarm, had
not stirred as far as Blood knew. The house was already heavily barred
each night after he closed. It had always been so. The only precaution
he took was to let the dog out each morning before Sally was up and
headed outside herself. This variation of routine so slight as to be noticed by no one. Except the dog who did not mind.

July turned to August. In the shortening summer twilight, the sky through
the open tavern door a broad smutch of green within the dark trees, the
green bleeding up to royal blue and then somewhere over the lake turning to black. The first star, a planet hanging low in the east. Inside was

light from the hearthfire and two candle lanterns, one hanging from a rafter of the public room, the other directly over the plank counter where Blood sat with his tally sheets and dram measure. The light soft, the color of pumpkin flesh, thrown spots on the log walls from the pierced tin of the lanterns. What air sifted through the open door was cool.

Sally perched on a hogshead behind the counter, her knees drawn to her chin, her skirt pushed down between her thighs so the cups of her kneecaps shone in the light and the light ran long ravels down her slender shanks. Her feet bare. Not talking to anybody, not yet. She'd commenced working again but only for the very few, usually not until the end of the night. Blood was watching to see if a favorite might emerge. He'd cut that quick. So far it seemed only who took her fancy evenings; what repeats there were had been short encounters during the day, which Blood rightly read as the result of convenience. He was confident that whatever thoughts she kept from him, it was not this. Not yet at least. She was forming no alliance save what trust lay between herself and Blood. Such trust a thing Blood would not attempt to measure or verify.

The men were working long days to get their rowen up. If the weather held, if the month did not turn damp and cold, if the killing frost did not arrive until mid-September, there was hope for a scant but rich third cutting. The heathen fear had died before this stark realization. The endless dream of summer gone. Still, the patrols went out, down now to the same half dozen hard men once or twice a week, their circuit varied each time. They were relentless in their conviction to maintain this show into autumn. If the savages lingered, they hoped this resolute attention might move them along, even as they knew they'd as well be tracking day-old smoke.

Blood drifted down the plank counter to where Sally sat. Gandy was leaning across trying to talk to her. He hadn't given up, it didn't matter what Blood had told him. Still, she wasn't having any of him. Even the week it seemed there was no man she wouldn't take she'd refused Gandy. It was a curiosity to him—Gandy seemed no less likeable than a fair number of the men. He guessed for each of them it was a form of game, at least they kept it that way. Blood knew Gandy burned. But that was all right. Sally could handle him.

Blood said to Gandy, "Are you pestering her?"

Sally said, "He's a pest but he's all right."

Gandy grinned at her. Blood said, "What's the matter, those girls down to Bath get sick of you? Winter's coming quicker than you think. Be worth the trek down there once more I'd think. Better than hanging around here where there's no hope at all for you."

Gandy said, "I'm afeared I'd lose my head on the way. Or end up in some godforsaken bog. I ain't going nowhere. My money's run down too. I need to hold what I got for the winter stores."

Blood said, "Spend it. You know I'll set you up."

Gandy grinned, his mouthful of black and orange shards. He said, "I'd bet you would."

Blood said, "It's up to you. Just don't moon around this girl so much you drive serious fellers away. But it was me, I'd take the trip to Bath. Those Indians aren't going to bother you. They was, they'd long since of done it."

"I'm not going. One of them girls give me the pox." Then he looked quick to Sally and addressed them both. "But I ain't got it now. I took the cure."

Sally shook her head, an amused dismissal.

Blood said, "The mercury salts?"

"That's it. Cleared the pox from me and near everything else I figger. I was struck low by it. Hard to say which was worse, the pox or the cure."

Blood nodded. "I hear the salts work. Still, you stay away from this girl here."

"Now you and I both know I'm right now as close to her as I can hope to get."

"That's right. Just don't forget it. And be grateful for that cure. There's men gone blind and lost their minds, their bodies rotting away long before they're dead from the pox."

"I heared that. I never seen any."

"You don't want to."

"Can't you two talk about something else?" Sally slid down from the barrelhead and came up beside Blood.

He said, "It's a fact. I expect you already know it."

"It don't mean I want to set around and talk about it."

"Well, just check each man good for chancres or the drip. Especially those old reprobates like this feller here."

Gandy grinned. Blood guessed Gandy didn't know the word but was glad to be included in some rare form of company.

Sally said, "I know how to watch out." Then she said to Blood, "Come over here a minute. I want to talk to you."

He looked at her. She was serious, rapt, something lit in her eyes. He stepped back against the wall by the stockade door with her.

"What is it?"

She worked a hand in her hair, a nervous twitch that aggravated him but one he would not speak of. It was not a thing she even knew she did. She said, "Well, it's about my birthday."

"What birthday?"

"I never had one. I mean I did. I wasn't hatched I guess. But I never knew when the day was."

Blood waited. She was looking down, away from him. And when it was clear he would say nothing she raised her face and her color was high, her cheeks like sunburn.

She said, "So I thought I'd just go ahead and pick one out."

"Is that so?"

"It is."

"I see. You got any particular date in mind?" Something in Blood constricted, turned over, some thing he would not name. Or could not.

"I was thinking maybe this Sunday?"

"You asking me?"

She looked down again. Then back up fast. Her words out quick as if she had to do it that way or not at all. "I was thinking maybe do something nice. Something quiet. The two of us."

Blood stood looking at her. He didn't know what to say. She didn't know what she was doing to him. He knew that. And so he went on the same as before.

"This Sunday?"

"Yes."

"You want your birthday to be this Sunday?"

"I do."

"Well. Can you tell me what day of the month this Sunday is? A birthday is supposed to be the same day each year. I can't see it would help to pick a day and not know what one it is. Idn't that right? So, can you name the day of the month?"

She looked up at him. "That's where I was thinking you might help me out."

"I see. Well. You know the month?"

"Don't torment me," she said. "It's August."

"That's a start. So this coming Sunday in August. Now tell me. You decided how old you'll be this next Sunday coming in August?"

"I did. I'll be seventeen."

"Could be sixteen. What you told me."

"I feel more seventeen."

He paused and rubbed his hand over his face. He looked at her and said, "It won't be so long, you might regret that extra year."

She nodded. "I can always change it back if I want, can't I?"

Blood shook his head. He said, "Sally."

She frowned. And he saw her uncertainty and let her have it. Her voice low but her eyes still clever she said, "What?"

Then he said, "This coming Sunday would be August twelfth. Do you like that number?"

She beamed at him. "I do. The twelfth of August. I like the way it sounds."

"All right then," he said, already wondering what he was agreeing to. So he said, "Now get to work. Do something. Wipe down this counter." She nodded and turned away from him, reaching for a piece of old sacking folded on the lip of the kettle behind the bar where he rinsed the cups. He said, "Well. Happy birthday, I guess."

She turned back. Her face ferocious. "No. It's not til Sunday."

What she would not know, could not know, was the date she plucked from the air was the date his wife and eldest son drowned. And not only the date but by the unlikely coincidence of the simple cycle of years, this twelfth of August fell on the second Sunday of the month, the day of the week of that event. As always Blood would pass the day as all previous—he would not allow the sentimentality of grief to besmirch his burden. But could not but wonder what tender providential filament had provoked Sally at this moment and time—if the air she plucked did not flow outward from him thicker than he thought or if it was indeed some greater authority. Either way he determined to hold his faith in silence and somehow allow the girl the day. This simpler than demanding a different choice.

Sometime after full dark a stranger came in, a small man with a white beard spread down onto his chest but no hair on his head which was covered by a small round cap of colored triangles of cloth sewed together and wearing a vest of the same outlandish design over a simple white blouse. Full-length trousers of wide red and white stripes and however small he was he was smaller than he appeared because on his feet were high wooden clogs of a type Blood had never seen before but long ago had read of. The man had a silver hoop in one ear and a small battered squeezebox slung over one shoulder and on a leash held in one hand was a monkey dressed in miniature duplication of his master. The monkey came into the room on all fours and when silence had spread complete throughout the room and all were pondering this apparition out of the night the monkey stood on his rear legs erect like a man, slowly surveyed the room and deeply bowed as if overwhelmed with the honor of the company it found itself amidst. And the old man at the other end of the leash spoke.

"Gentlemen." He addressed the room, his voice at once persuading and commanding. "Gentle men. Forgive my intrusion, forgive my interruption of your evening but pray you allow me a moment to introduce myself and explain my unexpected presence here before you. An unexpected presence. For what else could it be. It could be many things, gentlemen, it could indeed be many things. It could be pleasure or simple amusement. But it could be more than that as well. Yes. Indeed it could very well be more than that. But I race ahead of myself. First things first, first and always. So it is that the world demands and rightfully so. We wish to know not just what but who we are dealing with. And always, gentlemen, always we must begin with the who. Even though I could name myself anything but my true name and you would have no way of knowing otherwise. But so it is. So it always is. We begin with the who and then can hang bits of the why upon the who and therefore we come to know a man. So. Indeed. The who." Here he paused and reached his free hand and swept the round cap from his head as if his naked pate indicated not only his integrity but his vulnerability as well.

He said, "I am Phineas Vitalis. It's my true name sirs. Now you have that and the rest follows easily enough. I have seen the wonders of the known world. The known wonders of the world. I've stood before the humble cottage in Stratford where the great Shakespeare was born. I've walked the boulevards of Paris and bowed before Napoleon. I've been in Saint Petersburg by the grace of the czar and czarina. I've stood before the Great Pyramids of Egypt and seen the Sphinx. I've seen lions roaring at the breaking sea on white sand beaches of Africa and stood in the slave markets where black men sell their brothers and cousins, the daughters and wives they've tired of. I've trod the bazaars of Constantinople and drunk tea with wild men from the mountains of the Caucasus. I've sailed to the Indies both east and west. I've seen the mighty mountains of South America, mountains that make these mountains south of here, forbidding as they are, appear to be the merest of hills. All these things and more. Countless untold wonders. The world, my dear sirs, is filled with wonders. A man may travel all his life as I have and see only the least part of what there is to see. And I speak only of the places I have actually seen, make no mention of those wondrous places I've heard of, be they of myth or fable or just a day's journey away. No. I content myself with what I have seen. For my eyes have no lies within them. Lies are the work of men but are puny failures when tested before the real absolute world. Sights once glimpsed stay within the grasp of the mind and are beyond dispute."

"You're some kind of wonder, yourself." One of the men, the first to speak.

Sally came close to Blood and whispered to him. "What's that little creature?"

"It's a monkey."

"It almost looks human."

"It's the clothing it's got up in makes it seem that way. You can train one about like a dog. Get up next to it, you'll see it doesn't look a thing like you or me."

She said, "I ain't so sure of that. Except for his size he looks awful close to some men I seen."

Blood grinned at her. Then turned back as the stranger spoke again.

"No gentlemen. I am not a wonder. I'm lucky, is what I am."

Blood spoke up. "So far. Tell us what brings you here. This is no place grand or memorable. Why choose us?"

"A reasonable question from a reasonable man. I presume you're a reasonable man."

"I'm tolerable."

"The proprietor?"

"I am."

"I beg your pardon sir. I should have sought you out and gained permission for my poor spectacle before I launched myself."

"If my question's so reasonable why don't you answer. Right now you recall me of a frog leg in a hot skillet."

"A lovely dish. With a glaze of stock reduction and lemon peel and capers—"

Blood cut him off. "The only caper I see right now is you. Come to the point man."

"Precisely. My circumstances are somewhat reduced. Nevertheless I'm journeying north to Montreal where the King's Governor has extended an invitation to me. I have it here, in my pouch." He patted the leather rucksack on his back. "You're welcome to peruse it, although it is, in fact, written in the French language. Which is still, in some places, the language of the Courts."

"I read French."

"Indeed. I should not be surprised. You struck me as a worldly man when I first glimpsed you." The little man bent and extended his fist that held the leash-end and said, "Hugo, up!" The monkey jumped and squatted on his fist and the man rose upright and came to the counter and, with the monkey still on his fist, dug his rucksack around to the front, opened the flap and rummaged within and brought out a folded parchment and handed it over to Blood. Blood stepped down the counter so he was under the light and opened the vellum which was folded three times and bore a number of seals and inscriptions upon the top of the sheet. The paper was no longer crisp but soft with age. The dating had been reworked with a lesser pen. His reading French was not as strong as it had once been but the name *Phineas Vitalis* was in prominent enlarged script in the second line. The rest of it could have been near anything. He scanned over the lines which were smudged and largely incomprehensible anyway and then lifted his gaze to the man who was leaning forward awaiting him. The old man had bright eyes that had once been clear blue but were now watered and filmy and shot with blood. The eyes were at once eager and urgent. Blood decided that if he was not quite what he said he was, he once had been, even if that was nothing more than a charlatan of high stripe.

Blood said, "We have little entertainment here but what we provide ourselves. What do you propose?"

Vitalis nodded as if they understood each other, as if he'd read correctly all that Blood saw. He said, "It's not as grand as it once was. But it might prove pleasant enough diversion. Mostly I squeeze songs and Hugo dances. He has a broad repertoire. Most find it amusing. He will do tricks for a nibble of food. He's not particular. And if the evening goes well, he has a peculiar behavior that a select group of men might be amused by. There is nothing more than that. I used to sing but my voice is gone. It was sweet once."

"And remuneration?"

"Nothing more than what men offer to the cap. Nothing from the house. Although if my playing should satisfy you I'd not refuse a dram or two."

Blood held his eyes a long beat. Then said, "Do your best."

So the little man removed to the center of the room and unleashed the monkey from its collar and the monkey hopped to the floor and stood waiting gazing up at its master. Phineas Vitalis brought the squeezebox out before him and opened it and then rose on his toes in his wooden clogs and stood a moment poised and while standing so fingered the valve buttons and then pumped the stretched bellows half-closed and a pair of rusted notes wheezed forth and hung in the silence of the room. And Vitalis closed his eyes and raised them to the ceiling and waited a long pause for the residuum of the warped notes to die off and then sank back onto his heels and brought the squeezebox together in a furious rush of ululation and a wild wailing music sprang forth into the room that was no music Blood had ever heard anywhere before but seemed transported whole from some place exotic beyond reckoning. And the monkey begin to spin and whirl about the floor as a creature possessed, holding his arms upthrust over his head so the ends of his unbuttoned vest flew out and slapped against his sides as he turned, his hard-horned feet clapping a curious counterbeat to the music as they struck against the floor and the men in the room stood back a little tighter pressed to the walls, to make room, to leave distance as great as possible as if there were some danger in the phenomenon before them. And Blood watching remembered the man speaking of the places he'd traveled and thought I'll be damned but he learned that music somewhere. Unless he made it up out of his head. And even as he was thinking this the squeezebox slid into a long dying-away moan and then rose again this time in a slow lulling dreamlike tempo that was aching with sadness so pure and profound that the men grew even more still as the strains entered throughout them, beyond their ears and brains to the core beyond logic or reason that runs in muscle and tissue and blood and the monkey swung slowly as if a top driven by a breeze, with his arms extended before him and his wrists lank so his hands flapped gently as if moved by that very same breeze, the monkey's head tipped back toward the ceiling now and like his master he moved within the music with his eyes closed.

As Blood watched this he sensed as much as saw the men in the room begin to loosen, not moving, not swaying, certainly not dancing but some reassembling taking place as the melancholic music completed its work upon them and reduced them to essential men—the dirge played out was for each of them alone even as it sang of their brothers, of their others, of all mankind around them and all those come before and all following. And Blood knew this was not his imagining, not something he was electing to see in the subdued group of hard men but some actual event he was witnessing. Was even in his meager way participating in.

Vitalis let the song fade and die away in a long trilling descent in which the last notes emerged whole and separate and seemed to hang in the air palpable as the motes of light thrown overhead from the candle lantern. The silence then was dense, monstrous, the sound of men breathing. And as if he'd given them this moment and this moment only to consider what they'd just heard and what had occurred in their souls so they might never forget. Immediately Vitalis once more swept his arms wide and closed them in short punchy waves and the high-pitched squeal of a reel came forth and filled the room and the monkey began to jig, kicking his feet forward even as he trod backward with his slender hairy simian arms folded over his chest. And almost at once one of the habitant farmers, a man known for his shy reserve as most of his countrymen were when out among the Americans, a man known only as Rouillard came forth into the opening, bowed either to the musician or the dancing monkey or both and began to dance as well, his heavy hobnailed boots clashing and ringing against the floorboards and then others came out also, first more of the French Canadians and then the Americans and the room filled with the thumping heaving riot of bodies.

Vitalis was running now, standing in place with sweat fleeing from his face as he snapped his head in time with the music and he went from reel to jig and back to reel again without stopping. Most times Blood could not even see him through the mass of bodies but the keening lament of the squeezebox came through as if the bodies were meant to only allow the music around them, as if the music was in fact swollen and diffused throughout the men and careened to the rafters and walls of the building and bounced back to join with itself, some great unwinding never-ending coil or spiral of sound. And Vitalis, small Vitalis, there in the center of the room, bringing this all out of the instrument that in the hands of another would do no more than croak and bray. At one point the crowd parted enough so Blood could see him. His head whipping with the rhythm of the reel, his eyes now bright and wide, his arms in fluid motion that seemed at once without effort and the greatest work in the world. The monkey had climbed up and sat perched on one swaying shoulder, the small hands locked tight in the man's beard.

Men began to break away from the dancing, coming to the counter for rum, leaning and drinking deep. Some asked for water and Blood dippered it up from the bucket handily and without complaint. Clear splotches of sweat gathered on the men's foreheads and chins and noses and beaded there and fell, lighting on the counter where they spread in dark ovals. The men would drink and slip away back into the throng and other men would take their place. And all through this the music continued without pause from one tune into another. As if Vitalis wanted to see how far these men might go, how far they might frenzy themselves, as if he even knew that none of them ever before and likely never again would know this peculiar condition where body and spirit joined flush together and mind was left aside.

At one point young John Burt came around the counter and leaned close to Sally where she sat on the hogshead and cried something to her and she shook her head No. He leaned and pleaded again and again she denied him and Blood was about to move down upon them when Burt reached up and grabbed her hands in his and tugged and she broke a smile, came down off the barrel and went around the counter with him out into the cacophony of the room and Blood understood and watched them go. Soon enough he saw her bobbing up and down, her hair flailing around her head, a sprite of a girl in the throng of men. Blood watched her, knowing she had never danced before, not like this, not in any way. For all that, it was a way Blood himself had never danced. And never would. But he leaned against the counter and sipped his first dram of the night and watched her.

Some time later he saw them pass together through the door into the house side that led to the door of her room. He drained his cup and made his way through the men still dancing and fed split logs onto the coals and squatted there for them to catch and adjusted them with the poker and watched the fire leap and grow. He stretched one of his hands down toward the base of coals and held it there until the heat was well through him. And held it there a moment more and then took it away. A rock wrapped frozen for ages set into a bed of coals will not warm but crack apart. He pushed himself up and went back to the counter and filled the waiting cups of men.

Suddenly, way too soon, Sally was standing close by him waiting until he was done. He turned to her and she said, "Get him out of there. Get him out of my room."

Blood nodded. "Did he try to hurt you?"

She shook her head. "He wanted to call me some other name. And he wanted me to say things to him. There is some things I won't do. Lay in for someone else is one. And my voice is my own, not to be ordered up by nobody. Least of all the sort of talk he wanted."

Blood said, "Mind the counter."

He went through the house to her room where a candle burned bedside. John Burt lay prone on the bed, his breeches off, his mouth open, turned sideways as he snorted to breathe. He was out. Blood leaned over the bed and slapped him awake. Burt came up ready to fight but Blood held his shoulder with one hand and backhanded him several times across his face and the fight went from him. Blood threw the breeches from the bed and ordered him to dress. John Burt held the breeches before his naked crotch and, awkward, got them on. He bent for his boots and Blood brought his fist down on the back of the man where his neck joined his shoulders and Burt sprawled forth onto his boots. Blood waited. Burt came up slow, holding his boots, wary, stepping back from Blood.

Blood said, "Out."

Burt said, "You got no reason to come after me. I didn't hurt the girl."

Blood shook his head. "Just go. And don't be bothering that girl again." He could hear the moaning of the squeezebox through the walls. That and the tromp of madmen.

Late, very late. The half-dozen men remaining stood before the counter with the monkey upon it. Blood had not seen it being passed but Vitalis's odd cap sat upside down by the monkey with a large double-handful of coin within. Sally was back on her usual seat, sipping the tin cup with the single dram of rum allowed her nightly. Blood had produced a stale crust of bread at the request of the itinerant and broke it into pieces and the men would offer a crumb held high and the monkey would perform a simple agile trick and then hold up his paws as a supplicant toward the crumb and take it delicately from the great rough fingers that dwarfed the diminutive creased wrinkled hands of the monkey. He could somersault or standing backflip or frontflip, walk on his hands or balance himself aloft on one downstretched arm. He did knee squats and then finally an imitation of a crippled man, standing upright, walking crooked along the counter with one leg dragging behind him.

Vitalis said, "That's it boys. He's done in."

The men were very drunk. They howled and showered the monkey with the remaining crumbs. Which the monkey chased over the bar gobbling as if he'd not seen food in a long time. Blood poured out another dram of rum for Vitalis and the little man bowed in thanks. There had been no mention of food for him and Blood offered none. He was tired.

One of the men spoke up. "Hold on." He leaned toward Vitalis. "Early on, you promised something else. Something, what was it?" His face trembled with visible effort of thought.

Some other man spoke up. "Peculiar. A peculiar habit was what he said."

"Oh yes," Vitalis said. "But it's very late. The monkey is exhausted. As we all are."

The men clustered close, loud now and vehement, wanting the rest of the show, not wanting the night to end, wanting something more to tell their fellows who'd already left. Vitalis listened, then looked at Blood. Blood shrugged.

Vitalis said, "Reach deep in your pockets boys. This one is not cheap but dear." He looked at Blood again and said, "Perhaps the girl should go."

Blood looked at Sally. She was flushed high and shook her head. He held her gaze and she shook her head again. He looked back at the performer and said, "There's nothing that monkey can do she's not seen already, one way or another."

Vitalis counted the coins offered to him and then emptied all his takings into his rucksack and put the cap on his head. He turned back to the counter and spoke to the seated monkey. "Hugo," he said. "Stand."

The monkey did.

The man said, "Sow the air, Hugo. Sow the air."

The monkey looked at him.

The man closed his hand so that his fingers and thumb made a circle. Then he pumped it up and down.

The monkey showed his teeth in a sharp baring. Then he clutched himself and masturbated, his teeth still spread, the air hissing from his lungs. The men stood back. Sally came off the hogshead and stepped down the counter for a better view. Blood turned and filled his cup once more and turned back.

The monkey spewed forth.

Blood led the old man out to the stable and showed him where he might make a bed on the hay. The night showing the etiolated pre-dawn light, specters of trees, grass, fernbank, hillside, all glossed gray-silver with heavy dew. The old man had a single blanket in his rucksack and while Blood watched he wrapped himself in it so he was swaddled like an infant, tucked tight, only his framed face visible. He looked up at Blood. The monkey was burrowed against his side.

Blood said, "So where to next?"

Vitalis said, "As I said. Up into French Canada. The townships. Those Canadians know how to have a good time."

"With precious little specie to spare."

"I require little. And as you saw, I make money appear."

Blood nodded. Then said, "Break fast with us in the morning. Then, I was you, I'd be on my way. Word will spread and there's God-fearing righteous people here will be dismayed over accounts of this evening passed. I can promise it. They will vilify me but I'm used to it. You, I believe, would make an easier target."

"It's an odd thing," Vitalis said. "I give them what they're seeking and they do not recognize it's themselves produced it. But save your concern. My feet are light and my need for sleep is slight, an advantage of my years. I'll be long gone before the first of them is rousing. But thank you for the offer of food. Some other time, perhaps."

Blood stood looking down at him. "Yes. Some other time."

Midmorning Blood was up with a mug of tea, taking the sun in the doorway. The old man and the monkey gone like smoke. High-building flat-bottomed clouds worked over the lake. It was the time of year when the heat of day clashed with the sudden chill night air and fabulous storms of yellow and blue lightning in shafts not streaks would bolt the early night sky, the air would sharpen with ozone and rain would pour slantwise from the sky for half an hour, an hour. And the sky would clear after midnight but by dawn mist streamed from the lake and spread through the valleys before being broken by the sun to drift and gather again as clouds overhead. On mornings before and after such storms the air was of a rare quality, so each breath was more akin to drinking fresh cold water than everyday thoughtless breathing. Blood sat enjoying this even as he watched the three horsemen descend the road from the mill and knew they were coming to him. He sipped his tea and waited.

It was Emil Chase and two other men, his brother Peter and Isaac Cole. All wore hats and Sunday clothing. They swiveled their horses to a refined calculated stop before the tavern door.

As a young man Blood had enjoyed cigars, one in an extensive list of things he'd long denied himself. Still there were times and this was one of them when he craved a long ash-tipped cigar to dab the air with. Instead he just sat silent and sipped his tea and waited. There was nothing of these men that demanded or deserved a pleasantry.

Emil Chase spoke. "We're riding to Lancaster to confer with the high sheriff. Enough is enough. You've breached every convention of decency. A man free of scruples cannot be expected to understand that, and you Mister Blood, or whatever your name would be, are such a man. But that fact doesn't compel us to sit idly while you corrupt this small outpost of humanity. In truth just the opposite. Action is called for. You own no discretion, no moral guide. So it must be imposed. Tis the nature of civil society."

Blood did not hesitate. "Your man Hutchinson is welcome. Bring him on. I'll enjoy speaking with him. As you should know, I tend to be quiet and mind my own affairs. But because I don't flap my tongue doesn't mean I close my ears. I'm sure the high sheriff and I could spend an interesting afternoon together. To be blunt, I feel the lack of intelligent conversation."

"Blood," said Chase. "You continue to needle me with words that could be taken as threats. Do you seek to provoke me further?"

"Why not at all," said Blood. He tilted back in his chair and crossed one leg over the other to study the sky. Then looked at the robust miller and said, "It's sure a pretty day for a ride, idn't it."

The party whipped their horses at a strong clip down the road and then pulled up sharp and sat conferring among themselves. Peter Chase had his hat off and was flagging flies away from his horse's head. After a time he turned and trotted back toward the tavern and a moment later Isaac Cole followed. Blood rose to stand in the doorway. Emil Chase watched his departed comrades a moment before booting his horse forward down the empty lonely road. Blood pushed the door shut and heard the two riders go by. They did not stop and he did not expect them to. He went to the kitchen hearth and blew up the coals there and got flames and began breakfast. He thought he'd do well to send Gandy with the oxen and cart over to the mill at Canaan, Vermont, and purchase a winter's worth of meal. And while he was at it, he might as well get enough to offer some in trade. There were plenty of first-year pitch holders and trappers who raised no grain so that Chase's practice of milling for shares would offer nothing. Blood could otherwise beat his price. He'd even be willing to lose a little, although with the trappers there would be no loss unless the winter was poor. He felt no misgiving should Chase grow more peeved. Him and his high sheriff: Fuck them both.

He stirred a bowl of batter for griddle cakes. And resolved that day to hike up Perry Stream to the farm of the big-bellied Dutchman Van Landt. The only man in the territory who passed as a livestock dealer, possessing a motley herd of milk and beef cattle and some half-dozen or so riding and dray horses. While Van Landt enjoyed the public house as much as any other Blood sensed a reserve about him that no others owned—as if Van Landt recognized or respected something of Blood the others did not. Perhaps it was only sharing something of the outcast about him—not just his heritage but also the fact that he dealt in necessities and so was resented by those that needed him. Blood thought he would see if the man had some pullets and a rooster. Blood was desperate for an egg.

Van Landt was pleasant if spare with words. Blood recognized this was the man's nature and not personal. They haggled briefly over poultry and in this exchange Blood, who was not inclined to argue even if the price was high, so badly did he want the chickens, also learned something of the man. Van Landt's being tight lipped was also in a sly way a measure of his scorn for the place he'd found himself in and the men around him. As if the Dutchman was amused at his own predicament.

As Blood was preparing to leave, the pullets and rooster trussed and dangling in groups either end of a pole to carry over his shoulder, Van Landt tilted his jowls toward Blood and said, "Some sort of frolic to your place last evening I hear."

Blood said, "It was a wonder. The men enjoyed themselves. I'd not thought they had it in them."

Van Landt studied the bounty of his barnyard and then looked at Blood. "These people," he said, his thick lips wrapping the words with distaste.

"They know little of what's in them. Perhaps they fear to know themselves too well. One thing certain, it don't stop them judging others."

Blood took up the pole, balanced it over his shoulders. A chicken feather came loose and floated in the air. He said, "Too little sleep and a ringing head always make a man contrite. It don't last."

"Perhaps," said Van Landt. "Perhaps."

In the long summer twilight Blood was in the never-used pig stockade fashioning a perch platform from interwoven poles when he heard the tired trot of a horse coming along the road. He ducked his head out of the low door, hidden in barred shadow to watch Emil Chase ride slumped toward the mill. The man plainly exhausted from his day's travel. As well, Blood guessed, as from his interview with the sheriff. Blood went back among the skittering chickens. He thought Of the two of us, I'd hazard mine was the more productive day. But he was tired himself and there was little satisfaction in the thought.

On Sunday August twelfth, a day on which no-one was sailing, no-one at all, Blood rose mid-morning and wrung the neck of one of the dozen pullets, dressed the bird and plucked it and roasted it bound tight in string hanging at the edge of the coals, all this before Sally came sleep-struck from her room. Hair tangled, wearing the old shabby shift she slept in when she slept in anything at all, places around her neck and shoulders worn through so it was almost less a garment than none at all. She looked at Blood hunched before the coals, turning the chicken back to front toward the heat. "Is that another partridge?"

"No," he said. "It's a roasted chicken."

"You just got em and you're killing em off?"

He turned to look at her. "It's for your birthday."

"Oh my," she said. "I forgot."

"Well that's good. It's becoming for a woman to forget her birthday. Even though it was a little quick in your case."

She walked across the room and looked out the open door upon the day and turned back. "I didn't forget. I just wasn't awake yet. We going to eat that bird for breakfast?"

"No we're going to eat fried potatoes for breakfast, with some green onion cut into em. This chicken we're going to let cool and wrap up in some clean sacking and carry with us. I thought we'd walk up Perry Stream and then go up one of the little feeder brooks until we find a nice pretty place and have our dinner there. Put up a closed sign. Take the day off. You wanted something nice. I thought a picnic might fit the bill."

"A picnic?"

"Yes."

"I ain't never been on a picnic."

"Well," said Blood. "We'll change that."

"I'm getting sick of fried potatoes."

Blood nodded. "A few more days, those pullets settle down, they'll commence to lay. Then we can have eggs. Fried alone or mixed in with the potatoes. That'll be good."

She said, "I never et an egg."

"Sally," he said. "There's plenty you haven't had yet in this life. There's no need for you to announce everything new."

"What if I don't care for em?"

"I imagine you'll like em just fine. And if you don't, you'll just eat up anyway and be glad there's hot food for your belly. Now why don't you go wash up and get dressed."

"You going to be grumpy on my birthday?"

"Not if I can help it. Go get dressed, however you please, pretty or plain. It don't matter to anyone but you today."

She took up the washbasin and a rag and started for the door and then stopped and looked back at him. "Well, I want to be pretty. I want to be pretty for you. There's no need for you to spend the day with a frump."

He stood and put his hands in the small of his back and stretched, kneading the muscles there. He said, "Go on now."

They passed a pleasant afternoon, settled in a dell of soft wild grass between the boles of ancient spruce where the headwaters of a trifling brook ran, bordered both sides with rocks mossbacked and marked with lichen both yellow and orange, the water in spurts of spatter and backsplash before running through a narrow channel into a slight pool deep enough to hold small trout. A bright circle of sunlight slid in crescent motion around the opening as the sun crossed the sky and the rest lay in dapples of shade. The air was pungent with the fernbank that grew across the brook and the scent of fresh water erupted up newborn out of the earth. They ate and lolled in the speckly shade close enough to the full sun so they were warm not hot. Blood napped a little. Luther stalked silent up the small brook after trout that flared ahead of him, some few throwing themselves into the air to scramble over rocks to the next layer up. While Blood slept Sally sat out in the heat of the sun with her dress hiked high onto her thighs and her bodice open as she leaned back on her elbows so her face was turned back for the sun full upon it. When he stirred she sat upright and did the buttons on her front but made no effort to pull the skirt down her legs. It wasn't like he hadn't seen all of her anyway.

Blood rose and walked a hundred feet downstream where there was a larger pool at the base of an overgrown hemlock, roots of the tree great bent knees forming the backside of the pool. He was not gone but screened. He undressed there and slid down into the water which when he was seated rose up around his belly. Then he inched back and found the place where the water ran into the pool in a thick rush between smoothed rocks and settled himself so the thrash of water struck directly on his shoulders and the back of his neck. His legs stretched straight before him; his heels dug into the fine gravel so the loosed pebbles ran and struck and fled over his toes. After a time she came down and stood looking at him. He did not move. She said something to him but all he heard was the water jargon breaking at his back. Perhaps louder than needed he told her he couldn't hear her. She studied him a moment and then began to take her clothes off. When he saw this he stood upright in the pool, the water scarce to his knees. He made no effort to cover himself.

He said, "There's not room but for one. Scooch yourself up like I was so the water hits your back and shoulders. It's the best thing. Like a hundred sweet little hammers working at every muscle."

He clambered out with as much grace as a naked middle-aged man could muster before the eyes of a naked girl. He shook himself and gathered his clothes.

She said, "Don't get too far away. I don't want no one coming upon me here."

He said, "I thought I'd just go up a bit and if that dog hasn't terrified all of em, see if I might catch a batch of these little trouts for our supper."

"I'm still filled up with that chicken." Standing right next to him, naked and sunburned.

"You set in that water a time, your appetite will come back. Go on, get in there now." And he turned and walked a little sideways around the hemlock and paused and dressed. Heard her gasp as she settled down into the brook.

He got his handline out of his pocket and pulled some cartilage from the chicken carcass for baits and told the dog to stay where he was sleeping in the sun, stretched out full on his side. The size of him like a prone pony, some beast of the veld. Luther raised his head and blinked at Blood. Blood tossed him the chicken carcass. The dog began to eat, champing the bones as a man might biscuit.

Blood caught a dozen little trout no larger than the palm of his hand. He cleaned them by opening the vent and prying free the gore with the point of his knife and then dug with his finger for any missing parts. He rinsed the trout in the brook and carried them back down to the opening. He could just see the whiteness of Sally under the heavy hemlock boughs. He made a small fire and impaled each trout on a crotched twig. He sharpened the other end of each stick and ringed the fire with the upthrust fish, as if a circle of them were swimming up toward the sky. He sat and watched them cook, time to time reaching with a piece of wood to rearrange the coals or add some small dry stick to the fire. He carefully turned each fish on its stick to roast the other side. The skin of the cooked side was just black, blistered, the black still showing some residue as a shadow of the trout's speckling.

After a while Sally came up from the pool, her clothes settled upon her as if the effort to dress had been near too much, her gait languid, all her movements slow as if the water had drawn something from her and left something else altogether new. She squatted away from the slender smoke-rise of the fire and grinned at him.

"You were right," she said. "That water emptied my belly out."

"Eat some trout?"

"I could."

"They're ready."

She looked at him and said, "This was nice. This was purely nice."

He began to pull the cooked fish away from the fire. Without looking at her he said, "That's good."

She said, "So what do we do now?"

He turned to look at her, a savage bouquet of trout gathered in one fist. "What do you mean?"

"Well. I guess what I mean is, I guess we eat and then walk down and get back to work. Idn't that so?"

He studied her a moment. He wanted to know what she wanted but hesitated.

And abruptly recalled the date, the demon-thinking squelched thus far and the night still before him. He thought Give over and see what happens. What he said was,

"There'll be men thirsty for a drink after a long Sabbath afternoon I expect. And it could be a party. We could announce your birthday. How's that sound?"

She said, "It's already cost a fair bit of business, this afternoon. It's your money we're talking about here. So that's all right."

He held out the fish until she took them. Then he turned back to the fire and gathered up the remaining fish, his own supper. With his back turned he said, "But what would you like? Money aside. How would you like to finish this seventeenth birthday of yours?" And did not move to look at her but waited. Keeping busy with the fish.

"You really want to know? Or you just being nice?"

He turned. "What do you want?"

She said, "This has been so peaceful. Just you and me and nobody wanting nothing. I'd like to hold on to it a bit more. What I'd like is to spend the evening, just the two of us, alone. Quiet. Easy. Like this." She paused and he heard the fear in her voice as if she were asking too much. She rushed on, "I'd work extra, as long as it took, to make up the difference. I would."

He stripped a trout from the stick and ate it and tossed the head and bones off to Luther who'd come close in the late afternoon shadows. He wiped his lips with his hand and looked at her. She had not yet eaten. Because he had to, he said, "That's fair."

Thinking, You know better. You certainly do. Blame no one else. You tempted fool.

*   *   *

That morning he'd nailed a cedar shingle to the door with the legend Closed For The Day scribed upon it. In a crude hand someone had penciled underneath *To your returned Health Mr. Blood.* He studied this in the thin dusk, then discarded any connection, however dim, with his own internal ravage as a vanity. He followed Sally in and shut the door. And barred the door from the inside but also left the dog out as caution against any so bold as to approach. There was nothing gained in an evening off if continual breaches were attempted. The dog would hinder any so brash.

Not for the first time, Blood considered the nature of the beast. Eight years old, he'd been with Blood from the age of three months. The man Blood obtained him from had both the Wolfhound sire and the Mastiff dam and so Blood knew both as stouthearted bold creatures and had picked the puppy from the littermates because of his size and reserve. Luther was a dog of slow appraisal and resolute loyalty. Blood would never speak of it to another man but sometime during that first year together he realized the dog held a perceptivity of Blood's needs, of the tenuous and changeable nature of circumstances. There was some alignment of his mind to Blood's that allowed him to comprehend without commands what was required of him. Blood wondered if this was some aspect of his own nature, some vibratory field the dog keyed to. Blood did not know and wasn't sure he wanted to. He had no desire to know himself through the mind of the dog. Otherwise he trusted him absolutely.

The air inside the house was stultified from the closed-up warm day, overlaid with thickened scents of humanity, the odors of living that life itself seemed to abate but absence magnified. Sally was getting a fire going in the kitchen hearth and that would freshen the air. Blood went to her room and opened her narrow high window so air might flow into the house with the door barred. Then out into the drawing night to squat near-blind by the side of the swollen cow, milked and left the bucket outside for the dog. They would need no fresh milk until morning. He entered the enclosure where the young hens and cock had run of the stockade and flapped his arms to drive them into the hutch that was meant to keep bears from hogs and shut and bolted the heavy door. Then back to the tavern. His home, he abruptly comprehended. His first, seventeen years to the day.

*   *   *

They sat in the kitchen with a candle burning on the table. There was a single ladderback chair and a set of plank benches. The fire was small, a single log resting on a heap of coals with the slightest fingers of flames working. Blood had brought in his two good pewter mugs half filled with rum and the pitcher of water and they sat quietly talking: Blood on a bench and Sally sitting on the table beside him, her feet resting on the bench.

He said, "You favor a high perch."

"What's that mean?"

"I noticed you like to sit up atop something. The stool behind the counter or up on the hogsheads. And look at you now."

"I oughtn't to set on the table I guess." She did not move.

"Sit where you like. It was just an observation."

"I like to see around me. I learned that young. It don't mean for sure I'll see what's coming but it don't hurt."

"Well, that's right."

"You're the same way. I seen the way you watch people. Like you're not doing a thing at all. I know how you work."

"Do you?"

"I believe so. The only real difference between you and me, Blood, is you got the bulk of a man on your side."

"You think that's it?"

"Mostly." She sipped from her cup. "There's men respect you and one's don't but there ain't one I seen yet that don't have a fear of you in them."

Blood smiled with no pleasure. He said, "And you?"

That girl grin. A glimmer of something else. She looked away. "I've got no fear of you."

"And other men?"

Swift, serious, she said, "I fear them all."

That was a good thing. He said, "There's not one you're a little fond of?"

"You think I'm a fool?"

"No. I do not think that."

She drank and so did Blood. She said, "I know what I am to these men. Some little bit of time they mostly feel bad about afterward. But it ain't me they feel bad about, it's theirselves. It's what they need I guess. But it don't have much to do with me. Others see it different most likely. But that ain't me either. Do you know why I charge on top of you?"

Blood studied her. Then said, "Everybody wants money."

Sally drank again and looked back at him. "No. Well, that's part of it. But I want them to look at me while they pay. I don't want any of em thinking every bit of me is yours, neither. I got to have some authority over em. But mostly I don't want the first one of em thinking it's anything but what it is. I don't want some idjit confusing fucking with anything else. That would be the worst thing, don't you think?"

Blood nodded, said nothing. Considering how she'd slipped in the bit about remaining someway separate from him. A small alert perhaps except it made sense.

She paused a moment, perhaps giving him time to sum this. Then went on.

"But the money. You know what it truly is to me?"

Blood drank from his mug which was near empty. He guessed hers was too. It was their one nightly dram. His mind was divided. He wanted more. Guessed she did too. He was apprehensive but mildly expansive. He said, "No, I don't know. What is it but money?"

She drained her mug and set it down on the tabletop with a precise thump. She peered at him. "You're going to think I'm mad."

"I doubt it."

She craned sideways to look at the fire and then back to him. She said, "I only take coin. Silver coin. I don't take notes, no paper money. You want to know why?"

He waited.

She went on. "It's the moon. Those coins in my hand is like a piece of moonlight captured. Or more like loaned to me," she said. "But I watch the moon. Up in the sky. And it's all its ownself. There's nothing there but moon. White and silver and just rolling across heaven. And it looks to me like a nice place to be. Peaceful. And the moonlight falling. Nights I look out at it and the world can be different. I see that the world is more than how it seems daytimes. And I can hold them coins in my hand. Like someplace I never been and never will go to but I know is there."

And she stopped.

Blood said, "Well, I'll be goddamned."

She rose from the table to stand on the bench and stepped to the floor. She turned to him and said, "Isn't that the worst foolishness you ever heared?"

Blood drained off his cup and choked and coughed. His throat a blistered tube. His eyes watered. "Not the worst," he said. "But close. Close enough."

He looked upon her erect up before him. Bent forward, intent upon his verdict, her face screwed tight, her arms folded over her chest.

"Oh Sally," he said. "Go ahead. Go right ahead. Love that moon. It's the most faithful thing you could ask for."

Much later. A tin pitcher of rum on the table now and a bucket of water with the dipper tilted across the top. A pair of new logs on the fire and the candle had consumed itself. Outside, Luther had bayed once and that was all. She sat cross-legged on the table with her skirt pulled down over her knees. Just room for their cups between them.

"They say you killed your wife."

"Is that all they say?"

"No."

"I told you not to pester me with what you heard."

"I know."

They were quiet. Both drank. The firelight was grown liquid, runnels lapping and receding as the logs settled and seethed.

"She died," he said. "In an accident."

"A long time ago."

"Yes," he said. "It would seem so to you."

"Not to you."

"No."

"I'm sorry."

"Don't you be feeling sorry for me."

"If it was a accident you don't carry blame for it."

"I didn't say that."

She paused then and drank, looked away from him. Then back. "So you was responsible some way for it? You caused it to happen?"

He considered rising and ending it. He wasn't sure he trusted himself to continue. He wasn't sure he trusted her. He wasn't sure he wouldn't hurt her. But he remained seated and took up his pewter cup instead, turning it in his hands, watching the light soft in the metal. Then he looked at her and said, "Not the way you think."

"All right." But he heard the warble of disbelief.

He sighed and drank and refilled it from the pitcher and drank again. He set the cup on the table, wiped his mouth with his hand and looked at the girl. Her eyes upon him the gaze of wisdom certain unto itself, the gaze of one who has witnessed most all the profusion of bad that life may offer its hostages. One whose notion of humanity extended not much further than ever-changing laws of behavior she must decode against what harm was coming her way. And Blood saw it was not re-demption after all that she offered, though he'd never truly believed that. She was a tender balance against the weight of his life. Thought unob-tainable and more than he'd dare hope for.

He spoke soft but clear. "My wife died doing something she loved. But at a time and place she knew better than to be. For myself, how I contributed, was being engaged in activities, had she known, would have caused her great distress. I had no reason to think she would learn of them. But life is peculiar and the forces that guide us are not random but of great design unknowable to any of us. In the end I can't say I weren't responsible for what befell her. I was. Certainly so. In every way but the most obvious."

Her face was knotted with thought. She said, "You think she done it on purpose?"

"No." Quickly.

"I don't understand."

"It was an accident. But it was not. It can never be so, in my mind. And there's no other authority for me to consult. God is silent to me. As He should be. Whatever mercy He might once have extended to me I quelled. As sure as that candle there died. I used up every drop with-out even knowing I was doing it. And once gone, it does not return. He is not limitless in His mercy, as the preachers would have us think. Like any Father, there is a point where He cries Enough. And I passed that point. I have not looked for any mercy and expect none. In this life or any other."

It was quiet then in the room. Some time passed. Blood had lived without clocks for a long time. Without markers of any sort time is allowed its own rhythm. It moves slow or fast depending on its need. Now it was very slow.

Finally Sally said, "Maybe it really was just a accident. Something that just happened."

"Oh it was. As far as that goes. I don't believe, and never have, that she intended things to turn out as they did. Most I can say, as far as she was concerned, is she was angry. Perhaps nothing beyond knowing something wasn't right. Even just thinking she could dance close and come to no harm. Whatever she did know, whatever she suspected, no blame lies with her. It's mine alone. Because, you see, she was not alone."

Sally considered this. Drank some from her cup. And then very quiet she said, "Who was with her?"

"A boy."

"Your boy? Yours and hers?"

"Yes."

"And he died too?"

"Yes."

"I hadn't heard that."

Blood stood. Struggled off the bench and back away from it. Took up his cup and drained it. This time he did not choke. He was very drunk and knew it and possessed of absolute clarity. Everything, all of it, was right before him. The upturned sunburned face of the girl the perfect confessor he'd been seeking. Not believing he'd wanted that until it appeared. In fact the opposite. But he was within it now and there was a surge, a joy unmistakable in the dropped bindings. For an instant he recalled the sound of the knifeblade cutting the sinews that locked the Deacon's mouth. He set the cup on the table before her and gripped his hands together.

He said, "Yes there was a boy died with her. But there were others as well. Whom I abandoned. A younger boy." He paused but went on, to have it out, all of it. "And another. The oldest child. A daughter. Have you heard"—he paused again to reconsider but the words would not—"have you heard that part as well?"

She was silent. She hadn't moved, still cross-legged on the tabletop. Her cup balanced on her folded knee. Her eyes away.

"I regret—," Blood said and stopped. He was crying. He wanted to believe his tears were pure. That being held for so many years they had gained a purity. He knew it wasn't so. It could not be so. He tore at his face with his hands as if to break it apart, to stifle this grief undeserved. It was no help. He finished, "I regret everything."

He fled the house. When he jerked back the door the hound Luther was lying on the step and Blood came near to falling but flailed with his arms to catch the jambs, kicking hard the side of the dog who raised up snarling and Blood kicked the dog again and then was past him, falling running off the step out into the night, around the house. Into the dark. Away.

He went up through the wildgrass dadewater and came to a stop at the edge of the stream where a long-fallen beech lay with several feet of butt-end up on the bank, the trunk a footbridge that led down into midstream, growing more slender as it went. A footbridge to nowhere. There was no moon, just the summer night sky, the bleed of stars white far overhead. Too little light to throw shadow upon the land but the water curled silver in streaks and backwash. The voice of the stream muted in the night, the land silent but for the faint water. It was cold. He straddled the log and sat gazing down its length to where it disappeared into the water.

It was as if he'd torn some indispensable sustaining muscle. The false clarity of the tavern rum was gone. The girl just a girl, a hard-raised young whore. Perhaps the apt confessor for him but he was not deserving of one, any at all. His broken silence was in fact a final violation, the concluding and irreversible measure of his failing. His silence had been his only memorial, his only true act of contrition. His silence had become his life and his life was nothing but dedication to the memory of desecration. His being was mere acolyte to muteness. Some meager offering of himself before the vast silence of the sea of night that surrounded him, always.

Long years gone he'd considered death by water for himself. And rejected it as a vanity, a clumsy self-serving action, puny and poor in sight of the enormous bile of his soul.

He sat broken watching the water move in darkness, carving its endless course into the earth, over the earth. His faint breath emitting the only discernable mark that he was there at all. It was cold enough so there would be light frost in the morning. He made no move to warm himself, did not even bring his arms up from where they hung lank to wrap his chest. The cold was little enough of what he deserved. He was absolutely free of sentiment or self-pity when he wondered if he would recall the sensation of being cold after his death when he had no expectation but to reside in everlasting fire.

Born Micajah Blood Bolles forty-seven summers before in New Bedford, the middle name after a never-known grandfather on his mother's mother's side. Into a family of ship chandlers that owned their own rope walk and a dozen sail-makers' lofts. They purchased the raw goods and sold the finished ones and paid only enough for labor to ensure the quality of that work. Along with these staples they could larder a vessel with salt-pork and brined beef, dense ship-biscuit, salt, sugar, tea, meal and flour, live crates of fowl, tobacco for smoking or chewing, rum for the crews and brandies for the captains, firewood or coal for the galley, candles and rope matches. Besides the sails from the lofts and the sheets and shrouds from the rope-walk they produced everything else needed, right down to seaman's bags and rope hammocks. The only thing they did not own was a forge, preferring to purchase outright finished fittings; forges burned down. They owned sheds on the wharves as well as a block-long warehouse of brick that had offices for clerks and scribes on the upper floor, as well as the main office where Micajah Bolles worked alongside his brother and father, all within the cataract-cloud of his grandfather's presence—the old man the only one who'd been to sea as a young man and eventual captain until he shipwrecked in the Irish Sea with a load of cotton from South Carolina bound for the English mills and who, saved, returned by passage and vowed to not so much as set foot in a dinghy for an afternoon sail on Apponagansett Bay. He would not even own shares in vessels. Ships foundered, ruined, wrecked, burned. If they made their return they would still require outfitting; if not some new vessel would need the same. He made this liv-

ing by the sea, from the sea but not on the sea. It could never take him
again. Every year the great autumn storms would whiten his face, as if
the sea were pursuing him inland.

Micajah Bolles attended Harvard College at sixteen and married
Betsey Marsh two years later and set up house at two blocks situate
midway between his parents' home and hers. The Marsh men whalers
of good local reputation and wealthy but the men who sailed under
them earned hard their wages and almost to a man would land swearing never to sail under a Marsh again but when the ships were ready
to return to the far-northern waters the crews were never difficult to
fill—the captains might be severe but the wages and shares premium
to the work. And Betsey Marsh loved the sea, loved it not just for the
life it provided her and loved it also not just on pretty summer days
when the Bay fluttered with the most trifling of breezes, but loved
likewise the storms and dark winter days when the harbor-bound
ships ran silver with ice on the riggings, loved the summer squall-lines
that spurted along the horizon or turned and ran inland, where she
would stand on the wharf and watch the falling sheets of rain split by
lightning coming over the Bay toward her, thrashing her dark curls
against her face, the thrill blood-ripened her cheeks and her eyes wide,
their burnished blue like the last piece of summer sky lost within the
onslaught of storm, waiting there, leaning into the wind until the very
last moment before the rain lashed her, dashing then for cover of the
wharf-sheds.

And Micajah Bolles would stand at the upper-story window of his
office ahead of those storms and spy her figure out on the wharf, stand
there flushed and hot and frightened for her all at once. It was as if
Betsey was something created out of a world that was unknown to him.
As if they lived in not the same place but two different places overlaid. And part of this excitement was in being able to end the day by
returning to his own house where she would be waiting him with
supper prepared by the serving girl but overseen by her and she would
be as delighted to see him as he was her. And she would sit and listen
to the details of his day as if it too, for her, was someplace almost beyond imagination. She was a year younger than he was and although
they lived as adults, when the candle lantern was cupped and blown
out for the night they were as children together, their nights wild rau-

cous romps of laughter sleek and slippery as their skins, which seemed to be not two skins but one shared between them. He could sleep four hours a night and work ten hours the next day. And come home not tired but exhilarated.

The only contention seemed so obvious as to be inevitable, as if the two bloodlines swept down neat straight lines for conflict at the sole place available within their world: the sixteen-foot dinghy day sailer that had been her father's when he was a boy and that Betsey began to sail at such a young age that she claimed never to have been taught; it was something she had always known. She would laugh at his fears, his determination not to go onto the water with her and not once would she consider giving it up. The one time he attempted insistence was after their first child, Sarah Alice, was born but he had no response when Betsey looked at him and said, "Who would teach her to sail, if not me?"

And there were the children, along with the not unexpected problems of child-bearing. Micajah himself had a brother and two sisters he'd never known. After Sarah Alice came a girl Rebecca who lived three days and then a boy child Hazen who survived and after that a miscarriage too late to be hidden from anyone but too young for proper burial and then came the next boy Cooper who thrived and then John who lived seventeen months and died of a fever. After that a period of three years where she did not conceive and they did not talk of this. Then the final child, another girl, was stillborn and without speaking of it they knew she would be their last.

She was born the spring Sarah Alice turned thirteen. Micajah Bolles was thirty-two years old. His grandfather sat each day blind in his office chair turned to the window open summer or winter so he could hear the sounds of the harbor and wharves, the groan of chocks and pulleys, the swarm of gulls, the cries of fishwives and stevedores commingling as if the tongue of the world rose up beside the sea to fall upon his acute hearing and keep it living for him. Other than this he did little and his grandson, his younger grandson, had somehow gained his ear. Years later Blood recalling this would consider that this grandfather had left one life behind and made another of the same materials, the only ones available to him, and perhaps could sense something of this same ability in his younger grandson. What else to explain his preference for Micajah over the older brother, Proctor?

Micajah could look out the window in his grandfather's office, the one near-always open to the life of the sea and spy the chimney pot of his own house and some afternoons he would pause there, the old man behind him talking, the words, issues, commands, already known to the grandson who felt free to peer out and within himself see the interior of his home, the wife, the children, and he would from time to time catch himself in some near-frightful daze, a spinning fall of the mind—how had he arrived at all this? How had it happened around him? At thirty-two he did not recognize himself in the looking-glass of his shaving stand. Strapping as a youth he'd gained the softness of middle age, his throat pouched beneath his chin, his waist slack but full against the stays of his moleskin breeches. He walked through his days and mostly felt this was the way of all men. Sundays he sifted each word of the sermons and homilies for strength, for the wisdom that might allow him to accept his life as it was. What he could not understand was that while all men struggled thus some few must brand themselves. Out cast.

He feared most a fault, an essential weakness—some ill-forged hinge that one day would give way: that the struggles of the mind were but a child's fright mask for the primacy of the soul. Where the fullness of a man resided.

This hidden being shamed him most before Betsey. Who had aged and thickened with child-bearing and raising, whose formidable lustrous curls had already fringed with silver but her eyes were the same vault of blue, of pure wet—night promise they'd always been. And who carried her motherhood silent but prideful, who seemed to accept the numbering of days, who seemed to him to understand that all life was thus; quick, abrupt, savory as well as sweet. Who was no longer the fleet young girl she had been and did not seem to wish to be. Or if she did he did not hear of it. Anymore than he broached to her his own tattered youth still squalling within.

Perhaps in the custom of calling each other Mother and Father they had also annulled their true intimacy and assumed portrayals of themselves. He could imagine all too well the look on her if he were to suggest this.

She would still sail the Bay on a bright summer day, often with one or another of the children with her, coming in all of them shimmering and sunburnt, hair and skin filmed with salt, eyes bold as if gained something of the depth the little dinghy skimmed over. And those times he knew she held her own secret, one he could never know. He did not begrudge her this. His own mystery so vast he thought unknowable, fully, even to himself. A restless soul. He drifted. Silently, as if by chance.

And so, as antidote or disguise or even clearly a step considered but not yet named, he joined fully into the society of men. Politics held little interest but the alehouses and taverns, where all politics began and often ended as well, offered more than rhetoric and self-promotion—there were men like himself seeking respite from the silent insidious dust of each cloying day, ones who would come in and sit silent with their brown bitter ales or rum toddy before them and he could sit and watch the dust slip from them as the level of their drink went down and most times after calling for another they would turn and speak to the man next to them and so step tentative into the day made newly bearable.

There were drunkards and men who could hold their drink and Micajah Bolles knew which of these he was and which he intended to remain.

And all the while, it was not even the company of men he sought. That company only offered the pretext, the deep woods that his single solitary tree might blend within.

The girls were daughters of fishermen or in from the enfolding farmlands and sick of fishguts or the stink of cattle. They came in every stripe and check and for the longest time he would allow no favorite, not only from the determination to keep his heart if not his body pure but also because there were so many of them—as if the Lord God turned out on the face of the earth these lovely creatures not so much for the delight of man as for His own delight in His making—a notion that struck Micajah Bolles with the force of a gale wind. Not that he was reckless or abandoned like other men he witnessed. He would go weeks, sometimes months between girls. Most days and not only Sundays swearing off them completely.

But there were so many and they were so beautiful and Micajah Bolles did not yet understand it was his own delusive heart he was trying to fill. And did not yet own the gauge to fathom the depth of that void. Although the sickness for him was less of infidelity—he believed he held his heart pure to Betsey—but the necessity this prompted; the girls owned names he forgot even as they removed their clothing, these girls lacked not only names but history or future or anything at all beyond the moment. All he wanted was that moment with them. And it was this above all else—before, during, after—that proved the sickness of himself.

So she was the last thing expected. Called Molly and again he did not ask her details, did not want her history or sad dreams and this girl seemed no different in that she understood this. Even when the inevitable time came lying beside her spent but for the first time desiring to know her, wanting her selfness, every cranny of hope and to salve every wrong. To listen to all she might say. To talk himself. It was this last that stopped him, not able to reveal himself. He had already given her more than he knew was prudent. So he believed.

She had scant lank hair the color of weak sunlight, small feet and hands and long white legs. The first he saw of her was a forearm coming over his shoulder to set a tankard before him, and the fine drift of hair over the perfect swell of muscle from the sharp bone of her wrist toward the point of her elbow was so lovely that he wanted to take it between his teeth. The rest of that night he did not speak to her but watched her. Her face was pleasant, neither round nor sharp featured, her mouth with just enough curve to her lips to draw him, her eyes pale, a color he could never recall, could not in fact, looking at her, name. She was no beauty but was not homely or ill-made, just a girl who passed on the street he would not have looked back at. And yet from that first glance of forearm she was lodged in him as firmly as the fabled heathen arrow. An axe, it might as well have been.

To his surprise she preferred to make her assignations in the morning hours, when the sun was well up but she had not truly roused from the bed in her cheap room. He was the only man she saw and he paid her well enough to ensure this. Twice a week, on Wednesday and Saturday mornings he would visit her, on the weekday arriving late at the office claiming he was needed at home and Saturday having to say nothing more to Betsey than just once telling her it was a time he could work undisturbed. And Molly would still be abed waiting him, her hair tangled with sleep and her eyes slow but her breath sweetened from the night by a tin cup of milk. She had small teeth, perfect but for one canine that gaped and jutted a little forward. When her lips shut over it, it appeared that she was concentrating hard upon some unknown thing. That same mouth would astonish him each time with the ferocity of her appetite, her lips firm and flicking against him at once, the small point of her tongue running the inside of his mouth as if it would run down his throat and into his belly if it could.

She had very small breasts, nipples the color of her tongue and only enough body hair to know it was there. The one time he saw her by candlelight it could not be seen at all. It was only after he was forever done with her that he understood something of the significance of his attraction to this woman as child. And would recall that evening by candlelight when he was dressing and she lay curled, her hip jutting a shadow, the rest of her pink, when of a sudden she said, "How long do you think, Mister Bolles, before you come to despise me?" Her tone placid, no different than if she were asking when she would be beaten. He stood a moment, stopped. Then more tender than he knew he said, "It's myself I'll despise." She turned her face away and was quiet. He finished dressing and was about to leave when she spoke again, her face to the pillow, words all but muffled. "I guess that's right. I guess I ain't even worth your spite." He went to her and sat on the bed, gathered her and held her. Later, going from the boardinghouse, his heart was terrible and dark. Not knowing better, he believed himself fully lost.

And so he was with Molly the late summer Saturday morning following the spring stillbirth when Betsey had taken the older boy Hazen for her first sail since her confinement and it may have been the urgency she felt to grasp what was left of the summer's rare weather or it may have been just bad luck. Or, Micajah Bolles would later think, it might have been some wisdom in the blood that some way she sensed where her husband was. Because the one old man out handlining on the Bay swore later that when the squall line bloomed out of the horizon-fallen and gloomed cumulous and built out toward the open ocean beyond the reach of the Bay and held there as summer squalls would do, livened with lightening and the dark gashes of rain visible but offering nothing more inside the Bay but a freshened breeze, it was then, the old man testified to all willing to listen, that Betsey Marsh Bolles turned the little dinghy into the wind and sailed out toward the swells and dark water and heavy storms of the squall. Kneeling on the seat with one hand on the tiller and the other stretched to hold taut the sheet at the end of the boom, her face lifted so the wind drove back her hair and

her mouth was cut open in broad unheard laughter. He also said the boy
Hazen was not then in sight, likely hunkered low against the decking over
the bow.

They were missing three days. Micajah Bolles sat silent and unsleeping
through this time in his house while his mother and mother-in-law tended
Sarah Alice and Cooper, and whatever other arrangements the household
needed were conducted silently, without his knowledge or caring. And
the men of both families came in groups or as the days passed one by
one to sit with him and speak to him and he would answer not the least
query and they accepted this as his right. Not knowing they were dealing with a man who had abandoned all rights that might have once been
his. The only time he spoke was when his grandfather was led in to see
him, the two of them left alone and the old man dug through the air
between them until Micajah Bolles lifted one hand and the old man held
it between both of his and was silent a long time, long enough so Micajah
Bolles believed the old man understood all that was appropriate was
silence. But then his grandfather spoke.

"God," the old man said, "is a manure heap."

"No," the grandson said. "He's fair."

The grandfather removed his hands and pushed himself from his
chair to stand looking where he thought the younger man was seated.
He said, "He relinquishes us all, all creatures in our hours of need. We
desire Him so, yet He repudiates without hesitation. I'll have a word
with that son of a bitch soon enough." Then turned and began to call
the name of the nephew who had led him in, his voice shaking as if to
tear the house down around them.

The bodies were found Wednesday dawn, thrown up by a desert-
ing tide. Bloated, feasted upon by fish and crab, the boy naked but
wrapped in kelp as if the sea at the last moment had taken some measure of pity upon his innocence. They were carried up by fishermen
and laid out on planks supported by ladderback chairs while the women
washed the bodies and a younger Marsh brother was sent for the cabi-
netmaker to come for measurements. The Congregational reverend
was in the house, had spent time seated praying beside the silent Micajah
Bolles until the bodies were brought and then went to attend the women.
And so left him in the rush-seated chair that over the days and nights
intervening had burned blisters where the sides of his thighs rubbed

back and forth as he swayed with the awful rhythm of his heart. The rhythm of his guilt.

And then Sarah Alice came timid through the door, her own face swollen and discolored but a young woman nonetheless and bound to the duties of the house, mysteries he no longer understood. As if he ever had. She was the spit of her mother, even in grief. Perhaps even more so right then than ever before: almost the girl he had married—now, because it was what she understood she must do, assuming responsibility. As if she could see the future more clearly than he.

"Father," she implored. "They'll be removed soon. Won't you view them a last time?"

He could not refuse her. As if she knew best. Engaged in a dream, he allowed her to take his hand and lead him to the matched coffins where the powder and rouge and new clothes cut large did nothing to disguise the bleak corruptions before him.

He fled the house.

And went off in the shattering daylight where he had never been before, into the southwest end where the lanes were uncobbled and narrow, twisting between the shacks of fishermen and sailor's widows and those useless with age or crippled and unable to work, to where if any soul recognized him they would not speak his name and where a man such as himself would not be safe after nightfall from the hungry roving gangs of young men who cared nothing for his name but only for the wallet the cut of his clothes would announce. Strode hard upright through the middle of the day, looking not left nor right and meeting no eye but cutting through the ragtag crowd, each bootfall hard as if digging forward into the earth. The last time he would walk this way as the man he then was. Those who saw him shied away and it was not from the implausible presence of a man such as himself but his oblivious strident purpose. He passed by several gin-houses because he was not far enough away into this bowel of the town and then turned a corner into another ragged lane where a great sow lay blocking the way as her dozen get tumbled at her upturned teats and here he paused and looked about him and entered a poor public house with no name but a signboard swinging in the shape of an hourglass and he thought there could be no more propitious augur and later he would recall this and know he was indeed seeking all that would befall him. Almost, guilty heart and soul, as if freed.

Benches lined the walls and a pair of trestle common tables were set out in the small room and behind that was a plank bar set across a barricade of hogsheads with a rack of tin cups on the wall behind. There were no windows, what light there was came from cheap ill-made tallow candles, the room bleared with smoke from the burning wicks. This time of day the room was but half-filled, with young and old alike and none did more than glance at him. It was quiet, nothing like the noise of the tavern public rooms he was used to. He took coins from his pocket and stood at the plank bar and drank his first-ever cup of Holland gin and then another. And after that another. It was common lore that gin offered illumination unlike any other kind and the joke among his own sort was that it must—the gin-sots otherwise so miserable in appearance and health there must be some gain not otherwise obvious. It was for the very poor.

A boundless time passed. Later, he would reckon it in some number of days but would never seek greater accuracy for he needed none—it was a hole he stepped into and once out again it was into another life altogether. At some point he moved from standing to a bench at one of the tables. He spoke only to the proprietress, a toothless ancient with miserable rheumy eyes. The room filled and emptied and filled again around him. He woke once, face turned sideways down in a pool of curdled vomit that might have been his own or another's. There was no way to know. He wiped himself with his pocket handkerchief and waved for more gin. He ate nothing—there was nothing offered and even if there had been he wanted only the hot breath of oblivion within the gin. He woke a second time curled under one of the benches and found that his wallet was cut from around his neck and his pockets emptied and his watch stripped from his waistcoat although the thieves had somehow missed a single gold piece in the very same watch pocket— likely having jerked the watch out by the chain last thing.

That gold piece bought more gin, enough this time to send him down into the hole, a blackness so complete he would never know its face, or his own within it. It was not sleep this time but some walking condition of gone. What brain peered from his eyes throughout this time was a brain forever again not available to him. There were no splinters of light, no half images recalled afterward. It was as if he had entered the realm of the dead, although it was only later that he would comprehend the blackness that way. Only later when he wished it had indeed been that very thing rather than the living vacancy he occupied for those unknown hours.

He woke to a piercing crackling and crazed summer dawn with the open-window birdsong great jabbing probes into his brain. He woke in his own house in a bed other than his marriage bed. He was alone but the furniture was tumbled and the covers torn off the bed save for the sheet on which he lay, naked from the waist down. The room of his daughter. Of Sarah Alice.

The house was quiet that very early morning he escaped New Bedford. He made his way swiftly to the harborside and found passage on the first ship with a captain he did not know, the ship only bound for New York. Which it turned out was the farthest he went from home. He spent a year in New York mopping barroom floors in exchange for green cheese and stale crackers and buckets of flat beer. And busting heads of sailors or piece-work tailors or whoever was fighting in the bar every night. And there was always a pallet to sleep on during the hours the bar was closed. He was better than a watchdog and, whatever else they saw when they looked upon him, the men he worked for knew he could be trusted. He was badly beaten twice but his hard fare and harder life soon replaced the physical man with a version suited to the otherwise new man; he lost no weight but grew hard and thick-muscled as his soul did not heal but annealed. His mind became inured not only against himself but all humanity—concluding all efforts otherwise, by anyone, were delusions of the self. That the exercise of free will was a mere mask for destiny or fate. He doubted the hand of God but did not discount it—discarding only the God of the pulpit and the pious.

He left New York on foot with a hand-drawn peddler's cart in the fall a year later and went into the hills of western Connecticut and Massachusetts, calling on the backwoods forlorn farmwives, taking what they had for what they needed. The cart was fully loaded when he acquired it and so that first winter of hard hauling was pure profit. The only cost the curses of the old peddler, beaten and robbed of his purse, who had thought Blood his savior as the first light of day smoked through the mist off the Hudson and rats overran the streets. Blood pausing only long enough to assess the opportunity before dragging the old man to a slumped heap against a coal chute, paying no mind as the mutter of thanks grew to mingle and include Blood with the cutpurses and thieves, a mewl easily left behind. The only sound then the trudge of hobnails and the faint creak of the wheels. The cart was well made, balanced so with a full load a man could walk easily all day between the shafts.

So began seventeen years of cycles and half circles, all radiant from New Bedford as the hub of unseen spokes, the opposing magnetic pole he could neither approach nor leave altogether.

When he wearied of peddling, of haggling over pins and tea with those too poor to afford such goods, he gave it up and for a number of years was a drover for the Boston or New York markets, hiring local boys eager for a time off the farm to attend the herds of cattle, swine, sheep, turkeys—whatever was in season or demand or supply. Then, sick of this he made charcoal for a year but did not like that either for although solitary it meant being in one place. He needed to move. Motion was the only thing that would still and steady his mind. For a brief period he traded in cowhides and was left alone, dealt with quickly when there was a dead or dying cow, his oxcart swarmed with flies and about him was the putrescence of decay but the market was poor—the tanneries wanted fresh hides and it took him weeks through the countryside to build a load. He had roughened to his true nature but even such has limits. He went back to driving livestock but no longer could tolerate such close company as that of the boys and down-at-heels men he had to hire.

More than once he regretted giving up the peddler's cart. Of all things it seemed to suit him best. Even, as he grew older and more solid within his new self, his true self he believed, he thought now he would not mind so much taking what could be had from those who could not spare it. It was not for him to judge another's desires. And so was up in Maine when he heard of the Indian Stream country from a man who had a cartload of goods ready to make the journey and a broken leg that would journey nowhere soon.

It seemed to Blood it was the time in his life for a new venture to strike someplace fresh and see what yield might come. And it was not whim that led him to the bawd-house and the game of careful calculated cards that won him the girl he'd glimpsed once the year before. For in the intervening time she had come to him in dreams, and while he could scorn her silent pleading gaze for he did not know her, he could not ignore the dreams themselves. For they were the only dreams he woke from, ever, that did not leave him sweating, abject, enthralled with terror and humiliation and hatred of his own flesh, his relentless pumping heart, the very life that carried him forward. Once, briefly, waking from a dream of her, he considered she might be placed before him as some possible redemption, a notion he rid himself of before even rising that day. He regarded the girl as a prospect, an investment not pure and only momentarily simple. There was no purity and simplicity was always a disguise for something not yet understood.

Sally found him on the log by the stream some time later. It was still full dark although off in the brush a sparse few birdcalls trembled as if the birds were just trying them out. She had her shawl over her shoulders and came and stood without speaking beside where he sat. He did not glance or acknowledge her and she stood looking down into the water as well. He had nothing to say to her and did not want to hear what she would say to him. But he could not send her away. She had heard him and waited and followed him out. She had something of him no other being, living or dead, had. He wondered if she realized that yet or when she would. And what she would attempt to make of it when she did. His wrists and hands and ears ached with cold.

Finally she said, "After I got used to whoring there was a time when every man that looked old enough, when I took him in the bed, I told myself this could be my father. I never questioned one of em, not like I did you when we first started out. And so what I done was, each one of em that seemed like they might be it I worked extra hard for em. It wasn't all that many, not just ones that might be old enough. There was ways I picked and chose. You know I don't favor my mother much. I looked for men with fair or reddish hair. Or hair had once been that way. And you always talk a little first. So the ones that had never been to the house before I could rule out pretty much. Now some men will lie about that sort of thing, even to a whore. But you can usually make out when a man's lying. The men off ships didn't never lie about it; it was only men from Portland or nearby places that would lie. There wasn't any other reason for em to lie—they just feared being found out by their wives someway. Now my mother didn't likely know but if somehow she had she sure wouldn't have announced it, either to them or me. So, I did that. I figured there was no way for em to know me but at least they might remember me. To make some man who might be my father remember me. So I done that for a while and then I quit it."

She stopped. When he finally looked at her she was staring down into the stream. He said, "That's a sad thing."

"I know."

"Is that why you quit it?"

"No. I quit because it was making me too popular with certain men and the other girls got lathered up and a couple worked me over and told me not to holler and moan so damn much."

"I see," Blood said. Looking at her now. Then he said, "So when did you discover it was sad to have been doing that?"

"Why," she said. "Just tonight."

They were quiet together then.

After a time she said, "Life is terrible sad, idn't it?"

"Yes," he said.

She reached then and touched his bare arm, just laid her hand flat on his forearm. She held it there a moment, then reached and touched his chest through the neck opening of his blouse.

"You're awful cold," she said. And took her shawl off and wrapped it around him. He did not move while she did this. Then she reached again and lifted one of his hands from where it hung down and held it between both of hers and bent and breathed into the cup of her palms to warm him. Then she tugged at him, a small gesture that she could have quit if he resisted at all.

"Come on," she said. "Come in the house."

* * *

He sat on the bench with her shawl around him while she blew the fire up and sat also when she opened the door and spoke the dog's name and waited until the dog came in, where once inside he looked at Blood and went into the tavern and Sally shut and bolted the door and knelt again and pokered the fire flat and added logs on top. Then she came to him, took the shawl from his shoulders and folded it and placed it on the table and then took his hand and he stood and followed her into her room. Where she undressed him while he stood motionless and then let himself be led to the bed where she covered him with the soft bearskin and he lay shivering in the dark while she reached up to close the shutter of her window. Lit only by reflected fire from the next room she undressed and came under the cover.

She knelt up under the robe which tented over her and spilled down to cover him and he could not see her at all but felt her hands running over him, just sliding at first over his chest and arms and then down his stomach to his thighs and on down his legs until she was hunched at the bottom of the bed with first one foot and then the other between her hands. At his feet she began all over again, this time gripping and stretching and working the muscles between her hands, doing this all the way up his body, this time much more slowly, and he was warming as she went. As she worked and moved over him some part or another of her body came against his briefly and he knew this was not provocation but still each time something other than her hands touched or brushed him he clenched hard his teeth against that impact. It was the first time in years anyone had touched him so; the first time he would have allowed it if any previous had tried but none had.

When she came again to his arms and chest and shoulders she did not stop there either but worked her hands over his face and he felt his face coming apart much the way he'd wanted it to earlier. But nothing like that for this was a loosening, a gentle breaking into parts that once broken could then readhere.

When she was done with that she paused. In that brief moment he heard both of them breathing and nothing else. Then she went down the length of him once more, this time her fingers spread flat and easy, serving only to guide her head as she worked him with her mouth, the lightest of kisses and licking, at his armpits, his nipples, navel, the bones of his hips, down the inside of his thighs and then lifted his legs to run her tongue in broad slow swaths against the backs of his knees. And on down again to his feet where she took each toe separate into her mouth and laved it with her tongue. Then holding one foot in each hand she spread his legs and came up between them to his groin and took him in her mouth and his teeth unclenched and he groaned. In an agony pure from a deep recess of his soul.

She rose up over him and with a sweep of her arms threw the robe off, at the same time leaned her face toward his as she arched the small of her back and without needing any hand to guide fitted herself around him. She stopped for one long moment with him just inside. Then she rocked back and forth again very slowly until she was all the way down pressed tight against him. His hands came up and cupped her buttocks and she paused and through her teeth said, "Let me" and he did, keeping his hands upon her but only to feel her movement. She took his lips with hers and her tongue pressed through and scoured the inside of his mouth with its tight hard probe and he was inside of her and she was inside of him. She did not take her mouth away even when she began to speak words of some language that he'd forgotten he'd ever known but recognized and arched up to strain his mouth against hers and began to answer her. Both muffled and both insistent. Both known to the other. His hands slid up to her back and shoulders and drew her against him, to hold her as tight to him as he could. Their hips rocked. His toes strained toward the inevitable sky. His mouth filled sudden with only her hot breath. His own was gone.

After a time they just lay against each other. Not either of them wanting to move. Both very still, neither one poised or alert. The precise clever inertia of satiated bodies. The air beyond the log walls flecked with birdsong.

Finally Blood spoke.

"Thank you," he said, his voice rough, his throat barely able to work.

She raised her head and then pushed up on her elbows to look down at him. Her hair streaming down to shroud his face.

"Don't you ever," she said, "thank me."

He was quiet some time. Then he said, "Why not?"

"Because," she said, "it's like getting paid. Don't you ever try to pay me Blood. Not one way, not another. Not no way at all."

Three

A few days later the Coos County high sheriff rode up into the country looking for a man he would not name. And Blood waited patiently to see if the quarry was in actuality himself. Mose Hutchinson spent several days, taking board with the miller and his wife but otherwise riding the hinterlands, tracking the smoke of campfires at dawn and was reported to have covered the territory deep past the lonely outposts of the most ragged of trappers, finally taking the scrabble of a trail all the way over Halls Stream into Canada and still came back without his man, riding in a thunderstorm. It was that night he tied his horse in Blood's barn and came into the tavern to shed his sodden woolen overcoat, hanging it topped by his wide-brimmed hat on a peg by the fire before coming to the counter. What few men lounged leaning there stepped aside to make room for the sheriff, each maneuvering to give ground in such a way so it seemed they were not moving at all. In the corner there was a single improvised table with keg seats and here Gandy sat at cards with Cole and Van Landt and Peter Chase and these players glanced up at the sheriff and then went back to their game. While none knew whom he was seeking all knew it was none of them. It was someone new to the territory. This much was clear from where and how he rode.

Hutchinson was a lean man with long arms and a slab-sided head with thick hair the color of lead. His vest was dry but the collar and sleeves of his shirt were wet where the water had come through his overcoat and his hands were red-chapped at the ends of long wrists that lay on the counter as if there were too much of them, as if his hands were clumsy and difficult for him to use. He leaned his weight onto his elbows so his face came most of the way across the counter and introduced himself to Blood. Sally was up on the stool at the end of the counter and he did not glance at her.

"My pleasure," said Blood, who did not reach out his hand. "And yours, as long as it's rum. It's all there is."

"A tot."

"A tot. Yes." Blood poured a dram into a cup and placed it between the man's hands. Hutchinson took up the cup and turned it as if seeking unknown alignment and drank it down.

"Another?"

"One more."

Blood poured. He said, "It's wet out."

"It's better than ice."

"That's so."

Hutchinson said, "I could do with one more of these. Can you supply provender?"

"I can not," Blood said. "It's still a jackleg setup. I don't have the kitchen for it. I should. Come winter, men would welcome it."

"Other times, too," Hutchinson offered. For the first time he looked at Sally. "Perhaps the girl could find some sup for me. I'm chilled through and feeble with hunger."

Blood gazed upon the sheriff without blinking. After a beat he said, "The fire will dry you, the rum should take the worst of the chill. You sleep at Emil Chase's. Does not the wife lay an ample board for you?" Then poured the requested third dram.

Hutchinson spread his lips thin to bare his teeth. A smile of sorts. "She does. But the cost is dear."

"No less dear than here. If we did such."

"It's not the money, man. It's the chatter goes with it."

"I always found Emil Chase tight with words."

"I wasn't speaking of the miller."

"The wife avoids me."

"Emil Chase is no friend of yours either."

"Each man lives as he knows best."

"It's so. You seem to offend few others."

"I can't swear I'd hear of it if I did."

Hutchinson drank off the dram and wiped his mouth with his yet damp sleeve. He said, "It's the curse of public life. Most men tell you what they think you want to hear. Or they do not speak at all."

"So you think I undervalue Mr. Chase's opinion?"

"I would not go so far."

Blood studied the man across from him, making no disguise of his perusal. The sheriff's face was open, placid; also giving nothing of himself. He was mild and without concern throughout Blood's penetration. A man used to such. Blood saw all this and it was useful in its way. He reached for his pitcher and poured another dram into the sheriff's cup. Then said, "I'd feed you if I could. But then every other man would expect the same. Like I said, I'm not set up for such custom yet."

Hutchinson nodded. "A man in your line can't afford exceptions."

"Not any man can."

"Not all know that."

"That," Blood said, "is not of concern to me."

The sheriff took out a purse and opened it and placed a dollar on the counter. He said, "You were right. I'm warming up. And in less of a hurry for my supper. There's a drink or two left in that coin, isn't there?"

"More than two. If you want them."

Hutchinson looked at Blood. "I believe I do. But tell me this, Mister Blood. My horse has no fire nor drink to warm himself. Could I purchase fodder for the beast?"

Blood did not pause. "Did you not see the haycock as you rode in?"

"I did."

"Go feed what he'll eat. A horse is not a man. There is no need for him to be hungry with good feed five steps away."

"I'm grateful."

Blood said, "Let your horse be grateful. There is no charge for him. Go tend him and then come back and drink the rest of your dollar. Or however much you want. That was not the lone coin in your purse."

"You're shrewd, Mr. Blood."

Blood shrugged. He said, "I'm in business."

"I guess I am too. After a fashion. Sometimes with more success than others."

"All ventures are such."

"I've worn my ass raw riding after some fool boy. Sold his cattle and ran rather than settle honest debts. No one but himself made the trouble."

"What makes you think he'd come this way? There's not much to spend money on, here."

Hutchinson leaned across the counter to speak to Blood. "There are those who think I've no jurisdiction here. I myself am not clear on the matter. What you people do to one another is not my concern. I recently tried to explain that to Emil Chase. But if someone, from here or there, does wrong in Coos County then I'll ride into Canada after him if that's what it takes."

Blood studied the man. Then he said, "It's summer. There's young men all over this country taking a look at it. Some serious and some on a frolic. I imagine you've met a good number of them these last days."

"I have."

"And none seen your man?"

The sheriff shrugged. "If they had, none was in a hurry to tell me."

Blood said, "A young man with motivation, I couldn't see him stopping here."

"I guess not. I thought it was worth the ride."

"At least," Blood said, "you had a chance to look the country over."

Hutchinson paused, showing he understood Blood's implications. Then said, "No, I expect you're right. A young fellow like this rascal Gibbs, had that much money, I guess he'd push right on through to Canada. He could travel west up there and come back into the country and no one would know a thing about who he was."

Blood said, "Or stay right there in Canada. There's a lot of it, is what I hear."

"There is. There surely is. Why, who knows? Someday this right here might be a part of it. Not if New Hampshire has a say in the matter, but no one much listens to us. It's up to the men in London and Washington, I guess."

"Being here in the middle of it, it's hard to imagine who would make much effort over it. But then, it's almost never about the actual place, is it?"

"Sometimes," said the sheriff. "But not very often."

Blood nodded. Thinking whatever invention the character Gibbs might be, this short interview was not enough to justify the time spent hard riding in bad weather—that whatever Mose Hutchinson sought encompassed more than Blood himself.

A week later Sheriff Hutchinson and four men from the Coos militia rode up from Lancaster under cover of darkness and at first light arrested a pitch holder called Watkin up on Indian Stream under a warrant from the Coos County judge for bad debt. Watkin would not go with them and so was clubbed with the barrel of a horse pistol, strapped across the back of one of the men's horses and led out of the dawn dooryard with blood running down matting in his hair while his wife and children stood watching, listening to the sound of their husband and father coughing and choking on his own blood. His older boy ran then the half mile to the nearest neighbor and roused the man who rode first back to the Watkin house to speak with the wife before turning his horse with the Watkin boy behind him to race to Emil Chase. He reached the mill as the sun came over the hills beyond the lake and spread the still water with a broad path of fire. Chase was grinding early Canada corn. The miller listened and then sent the Watkin boy and his own off to alert neighbors and have them spread the alarm.

By midmorning there were eighty men and youths in disorderly and boisterous assemblage at Blood's that filled both the tavern and domestic quarters and spilled out into the yard, men weaving their way back and forth through all those clustering so the multitude reminded Blood of a swollen and maddened hive of bees kicked into a swarm but lacking the presence of the antagonist. The Watkin woman had been brought down by a neighbor and she alone was very still, seated at the kitchen table with tea grown cold before her, her hands engaged in her lap, turning over and over as she worked her fingers as if to divine something in the red-blistered digits.

Emil Chase arrived with his wife and stood in the doorway and called out for silence, for order. Then his wife brought Mrs. Watkin to the door and tried to leave with the woman but men called out for her to stay, that they would hear from her. Mrs. Chase surveyed the crowd and did not look to her husband but addressed them all.

"She hadn't ought to've been brought here in the first place. Shame to all of you, those who brung her thus and those who left her so." Then the Chase wife raised a hand against protest and finished. "Consider her needs above your own. Put down those cups and listen. She'll tell you once and not again. Then I'm taking her from this place." She looked at the stricken woman beside her and placed a broad hand in the small of the woman's back and moved her up so they stood side by side. Mrs. Chase said, "Tell them, Cilla."

And the sun-red grief-smirched woman tilted back her head and cried out. "They come and burst through the door with axes and took Paul from the bed. He was in his long underwears. He would not go with them and they was shouting at him and the sheriff had a paper but would not let Paul hold it to read. Maybe he was afeared Paul would throw it in the fire. Or maybe there was nothing about Paul on it at all. The children was crying and the oldest boy Edgar kicked one of the men and that man swatted him down like a bear cuffing a dog. And Paul still would not go and so another one of the men broke his head open with the long pistol he was waving and Paul sagged down and they carried him out the house and strapped him across the back of a horse like a carcass and rode out of there. It was my boy Edgar ran down here with word of it. There is blood, the blood of my husband, seeped to stain the floorboards of the house. He could be dead," she said and paused. Then said again, "He could be dead. And any one of you could be the next one battered or killed. We been too long without any authority in this country. We're betwixt and between. What kind of men are you to let it come to this? What kind of men? Just answer me that."

And Mrs. Chase led her down off the step and through the crowd of men who stepped back for the arch procession of the two bold women and some looked upon her and others dropped their eyes and not one spoke but all stood and watched as the women went up the road through the soft churning dust and sand until they entered the house beside the mill. The men stood, shamed.

Behind the counter in the tavern Blood listened to the woman speak and watched the stiff set of her back and when both women stepped down into the yard they passed from his sight but he heard the silence of the men even more clearly than if they had been raging wild and he thought There, that's done it, as the click of apprehension that he always paid attention to turned over in his brain. A physical sensation, the mild disturbance a bat-wing passing close in the dark brings to the cheek. More than what it was. A signal of some kind. One he could not fully read.

Sally came beside him. She said, "What's going to happen?"

"You watch close, you'll know as much as me," he said. "But, I had to guess, I'd say you're about to witness mankind striving toward the best it can do and most likely failing utterly."

"What's that mean?"

"It means look sharp."

"I always do." She stepped closer so she was just against his side. "You know that."

He put his left hand on the counter edge and left it there and stepped away down the counter, leaving his elbow out between them. He said, "Here it starts now."

Emil Chase shouldered his way to the counter and stood across from Blood. He said, "Will you suspend sales while we call a meeting? If not, I'll make it the first motion."

Blood surveyed the room. Looked at Chase. "Your motion wouldn't pass. But you need men sober as can be hoped for. For your goodwill, I'm happy to have your meeting run dry. They'll drink up after." And be looking to fill their ammunition pouches, he thought.

Chase said, "I have no goodwill today. The Watkin woman was right—we have no authority to rely upon beyond ourselves. And we have failed."

Blood said, "Perhaps. It may serve to see it that way."

"What do you imply?"

"Only that it seems to me that any solution arrived at has the potential to be worse than the problem."

"The quandary with you Mister Blood is you lack all sense of the brotherhood of man."

Blood nodded agreement. "True enough."

"We have no recourse here. We are not the keepers of our fates."

"Why certainly all men are."

"The State refuses us right of citizenry. We have thus an obligation to protect ourselves. To organize ourselves."

"The Watkin man abandoned obligation himself, it sounds like."

"Perhaps. This does not mean the man should've been bludgeoned before his wife and children and strapped like carrion over the back of a horse."

"I'd guess those Coos men felt they had no choice. They were a good ways from home. It was not that many of them, compared to this group here."

"If we govern ourselves there will be ways for such complaints to be resolved."

"You have no authority to govern yourselves."

Chase stared at him. Then said, "We assume the authority as free men."

Blood shrugged. "I wish you success, Mister Chase. But not one of us is a free man."

Chase studied him. He said, "I had no reason to believe you to be a man of God, Mister Blood."

"I was not speaking of Him," Blood said, then turned away.

In late afternoon a company of seven men led by Peter Chase and Isaac Cole departed by way of ancient Indian foot-trails for the ten-hour march to Lancaster, carrying with them armament rustic and deadly: a pair of long guns, a single horse pistol holding a double charge, two swords, a sickle, and sturdy ironwood clubs. Each man wore a belt knife of varying quality. They carried also a quickly-scribed copy of the constitution of the newly-made Republic of Indian Stream, as well as a writ issued by the new and duly elected magistrate Emil Chase charging the party of seven to secure the person of Paul Watkin, said Watkin being detained against his will and the will of the Republic. All measures necessary were to be employed and no man was to stand in the way of the party. So help them God.

At dusk there was a thunderstorm which dissipated into a steady drizzle and the men, all young and work-hard, handpicked by the brothers Chase, fell into a steady dog-trot with the lead men calling out warnings against the inclines and obstacles of the trail. They waded through a bog rather than skirt it and came upon Nash Stream and traveled down that along the eastern slope of the escarpment of cliffs that rose above the stream and at midnight came out onto the open road north of Devils

Slide that ran west into Lancaster and they kept that pace until a farm dog barked at them as they approached the village. They slowed to a walk and the drizzle covered all sound of their passing and no more dogs barked although one came out from a yard and trailed after them until one of the men bent for a stone and the dog retreated.

The jail was in the meetinghouse cellar and the front door of that building was shut against the night but not locked. In the dark they went down the stairs and came into a room lit by a guttering candle-lantern. The jailer was asleep with his head down on a table and one of the men tapped him on his nape with a club and the man groaned and spread his arms wide over the tabletop and did not move again. Watkin was awake in the single cell. His face was crusted with dried blood so he looked like an African and one eye was swollen shut. A simple bandage of rough woolsey was wrapped around his head, the cloth soaked through in spots like smallpox. The key to the cell was on a ring on a nail. Watkin was steady on his feet but weak. Cole fed him rum from a clay bottle he carried. Peter Chase unrolled the documents that he'd carried dry inside his shirt, gently lifted the jailer's head and slid them onto the table and lowered the man's head back into place.

One of the young men, the one with the horse pistol, said, "Shit. Is that all there is to it?"

Isaac Cole looked at him. "We ain't home yet."

There was a pot of cold beans with molasses and salt pork on the table and the men ate it with the single spoon already dug into the beans, passing it turnabout. Then they went up the stairs again in the dark and did not pause at the meetinghouse door but walked out like it was midday and they had just come in on ordinary duty. They went out through the town as silent as they came in. It was like they had never been there. Except each one of them knew it was nothing like that at all.

Once out away on the road they spoke briefly, voices taut with excitement as they moved.

"I'd hate to be that feller when he wakes up."

"He'll be out for a while."

"It'll still be some knot."

"I tapped him gentle."

"It'll still be a knot."

"Nothing like the knot the sheriff leaves on him I bet."

"That sheriff ain't going to like those papers."

"They ain't meant for him to like or not."

"Still."

"Watkin. How you feeling?"

"Better now. Some kind of sore though."

"You believe you can trot a little?"

"If I had to."

"What I think is, it would be a good idea."

"Let's do her then."

Late that afternoon Mose Hutchinson and a party of men came up the road beside the river. There were a dozen men and they were all mounted and well armed. They turned off the road at Indian Stream and rode the three miles up to the Watkin house which they found empty, with even the livestock gone. They sat their horses in the dooryard and after some discussion three of the men dismounted and fired the house and barn while the other men wheeled their horses about, watching the fields and woods around but it was silent as Sunday. The house caught quickly and burned with hard snaps and clear flame but the barn was full of new-made hay and so was slower to catch and when it did it sent up a roiling glut of dismal smoke and Mose Hutchinson watched this knowing a critical error had been made. But the jailer was his brother-in-law and when they left Lancaster midmorning was still speaking in a gibberish none could understand. They returned down to the Lake Road and realized there were no people at the neighboring farms or new pitches and no livestock in sight either and Hutchinson rode in front of the party with his big roan gelding reined in hard so the horse moved sideways. The dawn had come clear after the night of rain and the air was still and fresh and they could smell hay curing somewhere and heard the raw screech of crows and the lone single bark of a raven answering and that was all.

At the Lake Road they turned northeast toward the mill and followed the river deeper into the settlement. The river ran along the righthand side of the road and although it was late in the year and the water was low there was enough of it moving over the rocks so the sound was a constant rolling growl against which the hoofbeats seemed to echo as if the country had determined to announce the party.

They came over the slight rise of land that hid Back Lake and saw Emil Chase in his suit of dark wool and his broad brimmed dark hat standing alone in the center of the road. The river here was a jumble of great slabs and blocks of granite and the road was narrow with thick scrub woods along the other side. Hemlocks grew both sides of the road and the light that came here was speckled—a step forward or back could dazzle a man's eyes. Hutchinson silently swore and sat his horse to a standstill and the party stopped behind him. Chase was fifty yards away. When the party approaching stopped, he reached up and removed his hat and held it down before him with both hands. Hutchinson did not know if this was a signal or manners.

He called out. "Come down the road, Chase."

Chase said, "You're in trespass, Hutchinson."

Hutchinson spurred the horse forward and the company followed close. The sheriff sat his snorting horse in a tight sitting trot, the reins gathered hard in his left hand. His right hand he kept on the long pistol snugged under the belt wrapped high around his waist. With his eyes on the miller before him he also swept the underbrush but there was nothing to be seen. All the horses of the company were jittery. There was no way to know if this was transmitted from their riders or some outside force. He rode within ten feet of Chase and pulled up sideways, his horse pointed toward the woods. If there was trouble coming it would be from there. The horse slung itself back and forth in a sideways motion and Hutchinson let it—it offered excuse to watch about him even as he spoke to the miller. Who stood right where he was, hat in hand.

The sheriff said, "There is no trespass. I'm the representative of the State of New Hampshire."

Chase said, "Which State has made no effort on our behalf. Save to beat a man senseless and take him from his home without showing just cause. As if such treatment would have just cause. England and Washington show no desire to address the issue of this territory. New Hampshire wants us but will not treat us as citizens. We have taken the usual step reasonable men must take to protect their families and holdings under such conditions. We are sovereign and thus you have no authority here, now or before or ever again. I ask you this once to leave. I offer that chance. Which is a single chance more than you provided poor Paul Watkin. Who was guilty of no more than many men and less so than some."

Hutchinson looked down at the stout miller. "Are you the king here then?"

"I am the magistrate of the people. Nothing more than that."

"And if I do not leave?"

"I shall arrest you for general trespass and gross bodily harm inflicted upon my fellow citizen Paul Watkin. You may submit freely to the arrest and be assured you'll receive fair treatment. But I also offer, this once, the opportunity for you to quit the country, upon your oath you won't return."

Hutchinson said, "Where is the Watkin man?"

"He's safe and resting. He's been evil mistreated."

"If you'll turn over to me the men who broke him from the jail in Lancaster I'll see Watkin is well tended."

"I know no such men."

"Are you not in charge here?"

Chase looked at him. Then said, "I'm the voice of the people. That's all."

Hutchinson said, "You risk arrest yourself, Mister Chase. You can not interfere with the discharge of my duties."

"You have no duties here. Mister Hutchinson."

"You know it well, Chase. I'm the sheriff of Coos County."

Chase turned his hat over in his hands and studied it a moment. He said, "But you are not in New Hampshire now, Mister Hutchinson. You are in the independent Republic of Indian Stream. And so I arrest you in the name of that Republic and the people who have created her and the Lord God who blesses us with the freedom to do so."

And he did not wait for an answer from the sheriff but placed his hat on his head and stepped forward and seized the reins below the bit of Hutchinson's gelding. And as he did this men rose out of the rocks and trees and brush and woods both sides of the road, some it seemed coming from the river itself. Armed in every way possible and some ways Hutchinson had not thought of before. One man with a fencepost with a great iron spike driven through the top end. Men with hatchets and sickles and horse pistols in their belts. Clubs of firewood. Plenty of muzzle-loading hunting rifles. A man with only a scythe. That with one broad sweep could gut a horse and hook up to bring the man from the saddle like a fish gaffed. More men than he could count but he guessed between thirty and forty. As he reached to drag his pistol from his belt he turned his head back to his company to call out, to tell them to hold themselves steady and, as he did, Emil Chase reached up and snatched the pistol by the barrel. Hutchinson jerked back and the miller kept his hold, letting go of the reins to bring his other hand up and the gun discharged. A roar of human voice went up and then was muted by a shabby volley. A horse screamed and stumbled and fell and the other horses broke apart, wheeling and slashing as their riders fought them and fought also to discharge their own weapons and the men on the road waded in amongst the riders. As they came the riders fired and a new sound came into the air, the sound of men crying out as they kneeled or reeled or fell prone and still. Hutchinson had only the empty pistol which he now used as a club as the woodsmen surrounded him, three or four of them, one with a pistol of his own. Then a man came close and slipped under the club of the pistol and sank a sickle deep into Hutchinson's thigh, pinning his leg to the saddle and another man stepped up and with a wooden club held in both hands struck the horse behind the eye and the horse went down. Hutchinson tried to roll free but could not with the sickle in him and so felt his other leg crush beneath the horse that tumbled over as if struck by a black wind. The horse kicked once and was still.

Hutchinson lay pinned by the horse, his cheek in the sand of the road. He was looking back down the road. There were other men lying prone. One up on all fours trying to crawl to the bushes, puking as he went, his head down as if what he could not see could not hurt him. Hutchinson recognized this man as one of his own. Beyond that he saw that most of his company were off their horses and had formed a tight circle, backs against each other, facing out. Some had long guns, others pistols. Those with pistols held swords in their free hands. The horses were running down the road. Some stopped and turned to watch behind them. One horse stood near the band of men, its legs splayed and trembling, its head down. Immense pink and brown loops of intestines spilled from a gash in its stomach, down into the road dust. His men were not attempting to reload their weapons but using them as clubs to batter off the attackers. As he watched he saw one of his men step forward and bring his pistol up toward an approaching man, a farmer Hutchinson knew by sight, and the pistol went off and the man had no face at all but sat on the ground and held his hands up where it had been and then folded sideways. The same member of the company turned then and went after another man coming toward him, charging him with a wild roar and slashing with his sword. The man threw up an arm to ward the blow and the swordsman dropped his blade and swiped hard against the man's ribcage. Then one of the circled company stepped forward and pulled the attacker back into the group. For a moment it was quiet but for the suck of breath and a feeble moaning. The gutted horse wrenched its head in a terrible moan and collapsed with a wet bursting sound. All the men turned to look at it.

Hutchinson called out, "Cease, by damn. All of you."

At the sound of his voice the militiamen moved together in a clump down the road toward him. He wanted to tell them to remain where they were but his voice had exhausted itself. When speaking his lungs shot with pain and he knew he had broken ribs as well as the crushing his leg endured, where he could feel nothing. As his men approached he saw one of the attackers step close and recognized him. It was Peter Chase, the brother of the miller. His face was black with powder smoke and one eye was closed with a deep bruise and blood welling. Hutchinson drew breath and winced and said, "Where is your brother?"

Peter Chase said, "Why, it's the sheriff. How you doing down there, Sheriff?"

"Where is your brother?"

"You put a hole in his hand. He's being tended."

"Are you in charge here, then?"

Peter Chase looked at him. "We're all in charge here."

A mob, thought Hutchinson. His lungs seemed to be filling with blood. He forced himself to speak. If they were talking, they were not killing each other. He said, "This is a mess here. A useless mess."

Chase said, "It don't look so pretty from your angle, does it."

Hutchinson said, "Will you kill us all, then?"

Chase said, "We hadn't talked that far. We thought you'd have the sense to leave."

"We'll leave now."

"Will you, Mister Hutchinson? It's quite the load atop you right now, is how it looks to me." Chase was squatting to look close into the sheriff's eyes.

Hutchinson said, "It was my brother-in-law got brained last night. He can't talk right at all. Like a moron, he is."

Chase said, "He wasn't much of a jailer anyhow." Then added, "Is what I hear."

One of the farmers cried a warning but it was too late. The men of Hutchinson's company had drawn close, then rushed in to surround the fallen horse and sheriff. A pair of them caught hold of Peter Chase and pulled him to his feet where he struggled briefly but was held with his hands behind his back and a blade against his throat. The man with the knife called out.

"All of you get back. Up the road. All together. Now. Or I swear to God I'll cut this man's throat and then we'll kill as many of you as we can. If we all die trying. Get back now." His voice the high pitch of a man gone beyond reason but crimson with rage.

Another voice came. Steady, firm and calm. "All right. All of you."

Hutchinson could only see heavy boots coming across the road. All else was blocked by his own men. But he knew the voice.

Blood stopped in the road between the two groups of men. He carried only his ox goad. The hound was with him. He spoke to the farmers and trappers.

"Pay no attention to the militiamen. They are surrounded and you could kill them easy. They're not the proud bunch rode up here with wrong ideas in their heads. They've learned something here today. Kill them if you will, but then there would be a new bunch come after them. Let them gimp home and it will be some time and more than a little thought before they'd try it again. That's what I think. Isn't that right, Sheriff?"

Hutchinson said nothing.

Blood did not seem to expect an answer for he went right on. "Kill them, or leave them as they are to gather themselves and make their way home best they can. It makes no difference to me. But when the work is done here, there's drinks for all. And no charge for it. Mister Chase himself is right this moment setting at his table with his hand wrapped and the fight out of him. It strikes me enough work has been done this day." And Hutchinson saw the boots turn and begin to walk up the road.

It was quiet. No man on either side spoke. In the woods somewhere a woodpecker drummed.

Hutchinson worked his thick tongue to moisten his dirt-caked lips. He tried to speak and croaked and paused and swallowed and then said, "Let him go."

His men looked down at him. The one with the knife bent his head around to look at the sheriff.

Hutchinson strained and lifted his head for all the authority he might summon and repeated, "Let him go."

After a moment the men holding Peter Chase released him. Chase stood a moment where he was, rubbing his wrists. Then stepped away, toward his neighbors. He stopped also in the middle ground. No one spoke. Peter Chase turned and began to walk up the road in the direction Blood had gone. Blood was no longer in sight. Then the other farmers followed after him, some carrying other men, wounded or dead. None speaking. As they went several kept turning back to watch the militiamen left behind. Who did not move. Just before the farmers went from sight one turned and sent a rifle shot toward the company, aiming high. The militia heard the ball slash the foliage over their heads.

After a few minutes the men of the company broke apart. Some went to look after their casualties: one man dead, two wounded. A pair went down the road to collect the spooked horses. The rest stood guard and worked together to get Hutchinson's horse off him. They had to pull the sickle free first. Fresh blood ran from the wound and they tied a cloth tight high around his upper thigh. The femur of his other leg was broken. There was no way to know if it was crushed or a clean break. They splinted it as best they could with torn shirts binding in place the short ramrods from three of the horse pistols. Two of their horses were dead. They roped the dead man on behind a rider and tied Hutchinson into the saddle of the dead man's horse. The two wounded men rode doubled behind others. Once all were mounted they rode off, down the way they had come. They met no one, passed no one. As they went by the mouth of Indian Stream they could see smoke still rising from the house and barn they had burned. It did not seem possible to still be burning. One of the men dug out a pocket watch. Little more than an hour had passed.

Blood poured free drams of rum and then sold more for the next hour, watching the men emerge from the pallor and shock of what their actions meant to raise toasts to the dead man, and the wounded men, and from there refight the battle with words and finally proceed to threats and ill-made wild plans for future engagements. It was then he ordered all out and shut the tavern for the remainder of the day. Regardless of the rum the men were still sober enough from the engagement of the afternoon to understand this and they left easily, suddenly wanting the comfort of the sight of their homes. Before they departed Peter Chase called for a meeting at nightfall for the Committee of Safety. New patrols were needed. A new vigilance required.

Chase then spoke to Blood. "It's a good location to meet. It's central to all but the most far-flung."

Blood said, "I'd not turn down opportunity for business. But it strikes me, the sort of work you're at now, strong drink is not the best ingredient served into it."

Chase said, "What do you propose?"

"The first meetings, when those trappers was killed. They were at the mill. It's big enough. What's wrong with that?"

Chase studied him. "My brother's in this deep enough."

"Aye. And he stepped freely there."

"Are you not with us then, Blood? Are you against us?"

Blood gazed upon Peter Chase. He said, "I chose this place as you all did. So I accept the decisions of the majority. Be they made in wisdom or not. But as far as seeing men killed or damaged, it's not a way I wish for."

"You think I do?"

Blood ignored this. "There is never enough, once it starts. No one side is just going to say quit. Already there are men talking that it should not've stopped where it did. That Hutchinson should've been finished there and then. As if he would be the end of it. But there is always another Hutchinson."

"They will think again before riding back up here."

"To be sure. They will at least reconsider their numbers. But you, Peter Chase, have only one head to lose."

Chase colored. "I'm in your debt, Mister Blood."

"No," said Blood. "I assume no debts of that nature. It was not you I was saving anyway, but every man there. It could've been done by any one of you. If any had been thinking. That's what I dislike about this business. Men cease to reason."

Peter Chase said, "They came upon us with their intentions set. We would be less as men had we not acted."

"I'll not dispute that. But a critical point has been reached. Which is why I ask you to move your meeting to the mill. Let the men understand fully the gravity of what they choose, how they vote. What action they call for. When that is settled, then let them come drink."

Chase said, "You'll still see your profit then."

Again Blood ignored him. Locked his lockbox, placed it on the shelf under the counter, returned the key to the small pouch under his blouse and stepped to take up his goad.

Chase studied him. Then said, "Where are you bound now?"

"The same place as you. To see how your brother is faring."

"There is no love lost between the two of you."

"Our relations are not the issue of my visit."

"He will not like to see you now. Why not wait a day or two, until he's recovered more? He'll feel you're there to witness his misery."

Blood smiled at Peter Chase. "For his faults, your brother is a wiser man than you. He'll understand I come to him from necessity." He walked outside. Peter Chase followed and spoke from behind.

"And what could that be?"

Blood turned and called into the tavern. "Sally! Bolt the door until I return." Then to Peter Chase. "If there is a time to end this before more men die, it's now. I've no relish for the job but it seems I might be the one for it. If you know me at all, Peter Chase, you know I do my best to avoid meddling in the affairs of others. But it would be vile indeed if I were not to attempt peace. You were not the only man saved this afternoon."

"You speak of Hutchinson."

"And the others of his party as well."

"Do you think Hutchinson will see things that way?"

"I could not say. The man will be angry. His pride is worse than his wounds and those wounds are considerable. There's no way to know but to try."

"There's risk for you."

"I know it. But if I go or stay, it's still risk. Is how I see it."

Peter Chase looked at him. Then said, "It's your own hide you're out to save, isn't it?"

"Why yes. It is. But, if I save my own others will be saved as well. I go to make no deals."

"And how are we supposed to know that?"

Blood gazed upon Peter Chase a long moment. Until Chase turned his defiant eyes away. Then Blood turned and began to walk up the road toward the mill. It was late afternoon and the birds in the underbrush were settling in to call forth the dusk upon the land. He heard the trudge of Peter Chase behind him. As he came up to the mill he saw a loon working the shallow water near the lake edge. The bird dived and Blood stopped to wait for it to come up, trying to guess where it would. Peter Chase passed him wordless and went into the mill.

The loon came up a far distance out in the lake, nowhere near the spot Blood had chosen. He shrugged. It was only a loon, not a portent. He walked on past the mill to the plank house with the gun-slits in the upper story. On this warm day they stood open. He wondered if they had ever been used for other than ventilation. Or if Emil Chase was just the sort of man to think farther ahead than others.

The front door was shut tight and he rapped hard upon it with his fist but did not call out. He saw no reason to announce himself.

He left before first light the following morning, riding Emil Chase's bay gelding. Blood had not been horseback in years but the horse was well trained and the rhythm came back to Blood quickly, as if it had slept quiet in his muscles and bones and brain throughout those years. Once comfortable he briefly considered what else might lie hidden in a man to bloom forth once more. Then stopped that thinking and held steady focus to where he rode and what lay before him. The day was fair with some few high clouds that he guessed would draw together as the day went on and bring other, lower clouds after them. But for now it was a mild day, the air just tasting of the edge of dampness. He could keep the horse at a steady trot as long as he could tolerate it. He felt strong, as if he'd never been out of the saddle. Still, he expected that once he stepped down, his legs would quiver from the unused muscles.

He rode along the Connecticut River as it wound west and then south out of the Indian Stream country. Once turned south the valley spread wide, the farms were large with broad meadows and stands of Canada corn and flax with men out working and he raised his hand to them and some few responded while most turned back to their work. So the word was flown out. It was nothing less than what he expected. There was also the possibility of meeting a party of militia riding north from Lancaster but while he did not discount this he doubted it—Blood knew enough of these matters to suspect it would take days to organize such a party. There would be officials of the state to be consulted. There would be writs for the judge to draw up. And perhaps most important would be the condition of the sheriff himself. Blood did not see Hutchinson as the sort to easily abrogate his own authority and hand it over to another.

He came down the valley where the land rose more steeply to the east, the great escarpments breaking through the spruce and hemlock and hardwoods to show the white shimmer of quartz outcroppings and the sun was overhead now, the thin clouds of morning burned back to a faint smudge on the horizon. Where a feeder brook ran down between birch and rock maple and there were no homesteads in sight he dismounted in the shade and led the horse to water at the brook and knelt himself to scoop water. From a cloth sack tied to the saddle he ate a piece of wheaten bread and brine-cured pork shoulder and then knelt and drank again. He stretched his legs and mounted the horse and went on.

He had no weapons with him. Not even the belt knife that he wore all other times. He would've brought the dog but thought himself better served to leave Luther with Sally. If anything were to happen to him, she would need the dog more than he. She had baked the bread he ate. She was learning her way around the kitchen.

A little past the noon hour he rode into Lancaster. There was a church spire and the belfry of the meetinghouse lofted against the sky. The houses were all frame and most were painted and surrounded with gardens and flowers and the barns were the small barns of townspeople who needed only shelter for a horse or two, a milk cow, perhaps some chickens. The streets were broad and smooth and overhung with the lace-crowns of elms. There were cobbled walks. It had not been so many months that Blood had been in his raw country but he felt dislocated. As if he were in a place he had no business being. It was nerves he told himself.

He knew Hutchinson would not be at the meetinghouse and it was the last place he wished to inquire. He made his way toward the mercantile block and began to pass more people, on foot and riding, some driving carts pulled by horses or oxen. Some people looked at him but only with the mild curiosity of the stranger. He drew up the horse before an old woman coming from market with a basket of foodstuffs over one elbow. She wore a plain skirt and threadbare apron and a faded purple bonnet. He took off his hat and bid her a good day. She bent sideways to peer up at him.

"A day as good as can be hoped for," she said. "Age is naught but a multitude of small deaths. If you can manage it, die quickly, young man."

Blood smiled at her. He said, "Goodwife, a smart tongue is the product of a quick mind. You seem blessed to me."

"You say that now. See how you feel when all is lost but your quick mind."

"Aye. I know something of which you speak."

She glared at him. He held his face still, meeting her eyes. After a moment she did not look away but said, "You did not stop me for wasted compliments. What's it you seek?"

"I come after the high sheriff. He'd be at the meetinghouse?"

"Oh, a bad business that. He'll not be able to help you today."

"Is he ill?"

"He's abed with grievous wounds. They say he'll live but is in great agony."

"This is bad news. I have urgent business. He'd want to see me if he can. What's happened to him?"

"He was set upon by brigands in the far north, in the wild country. He was used most severely."

"Is he at home?"

"He is."

"I see. Is he conscious?"

"His moans are terrible to hear."

"Then I must go to him. As I said, if he's awake, he'll want to see me."

"Well, go then. Or carry my basket home for me."

"I would if I could spare the time. But I need the sheriff. I must speak with him, only—"

"What is it?"

"I've only seen him at the meetinghouse."

The woman pursed her lips at him. A dry shrunken grimace of distaste. As if he had revealed himself to her. She said, "A word of advice from one close to the grave. Don't waste so much time buttering the sheriff. He'll not stand it as gracefully as I. He lives two streets off the north side of the common. The third house on the left. If you can get past his wife and the militia boys, wish him well from me. The widow Colburn."

"Thank you Mistress Colburn."

"Get along," she said. "You've used me up."

He followed the directions of the widow woman even as he considered her words. He'd not counted on any militiamen attending the sheriff. It was not a good sign if they were so spooked as to post a guard at the man's house. He considered the possibility there might be a man or two among them that had been present at the fight the day before but told himself it was unlikely; those men would be home resting. It would be other militiamen with the sheriff, likely only a pair or three for public show, was what he guessed. He could tie the horse elsewhere and scout on foot but turned away the thought. He was bound to be bold.

He was wrong. Before the house was a plank door set on sawhorses to make a table and plank benches with six or eight men seated there. On the table were the scattered leavings of a meal on pewter platters and the men were drinking from tankards. He pulled up the bay by the hitch rail that ran along the street and stepped down and tied the horse by the reins as the men watched him. Then one said, "Why, there's one of em right now."

They came upon him in a pack. They had been drinking beer and he let them bring him to the ground without a struggle although they pummeled and beat him with their fists. Once down some of them began working his lower back with their boots and he felt the sharp flush of pain in his kidneys. Then that stopped as one crouched to tie his hands behind with a rawhide lacing drawn from a boot. They rolled him onto his stomach so his face was down in the packed dirt of the yard and he twisted his neck sideways to breathe. Then one sat on his head and two more on his back. Another leaned down and said, "You're either the dumbest bastard or the bravest. Did you think you'd find the sheriff alone to finish what you failed at yesterday?"

Blood said, "I come to talk to him."

"Is that so?"

"It is."

"Hold on," said another man, leaning close. "This is the one told them farmers to quit. Idn't that you?"

Blood said, "That's me."

"He didn't have a hand in it," explained the veteran. "Except to call the mob off us when Mose was pinned down under his horse."

The man beside his head said, looking at Blood, "If he could call em off like that, he had some authority all right. Is what I think."

Blood said, "All I was, was the voice needed at the time. Not any of it was what anybody figured on."

"It was quite the murderous bunch to not have figured on it."

"They were prepared, it's true. But I had no part save to walk in at the right time to stop things from going worse. For everybody." And he craned his head up to meet the eye of the veteran.

"What do we do with him?" the first man asked.

"Thump the bejesus out of him and haul him over to the jail, is what I say," said one of the men on his back.

"You can do it if you choose," said Blood. "Even if I was a mind to, I couldn't stop you. But, before you commence, why don't one of you run ask the sheriff what he wants done with me. My name's Blood."

"You're Blood?"

"I am."

The man sitting on his head stepped off. "I heared about you," he said.

Blood said. "I ain't going anywhere you don't want me to. But you might do yourselves a favor before you start in. See the sheriff, make sure he supports your plan."

"You seem pretty damn sure of what he'll want, Blood."

"I got no idea how he'll receive me. But I know this—it won't be me he's pissed with, you treat me a way he wouldn't want."

Mose Hutchinson was in a four-poster bed that had been set up in the sitting room on the first floor. He was upright in the bed, supported by pillows and bolsters. His bare chest was bound in tight strips of sheeting and his left leg lay outside the covers, a thick white grub of cedar splints and layers of taut wrappings. His shank and foot emerged, seeming small and dirty-white below the swaddle of bandage. Facing him, Blood realized he had watched the whole incident from the window beside the bed, that the sheriff had not intervened but waited to see what Blood could accomplish alone. He wondered at what point the sheriff might have called out, if things had gone badly. Then knew the sheriff would have remained silent if Blood had failed with his men. This did not alter Blood's opinion of the man. That opinion still shaping.

He said, "The leg will heal all right?"

Hutchinson said, "It's what the sawbones tells me. Though he claims it will ache with the weather. As if the rest of me don't already."

Blood said, "I rode down here to talk to you."

"Under what authority?"

"None but my own."

"As a citizen of New Hampshire?"

"As a free man who desires to remain an American. But that choice doesn't lie within my hands. Or for that matter with the State of New Hampshire. My allegiance right now, by necessity, lies with the community of men with whom I reside. It does not mean I approve of their actions, some or all. But it binds me to respect those actions, if not the consequences."

"A pretty enough answer."

"I'll not tell you what you want to hear."

"That would make you a rare man. What's your interest?"

Blood said, "Beyond no great desire to see men killed or maimed over little? Beyond that, my interests are simple—I have a business established in a place I wish to remain."

"Cut-rate rum and a underage whore."

"Paltry compared to the spires of Lancaster, I admit. And the girl is of age."

"It's true. Lancaster is no busy seaport. As for the girl, I don't care."

Blood said, "I don't brag over my past. What other men know is not my concern. Nor what they think."

"Did I cause offense?"

"I'm not here to discuss myself."

"Fair enough, Mister Blood. Enough of pleasantry I say. Shall we get to the meat of the matter?"

Blood nodded. "I'm not used to the saddle. I'm a little sore myself."

"Your treatment did not go unnoticed."

"I don't blame your men. I'd ask you let the matter drop."

"Mister Blood. Men are nothing without discipline. Now speak your piece or leave me to rest."

"All right," said Blood. "The problem is the border—or the lack of one. Between the United States and Canada. Britain. No one knows if it'll be the Parallel or up farther north to the headwaters of the Connecticut. There's no one doubts, that if the territory is deeded to the States, it will become part of New Hampshire. Except for a Canuck trapper or two, maybe a couple of fellers like the Watkin man you come and took, most all the men hope that's the way it ends. The question, in their minds, is a simple one. There's conflicting deeds to most all that land. There's two companies downstate that each claim it all. But no judge will look at those claims until the boundary issue is decided."

"I know all this."

Blood went on. "But the men up there—some with one deed, some with another, some with both, some with none at all—the way they look at it is they've done the work in good faith. They've cleared their pitches, built houses, barns, cleared fields, sowed and harvested them. Established trade and homes and brought their families in or made them there. Any man, in such circumstances would feel the right of establishment is in their favor."

"For some more than others."

Blood continued. "The rest is simple. Because they don't know which way it will go in the end, what Washington and London determine, they feel if they allow either side to establish jurisdiction, it would threaten their deeds if the other side prevails. They would be looked on as suspect. All they're really trying to do is remain neutral until the issue is resolved. Looked at that way, you can't blame them."

"It's an interesting case, idn't it?"

"It's toil and livelihoods is what it is."

Hutchinson nodded. He said, "I understand that Daniel Webster himself has taken an interest in the case and is speaking to others in Washington. So it may not be so long before the boundary is settled."

"Are you speaking of months or years?"

"It's politics Blood. Stones roll uphill faster."

"It makes my point. These men live each passing year in great frustration, in the fear of working for naught."

"Perhaps," said Hutchinson. "But I do not. I've been told the country up there is within my jurisdiction and until I'm told otherwise I intend to treat it that way."

"I know that. I know you aren't the sort to act where you hadn't ought to."

"So what do you suggest?'

"Some compromise. If you have complaint against one of the inhabitants then bring it into the country. There is a Committee of Safety formed. They would listen to you and if the justification is sound they would cooperate with your needs and turn over to you whomever you sought. They can be reasonable men."

"Will you name them?"

"Not until we have agreement."

"There it is Blood. You're protecting men you know have no authority. How could I do business this way?"

"A handshake would gain my trust."

Hutchinson said, "But I have no trust in you, Blood. It's too late for your proposal. I have other accounts to settle."

"Give me the writ against Watkin. I'll carry it home and if it's judged to be fair, he'll be turned over to you."

"And the others?"

"What others?"

"I returned here with a dead man and two others with dire wounds. Not to mention a man turned into a simpleton when your Committee of Safety broke Watkin from jail. It has moved beyond some simple compact as you suggest. The people are angry. I share that anger. You see, you come too late. With too little. Under the circumstances, you come with nothing at all."

He was quiet then, his eyes oddly mild upon Blood.

After a moment Blood said, "Many had no desire for it to pass as it did."

The sheriff said, "You have no idea how many times I've heard that."

Blood said, "I had hoped to reason with you."

Hutchinson said, "This is what you may tell Emil Chase and the rest of them: Tell them to take pause and consider it well. Tell them to surrender themselves to me here, all of them, every man-jack that was in the fight yesterday, every man who broke the fugitive Watkin from jail, Watkin himself. Within the week. If they do that, I'll consider it an act of good faith. Otherwise you may happily inform them that the sheriff sends his regards and when we meet again it will be with overwhelming force and we will arrest every boy over twelve and all men of whatever age. That we shall burn the country over so the women and children will have no choice but to return to their families downstate if they have them or go to the poor farm in Bath. That when we are done there will be nothing left but charred timbers and black stones to show men were ever there."

Blood said, "That would be a terrible wrong."

The sheriff said, "It's my decision. They have a week."

Blood studied the sheriff. "I hope your leg mends well."

"Those strike me as the first false words you've spoken today, Blood."

"Perhaps," Blood said. "Tell me. Will I be able to ride out of here safely?"

"I don't know," Hutchinson said. "Why don't you try it and see?"

It was well after midnight when he crossed over Halls Stream, considered the westernmost headwater of the Indian Stream territory. As he did a party of his neighbors rode out from the woods but he did not speak to them and they did not press him but all rode together some distance before the men turned back to watch the road leading from the south. Blood rode another hour, passing the darkened tavern and came up to the mill and the house opposite and stabled the horse and went to the dark house where a single window showed candlelight on the ground floor. He knocked lightly and Emil Chase let him in. They sat at the table and talked in low tones. Blood told him all. And finished by declaring that he was done with it, that he had failed at what he could attempt and would offer nothing more. As far as Blood was concerned the men of Indian Stream had not thought things through. That they had prepared their own destruction. He kept his eyes hard upon Chase as he spoke.

Then went out into the night with a half moon beaded on the slight chop of the lake and walked down the road to the tavern. Where he knocked and shushed Luther through the door while waiting for Sally to rouse and unbar the door.

He told her nothing but sent her back to bed. Stirred up the fire and stretched before it, seated on a low stool, his legs extended toward the flames and crossed at the ankle. He was sore all over. After a time he went into the tavern and poured a noggin of rum and went back and nursed that down. He set a small spider to heat over coals raked onto the hearth and fried two eggs while toasting a hunk of bread speared on a long fork. He ate the eggs from the pan and wiped it clean of yolk and grease with the bread. Then climbed the loft ladder and lay on his thin mattress stuffed with marsh grass. He had no sense of being tired but passed immediately to sleep.

He woke sometime later, jerked out of bed with a searing cramp in his right leg, a pounding knot of flesh. He hopped around the room, crying out and beating at the rigid flesh to try and break the cramp but it would not cease. He went down on his knees, then his side. His toes were curled back so tightly he thought they might break. It was as if every insult his body had taken throughout the day had arrived and joined force in the muscles of this one leg.

Sally's head appeared at the top of the ladder. Alarmed she cried, "Blood? What's wrong?"

He'd bitten his tongue. He moaned, "Help me, girl."

She came and eased him to the bed where her hands worked his leg as he clenched his teeth until the cramp was gone. Her hands continued over the rest of him until he reached for her and turned her roughly so she was under him and she cried urgent to him and he responded.

And then there was the long slow time both had learned with the other in the ten days since her birthday.

She was all he'd ceased hoping for. Everything he did not deserve.

There was a second frost and the white pease wilted. Sally pulled the plants by the roots and tied them in bundles and hung them upside down in the barn to dry them in their shells. The carrots and parsnips could stay in the ground yet. There were rows of beets to contend with. She pulled a handful and took them in and put them on the table before Blood.

"What do I do with these?"

"They for dinner? Just boil em. You know how."

"No. I'm asking what to do with all them out in the ground. We'll never eat all of em before the ground goes hard."

"Pickle em," Blood said.

"Pickle em? You going to show me how?"

"How? You just—pickle em. Slice some onion to put in. And pickle em."

"I don't have the first idear how to pickle."

Blood studied her a moment. She thought It's not my fault I don't know. She returned his empty gaze. And realized he didn't know either.

After a time he said, "The first thing we do is set down and make a list of what staples we be short of. For the winter. I'll write it up for you. Then you carry that list up to Mistress Chase and show it to her and ask if there's anything come to mind she'd think to add. Then, ask her how to pickle your beets. She'll tell you."

"I ain't going anywhere near her."

Blood went on, "I can't trade in Lancaster. Or Bath or anywhere else downstate. So I'll yoke the team and go over to Canaan Vermont. There's a store there. What they don't have they can order for me. It's time now. I've been setting lazy all summer but things are tightening and there's supplies we'll want come winter. Maybe I'll take Gandy with me so he'll know the way and I can get things set up with the men there to do trade with him. Although Gandy's days are numbered. He'll be gone into the woods and bogs pretty soon. But he'd make the trip with me. There'll be things he wants too. So, let me get a piece of page from the tally book and let's make that list."

"I told you. I ain't going near that woman. She despises me. And I got no use for her, neither."

Blood looked at her. "Do you know how to pickle beets?"

"No."

"Then you got a use for her."

"There's others could tell me. You could find out yourself."

Blood said, "Sally. When there's someone don't care for you, someone maybe even that's an enemy to you, the best thing to do is go to em and ask for something. It makes them feel good, like they got something on you, just the littlest jeezly thing is enough. What they thought all along is confirmed—that they're better than you. See?"

"I don't want her thinking she's better than me. She ain't as far as I'm concerned."

"That's right. But see, if you didn't know she felt that way, and you went asking something, then she would be the one wins. But. If you go knowing you're going to make her feel that way, and don't care, then you're the one wins. And she won't even know you beat her. See? It's a clever game."

Sally thought about it. She said, "But nobody but me'll know I won."

Blood said, "Nobody but you matters."

Blood bolted the door after her and went through into the tavern and unlocked the door of his storeroom and took a candle-lantern in and made inventory, tried to calculate sales. And his own needs; he would not underestimate those. He had ample rum but would try to obtain more. It could be a hard winter. He was more concerned with powder and lead. There was enough for an ordinary winter but the coming fall and winter held the possibility of being not at all ordinary. He counted and added weight in his head. He would try to buy or order more pigs of lead, more kegs of powder from the men in Vermont but had no idea if they'd be willing or not. Until he went there was no telling how they felt about the recent events. Humor was what he counted on. He could always go to Canada. It occurred to him he might be forced to buy in small lots, meaning several long trips. It was time to find Gandy. He sat at the counter, using the last of the fresh-made ink to write out the quantities he hoped for, scattered sand over the page and waited and blew it off, folded the paper and tucked it into the back of his tally book.

He went again into the storeroom and carried out two kegs of powder and took them one at a time on his shoulder up the ladder to the loft and set them behind the carriage of the swivel gun, behind the supplies of powder and ball already there. Back in the storeroom he set aside an equal amount of lead pigs and swore to himself that before the week was out he'd dig out the iron crucible and mold the lead into balls and store those overhead as well. It would be a vast amount of firepower, enough so if he failed to procure more powder and lead he might not have as much to sell as would be demanded of him. And so resolved one day soon to replace the simple loft door with one of thick hemlock planks. To loosen the ladder from the wall, so it could be drawn up into the loft. It was not perfect—he could still be burned out. But he was willing to believe the eight-pound gun would forestall such effort. He considered filling empty kegs with water and hauling them also into the loft. No. If it came to fire he would already be lost. But he would cost them dear.

He was gambling. For the first time in years the whims or actions of other men might impact directly upon him. But Blood was not ready to quit, would not allow himself to flee. It was not pride but something else. What bothered him most was he could not say what that might be.

Sally came back in. Her face was serious, her mouth twisted, clamped shut. She carried hugged against her chest a three-gallon pottery crock with a woodstave lid. She set it on the table, got the bucket and went out and some few minutes later returned with fresh water which she sat next to the crock. She took up a tin dipper and drank it down and filled it again and drank that too. She wiped her mouth with the back of her hand and looked at where Blood sat at the table. She dug his list from her skirt pocket and unfolded it and passed it over to him. At the bottom of his list of things was written in a spiked uneven hand *The vinegar is a gift, the crock a loan. Get this girl some stout winter boots and heavy woolen clothing in respectable gray or brown. It's not right to mark her so with tawdry raiment. Not suitable for her nor the other children & women.*

Blood indicated the crock. "That's vinegar?"

"To pickle the beets. You do em in a crock. With salt."

"I knew that."

"Well I didn't." She stood, twisting a strand of hair between her fingers.

"So how was it?"

"It wasn't nothing like you said."

Blood thought I'll walk up there and strangle that woman, she was cruel to this girl. He said, "How so?"

"She was grim when she saw me at the door. Shooed her children off to another room. There was one girl, nine or ten, kept peeking until she told her shut the door. Then she was kind to me. She didn't invite me to set for tea or nothing like that but she was kind. Tight with words but they all are, these women. Asked me my business and I showed her the list and she read through it and then looked at me and asked if that was all I wanted of her and I asked about the beets. She took me into the kitchen and got the crock and vinegar, all the time talking about how to fix em. And all the while she was doing that I felt like she was trying to say something else to me. But she didn't. She had me tell it back to her and then she set at a little desk and wrote what's on the bottom of the list and told me give it to you. And she looked at me a minute before she handed the list back to me. At the door she stopped me. Put a hand on my arm. And told me if there was anything else I needed to know, to come to her anytime."

Blood studied her. He said, "That don't sound so terrible."

"It wasn't. It was just—"

"Just what?"

"I don't know." She shook her head. "Peculiar someway. I sure don't feel like I won anything."

It was the company of women, Blood thought. Something she had never really known. Not in the everyday-world sense of things. What she knew of women was the underside, a world of women made more by the world of men than of women themselves. And thinking this, he realized the world of women was one he'd never truly known himself, that his marriage ended before he gained sufficient sense to comprehend fully the woman who had been his wife. And thus all others. He knew little of women, beyond the ever-more-vague memories of Betsey and himself before what he thought of as his troubles began—a time when they were more children than Sally herself. He understood men, he believed, better than most. But of women he knew almost nothing. It was part of what he denied himself, save for those creatures of the underside sought only for the occasional release it seemed no man could live without. And even those times infrequent for they left him foul and rancorous for a week or more afterward. As if he'd indulged himself. This through the long score of years. Until Sally.

He sat looking at her. She stood watching him, waiting for something. He didn't know what it was. He didn't want to know. He was angry, some sort of fool. He stood and said, "Do you know what she wrote on the list?"

"No."

"Do you want to know?"

"I guess."

"You guess? Don't guess girl. Be sure of what you want."

She tilted her chin up a little. "What was it? What she wrote."

"That you shouldn't dress like a whore. That it's bad for the children. That I should wrap you up in brown woolens. How does that sound?"

"That's what she said?"

Blood went to the fireplace and took his hat from a peg and went to the door and stopped and looked back.

He said, "I'm going to see if I can run down Gandy. Go on, make your beet pickle."

She said, "She hadn't ought to've said such a thing."

Blood breathed deep and easy, three times. Then said, "We need some winter clothes though. They say it gets cold enough to crack iron. So, consider what you want."

And went out. Not liking himself very much and not quite sure why. Beyond the usual multitude. Although it would be interesting to see what sort of winter goods she decided upon.

He would've knocked down the man who suggested it, or even the girl herself if she were to voice it but he wasn't sure anymore what to make of her whoring. Most nights she slept through with him but afternoons and evenings she worked when work came her way. It irked him that this bothered him; it irked him that he allowed her to continue. There was no peace.

Four

As if the weather knew the calendar the last day of August broke with a hard killing frost. Where the sun fell the world spangled, autumn arriving in glacial brilliance, almost suggesting snow over the grass and low shrubbery. Where the sun had not yet struck it was ghostly, a pewter finish over the sagging grass and wilted goldenrod stems. The pods of milkweed were brittle and broke open to release their slight spherical webs of seed onto any straggle of breeze. Smoke streamed white straight up from chimney tops and mist obscured the lake, hanging in sheets of cold vapor that disintegrated slowly from the top down as the sun came over the hills. A third-quarter moon hung against the endless fathoms of a cobalt heaven, the moon a quartzite river stone.

Blood woke early with the chill. Sally was pressed against his front but had dragged the covers over her so his backside was cold. He slid from the bed, gathered his clothing under his arm and went into the kitchen. Luther was sleeping against the door. Blood knelt and blew flames from the raked coals to kindling and then dressed. When he pulled his blouse over his head he heard a low thrum of sound coming from the dog. He looked and saw he was not asleep but was lying with his body pressed against the base of the door, his nose deep and hard against the slim crack where the bottom of the door fit the sill. The hair on his back quilled in a ridge.

When Blood approached the dog rose and circled around to be behind him. Blood took up the ox goad and slid the bar off the door and stepped out into the smoking dawn.

The pea-eating savage squatted against the side of the building. Dressed in leggings and loincloth and a rabbit-fur vest, hide-side out. His hair was oiled and hung straight onto his shoulders. There was the beginning of a new scar running down one cheekbone—a thick crusted scab of wound. Between his chin and mouth there was a broad swipe of bright yellow. An odd place for paint, Blood thought. Then saw the half-dozen broken eggshells littered between the moosehide covered toes and realized it was a simpler paint than he'd guessed. My goddamn breakfast is what he thought.

"We ran right out of peas. But there's potatoes and other such in the garden," Blood said. "I guess you don't care for that rough fare. Maybe you got a delicate stomach."

The man studied Blood a moment and then spoke a short burst of language that Blood did not know.

Blood said, "I'm not buying that. I'd bet a penny you know plenty more English than you let on. You eat that many raw eggs, you'll get loose bowels."

The man stood, a fluid effortless rising. He stepped close to Blood, not in menace but rather as one studying some mystery of an unknown world. A curiosity. He reached and touched Blood's chin with his fingertips and took his hand away.

"Dead," he said.

Blood's bowels jellied. He said, "I guess someday. But it won't be you brings it about."

The Indian gazed upon Blood with a face made from the scarred stunted hardblown land itself. He was silent. A long stare. Blood stood under it.

Then the Indian turned and trotted up the rough road running north along Perry Stream. He did not look back this time.

Blood stood watching some time after the man had gone from sight. Stood out in the dull silver stilled morning, his breath visible clouding out from his mouth. Finally he bent and gathered up the eggshells and walked as far as the bridge where Perry Stream ran into the river and closed his fists on the shells and then opened his hands out over the water and let the bits go. Like fragile broken brown skin the shell-pieces drifted down to the cold riled water and were gone.

* * *

Sally was in new winter clothing ordered from a dressmaker in Wells River Vermont through the store in Canaan, the materials all in grays and browns but for one skirt of dark moss green and a heavy shawl of deep cranberry. Blood scanned these wraps with mild amusement for while she had followed the Chase wife's advice in tone the fit of the clothes was snug and spoke clearly of her form as well as her absence from the bitter chapping work that the other women of the settlement were accustomed to. And the goods were fine, warm enough but not the rough hand-loomed apparel the other women wore. Blood supposed Sally could be set down anywhere and she would thrive. The thought was not altogether cheerful.

She had a basin of warm water set up on the table and was washing out the half-dozen sheaths of lamb intestine that she used with men, her sleeves pushed up to her elbows as she bent over the job, her hands working each sheath inside and out very gently. It was the basin he used to shave with but couldn't say anything to her about it—what else was she to use? So he said nothing but each time she finished this weekly chore he took the basin to the river and scoured it with sand and brought it back to the house where he filled and emptied it not once but twice with boiling water from the iron kettle that hung from the crane. The thought of the crusts of other men's sperm in his shaving water tumbled his stomach but he could not forbid her the use of the basin. If he were to regard this part of her work as so unsavory he must see it all that way. Even his scrubbing of the basin betrayed something of himself. Some hairline fault in his frank appraisal of the world.

She pressed each sheath between folds of a piece of soft old dress material, the same dress he'd brought her north in five months ago, before hanging them over the back of the single upright chair which she then positioned far from the fire and out of the sun so the sheaths would dry slowly and not become brittle. Later in the day she would work a dab of the grease from sheep fleece into each one to keep it supple and less likely to tear. He guessed the lanolin made her work more pleasant for her. Perhaps simpler as well.

Swiftly foul of spleen he said, "It's nice work you do on the table where we sup."

She said, "I could set on the stoop and wave them at passersby, hang them on a bush to dry if you druther. I'm not ashamed."

"Watch your sass, girl. I'm in no mood for it."

"Don't vex me then. It's a bad enough job as it is without you pestering me. A week's worth of men groaning and heaving. In a way, it would be funny, if it weren't me it was happening to. But at least they don't fill my belly. What would I be worth to you then, Blood?" And she met his eyes full with her own, boring into him as if she dared to know the answer. As well as silent somewhat hostile reminder of his own refusal to wear them with her.

He turned away from her and took down his long gun from over the mantel timber and his pouches from their peg. He slung the pouches over his shoulder and turned back to her. "I'm going out. A deer or young moose is what I'm after. You keep Luther close about you, in the house or out. I don't like the feel of the day."

"What don't you like about it?"

"I couldn't say. Just stay close to the house."

"You're in a foul mood, Blood."

"I am," he agreed. "Keep an eye sharp and stick tight. That's not too much to ask, is it?"

"No," she said. "My eyes are sharp enough. I don't rely on you to warn me. As for sticking tight, I'm not going nowhere. Not anytime soon."

He paused, knowing his face was sour. Then said, "It's a burden off me. To hear that." Then turned and left, shutting the door behind him.

She waited half an hour and went into the tavern side and poured a dram of rum and drank it down. Then reached below the counter and took up the short tapered bludgeon of smoothed pig-lead kept there and put it in the apron pocket of her skirt and went back into the house side and spoke to Luther and they went out together into the morning.

It had warmed enough so the frost was gone although passing into any shade was to go into a cavity of chill air. She went down to the road and walked over the bridge and came back up on the far side of Perry Stream where there was only a crude track to follow through the big hemlocks that bordered the stream. But fifteen minutes walking took her to a feeder brook that ran off to the west and following that another fifteen minutes she came into a wide bowl of open marsh.

Here sumacs flared and some rock maples were balls of fire and birches the yellow of butter. Cattails grew in crescents along the shorelines of open pools of slack brown water and hummocks of dry grass lay stitched together throughout the marsh and she made for one of these and sat back to survey the day. She had been here twice before, both times without Blood's knowing, after hearing of the place in passing one night at the tavern. It was trapped out but there were big trout in the deeper pools. She wasn't after any of that but just the stillness of the place. It was a different stillness from the quiet of the tavern mornings. This quiet was a thing all of its own. It was here without her and yet it allowed her to enter into it, to become part of it. At least to tolerate her sharing of it.

She sat on the dried grass of a hummock and hiked her skirt to her thighs and leaned back on her hands and tilted her face toward the sun. A flock of red-winged blackbirds swarmed the marsh, cutting and swerving each one but also all together as a group. She wondered how they did that. She sat in the sun until it was as warm as it would be that day and the grass around her was dry and then lay back upon it with her hands under her head. She did not close her eyes but looked into the open sky that was spread with high thin clouds made from the morning lake mist. This was the only thing outside of herself that she kept from Blood. It was important to have; it someway made what else she kept from him more substantial.

The blackbirds roved over her. She thought it must be fine to be a bird. To go wherever you wanted, whenever you wanted to. Then again, noting how they moved each in some relation to the others, she wondered if it was not that way with all creatures—all can fly but only so much as allowed by their fellows, as if each was born to fill a slot allowed in the world. It was a mystery. A girl is all I am, she thought. And wondered what was a woman for? A wheel on the cart of man is what it felt like, and she snorted out loud. Yes there was that brief time when she knew how a man worked. At least until he rolled off and got his breath back into him and was already gone from her. It was a mystery all right. And decided if it was a mystery made by God then she wouldn't like Him very much. Maybe just another man was all He was. The Head Man—the Boss of them all. She didn't know. She didn't know much about God and didn't really want to. From what she could see God wasn't much more than a torment to men. Women too. Maybe women even more.

She watched the birds, the slashes of redwing markings when they turned. The two times previous she'd climbed up here there had been far fewer of the blackbirds and she marveled over the number now. Then studied again the color on the few trees changed from summer green and realized the birds were gathering to travel southward, away from the coming winter. She wasn't even sure how she knew this—some mention sometime by someone regarding the changing of the seasons, spring to summer, summer to fall, the movements of the birds. Remembering the great flocks of geese and ducks and pigeons she had seen the spring before while traveling here with Blood. She did not know where the birds went. Some great distance. Some place she did not know.

She considered what she'd told Blood: that she wasn't going anywhere soon. A small lie, since she was here at the marsh when he clearly meant for her to stay at the tavern, but a larger lie also. Not that she had a plan. Plans, she thought, were what other people had. She'd seen her share of those plans fizzle to air. And what use was a plan when she barely knew where she was? What she had instead was a notion, a notion tucked tight, hidden like a coin in her boot. It was very simple: to pay attention to what was passing around her and watch for that opening, wherever, in whatever form it might take. Most likely a stranger. But nothing like Blood, nothing even close.

What of her own tenderness for Blood? This the greatest danger of all, she thought. A tenderness mostly of proximity, of knowing one another, sharing in fortune, fate even. No. It was not that simple. She cursed him. Her tenderness for him was genuine—she cared for him. She cursed him again, cursed herself. Because she was no fool. She was not a girl smitten and there were two things she believed certain of Blood. The first being that it wouldn't last and that however it ended Blood would abandon her altogether, even if that abandonment were only to relegate her solely to whoring again. Although she suspected that if Blood soured upon her he would sour thoroughly. She had a moment where she saw him sending her off to winter with Gandy or one of the other trappers, a meanness pure and simple: Blood's revenge. And revenge for only being herself. Whatever she was to Blood, she thought, didn't have all that much to do with who she really was. She guessed he saw her as something he might make amends to, amends for a fester tracked back to before she was even born.

The second was less simple to parse. Opportunity, when it came, would demand she notice it first and lock it tight before Blood even guessed it might be coming. The idea sent a shiver through her. To outsmart Blood. All of this and to make the right choice. It was almost too much to consider. But it was within her now and not something to be cast off. It was not just paying attention. It was about how smart she was. Blood was the first person to make her feel smart. Again, the shiver of doubt. Against it, out loud she said, "I guess maybe I've learned a thing or two. On my own. It ain't all from Blood."

The trick she thought was to be patient. But not too patient. She could patience herself right into the ground, she wasn't careful. An important fact in this was that things weren't working out for Blood the way he'd hoped—he hadn't told her directly but it was clear that whatever it was he'd attempted between Chase and Hutchinson had failed. And perhaps even diminished Blood someway. She sensed it from the men around the tavern. It was nothing obvious but a slight loosening on their part, as if they feared Blood a little less. Or discounted him some other way. If he saw this she could not say. Again, she told herself, It idn't all that much about me. In its way this only impressed further the need to jump. To pick and choose carefully. Because when she jumped it would be all the way.

She thought If people could see their future all the world would be different. But it didn't mean she wouldn't try. Try was all she had. That and a sockful of money. And perhaps, the lies of love. A different sort of whoring. She could do that. She looked down at her thighs, white in the sunlight, tight and strong. She pulled her skirt down to cover herself and sat upright and watched the birds circle and cry, the light glancing off the still ponds, the sweet smell of the moist earth. Something was possible.

She called the dog over and he sat beside her. Gazing off into the day, his brown eyes as liquid and unknowable as the marsh water. She put one arm over his shoulders and pressed against him. The dog did not break his gaze to look at her but allowed her to hold him so. They sat that way awhile. The day had lost a little of its warmth. There was a breeze breaking in short gusts over the marsh. The yellow birch leaves flipped over and some few came loose and tended toward the earth.

*   *   *

By noon Blood was far up Perry Stream. He crossed over Otter Brook and then left the waterside and began to work the triangle of land between the two streams, thinking this time of day the deer would be bedded but not up too high—it was warm enough so they would stay near the water. He moved slowly, working his way back and forth between the streams to cover the ground thoroughly. A bedded deer would stay right where it was unless he was close enough to alarm it. Especially a young one, what he was after. The spring fawns would be gaining size and weight but would still be with the does. The woods were big here: old trees, hardwoods. High enough so there were stretches where he walked with ease. It was the blowdowns and otherwise fallen trees he was hunting toward. In the scant openings there would be new growth of alder or larch or popples or hemlock. Good cover.

He was back alongside Otter Brook making his way upstream toward a hillside thick with young alders when he saw a flash of dun movement. Low to the ground. Something springing up and away. Even as the powder smoke burned his eyes he could smell the blood and the part of his tongue that ran direct from his stomach to his imagination could already taste the roasted young meat.

So he pressed hard up the slope through the stinging whips of young trees and found the egg-eating Indian thrown back on his side in the brush. The hole in his chest as neat as if made by an auger. His back was blown apart where the ball had gone through. His eyes strange blanks. One hand pressed just below the hole in his chest as if he'd reached but missed the mark. His hand covered with the flow of blood. His loincloth was twisted aside from his crotch. Closeby, from where he'd toppled, was a thick spatter of loose stool.

Blood, panting with the effort of his climb, recharged his rifle. Then bent low to the ground and squatted there, watching the woods around him. After a time the squall of a gray jay came and went, came again. Some crows. Smaller birds. Beyond sight the first cries of southward geese. Blood watched awhile longer. Then stood. Looked once a long time at the dead man.

Blood said, "I warned you against those eggs." Then went down to the brook and knelt and drank quickly with one cupped hand, the other holding his rifle. Between weak sips he continued to watch around him. With some water in him he rose and hiked downward along the brook.

* * *

The body of the Indian was carried south and hung from a limb over-looking the road to serve as warning for any party passing the blazes that marked the northern boundary of Coos County, indicating entry into the Indian Stream country. Blood had argued it to be needless provocation but would not say whom he feared provoking. So it was displayed and the small patrols that skirted back in the woods near the border to watch for men coming into the country could smell it as it twisted slowly on its rope and daytimes the ravens came to perch on the shoulders and eat out first the eyes and then the rest of the softening flesh of the face and at night when the air stilled and the frost came down the smell ran through the air in a broad grope of putrefaction. On the fifth dawn when the patrol arrived to relieve the chill-stiffened men lurking in the underbrush without benefit of fire, it was the newly arrived who discovered that during the night the body had disappeared. There were no footprints but the rope was cut and left dangling. None of the night-party had heard any disturbance, all swore to wakefulness.

Blood went to Emil Chase. "It was his own people got him you know. It was what I feared."

"Feared they'd take him or feared they'd find out what happened to him?"

"Feared that with it done every man we know is going to be jumping out his skin at the least sound in the woods. If it's just a stray ox gets shot we'll be lucky."

Chase held his chin with his hands. His wound had healed. "It pleases you to be right, don't it Blood?"

Blood said, "There's no pleasure in this."

"I wonder how that sheriff's leg is serving him."

"It was a bad grinding he took. Could be he'll not walk again."

"Perhaps," Chase said. "Do you think that'd keep him off a horse?"

As if the death of the Indian had conceived a final severance of faith, two nights later the five families of Canadian habitants loaded their carts and departed soundless in the dark up the track that led toward Halls Stream and the Canadian frontier, leaving behind crops and the houses and outbuildings of logs that once empty immediately seemed derelict, cobbled roughly, as if they had ever known their fate would be thus. The remaining habitant was the bachelor Laberge who had been in the country as long as any other man and who moved with the established gait of a man who knew no other land, wanted no place but the one where he stood. Of his own now-fled people he would only say that the turmoil was nothing more than the excuse all had been seeking to return to the townships and impose themselves upon already straitened brothers or fathers or in-laws. "It's the women," Laberge said, "who suffer the burden most. It's them will hear the talk not so careful hid. I'm lucky, me. No woman, no talk, no fear to stay right here."

It was evening of the day the abandoned pitches had been discovered and the tavern was thick with men. One of the young men, Burt or Bacon, wondered aloud if those departed men hadn't held some private knowledge of intent of invasion by the Crown or provincial forces and Blood looked up to watch Laberge remonstrate, "You damn fool why'd they run off if that was coming? They'd be the roosters over you little hens, that was to happen."

It was Bacon. "You greasy fucker I'll cut your nuts off and see who's the hen, you want."

Blood stood. There was an old reek in the room, the sweat-stink of anxiety like filings of some bright hard metal. It had been there all night. Blood thought it was his own.

Laberge was a grim small man who smelled of sawdust, wood sap. His smile was a bright rind of white against the plaited flecked wires of his beard and upper lip hair. "Don't talk so to a man. You a boy yourself. Just barely discover your own nuts, eh."

Bacon started forward and Blood began to go around the counter with the little lead bludgeon but Sally came off her perch which slowed him down and when they both came through the opening of the counter they saw Bacon snake one arm out lazy and slap at Laberge's face and come away leaving a sickle of white showing through the beard that then filled with blood. As Bacon stepped back Laberge groaned and brought both hands up before him and Bacon came back toward him and Laberge stooped swiftly and side-kicked one boot out and snapped Bacon's elbow. The knife skittered onto the floor.

Bacon howled and Sally surged past Blood, running across the sudden opening toward the door to the house side. Laberge also was moving, bending to scoop the knife, a spray of blood tossed off his thrown-back head as he came upright. Bacon went sideways and dropped his broken elbow, bellowing. But with his good arm he snatched Sally by the waist and drew her against him, so she faced the advancing Laberge. Blood stopped.

Laberge glanced around the room. He smiled. His mouth filled with blood and stained his teeth and dripped into his beard. He said, "Aw fellers. Look at this." Then he spoke to Sally captured by Bacon. He said, "I never did no dirty work upon you girl. Never harmed you. Don't plan to start now." And bent again as if to study the knife blade in his hand. Blood stepped toward him but like a wejack Laberge lunged forward and with one hand grasped the top of Sally's head and pulled it down and with the other swept the knife across Bacon's throat.

Blood caught up to him and bludgeoned the lead just behind the man's right ear. Bacon was dead on the floor and Laberge caved sideways. For a moment Sally stood between the two, her dress wet with the shower of blood. Blood spoke her name. She looked at him and then with one hand lifted her skirt hem a few inches and stepped over Laberge and went from the silent room. All watched her. All heard her go through the kitchen side to her room and the bar fall after she shut that door behind her. Blood looked at the ruins on his floor. He tapped his thigh with the lead and looked at the men in the room. No one spoke. Stunned, but not for long.

Rain began during the night and sometime before dawn turned to sleet and then ice so when the light came paltry and sullen over the land the body of Laberge was a swollen polished figure of encased darkness hanging from the rock maple outside the tavern. The body did not swing or twist but was inert as the light. Only the sheen of ice over it. Blood waited until the ice turned back to rain and cut the body down and hauled it by the feet down to the garden and dug a trench where the peas had been and buried the man there. He finished the work and turned to find Sally wrapped in her new shawl watching him.

"You think I'm going to garden there come next spring with that in the ground?"

He was breathing from the shovel-work. "What makes you so sure," he said. "We'll even still be here come spring?"

She looked at him awhile. Drew her shawl tighter about her throat. She said, "You ain't going nowhere Blood."

He watched her walk back toward the tavern, watched her go around the corner out of sight. Just like that he knew she would bar him from her room again this evening. As if she blamed him for the violence around them. Or, he considered, there was something else at work within her. He was suddenly greatly fatigued. His hands were caked and raw, clublike with cold mud on the spade handle.

He went that afternoon for the funeral of young Bacon. The rain had stopped and the clouds were quilted inkstains over the sky which the wind ripped sideways. The lake was a churned frothing. He climbed the hill to stop between the uprights of the granite entry posts. The funeral group was at the far side of the meager plot and he realized he was late for the service; men worked in turn to fill the grave. He did not advance but watched as a visible ripple went through the group and they turned one by one blank baleful faces upon him.

Blood understood they conferred accountability upon him for the fate of young Bacon—these the same men now hungover, their shame turned outward to anger—who the night before had brutally taken up the unconscious Laberge and carried him into the darkness and called for rope. When Blood would not supply it some one of them took a candle-lantern into Blood's barn and cut the length they wanted and brought it back. Blood had stood in the doorway watching. Silent. Several bad throws until the rope end went over the limb and then they noosed Laberge and held him upright while one man threw a bucket of water hard against Laberge's face and he stuttered into consciousness as the group of men took up the free end of the rope and hoisted him off the ground. They tied the rope to an iron ring set into a stone post beyond the tavern door and all stood then watching silent as Laberge kicked his feet angry into the empty air, watched in the sputtering lantern light as the hanging man fought with his fingers against the clamp of hempen fiber choking him. Stood until the motion was over, the last spasmodic absurd antic drifted to stillness. The rain had started. Blood had gone inside and barred the door. He expected some among them to hammer upon it, to call out for drink but the men went away noiseless in the rain. Morning first thing Blood found the candle-lantern on the single stoop. The pierced tin sheathed in ice.

He did not enter the cemetery but turned back and walked home. It was time to build fires. He'd let them go out that morning, feeling there was no reason for him to be warm. If Sally wanted warmth, let her kindle them. She'd spent the day locked within her room. He'd not seen her since he'd finished his own burying in the garden that morning. Cold as he'd been then he'd not wanted a fire. Disgusted with himself, with his failure to act the night before. Even as he knew it wasn't for him to intervene—his place in the community now fully relegated to the suspect position of witness. It was the service he brought that saved him and that only so long as he stood clear. If he'd tried to stop them, the men of the night-mob wouldn't have paused long before stringing him as well. Blood still sure he wasn't deficient of courage—he just wasn't stupid—there had been nothing left to save anyway. He'd scrubbed in the ice-rimmed water of the stream. Inside, chilled, had used the same cold water and meal sacking to halfway clean the bloodstain from the tavern floor, thinking it not a bad idea to leave some reminder for those same now righteous men. His heart was not in the job.

But it was time to build fires. Look at him as they would, he knew that as night fell the small log and plank houses would grow too close to contain all that had happened. The single men would leave their solitude grown too close, the married ones under bald pretense and all come to the one other place there was. So he came down the road and saw the smoke boiling from both center-chimney flues and he thought There, she's up out of her gloom now. He discovered his door barred and had the wry pleasure of pounding for entry and hearing his own dog bellow dire from within and other than that only silence. The wind was hard upon him and he was truly cold now, cold beyond the vehement deserved chill of the morning. And Blood stood a long moment. Loathe to call out to plead entrance. As if his voice before his own door would someway verify his lessened standing to himself. Calling for Sally. And some small spit of thought wondering what she was up to that she would bar him out.

So he called out to Luther. Once, loudly commanding silence. After
a beat of pause calling again as if speaking not so much to Sally or the
dog but perhaps the house itself, a mild query if all was well.

And still he stood some time more on his own step. It began to rain
again, a hard slantwise rain that stung his face and wet him through
behind. He stood there as a forlorn penitent before the sanctuary that
would not admit him. With his head tipped down and sideways a little
to let the rain strike him. And saw down off the stoop where the water
fell from the eaves a small trench filled to a small canal from which
water struck and pocked up off the surface. And recalled his daughter Sarah Alice not quite two years old squatting beside a puddle in
the rain and reaching trying to snatch those drops fighting upward.
Her face a glower, unable to fathom the way they seemed to disappear in the air inches from her face, her swiping hand. Scowling at
him as if she blamed him for this failure.

Sally opened the door wrapped in a blanket. Steam boiled out around
him. He stood looking at her. Behind her he saw the heavy pot hung
from the cradle swung out into the room off the fire. The floorboards
swashed with water stains. He could smell the hard lye soap and also
the scented rose-soap that someone—he'd not asked who—had given
her. Her hair was wet and her face was pink. Water ran drops down
her legs and outlined her bare feet. She waited a moment and then said,
"You going to just stand there letting out all the warmth or you going
to step inside and dry yourself?"

"What's all this," he asked.

"I was washing myself."

"Washing yourself."

She frowned at him. "That's right. It's something people do time to
time. Something might not harm you, you was to try it."

"What for?" His brain suddenly thick, as if all the night and day had
curled there and gone to sleep.

She shook her head. Stepped back and said, "What's wrong with you
Blood?" Then went right on, "No. Don't tell me a thing. There idn't
nothing more I want to know. But I worked too hard to get clean and
warm to stand here. You want to come in, come in. I'm getting dressed.
I'll push the kettle back over the flame. It's most full if you want it."
And turned from the opening.

* * *

It rained on. Hard rain that popped against the shingles, but there were no leaks. It was a sound roof. Well after nightfall a few men came in, then a few more. They stood silent drinking or seated on the benches against the wall conversing in low sporadic utterance. Three sat at the hogshead-top table dealing softened cards, playing with a dour trifle of discussion. Blood ignored this moderate ostracism but sat behind the counter with a reeking smoking tallow stub lighting the sheets of his tally book. There was nothing to update beyond the night before but he went over the entire last week, not looking at previous final figures but doing the work all over again. He was not a man who ever had to add twice so there was no satisfaction in the work beyond the appearance of business. If he was reminding anyone in this silent way that his life held some portion of theirs then he was happy to be doing so. Let them be averse to him if they chose. Tomorrow as tonight they would need his rum, his powder and lead. The girl. Who sat motionless on her stool pushed far back from the counter against the back wall and was not hostile to those few who this evening chose to speak to her so much as vacant. He watched her without obvious effort. She was pretty in her moss skirt and gray bodice and gray shirt-waist with the cranberry shawl slipped back loose upon her shoulders. Her hair seemed to be the one spot in the room where all light chose to gather. He could smell her, even this eight or ten feet away. She sat straight with her back against the wall and her eyes nowhere at all that he could tell. As if she looked out upon some other place altogether. He poured her a pewter cup a third full of rum and without ceremony or words of any sort carried it down and set it beside her.

Several hours after dark two young men Blood did not know came in. They paused overlong near the door as they brushed water from their stained and roughened good clothes, studying the layout of things. Without any discussion they moved along the walls of the room to a free spot on the benches where the light was not so good and they sat. One had a young man's beard and he leaned to place his forearms on his knees and tipped his head to the floor as if greatly fatigued. Their clothes were dappled with mud and he guessed whoever they were they were camped rough. But, curiously, the other men in the room glanced up at the strangers and some looked longer than others but all seemed to discount them. As if they knew something of them that Blood did not.

After a moment the one with the shaven face rose and came to the counter, not directly across from Blood but a foot or two down from him. But the youth looked upon Blood. Blood glanced up and met his eye and went back to his figures and completed another useless column and stood off the stool and pressed his shoulders back and cracked his neck.

He said, "Rum."

The young man looked at Blood for a pause. A short moment but those eyes were filled with tremendous length. He nodded, "Two of em."

Blood turned for a pair of dented tin cups and poured from the pitcher and while turning back saw Sally looking at the boy. When Blood swung her way she looked up toward the smoked ceiling beams. Blood turned back and set the cups on the counter. He said, "Is this it, or will you settle later?"

The boy ran his tongue swift over his lips. Without taking his eyes from Blood. "I believe, if it please you, we'll settle when we're done."

Blood nodded. Then said, "I don't believe I've seen you before."

The boy took up the cups. "No," he said. "I don't imagine you have."

Blood watched him cross the room to hand one cup to the other boy who took it and held it on his knee with his fingers wrapped around it. The first boy sat and sipped and leaned to say something to the other. The other lifted his cup and drank and while he did his eyes landed square upon Blood a moment, then away and he turned and said something to the first boy. Blood was staggered by the look. Brief as it was it was a purity of hatred gathered and winnowed to a nugget. No man had ever looked at Blood quite so—there was no mistaking it. This was no general emotion but something pointed, specific, distilled. Blood took his eyes away from the bearded boy. And saw Sally look away from him and back toward the boys as if she'd seen something of all just transpired.

Blood went to where his tally book lay open and finished the page he'd been working and the figures did not match. He circled the lower one but did not re-add the columns. After a time he closed the book and snuffed the tallow stub between thumb and forefinger and took pause, was considering a drink even though it was early for him, when Sally rose to go around the counter to the fireplace. She pokered the fire level before adding a pair of logs. It was something most always done by one man or another, whichever among them felt some chill. When she finished Blood watched her turn to sweep the room, her eyes going across the two boys and the one with no beard was waiting for that look and grinned at her. The bearded boy ignored her. Sally did not respond but continued her spin and came back to her perch. She took up the cup Blood had set out for her and drank from it. To anyone but Blood she'd seem bored.

Peter Chase was across the counter from Blood, propped on his elbows, eyes upon some distant pale in the woodgrain of the countertop. Blood leaned. Just enough motion to edge shadow upon Chase's gaze. He looked up at Blood.

Blood said, "You know those two boys against the wall? They ain't been in before."

Chase swung his eyes without moving his head, already knowing of whom Blood spoke. "They ain't up to nothing. Couple boys from way downcountry come for a summer in the woods. Isaac Cole talked to em. The morning after you shot the savage it was. They come down off Magalloway Mountain and along the road by the mill. Just a couple of greenhorn boys was what Cole decided."

"Where they pitched?"

Chase nodded. He said, "Don't know. They're well soaked but wet's it been they could be near or not."

Blood nodded. After a time he said, "They from downstate, you said."

Peter Chase thought a moment. Then shook his head. "Further than that. Connecticut maybe. Massachusetts. One of them places. Half-baked city boys. All their gear was new, Cole said. There's nothing to worry over with them two. They don't know the first thing about Hutchinson nor any of his doings. Cole talked about it with Emil. Nothing for you to be concerned with, long as they put their bits down like anybody else. The way I see it, one morning soon they're going to wake to a snow-squall and that'll be the last we see of em. Boys on a summer lark. Maybe they chose a bad summer for it but that idn't their fault."

Blood considered Peter Chase a moment. Then said, "I guess."

The boys sat on the bench, working slowly at the tin cups. The bench was a great comfort after three weeks of squatting or seated on rocks. Their

wet clothes chafed and then warmed and steamed and fit again easy to
their bodies. After half his drink Cooper sat back a little and slid one boot
up to rest over the other knee. This allowed him to view more easily the
room while providing the mild disguise of akimbo arms and legs, his chin
lowered toward his chest. He'd unbound his brown hair and now it had
dried and hung about his face, lank twists around his new beard. His beard
was darker, in this dim light near black. He tasted the cup, set it on his
knee and locked his fingers around the kneecap. He looked sideways at
Fletcher who was bent forward a little at the waist. As if to leap or spring.

Cooper said, "How you doing."

"All right."

"You sure?"

"I'm all right. You?"

"I couldn't tell you. I don't quite know myself."

"You look easy enough."

"He's been studying us."

"Well. We're strangers. You can't make too much of it."

"There idn't nothing to make of it. It just feels queer is all."

"I guess it would."

"Don't it for you?"

"Some. Mostly my own jitters I guess. It ain't the same for me as you."

"I guess so."

"Listen," Fletcher said. "There's one thing he idn't ever going to do
with me. He idn't ever going to look me in the face and see or guess who
I am. I know that. We don't have to pretend otherwise. It's all right."

Cooper ignored this. "You know what I think?"

"What's that?"

"I think I'm going up there and get another one of these drams."

"I'll go."

"No. I want to. You ready for another?"

"You going to talk to him?"

Cooper stood. Reached for Fletcher's cup. "My name's Russell Barrett.
I ain't nobody to him."

"You think up close he idn't going to recognize you?"

Cooper said, "It idn't my worry I should happen to remind him of
anybody else. I'd like nothing more than to stir his dreams. Get something working under his skin."

"All right."

"Let go your cup. You got me standing here like I can't make up my mind."

"Shoot," Fletcher said. "Sorry." And let go.

Cooper grinned at him, the grin a little crooked. "Anybody asks, I'll tell em my little brother idn't sure of himself, it comes to hard drink."

"Go on. Leave me be. Who'd ask anyway?"

"I don't know," Cooper said. "Maybe that girl keeps looking at you."

The boy with the beard crossed the room and Blood made him wait while he ran a damp rag the length of the counter. Then wordless filled the cups and the boy paid for all four drams but when he held out the coin he did not drop it into Blood's palm but kept it until Blood took it from his fingers. The boy the entire time watching him, this blank study unsettling Blood.

So when he was done with the boy he did not watch him return to his companion but went past Sally, telling her to tend to things as he passed, not waiting her response but went through the tavern and house to her room. Where he took the bar leaned against the wall behind her open door and carried it with him outside. He walked out beyond the barn and heaved the bar into the puckerbrush and stood a trice with his head tilted back to the sky. The rain had let up but the clouds were still low and thick, pushed on by a bitter wind, broken only in spots. He briefly saw the cluster of stars that he knew were called the Sisters by men of the sea but to him looked like a blind bright great eye. And then it was gone behind clouds. As if the eye had closed. There was something about the boys, both of them but particular the bearded one, that disturbed him. More than her interest? He could not say.

She waited half an hour after the boys had left and he gave her credit for that but the one man that approached her as the night grew long she turned away. Blood could not hear but saw the way the man looked at her and guessed her words were more bitter than called for. She slipped from her stool and without speaking to Blood left the tavern and went out into the night. A short time later came back in but did not return to the tavern. She had gone to her bed. Surely she noted the missing bar but did not come asking about it. So a couple hours later when the last of the men were gone he wiped the counter clean and locked the small lead cashbox, put the key back in the pouch he wore around his neck and laid fresh logs on the fires before he finally went to her door where he did not knock but went in, expecting her to be awake and she was.

He stood beside her bed in the pale firelight coming through the door and said, "Why've you locked me out?"

She said, "I can't lock you out Blood. Ain't you just proved that?"

"I've not forced myself on you."

"Not but once."

He waited wordless. She was sitting up in the bed. Blankets tented over her shoulders. After a time he said, "Who was those two boys in here tonight?"

She said, "I never seen the two of them before."

There wasn't much she could be up to behind his back. He said, "You sure studied them pretty hard."

Before she spoke he saw her soften a little. He thought Oh Jesus. She said, "I didn't make no fool of myself."

He understood something but again wasn't sure what. He said, "Which one do you favor?"

She was quiet longer this time. Finally she said, "They're just two men I ain't seen before. I get tired of the same men all the time. I thought maybe they might take an interest in me, is all. In case you ain't noticed, the work's not been so good recent. Too much trouble on most men's minds."

He was silent.

After a time she said, "You been good to me. But whatever's wrong with you. I can't fix it Blood."

His voice came rough and sudden, caught upon itself. "I never expected you could."

He stood looking down at her. She looking up at him. Finally she said, "It's awful late. You going to just stand there til dawn or you going to come in the bed?"

*   *   *

For three days it rained and froze, rained and froze, the sky pressed hard upon the earth. When it froze there was a crust of ice a boot would break through into thickened mud. Trees and lesser shrubs encased in ice, then stripped clean with the rain. When the ice came, mostly but not always at night, it would build on limbs and some would give way under the weight, the sound an anvil of broken glass. At dusk on the third day the rain stopped and sometime later the sky cleared and it grew very cold. Throughout this time the tavern was busy and Blood began to feel more at ease. Perhaps the string of events, the bad luck, had broken. He knew that time moved, men realigned and while a grudge or sense of blame did not disappear it could be tamped by more immediate desires—the need of a drink perhaps. A tumble with a girl. She had stopped barring him from her room but was also working and he thought this good. For both of them. Some balance had been regained. With the cold weather settling he began to believe the winter might bring quiet to the round of days. Blood was weary of adventure. Although daily he paused over what others might be about. Mose Hutchinson for one. But each day that passed quiet was one more day gone through and he guessed snowfall would put an end to the turmoil. At least slow things down. Save for the impoverished and restless trappers, he guessed he was the only one truly craving snow. Cool them all off was what he thought as he took the first tipple of rum for the evening.

The two boys had found a good place to camp—directed there by Gandy whom they'd met on the road—they climbed the rugged track running up Perry Stream and watched for the trail that broke off and led up to a marsh of old beaver ponds and pitched their sailcloth tent back under ancient hemlocks that broke the worst of the rain. They had dug down through layers of needles until they had dry ground within the tent. The first night, with the camp fresh, they'd hiked down to the tavern. For the remainder of the ice and rain storm they huddled, keeping warm and dry with the abundance of dead limbs low on the ancient hemlocks surrounding them. It wasn't the weather that retained them so much as the quiet stun of how simple it had been to find him, which cast off like ill-recalled dreams the months of planning. They were suddenly marooned, not from the weather but an unexpected malaise. They didn't know what to do next.

On the evening that it cleared the younger boy dug into his packbasket to come up with his one clean dry shirt and put it on and then his damp wool blanket-coat, this done in silence while the older one watched. Fletcher stood under the tent-fly near the hissing fire, looked back at his brother and said, "I'm going down there."

"I'd thought I might be the first to talk to him."

A short pause. Fletcher said, "Well. We just been setting here. Like neither one was in a tear about it. Also, to talk, evenings when he's busy idn't the best time. I'm tired of setting here. Thought I'd just get out of the chill. I got no great plans, otherwise."

Cooper considered this. "I guessed as much. You want I should come along?"

"No. I believe I'd go alone. There idn't no chance of his recognizing me."

The older boy nodded and said, "You put on your clean shirt just to look good for him?"

Fletcher stood silent.

Cooper said, "It's that girl, idn't it?"

Fletcher looked at his brother and said, "I'm not sure just what it is. I get it figured out, I'll let you know." And turned and walked into the gathering dark.

So he stood before Blood and did not wait but spoke first.

"A measure of rum, if it please ye."

"A measure, is it," said Blood. "You're a sailor, are you?"

Fletcher shook his head. Fingered a coin down on the greasy wood.

"You're wet enough to've just come from the sea," said Blood. "But there's not a man here idn't."

Fletcher said, "It'll pass."

"A young man don't mind the elements as much as the older, idn't that so?" Blood had not yet moved to pour the dram.

Fletcher looked at the pitcher, then back at Blood. He said, "It's a little damp."

Blood reached and brought up a tin cup. He still did not move to fill it. "Where's your partner? A night like this, he didn't want to come warm himself?"

"He's my brother. He didn't care to make the tramp."

"Your brother? You do favor one another."

"Sometimes."

Blood nodded as if he understood this. He said, "So how do you find the Indian Stream country? You two going to lay out pitches, make farms?"

"We ain't decided."

Blood nodded. He said, "My name's Blood."

Fletcher nodded. "I heard that."

Blood waited. Fletcher looked again at the pitcher, at the coin on the counter. Blood waited a bit longer and poured from the pitcher into the cup and set it before Fletcher. Did not touch the coin.

Fletcher said, "I'm Fletcher Barrett."

"And your brother, Fletcher Barrett?"

"Russell. He's the older one."

"I guessed so."

"Do I get change from that or do we just wait and see if I drink it up?"

Blood shrugged. "Here on the counter or in your pocket, it's your money until it's gone."

Fletcher took up his cup. He said, "I'll trust you to keep tally." And turned away.

He passed by the table, not too close but enough so Cole saw him and nodded a greeting. Fletcher went on and sat on a bench with his back to the fire so he could see the room. He watched the men playing cards. Time to time Cole glanced at him. Fletcher worked at the rum. The room was hot and he was soon flushed. He stood and set his cup on the bench and pulled his coat off and hung it on the set of pegs that ran one side of the mantelpiece stone. As he did this a heavyset man came into the tavern from the other side of the house. His face held a skim of sweat and his shirtfront was stuffed awry into his breeches. He nodded at Fletcher, took down a heavy hand-loomed woolen greatcoat and pulled it over his shoulders so it wrapped him like a cape, turned away and went out, leaving into the night. Fletcher sat again on the bench and saw Cole lean across the table to speak to the other sportsmen before rising to approach. As he came he was paused by Sally coming in from the house side. She looked at Fletcher and frowned and went right by him. Cole came up.

"I'd a bet this weather would've sent you two downcountry."

"It idn't so bad," Fletcher said. "It's turning."

"I guess that means you ain't stopped for a farewell. So where'd you two land?"

Fletcher told him.

"Why that's a pretty spot, idn't it? I knew the old man trapped up there. I can't recall his name at the moment but he trapped it right out. My it was fine. I don't think he was there but two three years but pulled piles of fur. The spring it was finally done in he told me he was going across to Maine. Said it was the only other place on earth might be as good as that little bog. Beaver and mink and otter, not a trash fur in the lot. There's still deer a-plenty for fresh meat. And trouts in the ponds. A man can get awful sick of trout but he sure won't die."

"It's all right I guess. We're keeping dry mostly. Them big hemlocks help."

Cole nodded. "It's a peculiar territory. This time a year you can't tell. Could come off pretty for a couple weeks, could be a cold night and then more rain. Could be a foot of snow and hard frost by tomorrow evening."

Fletcher nodded. "I heard that."

Cole stood. "Some day perhaps I'll walk up and see you and your brother."

"That'd be fine. Can I ask a question?"

"A course so. But it don't guarantee a answer. This country idn't the best to be asking too many questions."

"Do those floorboards got some kind of rot or is that bloodstain?"

Cole did not look away from Fletcher. He said, "A man was killed there a couple nights ago. Another died on account of it."

Fletcher said, "Was that because of asking the wrong questions?"

"No," Cole said.

He sat on the bench a time and then went back to Blood. Placed his empty cup on the counter and was silent. The coin was gone. Blood filled the cup and put it before him. Fletcher drank from it.

After a bit he said, "How much?"

"We're square," Blood said.

Fletcher looked at Sally settled on her stool. She had glanced as he came up, then looked away. He spoke to Blood. "How much for the girl?"

Blood rubbed his stubbled cheek. He said, "It's a dollar for the girl. That's what you pay me. Another four bits to her. If she'll have you."

Fletcher kept his eyes on Blood. "What do you mean, if she'll have me. Idn't she yours?"

Blood said, "As much as she'll allow."

Fletcher said, "I never heard a whore run that way."

"What's a boy like you know of running whores?"

Fletcher dug again and got his purse out and set down a dollar. He said, "Enough."

Blood took up the dollar. He said, "That takes care of me. The rest is up to her. She won't take paper money nor notes."

Fletcher looked at Blood. He said, "At least she idn't stupid."

Her room was small but ordered: clothing hung on pegs, a candle-lantern with the door closed so it threw its spew of dappled light evenly from a small stand beside the bed. A basin and pitcher also on the stand. The high small shutter was opened to fresh air. The bedding was neat-ened, rough blankets with a warm bearskin over them. He followed her in and dug a dollar from his purse and handed it to her. She slipped it into her apron pocket without looking at it although he was sure she knew it was a full dollar. He sat on the edge of the bed with his hands loose on his knees. She shut the door and slid a newly-peeled pole into supports that should've held a bar for the door. Turned and began to unbutton her bodice.

He said, "Don't."

She paused her fingers and looked at him. It was the first time she'd looked at him since he'd paid Blood. She said, "There's things I won't do. One's to have some feller tear my clothes once he gets going. I can't afford that kind of rubbish. If there's something wrong with you that you don't want me bare I don't want to hear about it. Also, you get rough with me beyond what's tolerable, you'll go out. And Blood idn't gentle over that sort of dealing neither." She finished the buttons and took the bodice off and dropped it to the floor. She looked again at him. "You got to undress yourself, at least as much as you want. Usually it's the older men with their bellies that like to keep most dressed. But it don't matter to me."

He stood off the bed and bent for her bodice and held it to her. "Here," he said. "Put this back on."

She ignored this. For a moment her eyes flat upon him. "What's wrong? Your breeches is about bursting." She reached behind her and began to untie her skirt.

"Please," he said. "Get your clothes back in place, girl." He held the bodice as an offering, the garment a flutter from his hand.

Her mouth compressed as she studied him. Not sure what he was about. So she said, "It's the whole idear. Why else waste your money? You don't get it back, not if it idn't my fault you changed your mind."

He laid the bodice on her bed, stepped to the door and lifted the pole from the brackets. She came fast then and caught his shoulder. "Wait," she said. "What's wrong? Where you going?"

He stood like that with her hand on his shoulder. Then dropped the pole back into place and turned. He stepped around her and picked up the bodice and handed it to her. She looked at him and put it on. Did just the one button to close it over her breasts.

"There," she said. "Is that better?"

He stood pondering her. Abruptly she understood. She thought Maybe. But. Go slow. Take time. Something else she couldn't name ticked over inside her as well.

She said, "Now. You going to tell me what's wrong with me that makes you want to run off?"

"There's nothing wrong with you."

"You ain't never been with a girl?"

"It's not that."

She almost smiled at him. "That idn't what I call a answer."

Fletcher was almost grim. "I paid Blood so I could see you. I paid you so you wasn't thinking I'd waste your time." He took a breath. "I want to talk to you."

"You want to what?" Still thinking Go slow.

He said, "How long do I get?"

"What do you mean?"

"How much time did that dollar to Blood buy me."

"Most usually, as long as it takes. I ain't never had a problem that way. Although you're jabbering more than most."

He went back and sat on the bed. "Come over here and set down."

One corner of her mouth twisted. "It don't buy you all night."

He almost asked what that would cost. He said, "Why don't you just set down. I ain't going to bite you."

"I'd bite a gouge right back, you did. What do you want to talk about? I don't even know you. What're you called?"

"Fletcher Barrett. And your name's Sally, idn't that so?"

She nodded. There was something she needed to know. "Was that your brother come in with you the other evening?"

He looked away from her and back again. When he did this she thought she'd made a mistake. Careful, she thought, as Fletcher said, "Listen—." And stopped.

She stepped and sat on the edge of the bed. "What is it, Fletcher? What is it you want to talk about?"

He sat silent a time. Already wondering how much time he had left. He looked away from her. Then, his voice quiet he said, "Can I ask you something?"

"What?" Guarded.

"How'd you come to doing this?"

She looked away from him. Well there it was. Her voice emphatic, without sway she said, "I was born to it."

"It wasn't something you chose?"

She looked back at him. "I ain't never known anything else. There wasn't any choosing. Not for me. I heard all the hard-luck excuses some girls made but I never had that chance."

"Well—." He stopped and reached and took her hand. She let him hold it a moment, felt the heat there, felt all his intention and unspoken honesty and spiked desire at once in his grasp. His hand wrapping hers like it had been waiting longer than either of them knew for just this. She pulled free.

"No," she said. "There idn't a way out. You got to stop this."

He took his hand in his lap, joined it with his other. Neither looking at the other. After a bit, his voice not bitter or smooth but matter of fact as if speaking of the rain and cold, he said, "I guess my mother was one of those hard-luck girls. Except the way I heard it, it was just the one man, a man with family of his own. I don't know what she expected of him, but what she didn't expect was me. But by the time I come along he'd long since disappeared."

She also was easy. "Happens like that, more often than no. How'd he find her?"

"She come in off a farm, was working as a serving girl at a public house."

"So then there was you and she was stuck. That man gone like a Christmas orange and no hopes for another. Everybody has to survive one way or another."

He looked at her. "That's the part of the story you got wrong."

"How so?"

"Because he never even knew of me. When I was born she took me up to his family. Everybody knew who they were. She didn't even try to find my father. Because he was gone, long gone, not just from her you see but his own family as well. Didn't bother going to his father either. But went straight on and presented herself to my father's grandfather. Who was a fearsome old man but I guess knew simple truth when he heard it. And he done the right thing by her. By me too. It was him made it possible for her to live a different life than the one facing her. And me as well."

They were quiet awhile. Then she said, "What's that got to do with me?"

"I don't know," he said. "You tell me."

"It sounds like you was lucky. That's all."

"It was more than that. It wasn't luck. It was the viewpoint people took on the matter."

"What's that mean?"

"You seen that boy I was with the other night in here."

"The one with the new beard." Now she'd stopped thinking all angles, any notions. Was just listening.

"That's right. He's my half-brother. My father's son. We've known each other since I can remember. And he's always treated me just like his brother."

"Well you are."

"No. You ain't thought that one through. I was the brother he wasn't supposed to have. There wasn't any reason for him to even want to know

I was alive, let alone tolerate me as his brother. But instead, the way it turned out, when I was little, he was the one protected me from other children. He took to me and we grew up close. Still are."

"I still don't know what all that has to do with me."

"People don't always act the way you think they will."

"Well," she said. "You was lucky."

He was quiet as if considering this. "No," he said. "It started with that old man. He had a wisdom rare. And the strength to force it on those who'd as soon looked the other way. In the later years of his life he had more heaped on him than many a man all their lives long. And he stood up and faced it head on. Some part of that come through to my brother. And I like to think some part of it come to me as well."

She sat silent looking at him.

He stood. "I guess I used up my dollar. I got to get along. But I could come back, some evening, you wanted. We could talk more."

She shrugged, her eyes away. Then, propelled, she came off the bed and took his hand and pressed it and let it go. They were quiet together a moment. Then she said, "Fletcher. I ain't but a whore."

"Sally."

"No." Her voice tight, concluded. "You'd end up hating me. I'd not blame you for it but it idn't something to wish on either one of us. Please."

He reached for her but she stepped away, just back enough to stall him. Seated herself on the bed. His eyes bored upon her a long moment, then relented. As if he would not even do her that harm. Abrupt he swung toward the door, stopped and turned back.

"Don't you tell no-one what I just told you. Nobody. All right?" This tone new for the evening. She noted it but only tilted her head, her chin tipped at him as if defying him to question this of her. She said nothing.

He tried a frail grin that did not work. "Well." A last hesitation. "Good night then." And lifted free the peeled pole.

Quick, as if to keep him a bit Sally said, "Where is it you've pitched? You and your brother."

He said, "Why, right up the stream. Off the path some in an old beaver meadow."

"Oh," she said. "I know that place. It's pretty."

"Right now it's awful wicked damp."

"I can picture you there. See you in my mind, knowing that's where you are."

He nodded. Then cut his eyes away from her.

"Fletcher."

"No," he said. "I got to go."

And now looked at her seated on the edge of her crude bed, shoulders stiff and her knees together, her skirt smoothed down, hands limp fallen into her lap. Still silent he opened the door, stepped out and closed it behind him even as he heard her whisper good night.

The fire was burned down to a heap in the kitchen and he went through into the tavern that was lit only by a likewise fire. The room was empty but for Blood up on a stool behind the counter, a pewter mug before him. Fletcher went to the fireplace and got down his blanket-coat and put it on. Blood was watching him. Fletcher met his eye but did not speak.

Blood said, "It was awful subdued. Usually she's a screamer."

Fletcher said, "She was mostly quiet with me." He dug out his purse and stepped to the counter and laid another dollar on it. Blood looked at the coin and back to Fletcher.

Fletcher said, "I come to terms with Sally. But I figure I owe you. I just got going and couldn't stop. You was a young feller once yourself—you know what I mean."

Blood said, "Yes. A fool with a pecker like firewood. A pup, you could say."

"It must be hard, having her flaunting around all the time."

Blood said, "I get what I need from her."

Fletcher said, "I bet you do. I bet you do indeed." And without any final words walked past the sleeping hound and out into the cold starry night. He did not linger, did not walk around to the back to stand below the open port of her small glassless window to see if it was still lighted within, did not walk back to call her name once low into the night but strode hard over the curds of mud freezing on the road and over the

bridge and up the near-hidden trail, not once looking back, not wanting to know if Blood came to the door to watch him go or not. Guessed
that Blood would not do such a thing. Wishing he would, wanting Blood
provoked enough to step out to watch him walk away. And knew it best
if Blood did not. So he tramped up the uneven brockled path of stone
and mud lit only by pale starlight breaking through the layers of hemlock boughs, his right hand made into a fist that over and over he smote
into his left palm.

Five

∽∽

Following the days of freezing rain the skies remained clear, the air came from the south and the warm wind and sun dried the land. The lakes and marshlands filled with geese and ducks at dusk and at dawn they rose, breaking from the mass of water into clumps that fell apart into files ever more as they climbed and the sky darkened with the thousands of waterfowl in their chevrons. The eagles and falcons came off the ledges to feed among them, stooping from great height to clout the unknowing duck into a burst of feathers, scattering the flock. Daytimes the geese not flying would come off the water and into the stripped grainfields and meadows to forage the rare kernels or the tender blades of younger grass. Boys went among them with rawhide snares at the end of poles and women rendered the goose fat into crocks to store for winter when the cows went dry and there was no butter and the wild game was lean and so fat of any sort was not luxury but sustenance.

On the third day of this season a party of heavily armed mounted men in royal uniforms rode over the rough trails that ran west to east from Saint-Venant-de-Hereford in Canada along the upper reaches of Halls Stream, where they came out on the road running down Indian Stream and arrived midday at the tavern with a warrant claiming complicity of Blood in the murder of the habitant Laberge. The officer of this company was a whipthin horseman named Quigley and he sat his horse quietly while he explained that Blood must be presented to the magistrate in Hereford to answer in the inquiry of the death. His manner was pleasant and whatever he'd heard about the ferocity of the local residents had left little or no impression upon him. Blood stood in the temperate morning and related the events as they'd occurred while the officer watched and listened until Blood was finished. Sometime during Blood's retelling Peter Chase and Isaac Cole arrived on horseback from the direction of the mill but they stood their horses well back in the road and made no sign of interference or even great interest and Blood saw they expected no reinforcements, saw also they wanted none. When he was finished the royal officer removed a glove and leaned to blow his nose away from his horse's side and replaced the glove.

"I'm sure, Monsieur. It's a legal matter. My job only is to escort you to Hereford. It is, you understand, your deposing that is of interest to the magistrate. My own duties are freed from judgment."

"I did what I could to save him. It was self-defense on his part."

The officer gazed with interest upon Blood, as a man would a stranger's child caught in mild mischief.

Blood said, "You're out of your country. Nothing compels me to go with you." He looked at Chase and Cole. They were intent upon a pair of boys coming up the road from the river dadewater with a pole they dragged between them. The pole sagged, heavy with dead geese. Blood looked back at the officer.

Quigley said, "Dead, you'd be useless for questioning. Otherwise, your physical condition is of little concern to the magistrate."

Blood did not even bother eyeing the troopers but kept his gaze on the officer. After a moment he said, "There could be considerable havoc short of me dead."

The officer lifted his eyes to gaze toward some horizon. Mildly he said, "I've the men for it."

Blood drew breath and waited. The officer looked back at him. Blood said, "Resistance would be naught but loss for me but I see little gain in going freely—with no assurance of what waits."

"What waits you Mister Blood is not my consideration," Quigley said. His voice had clicked up to just short of command. Blood heard this and felt as much as saw the troopers gather themselves. Quigley said, "I'm charged with bringing the body as well as you. There is family awaiting."

Blood paused a long moment and then sighed. "I'm not digging him up."

The officer leaned sideways a little to study Blood. "But, as a Christian man, you'll be inclined to accompany men of my company to your burying ground and point out the grave. Yes?"

Blood said, "Shit."

"Sir?"

"It wasn't me killed him. It wasn't me strung him up. Left to their druthers, the ones who did would've left him hang till he turned black and rotted. So I buried him best I could. A Catholic—he'd never been allowed in the cemetery."

The officer sat his horse and glanced at Cole and Chase then back to Blood.

"So," he said. "Where did you bury him?"

"I wanted him gone. I was trying to do the right thing for him, best's I could."

"And so?"

Blood felt his shoulders give. "He's in the garden."

The officer glanced around the packed bare earth before the tavern as if he might discover a bed of flowers. Then he looked back at Blood. "The garden?"

Blood paused, knowing whatever authority or goodwill might have once been his was as good as gone. "It's round back of the building," he said.

When the party of three royal soldiers came around the corner of the tavern their breeches were stained with dirt and they carried Laberge as three men might a short length of log along their sides. The body was wrapped in heavy canvas and belted with hemp rope crisscrossed along its length. They did not look at Blood. They loaded the body onto a blueroan mule that stood throughout as if its life-job was to have dead men strapped over its back. Again without speaking, the three went to the stream and washed their hands and came back up to the party and remounted their horses. Sometime while they were gone on their digging, Chase and Cole had ridden off up the road, at the easy gait of a late summer afternoon, as if their only job in the world might be to catch up to the boys with the geese and get their share. Their observation and departure bothered Blood as much as whatever adventure lay ahead in Canada. Perhaps more.

Blood said, "I've this public house here. I'll lose trade."

The officer regarded him for the first time since he'd sent the regulars off with the spade. The intervening time he'd sat with one long boot hooked up over the pommel of his saddle while he smoked a pipe, gazing with mild disinterest at the hills around the lake. He'd said nothing when Cole and Chase went.

"If your records are meticulous you may petition His Majesty's government for what custom you may lose." He spoke mildly, as if uttering drollery.

Blood said, "It's not that. I've a girl'll tend things. I'd speak to her though, so she knows where I'm off to."

"Call her out."

Blood stepped to the open door and spoke her name. She came onto the threshold and without looking behind him Blood stopped her there. Swiftly he caught the thong around his neck and brought forth the pouch from under his blouse and handed it to her.

His voice low, he said, "You heard?"

She nodded.

"The small key in the pouch is to the strongbox under the counter. Go up this afternoon and find Van Landt. Don't dicker with him but make him name a price. Don't let him see any money first. What you got to do is get him to ride over with you to Hereford tomorrow and you bring the rest of the money with you. Make sure he comes with you. Don't trust nobody, least of all Isaac Cole or them Chases. You got no choice but to leave the house open but move the rum into the storeroom. The other key fits that lock. And leave Luther shut in. Make sure you bring an extra horse so I don't have to walk home. And listen. I don't want nobody but Van Landt. There's nobody can be trusted at all. But he understands money like none of the rest of these do. Is that clear?"

She nodded. Looking from him to the king's troopers and back.

Blood said, "Sally. I ain't got time to go over it twice."

She said, "I can't ride."

"You just make sure you and Van Landt are in Hereford tomorrow noon. Not first thing in the morning and not at dusk. You understand me?"

"You trusting me with all that money?"

"I am."

"You never did pay me that wolf bounty."

"Jesus," he said. "This ain't the time for jests, Sally."

"I weren't jesting." Then she nodded. "But if I break my neck trying to ride a horse to rescue you, you have the decency to put up a good stone for me, you hear?"

"Christ," he said.

"Sally Blood," she said. "No fancy words."

"You ain't going to break your neck. Or nothing else. At least as long as you're in Hereford by noontime."

"You got to promise."

He looked over his shoulder at the officer who was smoking again. But this time watching the two of them.

Blood lowered his voice. "I promise."

"You have no horse?"

"I do not."

"You'll have to ride pillion on the mule then."

"It's some load he's got already. I'm not sure he'd want me up there."

The officer smiled. "He's a mule. The two of you aren't the worst he's carried before. The question is, do we tie you on or do you mount yourself?"

Blood on muleback surrounded by the troopers on their black or gray or bay horses—the horses on short reins so they moved in a shifting sideways trot, the essence of controlled dreadful power, the war-horses and their riders groomed spotless, all leather and metal to highest polish so they moved through the day as bright spangling alert precise machines of annihilation- and Blood on the blue mule that marched as if blind to the display about itself, whose only job was to convey whatever cumber was laid upon it and this day it was the wrapped body of a dead man hanging down head and feet on either side and perched behind that burden was the heavy short man who had no choice but to wrap his hands in the shroud-lacings and ride with his knees spread to nudge against the sides of the body before him. Blood riding thinking not so much of what was before him but trying to discern what lay behind.

Chase and Cole lounging horseback the least of it. They were simply witness to what was ordained. So the question was not so much who had informed upon him but to what purpose? Not so he would name names, which was most certainly what the magistrate in Quebec would expect of him. And so, for what? He did not know. The mule's backbone dug at his scrotum. For the moment there was no divining what design consigned him to this ride. The only probability seemed to be regardless of what he did or said in Hereford, his own words might be used to drive him from the country later. But to the peril of how many other men? Who would risk that? None of them, he was sure of that. Least of all the men who'd strung his riding partner from the rock maple. There was no sense to be seen in it. Yet there had to be, for here Blood rode along. What mind appointed Blood this role? He did not know. So he rode, the mute mule his only guide for the moment. The rest awaited.

He wondered if he could trust Sally. He thought so. He listened to the high far-distant geese.

It was an awful pile of money. Took both hands just to struggle the lockbox off the shelf below the counter and hug it against her chest to heave onto the plank countertop. This after barring the door and lighting a pair of candles in tin holders on the counter. She dug the smaller key from the pouch and opened the box. It was mostly filled with coins and a small sheaf of banknotes and a larger stack of promissory notes. She could tell the difference. The banknotes were in different colors and sizes but they were printed and engraved. The promise notes were handwritten on scraps of various papers. She set those aside first and then the banknotes. Then scooped out by the handful the assortment of specie. All she knew were dollars and their bits. There were more of those than she could count. As well as a jumbled pile of other coins of copper and silver and the mysterious gold, some round and some with many short flat edges to suggest roundness. Stamped with the heads of men or women and some had numbers raised on their surfaces and all had some legend running around their edges or in bold letters straight across the surface and she knew they were mostly foreign but had no knowledge of their worth. The whores in Portland had talked of such monies, debating the values of such pieces as if value was in constant flux and not of any steady account at all and she wished she'd paid more attention but hadn't. All she knew was it was an awful pile of money.

She sat a time and moved the coins to stacks, the dollars first and then the others, by color and then by size, then back to color again. The least stack was gold. She'd not seen gold before but there was no mistaking it. It was a curious metal. Almost soft to the touch. When she closed her hand over one of the pieces it seemed to grow warm in her hand. She touched it to her cheek—it was still warm. As if something from her body ran out into the metal and stayed there. Soft to the skin but when she brought her teeth against it the metal was of a peculiar density, fooling her by its warmth and the softness to the touch. Her teeth struck another metal altogether, something hard and unforgiving.

Her first inclination was to take it and run. It was enough so she could go anywhere, do anything she wanted once she got there. But when she tried to picture where that would be all she could come up with was Portland. The only place she knew and the last place she wanted to re-turn to. No money in the world would change her life there. Once she understood this the rest tumbled apart easily enough. Most apparent was that whatever his predicament Blood would one way or another work his way out of it and the very first thing he'd do was hunt her. And however far she might get in however much time she had would not be far enough. She thought I ain't that stupid, just ignorant. But that's enough. Whatever else he was, Blood was not ignorant.

She poured herself the smallest of drams. Sat on her stool and drank it in sips. So she couldn't run. Not yet anyhow. What she wanted was some help. Some advice over how to proceed. Not yet ready to progress imme-diately to Van Landt. So she took three of the gold pieces and knotted them in a rag and put them in her apron pocket. Took a fourth and tucked it down inside her high shoe. Gathered the rest of the money and put it back in the lockbox. She used the other key and opened the fortress-storeroom and staggered in with the box of money and set it on the first powder keg inside. Considered Blood's directive to remove the tavern rum to this room and out loud said I guess not and locked the room and hung the pouch of keys around her neck, down between her breasts.

She took down Blood's rifle and the pouches of powder and balls and checked the charge and went to the door. The dog was beside her. She put a hand flat on his head and told him to stay. And stepped into the afternoon.

Peter Chase was squatting under the rock maple, the dry sunlight splintering down onto him through the inflamed leaves. He grinned when he saw her.

"Ain't you open for business?"

"I got other things to do."

"Didn't Blood leave you to run things?"

"Blood left me with work to do."

"You ain't got a quarter hour for me? Before you go off on your business and leave the house open to all? Seems to me you'd want someone kind to watch things."

She turned and spoke to Luther. "Anyone comes through this door ain't me, you rip his throat out, you good dog you." She pulled the door shut and turned again to Peter Chase.

"You can set there and watch the afternoon or you can walk down the road. It don't matter to me. But you move toward me once I'll blow your peckerheaded head off." She swung the long gun toward him.

He kept his grin. He said, "You're one riled bitch, idn't that so?"

Sally brought the rifle to her shoulder and held the barrel without waver upon Chase. She said, "Riled idn't the half of what I am. Now you get." And stood there until Chase rose slow and laborious and moved out to the road and she followed him all the way with the steady swing of the barrel. Once on the road he paused and looked back at her.

He said, "Your friends can change all the sudden. Enemies too."

She let the long gun down to her side, still pointed in an easy way at him. She said, "I got no friends, Peter Chase. Least of all the likes of you."

She came up along the brook out of the woods into the open ground of the marsh and redwing blackbirds swarmed up out of the tall grasses and cattails, the birds thrusting up and then turning as one so the sun caught against their underbodies and they were silverblue a moment against the sky before they were gone over the woods, their cries hollow splinters of challenge against her intrusion. She walked among the hummocks and pools hot from her trek as disappointment surged to anger that he was not here. He had misled her or worse had left the country without returning once to see her, already what she thought she'd believed of him twisting over against herself—that she should have expected anyone would see her as anything but what she was, that what grace she believed had extended from him had been some other thing altogether. Sympathy for her was what she thought it must've been. Some pity for her that caused him to be kind, a false kindness she now saw. At best he'd felt some curiosity about her and had misunderstood that as attraction until he got close enough to see the taint upon her and then repulsed had covered himself with some peculiar effort of courtesy. Perhaps only for himself, so he might walk away feeling he'd not further despoiled her. And she saw herself thus and was bitter with self-hatred, a loathing so pure it had a taste. She was some rare kind of fool.

Then saw the camp back in the hemlocks, the once-white sailcloth canvas tea-stained with rain and mottled with fallen leaves so it seemed not on the land but within it, hidden neat. She recalled the rising birds and thought the brothers must not be there, perhaps hunting or on some ramble. She realized she had no way to know their days, their purpose within this place. Her mood did not soften but turned again over her presumption she could simply walk up here and find him waiting. So she was stricken, seeking trust with no reason she'd find it. What she was aware of now was wasting time, sidetracking up here instead of making her way to Van Landt's. Of Blood taken, awaiting her, now looming in dismay and anger at her. It didn't matter he'd only been gone an hour.

So at first when he came out of the canvas lean-to and made his way toward her, hair loose and matted, his hands up rubbing his face and working at his eyes to bring them to focus, when she first saw him she was again confused, distracted, without a clear idea why she was here, what she wanted of him. She watched him come, feeling rough peeled. Not how she'd imagined this. A sudden tumbling of events and thoughts that left her contrary and doubtful.

He said, "I was laying back on my blankets watching this pretty day and fell right to sleep. All them birds put to fright woke me. I ain't used to a girl walking around in the woods. My, you look pretty this morning."

He finger-combed his hair mostly free and pushed it back behind his ears. His eyelids still swollen from sleep but he was grinning at her.

"Where's your brother?"

He heard her then. She saw his face converge fully upon her. "He's back there sleeping likewise. What kind of trouble's happened to you?"

"I ain't in any trouble."

"Well, what're you doing walking around with that musket? Hunting some venison?"

"I ain't the one in trouble. But I could use some help maybe." Watching him, knowing the next moments would reveal much of him. And saw he understood this.

"I was wondering why you looked so distressed to see me." He spoke with deliberation. "But if it's help you need I'm pleased it was me you come to. What's the matter?"

She told him of Laberge and Bacon, and the royal troopers ridden over from Canada after Blood, and how Chase and Cole had watched Blood being taken as if it was of only mild interest to them. How Peter Chase was waiting as she'd left to hike up here. Finally she told him of Blood's directive to her, of Van Landt and the idea of horses and her uncertainty of taking that on alone.

He stood awhile considering all this. Sally was patient, wondering if it was luck or fate that had brought her here. If it was all a mistake. If she should've gone it alone, if she still should. This boy Fletcher with his face too open, his desires still intact, easy to read. Not the best for what she required.

Finally he said, "We better go wake my brother."

This could be worse. She felt she'd already gone too far, said too much. "No. I don't want anyone else to know about this. I already told you enough for Blood to kill me."

He shook his head. He said, "Maybe you owe Blood enough to chase after what he says. But he's got debts hisself. There'd be satisfaction in riding in with you to help him out of his scrape. But it's not enough."

"What do you mean?" Now agitated as much as confused. Afraid she was about to lose what control she had. And determined not to even as part of her was popping with interest keen.

Fletcher said, "Here," and reached and took her hand. "Walk over here and meet my brother." He did not lead her but walked beside her across the marsh toward the lean-to. She let him do this a moment and slipped her hand away—knowing she needed his attention but resolved not to encourage it. Not now for certain. And guessing his imagination would serve just fine without her provoking it. Some part of her already tender toward him. An odd feeling for her. Something new and not at all disagreeable.

There was something about the brother that disturbed her. It was, she decided, in his eyes. While Fletcher regarded her with eyes plainly prepared to hear and accept everything about her, this brother she knew as Russell bore eyes upon her with hot flicks of motion as she spoke, not her body which was usual to her but as if he followed her words out and caught them up each one by one and examined them in his own time and fashion. As if she might speak for hours and he would lose nothing of what was said but would come to his own conclusion. When they'd come up to the lean-to Fletcher held her hand again while he called forth his brother but then let go and left her to stand while he crossed over and squatted next to the fire and said, "Sally. Tell him just exactly what you told me." And she thought If it's a mistake, I already made the jump and got no choice but to confide. And so she did.

When she was done she waited for Russell to speak and when he did not, she went on and said, "I don't trust that Dutchman as much as Blood does. I don't guess I got a choice but to get over there to Canada and bring what Blood wanted me to but I'm nervous about going it alone. I was thinking maybe you two might help someway."

Russell stood considering all this. She waited patient. After a bit he leaned to the stone fire ring to turn the coals and add hemlock deadwood for a quick fire and moved a blackened kettle directly onto the coals. He was now a few short feet from her. She did not move away. He set out tin cups and measured tea and when the kettle boiled he threw in the tea and took the kettle from the flame and rested it on a stone to steep. Still he did not look at her. Fletcher watched her and once flashed a quick grin at her. As if he knew her discomfort and was pleading patience. Russell merely squatted and watched the kettle, as if penetrating the iron wall to gauge the progress of the tea. After a time he poured out three cups that steamed in the warm afternoon. He looked up at Sally then. His eyes had drifted a little. He almost seemed surprised to see her there.

He spread an open hand to indicate the circle of rocks. He said, "Set yourself and have a sup of tea." Then, still serious said, "Lest you plan immediate destruction, you ought to lean that musket rifle up against something. It's a considerable weight to stand clutching like that."

She settled across from the brothers, facing them, her skirt tucked under her knees. She held the tea in her hand. The cup was hot through, too hot even to try against her lips.

Russell said, "You come up here trusting, idn't that so?"

"I guess. To see anyhows. We ain't made no deals."

"Fletcher here thinks much of you."

She was silent.

Russell nodded. She didn't know what this agreement signified. He said, "So it's only fair we trust you."

She blew again and made a small sip of the tea. She said, "You can."

"All right," Russell said, the tone of a man making a contract.

She was silent, agreeing to nothing.

A short pause. As of final assessment. Then Russell said, "My name idn't Russell Barrett." He leaned his shoulder to direct her toward Fletcher. "And he idn't a Barrett either. It's only a name we come up with. Although he truly is Fletcher."

She was watching Cooper close. Aware things were shifting toward some great weight. She made no response.

The brother was abrupt. "I'm Cooper Bolles. And he's Fletcher Bolles." She said, "All right." Placid even as a crack of recognition opened. "You don't understand. What do you know of Blood?"

She considered. "A fair amount, someways. But not so much, others."

"He's got more name than Blood." Cooper watched as if expecting her to understand something. She glanced at Fletcher. He was watching her also. His face was kind. He had a kind face. She looked back at Cooper.

Who was awaiting this look. He said, "He was born and named and still is Micajah Blood Bolles."

Without pause she said, "He's your father, Blood is."

Cooper nodded.

She looked at Fletcher. "And yours."

He drank some tea and nodded. Looking out the tent-fly onto the late summer dusk.

She sat silent a moment. When neither of them spoke she said, "He told me his wife and older boy died in the sea. An accident. But there was someway he held hisself responsible. He tried to explain that to me."

Fletcher turned his gaze up toward the canvas fly lit as a candle from the late sunlight. When he spoke his voice strained to stay even. "There's plenty men not callous enough to turn their backs on every thing in their lives. Like what children they left behind. Even just the ones they knowed about."

Her voice tentative, Sally said, "What was it then?"

Fletcher remained looking out, away. Cooper tossed the last of his tea into the fire and sat watching where the small jet of steam rose. Sally let their silence be.

Then Cooper stood under the tent-fly and so without apparent effort was closer to her, looking down upon her. He said, "I waited a long time for this. But there's not a thing we need to do this evening. There's time enough to hire horses in the morning and ride to Hereford to learn what trouble he's in. And see what he makes of us, and what we make of him. There's a pile of story you don't even begin to know yet girl. But I need to mull this some. I waited too long to hurry now and mess it up. I want to get it right. So, I thought I'd stroll on out and see if I can catch some trouts for a supper for us all. And I got to consider just where you stand with all this."

Without waiting response Cooper took down a loop of handline from one of the upright poles and turned and walked away. Fletcher was still gazing upward toward the screened sky. So Sally sat with her cold tea and watched Cooper tread his way out into the threads of the marsh. She was thinking We hadn't ought to just set here. But they were. Neither boy seemed in much of a hurry. Then she realized Fletcher was waiting for his brother to lead.

She didn't know what to think of Cooper.

Late in the afternoon the party of troopers and the twice-burdened mule came down the western ridge of narrow switchbacks above Halls Stream and sat their blowing horses at the streambank. One of the troopers wordlessly handed a canvas waterbag to Blood and he drank and handed the bag back and then without ceremony they crossed over the stream and were in Quebec. They rode north through the low rolling hills and broad valley past farmsteads with rail-fence enclosures and small well-built barns, the farmhouses all without exception painted in a variety of hues Blood had not imagined for a house: mustard yellow and chalk blue and pale pink, with sills and window casements in sharp contrasting colors.

The evening sun was lowering over the western hills and the light poured forth over this land as if onto some favored place and Blood could not help but wonder if he hadn't stopped some few miles too short on his northward trek the spring before. He recalled the Canadians dancing to the wondrous accordion music and thought perhaps he might have been more welcomed here. Among these Catholics, the men might've welcomed him more than the men of Indian Stream—the habitant trappers he'd met seemed now to him to have been reserved only by their minority. Perhaps their religion would have been benefit rather than hindrance. Even for the girl, although he expected she would have faced the same censure from the women. And there would've been the black-robed Fathers to contend with. It seemed no place was free of the righteous. In his own way, he guessed he was well righteous himself.

Blood thought all this trotting raw-buttocked on the mule with his hands blistered from the harsh ropes binding the corpse before him. Then a gaggle of children grew roadside and he realized it was himself they were peering at. A few flung pebbles and one struck Blood below the ear and another a trooper's horse and the officer swung about in the road and ordered the children off. If they spoke English as well as French Blood could not guess but the officer's message was clear in any language and the children fell back, calling names or threats lost in the soft twilight.

It was dark when they came into Saint-Venant-de-Hereford, the windows of the houses lit from within and only stray dogs to stir to the muted jangle and leather-creak of the troop and they rode through the town until they came to a plain one-story modest garrison house with a long ell of a stable. The captain remained mounted while three of the troopers took Blood down off the mule and held him by the elbows and brought him before the officer.

Quigley stroked his mustache and looked down at Blood. "You'll be placed in stockade for the night. I have yet to deliver this body and see no reason to offend the family with your presence."

"I thought I was here to see the magistrate."

Quigley regarded Blood. "By the hour it's plain the magistrate would be sitting to his dinner. Would you care to interrupt him?"

Blood said nothing.

The officer went on. "You may of course purchase whatever rations would otherwise be also available to the garrison this evening."

Blood said, "I have no money with me. But the girl is coming along tomorrow and will have ample funds for reimbursement."

"Will she," said Quigley. "In that event, you will be able to eat when she arrives." He turned to the troopers restraining Blood. "Make no concessions to his pleas. Irons, both hand and leg." Then he spurred his horse forward into a tight trot and the others of the company moved forward with him, even the blueroan mule trotting into the darkness. Leaving Blood as a minor hindrance of more solemn concerns.

The three cavalrymen led Blood to the end of the horse stables. The last stall did not have a half-door as the others did but one made of stout oaken planks with iron straps. While one of the men took a candle-lantern from a peg and lighted it another removed his horse pistol and struck Blood behind his ear and he went to his knees. The trooper struck again and Blood went down, his face scraping the hard-packed dirt of the floor. They rolled him face-up and one sat on his chest and held the muzzle of the pistol to his face while the others fitted his ankles with manacles attached by a short chain and then his wrists with a smaller set. The man stood off his breast and replaced his pistol in its chest holster and the three stepped out without speaking and shut the heavy door. A moment later Blood heard an iron bar being fitted across the door. Then boots receding in the measured uneven pace of horseback men walking. They had taken the lantern with them and he could see nothing but floating shapes of red and white pain sifting over his eyes. He was able to lift his bound hands and could feel a small blood-flow behind his ear. A knot stood out on his head there and the flow was already crusting in his hair.

He rolled onto his side and made his way up onto his knees and like an animal crawled around the enclosure. The inner walls were reinforced with planks like those on the door and buried well into the hard earth. There was a small pile of coarse marsh hay such as would be used for animal bedding in one corner. With the darkness it was already cold but he would not sleep in hay. He moved down the wall and sat with his back against it, his knees drawn up and his hands together down before him. Other than the pound of blood in his head he could hear nothing except the faint settle and tramp of the horse in the stall behind his back.

Some time later someone worked the iron bolting the door and the sudden pale lantern light near blinded him. Two men stood behind the light. Blood could see only their boots and legs. One held the light and the other advanced. He came only to the threshold and set down a tin plate and a pair of tin buckets, one of water and the other empty.

The trooper squinted at Blood. "Compliments of the lieutenant. If you drink all the water take care not to shit or piss but in the other bucket." Then the door closed and the men were gone. Although for some moments Blood still saw them etched before him, his eyes refusing to let the memory of the light go. Then a darkness even greater than before.

Blood crawled cautiously toward the door, toward the lode of food smell, a richness so vast it displaced all other senses. With his linked hands he carefully judged the water bucket and moved the empty slop bucket off to a corner and came back and lifted the water bucket and drank. Then very slowly and carefully outlined the rim of the plate with his hands, grazed the surface with his fingertips and then dug them in and lifted a wet portion of the food to his mouth. It was a stew of dried pease and ham, still hot enough so that he cooled the first mouthfuls on his fingers. After those mouthfuls he scrabbled around so he was squatting and brought the plate up to balance it on one knee and so ate his meal. Using his first and index fingers to pare up the last traces. Drank again and then shifted the bucket against the wall beside the doorframe. A place he could find in the dark if he moved prudently.

He still believed this was temporary. Whatever the magistrate was after could not include confinement of this sort for any length of time. It was a matter of waiting out the night. The morrow would bring all manner of light. There returned the question of what purpose he truly served being here. What master had approved this, brought it to fruition? It was apparently simple—Blood was the one who could answer most clearly what happened to Laberge. But there lingered the image of the lounging and unconcerned Peter Chase and Isaac Cole. To witness his arrest as something expected. There the mystery deepened. And Blood with no choice but to wait.

He scratched his wrists, the irons rattling in the utter black silence. Even the horse in the stall beside had stilled to equine sleep. For long moments he found relief pondering what dreams a horse would have— what dreams would visit a warhorse with no war? Carnage or pastures verdant everlasting? Would a horse, once shut into a stall, wonder if it would ever again be set free? Could it forget the expected routine of life and tremble over some horse-notion of being forgotten? Of rotting some slow death, away from all fields, those of war and those of browse as well?

The girl would arrive in the morrow. Sally and Van Landt. Blood was confident both would come. There was enough money, Blood was sure of that. Even as he calculated how much Van Landt might overcharge for the horses and his time, how much he could skim off Sally with her threatened to silence. But there was enough. Blood had done nothing that money could not smooth. He knew he could drip money out by the shilling, dollar, or pound until whoever had to be appeased was satisfied. The mystery of it all be fucked. Worst, he thought, I consign the tavern to Van Landt and walk out with only Sally and Luther alongside to start some place anew. Great God it would not be the first time.

In the enveloping darkness he was washed with sudden longing for the girl. Sally trusted Blood and depended upon him. She would resent him though, if not now then soon enough. But she would never be free of debt to him. The older she grew, however she ended up, he knew this was true. And the Dutchman was the only man he'd met in the Connecticut Lakes who was even close to an equal with himself—the only man who comprehended life as capriciously as Blood and so chose to stand apart from his fellows, to make of himself what he would or could and leave the rest to their own misconceptions and expectations. He would come. Blood could almost see him, Van Landt with nothing of pleasantry about him. Interested only in solving the problem before him, turning that solution directly to his own favor. What more could a man ask for in another?

*   *   *

Some uncountable hours later there was a visitation. What Blood had long since trusted to be mercifully unattainable. If it began in the familiar nightmare it continued unabated long after he was sweating upright strained against the stockade wall—some moments or even hours returned from that locked black closet of his brain between the long-gone New Bedford gin-house and his own home there, now within that home, in the entry hall as he fell against the wall trying to remove his boots and fell again until sobbing he got them off by kicking like an Indies juggler lying flat on his back with his feet up in the air and in this way recaptured a brilliant crystal energy, upright again, sock-footed, his mouth a web of drought, his brain luminous and distinctly attuned to nothing more than whatever lay before him, whatever now he might seize, to swallow of the old life and so suspend if not outright rend forever, casting himself already out, the old self out, destroyed.

So was wavering his vision-led feet toward the candle-lit but empty sitting room where his wife and son should still be in their caskets when he looked up and saw his lovely Betsey not dead at all but cringing halfway down the stairs, her hair tangled evermuch as always but not tangled enough, not the way he wanted it to be. Oh she was so lovely trembling in her soft nightdress and his head swung back and forth like a weight, like a bull with its throat cut but yet still standing and then cried out her name and went up the stairs as if his feet were only born for this and caught her as she turned away from him, Betsey drawing him on as always by her feigned shrieks and he tore the flannel from her and clasped her to him and then it was his own daughter Sarah Alice naked against his chest and beating at him with her fists as he carried her upward, her small breasts there just short inches from his mouth and his one arm scooped under her thighs feeling the heat of her run through into him and so when he reached the top of the stairs it was not accident but a deliberate thing that he turned left not right and carried her down the hall where he kicked open the door of her own bedroom and threw her on the bed and closed the door behind her— standing there as he removed his clothes watching her scurry back and forth over the bed trying to cover herself even as he worked his breeches off, not taking his eyes from her and then paused, watching her face turn up to him pleading her mouth silent as it worked and her eyes not able to not go between his face and his dreadful penis as he advanced upon her and then that last glorious wrestle around the room where he destroyed any objects she thrust in his path as if to prove himself beyond doubt to her and then that most perfect moment when he caught hold of her and her body arched away under the lock of his arms, the slow exquisite spell of his strength and then felt her succumb. Her body collapsing, failing, floor-bound. He kissed her hair as he lifted her and carried her to the bed, knowing she had to say those words, the way every one human has to deny what they truly desire. Papa Papa No No No—

Ripped sweating in the cold pitch night, the stink of manure and old hay, the visitation as cruel as the nightmares, vivid, actual, the moment of his life one second before him in each full realm of each exerted sense *for now as ever before as he entered her she faded, became some fluid greater than water, then gone, all lost.*

He found the water bucket and drank from it. Then vomited hot hard curds into it. On hands and knees again. The manacles clashing as to break bone. He swayed over the bucket. Retched and puked again and felt something splash blistering against his hand. Rocking back and forth. His stomach seethed and rumbled. He leaned forward and butted his head against the door. A too-small flower of pain spread red around him. He lifted his hand and smelt his vomit. Wiped the backside of the hand in the dirt, the iron bracelet cracking hard against his wrist. Then slowly fell onto his side and rolled away from the door to put his back to the wall. Got his back against the wall, his knees up before. So whoever might open the door in the morning would find him facing them. It was important to do this.

At dusk the three of them carried a stick of gilled trout down along the brook to Perry Stream and followed that as the twilight came on until they were in the moosewood bushes under the hemlocks across from the tavern. They crouched there in shadow some time, the tavern dark, silent, the chimney cold. They hunkered until past full dark when the owls began to call from their perches back in the woods. If anyone was in the tavern they had neither light nor fire—if there was anyone watching they had not revealed themselves.

Finally Sally left the boys and went down to the road, across the bridge and up to the tavern, approaching the gnarling threat from the dog within. She spoke his name and the sound changed to his greeting of low rumbled delight. She stepped in and made her way in the dark to the fireplace, stooped to blow up some coals and bring a splinter to tender flame and lighted the candle-lantern. It was she insisted if they were not to go on to Van Landt's then they must return to the tavern, to see if any mischief had transpired and to guard it against the night. Whoever the boys might be, and whatever might happen on the morrow, whatever chance or opportunity came her way she still was determined, until that final second when she broke from him, to give Blood no reason for rage against her.

She opened the door and held one hand on Luther's head and called in the boys. As they approached into the dim spread of light the dog snarled and she told him to hush and he did. As the boys entered the dog sniffed at each one and then Sally took her hand from his head and told him to go on and he trotted out into the night to prowl and paint his patrolled ground with urine.

"Can a one of you milk a cow?"

She and Fletcher went to the barn with a bucket and basket for eggs and left Cooper to build the fires up and fry the trout in the spider. And, Sally figured, poke around wherever he wanted or could. She still had the key pouch around her neck. She threw hay to the oxen and cow, disturbed the already night-roosted chickens for their eggs and shut them in. Went back to the stable to find Fletcher standing beside the stool with a half-bucket of milk while the cow switched her hindquarters at him, lifting first one foot then the other.

"I guess my touch idn't what she's used to."

"It's all right. You got enough so she won't burst before tomorrow."

They ate the trout with old bread toasted on forks over the coals and drank tea touched with rum. The dog stretched on the hearth, his eyes traveling from one boy to the other and back again. They had the bar on the door but no one came knocking. Sally guessed everyone knew Blood had been taken. It irked her none of the men beyond Peter Chase had come checking on her. Frightened her a little also. As if not only did all know what had befallen Blood but cared not what happened to her. For the first time she doubted Van Landt. But then he was not the sort to come but wait to be sought. He was also, she realized, save the odd trapper, the one man who might know nothing of these past events. Which made her wonder where Gandy was. He should be bothering her, trying to get free drinks for dreamed-up reasons. For the first time she was truly afraid.

As if he knew her thoughts Cooper said, "It's awful quiet. You'd think men'd be clamoring to learn what happened."

"Seems like maybe they all know."

"Some kind of deal was struck?"

She shook her head. "It seems so. But I wouldn't know what sort."

Cooper nodded. "Think Blood knows?"

"If he did he didn't show it."

"Maybe he does by now. Where he is, you said it's a half day's ride?"

"I ain't sure. It's how it sounded."

"A hard tramp."

"What's that mean?"

"It means we leave the Dutchman and his horses out of it altogether. Just go afoot ourselves and see what we can see."

"No," she said. "Blood idn't going to like it, I don't do as he says."

"It don't seem to me he's in a position to like it or no. We don't even know what trouble's upon him. Surely more than he'd guessed at when they come after him this morning."

She poured herself more tea. "How do you plan to explain to him just why it's you two instead of Van Landt?"

"We just say the Dutchman wouldn't come. And we come along and found you distressed."

"What happens when we get back here, he learns different?"

Cooper was quiet a moment. Then, his voice level he said, "Well. Horseback or shanks-mare, it's a fair piece of rough country to travel between there and here."

She said, "What is it you got planned for him?"

"I don't know. I won't know until I'm up alongside him."

"All these years, you don't have a plan made?"

His eyes flicked off her. "I've got lots of ideas. But until I'm face to face with him and he knows me I don't know exactly what I'll want to do. So, I ain't going to bother myself with a plan except to see what happens."

It was quiet awhile. Then Cooper said, "What we ought to do is bed down. If we got to walk we need to leave well on before first light."

"We ain't going to walk," Sally said. "I'm going up to Van Landt's first thing and get whatever horses he'll have to let."

Cooper said, "What makes you think you should come along on this?'

She gazed hard upon him. "Seems to me you got that question backwards."

Cooper was quick. "You got a little soft spot for Blood?"

"I've known worse men. Blood's hard but mostly he's done right by me."

They were all quiet a moment. Then Fletcher spoke. "She's got the right to come."

Cooper said, "That means you gave it to her."

"No. It means she's got the right to see what happens. So she knows herself and don't have to make up her mind from whatever she hears."

Cooper said, "Brother, you're in bad shape."

"No," Fletcher said. "I'm good."

Again it was quiet. All three watching the fire, not looking at the others. Sally thinking there was no good way to respond but to leave this mild declaration out in the air, hanging, unanswered.

After a time Cooper said, "What makes you think that farmer'll let horses to you and two men he ain't never seen before?"

Sally bent and unlaced her boot and took it off, leaning part of the time on Fletcher's shoulder and he reached up and held her upper arm to help hold her steady. She held the boot in her lap and reached in and brought out the gold piece and handed it to Cooper. She said, "How much is that worth?"

He held it. Then said, "That's a hundred dollar gold piece."

"Could I buy a horse with that?"

"I imagine most any one you'd want. Is this his?"

She reached and took it from him. She did not put it back in her boot but stood and placed it on the mantel. She sat back down and said, "There's more where that came from. If Van Landt's got three horses we'll end up with em. Even if we have to buy em just for the day."

Cooper said, "I thought we'd need four."

"I can't ride. I ain't never been on a horse in my life."

Fletcher said, "I thought you wanted to come."

She said, "I'm coming all right." She gazed now into the fire. "I thought I'd double-up. Ride behind one of you."

Fletcher said, "That'd be fine."

"Well," said Cooper. "I guess we'll have to see what those horses look like."

After brief discussion, doleful eyes from Fletcher that she ignored, the boys went to sleep in Sally's bed while she climbed the ladder and bedded herself on Blood's simple pallet. She lay without sleeping much of the night, the blankets steeped with the scent of Blood, not sour but stained with his agonies and night sweats. Unsure of herself, the boys downstairs, the day ahead, the day just passed, all other days to come. Whatever else, she saw herself severing from Blood, although without a guarantee of outcome or escape. Simply the inevitable turn, was how she saw it. She thought of Cooper speaking of the futility of plans. A swirl of a girl, guts cramped and brain aroused with trying to sort things out. The night passed, faster than possible. She must have slept some.

Still dark when she pushed the blankets off and went down the ladder into the kitchen and pokered up the fire to boil water for tea and broke eggs into the greased spider and knelt stirring them with just the light from the fire leaping out past her as it gusted toward the fireback and she thought There's air moving. When the eggs were cooked and the tea steeped she lit a candle and went to wake the brothers who were curled together in the bed, wrapped up one against the other almost like lovers and she stood over the bed a time looking down at them, considering the pair, wondering how they might fit or fall with her. Studying their love. Would she break that, enter into it? She stood long enough so wax fell hot onto her hand. Then tipped the candle just enough so she was burned again. To halt her self-pity. Whatever these boys had with each other was nothing to be envied. Born of and burdened with sadness. She had enough of that, herself.

She leaned forward and rocked Fletcher's hip until he turned and she stood watching him swim up from sleep. He grinned at her. She cut any greeting. "We got maybe half a hour of full dark left. I been thinking it's been too quiet and that's bound to change. Most likely today. We need to get out from here. I got tea hot and eggs cooked."

She let the dog out while they ate but he was quiet. She took a sock and went into the tavern and unlocked the storeroom and cashbox and filled the sock with the heaviest of the coins and locked the box and knotted the sock and went out and handed it to Fletcher. She went to the mantel for the goldpiece left there the night before and it was gone. When she turned Cooper was holding it out silent.

"You keep it," she said. "I got a couple hid on me. It won't hurt we spread it around a little." She went to the door and called the dog in and the three of them took up their rifle muskets and pouches and went out into the dark. The stars were out but smudged in the east. The air was warm and moving from the south. They went up the rough road along Perry Stream. She guessed they could make Van Landt's by dawn.

Blood woke to the concussion of horses maneuvering formations on the packed earth before the garrison, the blunt monosyllabic commands, the near-wet clash of sabers being presented and then ringing back into scabbards. The darkness within the stockade was no longer absolute but with no clear source had attained only a low murk. He got to his feet and did what he could to brush the dirt from his clothes and wiped his face with his sleeve, one wrist manacle finding a bruise from his handling of the night before. He regretted the vomit in the drinking water but there was nothing to be done but move the bucket over beside the unused slop bucket. He stood with his feet apart and his manacled hands before him and faced the door and waited. Determined to let the night be past and confront only what the day brought.

Sometime midmorning he heard boots approaching and the rod being lifted and he squinted his eyes against the light before the door opened. It was the same two troopers who'd brought his dinner. They stood in the door a minute studying him and he guessed he looked pretty bad. One nudged a boot against the dirt where his vomit had missed the water bucket and looked back at Blood. Blood met his eye and said nothing. The trooper spat and both moved in and took Blood by the elbows and led him outside. The day was bright, the air soft. As if summer returned. They escorted him along the stable and turned at the road that ran back into the village when he spied a well and he stopped, short enough so the men either side jolted against him.

Looking straight ahead he said, "You're taking me to the magistrate." It was not a question.

They gripped him hard and the one on his right said, "We ain't supposed to talk to you. Step up now." And they moved against his upper arms as a man will a horse frozen in a balk.

Blood said, "Unless you're taking me off into the woods to hang me without a judge I'd like the chance to wash myself. My hands and face is all. It'll do me no good to offend the magistrate further than I already have."

"Shut up," said the other trooper. "Get along."

"Wait," said the first. "He's awful ripe. They might not be pleased, we brought him in like this."

Blood waited, silent. After a moment the second trooper said, "I don't know they care one way or another."

Blood thought That's not good.

The first trooper said, "I'm for letting him wash. I'd like to think, it was me, someone might do the same."

The second said, "If he makes a problem, it idn't going to be on me."

The first said, "He idn't going to make any problem. Are you now?" And reached up and clouted the knot behind Blood's ear.

They cranked up a bucket of water and balanced it on the stone wellring. Blood scooped water with cupped palms and drank. Then scooped again onto his face and was savage with his fists against his skin. He washed his hands and finally lifted them still wet to run them through his hair so it was as flat and even as could be hoped. Sometime the day before he'd lost the leather string he tied it back with. He pushed it behind his ears. He turned to the first trooper and said, "I thank you."

The man said, "Come along. We wasted too much time already."

The village was smaller than it appeared the evening before and daylight revealed it to be more coarse and mean than the lit beckoning windows had caused him to think. The painted houses were peeling and blistering where the clapboards had not been allowed to season and the yards were irregular trodden dirt with meager flowerbeds already blackened by frost. Heaps of split firewood were piled in mounds by backdoors and chickens worried amidst the weed patches. A sow and litter were lying in the sun-warmed road and as the three of them went around her she lifted her head to cast a red ominous eye upon them. Laundry was spread on bushes with ends and edges and arms or legs lifted by the passing air. A man with an ox hauling a stone boat came up the road toward them, the boat loaded with dried stalks of Canada corn stripped already of their ears, the stalks to be stored to make a poor winter fodder. The man didn't even look at Blood or the troopers guarding him. Blood wondered if this was because he was of so little concern or if it betrayed some unknown attitude the citizenry held toward the royal troops.

They turned past a stone-post fence and entered the lane of a house no greater or different than the others but for the sweated horse tied to a rail before an ell-shed. Blood looked at the roan horse. He'd seen that horse before.

The officer Quigley came from the house into the yard to meet them. The troopers halted Blood. Quigley regarded him carefully, as if assessing the condition of his charge.

He said, "You look well rested."

Blood was silent.

The lieutenant said, "Or perhaps not. It makes little difference, I suspect, to a man of your stripe."

Blood remained silent.

"But enough of pleasantry," the lieutenant said. "Step up and enter the house."

The troopers released him and Blood passed the officer and one foot at a time went up the three steps as effortlessly as possible, as if the chain between his ankles were merely decorative. His hands clasped before him, he opened the door, the lieutenant close behind him. They were in a small chamber off the kitchen, a pantry of sorts, with crocks of pickle on the shelves of one wall and giant winter squash on the floor and an assortment of leather-bound legal encyclopedia on the opposite shelving. Through the doorway he saw a large fireplace and the corner of a table and there was the residue of voices that fell off as he'd come through the initial door. Without pause he continued into the kitchen.

It was an odd room. A kitchen in every way but twice the size of any he'd seen in this far north country. The table also was oversized, a massif of dark wood more rectangular than square with fine-turned heavy legs and inlaid scrollwork along the edges. At the far end of the table, next to the fire-corner, there was a small raised platform with a heavy armchair holding a man of slight build and fine features, with the pale wet blue eyes of a redheaded man. His hair was thin on top but a brush on the sides and back. He wore a white shirt and canary waistcoat and before him on the table was a leatherbound ledger opened to a page already half covered with a fine hand. A clay inkwell and soapstone stand held a pair of quills with a small trimming knife in a tray along the front of the stand. There was another clay pot of sand beside the ledger and beside this was a brass round-faced official die and a stick of sealing wax.

At the side of the table with his back to the fire, seated beside the magistrate, was Mose Hutchinson.

"Sheriff Hutchinson," said Blood. "I'm pleased your leg has healed to enable you to ride." The mystery of this affair had tipped open a bit.

"My leg throbs considerable and will never be sound again," the sheriff said. "I'm only here as witness to the proceedings. To ensure there is justice meted equitable to the satisfaction of the laws of both Canada and the United States."

"Ah. Well," said Blood. "I had not expected you to be my advocate."

"It's the magistrate you should petition, Blood. The grievance against you is his jurisdiction."

Blood bowed his head toward the sheriff. "I was not aware I was making a petition Sheriff. But your point is taken." He turned to the red-haired man and said, "My name is Blood. I know not yours nor how to address you. But I assure you that in the matter of the deceased Laberge my own role was passive. He murdered a man and was then set upon by that fellow's companions and hanged. All this occurred within or nearby the public house I maintain in the territory known as the Indian Stream, which is in dispute between Canada and New Hampshire. I was not in favor of his hanging but could not intervene— the choler of the crowd was too high and the deceased Laberge was rash perhaps but nevertheless guilty of murder. There is no dispute there."

The red-haired man studied Blood. After a time he spoke—an unfortunate voice, the shimmering whinny of an adolescent boy. Blood had to wonder who had chosen this man to mete justice. The magistrate said, "My name is Morris. You may address me as Esquire Morris or Your

Honor, as you choose. The rope used to murder Monsieur Laberge belonged to you, is that correct?"

"It was taken from my barn."

"You attended the hanging?"

"It was a tree before my public house they hung him from. I was there."

"You did not intercede."

"I already addressed that."

"You already addressed that."

"Your Honor. It was late. He'd killed a man. The men were riled. And there was spirits consumed."

"Spirits you provided."

"That I do commerce in."

"And you could not have stepped forward? As the proprietor. And suggested that perhaps these men wait until the morning. To consider their actions in the light of day?"

"I did not."

"And why not? Mister Blood? That is your name, isn't it?"

"It is."

"An unfortunate name, under the circumstances."

"It's my name," Blood said. "No, I did not step forward. There was a man with his throat cut open dead on my floor. And the others, they were a group of men—which can become something more than that. I felt a risk to myself. It was not just the murder Laberge done. Two nights before without farewell and in secret the rest of the Canadians making homestead in the territory had left. It made men uneasy. Why they did that. What did they know, to leave silent, in secret? Now, maybe they just decided it was time to go. There has been some turmoil of late. But to the men it didn't feel right. And more than a few wondered why Laberge had remained. It didn't look right. Like there was something more behind it."

The magistrate Morris inclined his head to one side. "And what might that have been, Mister Blood? That something behind it?"

Blood said, "For myself, I figured he elected to stay for reasons of his own; he was a trapper, a solitary man. I liked him well enough. But for the other men, it's a question of what fancies, what notions, that group of men might've had. With things edgy there and the other Canadians gone I imagine more than a few thought Laberge was an agent of some sort. I don't know. Foolish thinking but it's not my job to supervise what grown men think. Can't you see that?"

Morris said, "Are you the one now posing questions Mister Blood?"

"I just don't know what you want, is all. I wasn't the one strung him up. Why come after me?"

Hutchinson spoke now. "That's easy Blood. You were the one we all agreed upon."

"What do you mean by that?"

The magistrate frowned at the sheriff and returned his attention to Blood. As if there had been no interruption. He said, "The surviving sisters of Charles Laberge have petitioned for warrants against the men responsible for his death." He raised an eyebrow as if the rest was obvious. "You shall name those men."

"Why, I might's well cut my own throat as do that. But even if I was of a mind to I couldn't do it."

The magistrate regarded Blood. Lizard unblinking eyes. Waiting.

Blood said, "It's true the boy Laberge killed provoked it all. Drew his own knife out first and swiped Laberge with it. But then Laberge kicked that boy in the arm, broke it he did too. Kicked the knife right out of his hand. That boy was hurt bad, his knife gone, so he grabbed hold of the girl works for me. As a shield. It was over. I was moving fast to get to them when Laberge just stepped forward and slashed that boy Bacon's throat. That was the murder done, right there. What came after that was just a spontaneous reaction to a horrific thing."

"Why should I believe this version?"

"Why shouldn't you? It's what happened."

"Then the men I wish to question would confirm it independently, would they not?"

"It's not that simple."

"No?"

"Those men don't trust anybody. Not any authority. There's no boundary established yet. So, any arrests you Canadians might make, like any by New Hampshire men, they'd see it as greater threat than it was. The same way they mistrusted why all the Canadians left under nightfall cover. They're prickly and they've reason enough to be. So, however it came out, if I was to name you names I'd be done there. Even if they weren't to kill me I'd be finished in that country. Not a man would trust me, not a man would do trade with me."

It was quiet in the room. Hutchinson had a penknife out and was cleaning his fingernails, wiping the residue from the blade onto his coat sleeve. The magistrate glanced at him but Hutchinson kept his head bent over his work. Morris peered at the ledger before him, reading. Blood watched him. He seemed to be rereading the same lines. Blood wondered if this was a distraction or if the magistrate was coming to some decision over some or all of this.

Finally the magistrate looked up at Blood. He said, "And so the sisters of Charles Laberge. And their children—his nieces and nephews— all I can offer them is this tale of how their brother and uncle was a simple murderer who received a rough but true justice. And it took a party of the King's troopers to retrieve his body for a burial according to the rites of their Church. Is that what you suggest?"

There it was, thought Blood. Then considered the presence of Hutchinson and amended—This is the money part. Where the hell was Sally and Van Landt? He said, "I feel bad about that."

"Which part," the magistrate asked in a mild tone. "Do you regret?"

"I never gave his family the first thought at all. Most of the men, the single men, the older ones, the trappers and woodsmen, they left whatever family they might've had long ago. It's the unusual ones that take to the woods like that. I might not've done the right thing, burying him as I did, but I was showing what respect I could for him. There wasn't even a hope of burying him in the cemetery there. The others would've been happy to leave him hang to rot. I cut him down and did the best I could. I don't regret that. But I'm sorry to distress his relations." He paused. "Perhaps—"

"Perhaps?"

"Perhaps if you were to explain all this to them they might understand it better. Why I did as I did."

"You mean why you buried him in your garden."

"It wasn't the best choice. I just wanted him in the ground. It was bad weather. Everything was iced up. Doing the best I could with short judgment."

"Short enough," said the magistrate.

Blood ignored this. "The family? Are they well off?"

The magistrate studied him a time. Then said, "In this place?"

Blood nodded. Some ground had been established. He said, "Perhaps, as a token of my regrets and my intentions, my sorrow over the entire affair, I might be allowed to relieve the costs of the burial. As well as whatever attendant expenditures would be involved. Of course, we must consider their pride, so if you think it appropriate this could be accomplished silently, through a third party. The priest perhaps. Or even yourself, as you must know all the parties affected. Whatever course you think best."

The magistrate bowed his head over his hands folded upon the ledger. Then raised his head and his clasped hands so his chin rested upon his fingertips. He said, "It would not be an inexpensive proposition. To be done properly."

Blood said, "I would think not."

"How much money," the magistrate asked, "do you think correct?"

"I defer that judgment to you."

"My expertise is legal, not fiscal."

"I see," said Blood. "I myself know nothing of Catholic customs. Would five American dollars in gold be sufficient?"

The magistrate hummed into his fingertips, now up, pressed against his lips.

"But I should sorely hate to offend further than I already have. Perhaps ten would be closer the mark?"

The hum dropped a tone.

"But then again," Blood said. "The Catholics have a party for the dead, don't they? A wake. That would be expensive I'd think. And there is the question of a proper burial stone. So might fifteen be a better figure?"

The magistrate finally looked at him. "You have this money, this gold, upon your person?"

"You know I don't. I already told that officer of yours I carry no money and had no time yesterday morning to bring any away with me. But the girl works for me should be along soon. I instructed her to bring what money I have with her."

"You have no money?"

"It's coming I tell you."

"And where is this girl?" The magistrate glanced around the room as if to discover her.

"She is riding over under the safekeeping of a man I trust. A man of responsibilities. So they undoubtedly got a late start. Even so, they should be here within the hour."

Hutchinson folded his penknife and put it away and raised his hands one at a time and spread his fingers to inspect his work. Then looked at Blood for the first time throughout this negotiation. He said, "Would that be Emil Chase by chance?"

Blood said, "No. It would not."

"You'll not tell me who then?"

"I see no reason to. They'll be along."

Hutchinson stood. An awkward sideways struggle up with both his hands on the tabletop. Once up he stepped back from the table, the healed leg swinging out straight from the hip and making a half circle out to the side.

He said, "Has it occurred to you to question how the King's troopers rode in so easy to a place that cost me men and horses and the better life of my leg in order to bring you here?"

Blood was cautious. "I imagine their letting me be taken served some purpose. I'm tolerated in the Indian Stream but nothing more."

Hutchinson reached into his vest pocket and drew out a ten dollar gold piece and laid it on the ledger before the magistrate. He said to Blood, "You're in my debt now."

Blood addressed the magistrate. "No. I'll await the girl."

Hutchinson ignored this. "The girl will not appear. My deal with Chase was that if they would allow you to be taken I'd not ride into their country. I've kept that bargain, hard as it was to do."

Blood said, "I don't understand you."

Hutchinson said, "My wording with Chase was carefully chosen. I mentioned only myself and let him believe I spoke for all the New Hampshire authorities. And I'm here. Up in Canada. Attending to you. But this morning at dawn a Captain of the New Hampshire militia led a company of over a hundred men into the Indian Stream with warrants for the two dozen men we could name and orders to repulse all resistance by whatever means. In fact, Blood, you should count yourself lucky to be here. Wouldn't you agree?"

The magistrate Morris stood now also. The gold piece had disappeared from his ledger page. He said, "I would've done better to deal with this man alone than with you, Hutchinson. But I'm done with you both now. Take your business from my house."

Beside the hitching rail a single trooper waited. It was not the one who'd allowed Blood to wash himself. He watched Blood and Hutchinson come from the house and then wordless bent and unlocked the manacles from Blood's ankles and rose and took the irons from his wrists. Then stepped back and faced the two men and made a weak mockery of a salute and turned and walked up the road, the irons dragging from his taut sturdy arm, one of the leg circlets dragging in the dirt as he went.

The two men stood by the rail and the roan horse Blood had recognized earlier. He said, "I thought that horse was dead."

"The horse that died that day was the colt of this one. I still don't know what made me ride that young horse up there." Hutchinson speaking with the self-assurance of a man happy with his undertaking, with the results, almost relaxed.

Blood said, "You've killed me surely. You know that, don't you."

The sheriff said, "I'm half of a mind to ride over the notch and see what's left of the place."

Blood said, "If the girl's been harmed it will rest on you. Do you understand me?"

"You threaten me again, Blood."

"No. I speak only the truth."

Hutchinson put the reins over the horse's head and slowly led it to a block of granite set into the yard for children and women to mount from. He had to back and steady the horse some time to force it to stand stirrup-side by the block, Hutchinson hopping stiff-legged back and forth. He finally got his good foot into the stirrup and heaved himself across the horse that once the rider came up stood still as the stone. Hutchinson looked down at Blood.

He said, "Would you travel with me Blood? At least part of the way?"

"No."

"Think man. Away from here, you might attack me. I'm better armed but you're a resourceful man, are you not? You might find your revenge."

"That day," said Blood. "Is not this one."

Hutchinson smiled. "You ain't dead yet, are you Blood? That's a good thing, is how I see it. That's how little I fear you. But you, you recall you're in my debt."

"No," said Blood. "I'm not." And stepped forward and with all his freed might struck the horse across the head with his balled fist and the horse wheeled and farted and Blood struck it again on its fat muscled buttocks as the sheriff listed in the saddle. The horse snorted and burst out upon the road where the rider fought to control the horse, fought to turn it south and not north and so the two spun together a moment and then set off, the rider still not in control of the beast.

Blood walked out to stand between the stone gateposts until the horse was gone from sight. Then he began to walk south along the road. Hoping only that he would spot the rough trail that led to the ford and the notch and the land beyond. Telling himself to walk, not think; all thinking at the moment was worry. Put it into your legs, he thought.

Six

They heard them coming, the measured rolling rumble of horses in reined-in canter, the sound in the gray dawn light coming more through the earth than air and they scrambled off the rugged road up a hillside of scrub juniper and cedar where they crouched behind the circles of giant juniper and watched the horsemen pass below. Perhaps twenty men in white and green uniforms with cross belts and high boots riding into the filaments of daylight hazed in cold mist from the stream, the men and horses a bright slash of color made animate, the surging grand horses and the men upright under their black beaver tricorns, the sound some herald drumbeat sent forth onto the land.

The three crouched inert until the dawn smothered the passage of the horsemen and then looked all three one to another.

"What in the world was all that?"

"I'd guess a pile of trouble for somebody," Fletcher said. Then turned to Sally and said, "Was those the same soldiers come after Blood yesterday?"

"I don't believe. Those was different uniforms."

Cooper said, "Other than the Dutchman farmer, what lies upstream from here?"

Sally said, "I ain't never been up there. But there's four five others along this way, I know that. Seems like some trappers too, further along."

"I wonder who that bunch was going for?"

Sally frowned at Cooper. She said, "I don't know anymore about it than you. We should get on. We're wasting time setting here."

Fletcher said, "I ain't so sure. Maybe we should pause a bit and see if those soldiers come back with someone. Or what happens."

Cooper said, "Whatever it is, it's serious. Riding like that this time of day. Those horses was lathered, cool as it is. They been traveling some ways. I say we set tight too."

Sally said, "Blood idn't going to take it well I'm late from what he expected. He expects me midday: not earlier, not later."

Fletcher said, "You don't have to fret over him."

"I ain't fretting. It's a fact is all. I got to watch after myself."

"No you don't."

Sally said, "Yes I do."

It was quiet then.

After a bit Cooper said, "Well, might be nothing at all. But Blood, I'd guess he druther see you arrive a bit late than not at all."

Then came a snapping burst of riflefire. Cooper said, "That's something."

Fletcher lifted his head, rising from his crouch and tilting his head back and forth to listen. He said, "Let's get up the hill to the top. It's gunfire all right but I'd swear it idn't coming from where those men was riding. It's hard to tell, the way it's bouncing off the hills."

Halfway to the crest they heard another burst of sound conflicting with the first and then up on the large pinnacle rock ledges amid twisted dwarfed cedars there was a third and sudden volley, most definitely from the group just passed. The three stood in the drifting yellowed needles, turning their heads one way and then the other as new reports peppered the air. Now short bursts and single responses, other scattered shots. It was clear it was coming widespread—not just the cracks sharp and immediate upstream from them but also other clusters, down the river, toward the lake and the farms and mill there, the other pitches strung out far-flung.

Fletcher was turning his head each way, nodding as if confirming.

Cooper said, "Christ. It's everywhere idn't it."

None answered him but the rise and fall of gunfire, as a stuttering manifestation of the sun breaking dim light now upon the hilltop, a roundelay of distant yet close confusion, unseen, but with near as great an impact as if the rounds whistled overhead to sift broken twigs upon them. As if there were no safe place. The danger present, absolute. The three teetered upon their hilltop safe or unsafe, unable to say for sure.

It was Cooper who spoke again first. "This idn't a good place to be. Sooner or later those soldiers will ride back down. However it ends for them, we don't want to be found loitering about. By them or the ones drove em off either way."

Sally said, "We got to get on to Blood."

Fletcher said, "Sally. This is a big business. This is the whole country been invaded, is how it sounds."

She said, "You two can do as you please. I don't do as he directs, at least make some effort that way, he's likely to cut my ears off. Or worse." She turned to Fletcher. "Hand over that sock. I got to have the money with me."

"Sally," said Fletcher. "Listen. Listen to the sound of that. There idn't a way through this country you can go." He handed her the sock. When she took it, it sagged against her side. She straightened, opposing the weight. He said, "You insist on trying, I'll go with you. But it don't make sense. We wait some, maybe just a couple hours, we'll know better what we're up against. It's what Blood hisself would do. Can't you see that?"

She looked at him. Looked at Cooper. "That Dutchman might not even be a part of this," she finally said. "And you two idn't necessarily expert on what Blood's capable of."

The brothers were silent.

Cooper looked off into the trees. A sputter of gunfire came from the south and west. Then another sounded just north of them. As if it was at the base of their small hill. He said, "I just can't see it as happenstance that them other soldiers took Blood off into Canada yesterday and today now this."

Fletcher said, "You think he's behind it someway?"

Cooper said, "First, I don't even know what this is. Second, as the girl knows, the last thing I'd attempt is to offer to know his mind." He turned to Sally. "I think you ought to care a little less what that man thinks of you, of what you do or don't do."

"Why's that?"

"Why because you got the two of us."

"So far," she said, "I can't know if that's a good thing or not."

"Well," Cooper said. "Sometimes you just got to trust."

"I ain't done that once in my life."

He looked at her. "That's too bad." Then, as if done with her, turned to Fletcher. "I'm going to creep along the ridge here. Keep off the road. Make my way back to the camp. I can't see a reason for anyone to come through there. Hardly a soul knows about it and not many even know we're pitched there. It's out of the way. I was you, I'd come along. I bet you're going to follow wherever this girl trails. But all this going on, this is something beyond us. We need to let it settle. We both waited too long to misstep at the last moment." He paused, looked at Sally and away. "I'm going now."

Fletcher cleared his throat. "All right," he said.

Cooper stepped toward one of the giant cedars and turned back. He said, "You want one last piece of advice?"

Fletcher stood silent.

Cooper nodded. Then said, "You have to, scoop that girl up and sling her over your shoulder and follow me down." Then he turned and went down the hill, working his way along the side of the slope, moving quiet in the dead leaves and over the bracken and juniper clumps.

He wasn't yet gone from sight when Fletcher turned to Sally and said, "He's right, you know. We should stick together, all of us."

Sally studied him, took her lower lip and worried it a moment. "Seems to me, the both of you maybe need me more than I need you."

"How's that?" Fletcher was a little grim, as if he might not like her answer, whatever it might be.

She took her time. "Because," she said. "I know both Blood and this country better than either of you."

"It was you come seeking us, is how I recall."

She nodded. And said, "But things is changing faster than we can even guess." And was quiet then, letting him read that how he would. She watched his face, her own open, giving nothing. She knew how to do that.

Then, just when she saw he was about to speak, she said, "But for the time being, your brother makes sense. We go back to the marsh and hide ourselves there a bit. Later is enough time to decide what to do."

And saw he was growing more determined to speak his mind and so held out the sockful of money and said, "Carry that, if you will." He reached for it, as she knew he would, and as he did she turned and followed after Cooper. Who was right around the knee of the hill. Waiting. This did not surprise her either.

They followed the rough ground of the ridgeline downstream until the land fell away before them and veered west down through alder thickets and young popples that snapped back like whips at their passing, came through a boggy ground smeared with the whitewash droppings of woodcock and found the brook and followed it up, keeping again from the faint trail that ran waterside but climbing the steep hillside, moving slowly one behind the other and often stilling their footsteps in the leaf-fallen woodsfloor to listen.

Sometimes they heard gunfire, heavy or light, and others only the sound of their own breathing. By the time they came out into the marsh it was midmorning and hot. They knelt together at the brook and drank and went on to the camp, ever more hidden as the early leaves fell and swirled onto the canvas. Even the fire-ring was filled with yellow and red leaves. As if the land would cover them.

The air moved but slightly and they could smell smoke upon it, not the faint autumnal scent of burning that sunlight stirred from dying leaves but a keen series of twisted ropes of smoke, those smells not the clear sweetness of burning wood but the bitter rank odor of houses burning, barns—of clothing, foodstuffs, furniture shellacs and varnishes, feather-bed tickings, harness leather, the dense scent of burning fodder, of haystacks, of meal or corn—the burning of human works.

And still there came the rising and falling away again of gunfire, more distant here in this bowl of moist land but joining all the same, fainter and less often as if the fighting now was someway diminished, surplus, left over. Some resistance more token than effectual. Or of final desperation.

The three crouched under the canvas. Time to time Cooper would go out to stand in the middle of the marsh on the largest of the hummocks and tilt his head around as if to detect something of the direction of the smoke. As if to learn its source.

Midafternoon they ate the remains of the stale loaf-bread carried away from the tavern that morning. The gunfire died away and only the smoke remained, enough of it now to haze the sun. Sally was agitated.

"I ain't setting here anymore. I got to go down to the tavern and see what they done to it. If it's burned or looted or what."

"Or filled up with drunken soldiers," Fletcher said. "Might be best to wait at least til dusk."

Sally made a grimace near on disgust. "Seems to me you two are expert at waiting. If there's men trying to drink they're going to be sore disappointed once they go through the little bit out in the public room. Unless they take a axe to the door of the storeroom and get into what's there. Which is all the more reason for me to go. Blood'll be raging I was to let that happen."

"How can you go rescue him and still take care of things here? He idn't going to have a reason to get angry with you. It's all beyond your control."

She stood up. Flipped new-fallen leaves from her hair. "I ain't done a good job of either one. I ain't done a bit of it. You two do what you want, I'm walking down there."

Cooper was leaning against the front upright tentpole. He said, "I tend to agree with her. We need to poke our way down, take a look at things. Although if it's overrun with soldiers it idn't going to serve any of us good to go in there." He was looking at Sally. "You understand me?"

"I can take care of myself, drunk soldiers or whatever." She went to the other tentpole and took up Blood's musket rifle and the pouches.

Fletcher started to speak but Cooper held up his hand. He said, "Well, I don't doubt that. Still, let's go cautious. Try to see what's there fore it sees us coming. That's all I was thinking."

The dog Luther lay stretched in the trodden yard before the deserted tavern, a swarm of flies working at his destroyed skull, shot or bludgeoned they could not tell. A fragment of torn green cloth clenched in the remains of his jaws was mired in the dust, a grotesque tongue; even tongue-shaped, a coattail from a militia uniform. The door was open but otherwise the tavern was untouched. There was no obvious sign it had even been entered.

Sally was wild. She went down in the dirt on her knees and pulled the dog's body onto her thighs and circled it with her arms and bent over the dead dog, sucking air, sobbing, saying Oh Oh Oh through her crying. As she pulled him onto her, her head already bent down, the dog's head turned limp and brains slid out into the dirt. The flies teemed around her, their green and blue backs malignant jewels in the sunlight.

The boys stood back watching her. Then Cooper made sign to Fletcher and they stepped back out into the road. Up along the lake there were long drifting pales of smoke just beyond the mill. They could see the mill was unburnt but charred heaps lay where houses had stood that dawn. The road they stood upon was churned by horses.

Cooper said, "I'm going to walk up along and see what I can learn."

"I'll go with you. There's no telling."

"No. You stay here. Help that girl. Do something with that dog. We need to get her back thinking with us. She idn't no good at all right now."

"I don't like it," said Fletcher. "This place untouched, except the kilt dog."

"I know. That's why I thought to walk up there. Nobody connects us to Blood yet. I ain't going to linger. Whatever's happened here, my guess is people ain't had the chance to collect themselves yet. But it won't be long and some's bound to come along down here. It's curious, dangerous odd to me, that whoever those horseback soldiers was they'd leave such a ripe teat as this tavern untouched. And then Blood taken just yesterday by the Canadians. That idn't going to look good for him, people get collected. It don't even look good to me and I ain't lost a livelihood or a loved one. That's what I think."

"It don't look like just his bad luck, does it?"

Cooper looked at his brother, then passed over his weapons. He said, "I'll be quick as I can. Get that dog buried and get that girl inside. There idn't luck to any of this."

Fletcher found the spade left leaned against the barn by the royal troops the day before and walked out around the tavern, paused by the dug-up garden but did not like the look of it and so went along and found a grassy level spot with a solitary young paper birch. He worked there until he had a pit deep enough so as not to appear hasty, an offering of a grave not so much for the dog as for the girl. Back around front where she sat on her heels still rocking with the dog, her face lifted to the sky, her eyes puffed and her face dried with muddy tears. He'd left the spade by the hole but his clothes were spread with dirt and his hands crusted and he went over and crouched across from her and looked at her.

"Sally," he said. "Oh honey."

"You don't know," she said. "You don't know. He was Blood's dog but he gave some part of hisself to me. I could trust him. I knew he'd never let nothing harm me. I felt safe with him. I felt safer than ever in my life. Oh god damn Fletcher, he was a good dog."

Fletcher said, "I recall how he sniffed me over. And those great brown eyes."

"I know it," she cried.

Fletcher paused, then said, "I found a spot. A pretty spot."

"I can't stand it," she said. "I can't stand to let him go."

Fletcher was quiet again. Gentle he said, "You let me do the burying. You go inside, get yourself cleaned up. Then, I could come get you and show you where it is." He waited for her, then again offered, "It's a pretty place."

She ran her hands over the dog. Then looked up. "He was a awful good dog."

Fletcher stood from his crouch and without leaning extended his free hand to her. She looked at it and then eased the dog from her, reached and let him take her hand and bring her to her feet. He led her inside and turned to her and said, "Cooper went upstreet to learn what he could. To have a look and listen. It don't look good, with all the shooting and burning yet this place left wide open untouched. We got to be careful, right now." He leaned and touched the side of her face and said, "I'll come for you. Soon."

She was looking up into him. He held her eyes, gathered them into himself, and turned and went out, closing the door behind him. He'd have to drag the dog around to the grave and then come back with the spade for the brains.

She sat at the table with her head down on her crossed arms. It was not fatigue, it was not even the death of the dog although it began there.

Began there but ran through her distinct as a fracture—the course of hours just passed all gathered in upon themselves and collapsed upon her. Her head hurt with it. Failing Blood. Who, wherever he was, surely knew already of her failure. Trying to match his certain deadly anger against Fletcher and Cooper. And herself as well. Was it truly that way? Would she hold to the brothers when faced with Blood? She felt the three of them a match for near anything but then imagined Blood step-ping through the door behind her this very moment and could not say. Then recalled Fletcher come searching the father who did not know him. And Cooper seeking the father who knew but abandoned him. She wondered if she herself would be so brave. She wanted to think so. But every blown leaf that scraped against the rough shingled roof overhead was the footstep of the phantom Blood on the threshold. Perhaps, she thought, I just ain't so tough. Then realized she was, she was plenty tough enough.

She had no doubt of Cooper's resolve. Possible even that to achieve what he needed he'd turn her loose the first moment he had to. It was Cooper, she decided, she needed to watch.

She felt she'd left Blood but this did not have the clean terrifying feel of the jump.

Cooper came back down the road an hour later. It was all bad and the mystery was sinister. Emil and Peter Chase were gone, arrested by New Hampshire militia and transported to the Lancaster jail. Isaac Cole also. Others whose names he did not know. And men dead. A dozen. Five. Thirty. No one knew. Homes and barns burnt to flinders all over the country. At the mill had been a gaggle of women and children come in from the flung reaches, most without their men but for the wounded, the rest transported, some dead, others just gone, trailing the militia party, hid in the woods, lost, confused, frightened. The mill was not touched but the Chase house was burnt and so was Cole's house oppo-site. Even as he stood listening to the women and spare handful of old men and boys, others trickled in to the mill. All on foot. Some few car-rying belongings unlikely and tattered, grabbed up at the last moment. Family Bibles. A sack of meal and another of seed corn. An axe with a scorched handle. A linen sack of wool. One woman with a cooking spider in one hand and an infant cradled in the crook of the other arm. A boy with a musket rifle so long that he held it by the muzzle with the stock dragged on the ground. When one old man with burned-away eyebrows and fire-tattered pantlegs high over bare feet thought to ask Cooper who he was and why he was there, Cooper said he was seeking Van Landt. None knew what had befallen the Dutchman. None seemed concerned, as if Van Landt was a neighbor apart. Which made sense if he was Blood's choice. The mill was filled with crying children and sobbing women in consolation. Here and there he heard the name of his father. None outright blamed him but there was more murmur than outright question about his disappearance, his arrest into Canada just the day before. A murmur was more dangerous than accusation was how Cooper saw it. A murmur had room to seethe and grow to encompass all misfortune.

He asked once more about Van Landt, so that was what he left behind him, and stepped out from the mill and walked slow as he could down the road to the tavern.

The yard was clear of the dead dog and the door was closed. He went up and it pushed open easily. There was no one in the kitchen and the door to Sally's room was pulled shut and he heard quiet voices and felt someway a voyeur, even if there was no intent on his part.

He lighted a candle-lantern and carried it into the tavern side and set it on the counter. He went and dropped the bar on the outer door. He checked the rifles and pouches hung fireside in the kitchen, three sets including Blood's. Then returned to the tavern to sit behind the counter. He poured rum without measuring into a pewter cup and drew his stool close and pulled the candle-lantern up beside it and opened the tally book. He sat leaning over the entries and drank as he read. The handwriting was almost like a voice—he'd seen it before, studied it as a boy. Yet the voice had nothing to say. Items purchased, goods received. Balances due or paid off or monies paid out—a flat voice. He kept reading. One side of the pewter cup was black in shadow, the other glimmered with faint caught light. Time to time he lifted the cup and drank from it.

Outside, it wasn't even dark yet.

In the warm closed-up room Fletcher declared himself. Sally sat on the edge of the bed, hands twisting then still in her lap as he stood before her. It was like nothing she had ever heard and it frightened her. As if he had not only come to an understanding of himself but her as well. She wasn't sure she liked that part. She wasn't sure she liked any of it. It struck her as a strange time for it. Maybe that was how it was done. She didn't know. She was pulled, and not all the pulling was from him. It was getting hard to breathe, especially when he finally stopped and stood, his brilliant eyes finally away from her. Because she didn't know what else to do she stood within the great enfolding of his passion and silence. She stepped and kissed his cheek. When he reached for her she took his elbows. They were face to face. She said, "Fletcher."

He heard the hesitation. And nodded as if he understood.

Blood was sweating hard by the time he made the height of land at the notch above Halls Stream, hot and sore and hungry, and he could smell the smoke as he climbed that last five hundred yards and came to the eastward view of the land. But he was still not prepared for the extent of it: the columns rising, some pale and others inky turmoils, diffuse at all points before him, rising to join into a mid-level haze that stretched over the expanse of land, midway between the rough surfaced earth and the pitch-blue sky overhead. As if the smoke of the burning would hover over this place to mark it, ghosts of what was burned below. From the spread of it, from the numbers of fires still sending streams upward to thicken the pall he could begin to estimate the amount of destruction.

He sat on a rock to cool, then knelt at the headwater seep of the brook that flowed downhill to drink. He wanted to take his shirt off and rinse it in the water, wring it and wear it again wet but the days shortened this time of year perceptibly each one after the next and he would be traveling some hours dark and cold. With no idea of what he'd discover, he started down the trail.

He'd long since given up on Van Landt and Sally. Some part of him knew they wouldn't appear once Hutchinson revealed the true nature of the day. Still, walking the long Quebec valley to the ford at Halls Stream he scanned the road ahead for sight of the two coming horse-back. For no better reason than bald hope—that and mistrusting every-thing Hutchinson said. There was the chance the two of them might've got off before the militia arrived. That notion eroded as the time passed that they might have reached him and disintegrated altogether as he viewed the burning country. Perhaps the girl had made it to Van Landt's early enough in the day and was safe there. Blood doubted Van Landt was the sort to become entangled in any venture that would draw attention to himself. Whoever the militia would be after it was not likely to include the Dutchman.

If the girl was still at the tavern he had little hope for her. If it was still there it would only be because the militia had taken it as a headquarters, or as simple spoils. More likely they would've removed what rum they could transport and fired it along with all other buildings burned. If, somehow, they had left it untouched, it would be the end of Blood altogether. Regardless of the condition of his property there remained the deal Hutchinson had brokered with Emil Chase and the others, the deal violated in all ways but by the most narrow rendering.

He stopped. He was halfway down the trail from the notch. What point to continue? He was ruined there. Could he even hope to sift in through the darkness to survey and, if anything remained at all, make off with any of it? What money he could carry would be good, if it wasn't all with the girl, wherever she might be. Better would be his rifle, if that remained. The dog. And wherever he might go, the weather threatened—he could use his good boots and coat. All unlikely, all trivial.

Better to turn and make his way back to Canada. Or over to Vermont, to Canaan. The storekeepers there had done considerable business with him—they would take a note to fill his needs. And then? Wherever he had to go.

He stood thinking. Already the smokescreen over the valley was turned wine-colored from the angling sun. The day was failing.

A prick of conscience. Prick of something. What of the girl? Supposing she was all right, how would she fare, abandoned by him. Well enough he guessed. If he vanished it might go rough for her but that would pass. And perhaps she had his money with her, wherever that was. The money would help, if she was able to hold onto it and he guessed it would be rough going indeed for her to part with it. He considered briefly the strange boy come hanging around. No, Blood thought. He was the wrong sort for Sally. He might be smitten but he was soft. Too tender to know the use of a whore. Too tender to forgive her otherwise. But Sally, he thought. Sally would be fine. In the run of things she would survive.

But still he stood. And having considered everything he knew he would go ahead, down this trail and then over the rough land behind Back Lake and make his way quiet as a cutpurse down through the dark and discover what he could and take what was there to be taken. Even if it proved to be nothing more than a long night of woodsrunning and hiding from any seeking him, any lying awaiting him. He knew this was a possibility. But still to take away from the place the knowledge of what remained. To never second-guess himself. The worth of that was unassailable.

Down he went into the twilight land.

Cooper stood guard just within the barn door while Fletcher tried again to milk the cow and was swatted in the face with a shitty tail but brought back a full bucket to the house. There were fresh eggs. Once all were inside the door was barred and the rifles leaned against the table while they ate. Sally boiled a pot of new potatoes from the crane over the fire and they ate those broken open with butter and milk and salt, the fried eggs on top.

Cooper said, "I can't recall last I had a potato. They're awful good."

Sally said, "We had a garden this summer. Food I never had before, most of it."

This modest statement brought home their circumstances, forgotten briefly by the pleasure of homely food. After a time Fletcher said, "So they lay blame with Blood mostly?"

Cooper said, "I didn't probe too hard. But his name was spoken. Nobody was neat yet in their thinking. And it's mostly women and children, a handful of old men. I ain't sure where all the rest was. I can't imagine all the hardy men was arrested. At least some still off in the woods or scrapping with the militia boys I'd guess." He paused and went on. "Sooner or later there'll be some show up here. Looking for him or what they can scavenge in place of him, I'd think."

Fletcher stirred the last of the potato and milk broth together and lifted the plate and tipped it into his mouth. Set the plate down and said, "You think he's still stuck there in Canada?"

Cooper took up the pewter cup he'd brought from the tavern room. He was the only one drinking. He said, "I imagine he's struck a deal of some kind. He might've set waiting for this girl to ride in to rescue him but when that didn't happen I doubt he dropped his head in his hands and gave up."

"Sally," Fletcher said. "Her name's Sally."

"I know that."

"Then call her that. She idn't this girl."

Sally said, "Cooper's right. He wouldn't just set there."

Fletcher said, "Maybe he ain't got no choice."

Cooper lifted the little pewter cup and studied it. "Father," he said. "Father always finds a choice, always has. Even when it seemed there was none left to him."

"What do you mean by that?"

"Well brother. I wouldn't faint from surprise he smacked up against the door and commenced pounding and hollering any moment now."

Fletcher looked at the door.

Cooper drew his belt knife and smoothed the crumbs from the table-top and dug the blade with slow concentration and scribed the letters of his name deep into the wood. A wound, fresh and white. When he was done he leaned to blow off the shavings. Then stood and said, "That's a start. Even if he never sees it."

Sally said, "I'm afeared. Afeared of all this."

Fletcher looked at her, then at his brother. He said, "So what's next? He idn't going to show up tonight. Those British hauled him out of here with a corpse. That's not something he can just talk his way out of. Sally said he doesn't even have money with him."

Cooper said, "So tomorrow we start again where we was this morning. We seek out that Dutchman. There wasn't any news of him today up to the mill. I take that to mean he's likely all right. We get horses if they can be got. And we go looking." Then he took up the pewter cup and walked through into the tavern and Sally and Fletcher sat silent, not looking at each other.

When Cooper returned Fletcher said, "Thanks but no. I don't care for none."

"You did, you'd get it. I ain't the host here."

Fletcher shook his head. "It'd feel strange. Drinking his rum as if it were mine."

Cooper studied the contents of his cup. Swallowed some of it. Then looked at his brother. He said, "That's an odd scruple. It might be all you ever get from him."

Sally said, "We still got his money too. Don't forget that. We got that sock full and there's a bundle of paper money I ain't touched yet."

Cooper looked at her. He drank a little.

She thought I wish he'd stop pondering me like I was trouble. She said, "I got money of my own, too."

Cooper nodded. "Honest money."

She said, "I earned it, if that's what you mean."

"I know you did."

Fletcher said, "Cooper. Leave her be."

Sally said, "It's all right. He's got the right to be mistrustful."

"Maybe." Fletcher stood from the bench. "But I trust you. And you can trust me, too."

"I don't know," she said. "I can't say for sure about anything just now."

Fletcher was quiet a long pause. Then he dipped his head toward her. "Maybe you ain't thought that through." Then he said, "Excuse me." And turned and went into the tavern. Cooper stood looking down at Sally. Then sat across from her. After a moment Fletcher came back with a taper and bent to light it from the one on the table and without looking at either of them went back into the tavern. There came a me-tallic ring as he dropped something and then quiet and after that the sound of rum filling a cup.

Cooper said, "There. That's the drink he needs."

"Tell the truth, I'm thinking I could use the same."

Cooper pushed his cup across to her. He said, "Why don't you drink this." Looking at her as if he knew what his brother had confessed ear-lier, something of her reaction as well. "Could be, he wants time with his thoughts."

She nodded. She said, "I'd be happy he was to settle his thoughts a bit right now." Then quickly added, "Could also be he's leaving you and me a chance to come to terms."

"I got no problem with you."

Sally lifted his cup and drank. Set it back before him. "I don't really care," she told him. "If you like me or not. But you lying to me idn't going to help any of us. I been honest with you. I been trying my best with Fletcher. Maybe—" she paused and took the cup back and drank and set it again before him—"maybe the time's upon us, that you was honest about me."

Cooper took up the cup. Did not drink but turned it in his hands, the light revolving along the rim. Then looked at her and said, "I been fair with you. Honest enough."

It was hours after nightfall and bitter cold. The stars whitened the night, a spread of layers with some sporadic brighter glitterings. Blanched smoke rose straight toward the stars from the kitchen side of the center chimney. None at all from the tavern side. Time to time the smoke would break and fragment, then sparks would spew as someone pokered the fire and added logs.

Blood crouched in a stand of big hemlock across from the tavern where Perry Stream ran under the bridge. His arms crossed, hands under his armpits, his fingers senseless as stone. Three times in the dense backcountry he'd passed the fire-rubble of burned houses and barns but skirted these, tempting as they were for warmth. There'd been no sign of any survivors of these disasters but he expected none; those not arrested or killed outright would be with neighbors or more likely down at the more populated territory along the First Lake, near the mill and tavern. What he feared was anyone lurking to watch for such as himself. Or himself especial. What cabins he passed still standing were dark but this did not indicate they were empty—indeed throughout the entire country Blood felt a drifting presence of alerted inflamed men. Only twice did he encounter any—or rather heard small bands along the trails afoot and both times he slid into the brush and they passed without detecting him. Both times the men silent, tramping with the weary sideways gait of men stripped to senseless motility by the events of the day, weapons over their shoulders at angles of exhaustion. Blood not breathing while they passed. Earlier, at the fade of day he'd found and uprooted a dead ironwood—slender trees that die standing—and snapped the trunk about a yard above the gnarl of root. So he had a club of sorts.

Not much weapon and less desire to use it. Unless he'd no choice and then it would be fearsome in his hands. Or would've been before his hands grew so cold his fingers groped and clutched at odd angles.

The tavern was all wrong. Not burnt and not abandoned and yet with no trade at all, certainly, if left standing by the militia, not the crowd of dispossessed incensed men he'd thought to expect. But not the girl alone either. Twice the figure of a man had come forth to stand and piss on the bare ground, even in the starlight the piss steaming in the cold. He could not say for sure if it was the same man or a number of men. Too tall to be Gandy, even if Gandy was so bold. There was no hint of Sally. Both times Blood could hear the solid thump as the door was barred.

Swiftly he'd hiked up to the mill. He could smell the char before he saw the heaps of embers, what was left of the Cole cabin and the Chase house. The mill alone stood and he stopped in the roadside brush and could hear the voices from people gathered there, the survivors, women and children come in from their burnt-out homes, their men mostly gone in arrest. What Hutchinson had warned, and the viewed land revealed, this small huddle confirmed. A small group of men stood in the cold outside the closed mill doors and he saw the faint glimmer of starlight on metal but the men hunched together not so much on guard as in parley. Or yet stunned. He'd halted before they saw him, kept to the roadside and retreated to his grove opposite the tavern. The inexplicable tavern.

If he were to hammer upon the door and was not admitted what then? Or, if opened, to what numbers? What weapons? At least his own if nothing more. Not counting his clumsy club. Silent he cursed the girl and then stopped—it was possible she was at Van Landt's and the events of the day had forced them to wait. It was possible she'd taken his money and fled the country. He considered the hike up to Van Landt's but discarded the notion. He would not walk so easily from what was his. It was also possible Sally was held within.

Slowly he moved across the road, within the tree-shadow, and circled along the kitchen side away from the front. He could hear nothing but did not expect to through the log walls. Nor be heard, even the faint crunch of his boots in the mud-crusts of the yard. Except for the dog— Luther would hear that. So he stepped deliberate and eased alongside the wall and waited, hoping the dog would smell before hearing him.

Even so, there was the chance of being given away. He could see the great hound rising and lifting his ears, tipping his nose toward the wall beyond which Blood crouched. So he waited but it was quiet. It was all not right. Luther, he decided, must be with Sally and so she must be gone.

With this thought his anger organized. He took up position by the blind side of the door, where there would still be shadow from the firelight thrown out next the door was opened. Some bastard pissing away his rum. And squeezed his fists hard enough to feel the nails gouge his palms. Making pain was the best he could do to bring his hands to life. He stood then with the club held up against his chest and waited.

It was a strange thing. To hope a man drank enough to need to piss. Blood thought. Whoever it was hadn't yet thought of paying. Soon.

Do stars move if watched? Can a planet be tracked against the deeper field? Blood clutched his club and kept his eyes to the shut door, as if his eyes could assist his ears. Gaze into a half-full bucket and what looks back? Peer into a well and what then? He waited.

Somehow he missed the footsteps but heard the whisk of the bar being lifted and the thump as it was placed on end beside the door. He brought the club higher and the door opened and with an uneven caution the younger brother with the shaven face rocked in the jamb and stepped forward. Blood brought the club down, missing the proud young head but cracking hard against the side of his neck, collarbone, shoulder. The boy had his hands before the buttons of his flies and when Blood struck he lifted his hands as to seek something just beyond reach. Then gave a rending groan and heaved face first onto the frozen earth.

Blood leaped into the doorway, his club up again. Sally sat at the table, looking at Blood. Then she spoke his name as a curse as she rose from the table. Once up she stood trembling, her fists up. Blood gazed on her, not sure if she feared his attack or was about to launch her own. Perhaps she did not know herself. No matter. Blood had been diverted.

For at the same time the other youth, the older brother, spun from where he'd been standing fireside and snatched in a deadly smooth motion a long rifle leaned against the fireplace stones. Even as the boy was swinging and Blood saw the black eye of the muzzle grow as it came upon him, he was thinking, What was their name? As if it was the most important thing to know at the moment. The black eye flashed orange, the room convulsed and Blood was down. Then he heard the sound. There was no pain but he couldn't move. It was almost peaceful. As if he'd been relieved of all duties and he considered that if he was not dead he might soon be. Sally ran toward him but not to him, instead flying over him as if he were not there—an encumbrance only, a log of felled wood perhaps. He saw the white passage of her legs under her skirts from a boundless distance and then, as if brought or left by her passing, pain rose over him and for a blessed moment, the first in years, he did not know where he was or why. And then truly knew. A crimson and black-bloodied tide. Blood himself the wrack spread on beach shingle after a storm.

From outside, beyond his failing sight, he heard Sally beg to know if the boy was all right. From a strange distance Blood heard the boy respond, his voice striving to be measured, reasonable, and knew the boy was as concerned with her fear as with his own pain. Until that moment he hadn't comprehended that Sally was gone from him.

The boy said, "I'm struck down is all." His voice a-flutter.

Across the room the rifle was being reloaded, the slick swipe of ramrod driving home the charge a sound as pure a pain as if run into Blood. Into the hole in his right thigh where all pain spread from. Then footsteps.

The boy with the beard stood over him and looked down, the muzzle of the long gun swinging back and forth inches from Blood's chest. The boy said, "Have I killed you?"

Blood thought about it. Looking up at that boy. He said, "I know you."

The boy nodded. "It's Cooper." A voice simple, unbearably full.

"Yes," he said. "I know now." Hating his slippery falter, hearing some plea in it.

Cooper's face appeared fluid, an emotional teem. His voice cracked like a much younger boy. All he said was, "How you doing Father?"

"Not so good just now. And yourself?"

Cooper said, "I couldn't say."

"Failure"—Blood paused to groan, a sound involuntary. Clenched his teeth, released them and continued—"failure's hard to face. Be a man about it."

"What's that supposed to mean?"

"It's always harder to finish a botched job. But you're set. Just don't torture me with words is all."

The boy said, "I didn't know who was coming through that door. I acted without forethought. But it wasn't you I meant to shoot. I got no plans to kill you. This country is all gone crazy."

Blood groaned again. He said, "I hadn't figured you to be soft."

Cooper stood a long moment, his face a puzzle. Then, understanding something, he leaned to place his rifle against the door. "Father—"

Blood roared, a rejection absolute. His body pierced, fragmented with pain.

Cooper stepped back, his face changing again. The puzzle adjusting again. He said, "All right. But all you got is a flesh wound, it looks to me. You don't bleed from laziness, you'll be fine." He bent close, examining the wound, began to reach to touch it, then took his finger away. He said, "You don't want help with that anyway, do you? Leastways not mine."

Blood was silent. He looked away from the boy, let his eyes go up. The rafters were smoke-darkened bars against a blacker field.

Then Sally came through the doorway, standing near Blood, who shifted his eyes to her. She ignored him, her eyes on Cooper, her face white and clamped. She said, "Fletcher's hurt bad. I can't tell if it's his skull that's broke or what. I need help." Then her eyes flickered down to Blood, the wound in his leg, blood pooling and thickening, the soaked fabric over his thigh.

Blood could not help himself. The word croaked. "Sally."

Sally opened her mouth. Silently breathing, looking down at him. Then low as if the words would barely come said, "Blood. I can't."

Blood gained a bit. "So that's how it is."

She stood a moment more. Then, oddly, shook her head. As if to deny what he already knew. Turned and went out the door.

Cooper took the gun up again, cradled across his chest. Prepared but free of threat. From outside there came a string of murmur from Sally and small gasps from the other boy. Cooper looked over Blood, out the door. Then back to his father.

He said, "That boy out there's my brother. He's the one gets the help right now. Your son also. One you never knew of. Or would've denied if you had. But he's my brother sore hurt. It's like you can't quit, idn't it?" And stepped over Blood to the door.

Blood lay so the door could not be shut and Cooper again leaned his rifle. He knelt and eased Blood's legs aside, holding them just above the knees so they moved together with pain remarkable so gentle and thoughtful was his touch. He squatted like that a moment, his hands resting on his father, Cooper looking only at where his hands lay, Blood breathless again. Then the boy stood. He did not look at his father but took up the gun and reached one hand to grip the open door. The bitter air flowing around him, his breath the smoke of life.

Blood said, "Wait."

Cooper turned only his head over his shoulder. They looked at each other. Cooper stepped out and shut the door.

Blood lay some time. From beyond the door he could hear undertone voices and the groans of the boy he'd struck down. A single shrill yelp as he guessed the boy was brought to his feet. More murmuring. Then silence.

He probed with his finger the sticky rend to his thigh and found there was a topside and bottom. The ball had gone through. The wound was on his right leg, in the thick muscle along the inside of his thigh. Best he could tell it had missed the bone. At such short range if the ball had struck bone it would have shattered and he guessed he'd not be awake to know it. Even so the pain was a red rage encasing him as if he were nailed through to the floor. His neck a warped iron bar striving to hold his head off the floor. He studied the blackened beams overhead and tried to assemble himself. The wound was bleeding, not greatly—no artery had been struck—but enough blood to soak through to pool on the floorboards. He had to clean the wound and stanch the flow. Such a wound he knew could either heal clean, or fester and suppurate and rot the limb. It was chance mainly. He could help luck but not by laying on the floor.

He rolled to his left side and got his good leg out from under the bad, the knee bent so he could push with his left foot and so shoved himself by clenched inches until his head was against the table trestle. He reached with both hands and grasped the trestle to pull himself upright. Enough to get his weight onto his left foot and rise the rest of the way. Stood panting with both hands flat on the table as the room swam and gave about him. When his eyes came back he held the ladderback chair, rested himself against it and then pushed it forward, hobbling a hard hitch toward the fire. The crane was swung out but the kettle was upon it and he prayed for water and the kettle was half full. He pushed the crane back over the fire and while the water heated he faltered against the chair into the girl's room and one handed dug through her meager clothing and found a newer dress he guessed was clean and pressed on back to the fire, the dress held between his teeth. He positioned the chair where the kettle would be in reach once swung out and gimped around the chair. He got his belt knife out and eased himself down into the chair so his wounded leg was stretched before him. Again for moments he could not see, the pain an elastic upheaval from whatever core lay in the midst of him. When this passed he discovered the dress still clamped in his teeth and he kept it there, reaching down with the knife to cut away his trouser leg above the wound. The cloth was infused with blood and keen as the blade was he had to saw to split the fabric. More dilations of pain; then the cloth was gone and his leg was bare.

Something to see: a hole in your body. He probed with his fingers around the edges but learned nothing from this but some little more about pain. He cut the dress in strips and laid them over his shoulder and reached to draw the crane with the hot kettle out. Took up a piece of the cloth and soaked it in the water and without hesitation brought the hot wet cloth down onto the hole. At the same time bit his own tongue.

Sometime later he was able to stand with the leg swaddled tight with strips torn from the dress. The rest were bloodied wet clumps about the chair. The pain was still distinct, ringing. But changed. As if his cleaning and dressing the wound had given him back a portion of mastery over his body. By degrees he was able to get the boot from his right foot. He hopped onefooted to the door, barred it, and took up the ox goad to use as a crutch. Back to the fire and struggled a log onto the heap of coals. Used the goad-tip to sweep the bloody rags onto the fire. As if neatening was of dire need. For the first time regarded the table: the pair of pewter cups, whose dregs he poured together and drank down. There was a sock he did not have to touch or heft but could see by the bulges was filled with coin money which he knew was his own and wondered

if she'd forgotten it, not left it on purpose. Then saw the rough white
sharp gouges, the rounded letters crooked, the straight parts deep slashes:
COOPER.

He leaned and studied the legend before him. Understanding the boy
had already determined a course of action, of revelation, of confrontation. How long, Blood wondered, would he have awaited Blood's arrival? Would he have come looking, come to Canada? Come with Sally?
Or been content to leave this mark and quit the country, taking the girl
with him, perhaps the money as well.

No. Blood knew it would not have been the last.

Then recalled not only the other boy but what Cooper had said of
him. Something of that. Only enough to make no sense of it. He had no
other son but for the one already and long dead. Whose name Blood
would not say, had not spoke in years. Would not even allow of it more
than a sudden capricious skip across his brain before re-stoning that wall:
Hazen. Gone. A water shade. Nothing.

But Cooper. Cooper.

He upended the pewter cup over the top of the goad and made his
way into the tavern, hauling also the sock of money. Sally had his keys
so the best he could do was drop the money behind a hogshead. A solid
thump. A taper was guttering in its saucer. Just the right light. He
poured from the pitcher on the counter. Eased his left buttock onto the
stool-edge and stretched his right leg at the most comfortable angle.
Already the muscles were seizing against the outrage done them. The
morning would be bad. He drank from the cup.

Cooper. He would not attempt to recall him as a child and yet could
not help himself. The final glimpse of frightened boy-face peering from
a dark hallway one morning while waiting the dead. And with that came
the other children. He drained the cup and poured again. Stop.

So, Cooper. Had Blood believed he would never come? Or was this
what all those years of circling had intended? That opportunity: *Find me.*

Cooper. Blood throbbed. Come finally after his father. Whom he had
not killed but could have. Cooper had already bested him.

And the other boy. Who was he? He'd introduced himself. Barrett.
Fletcher Barrett. Whom Cooper called his brother, named as Blood's
son. Blood knew no Barrett. In New Bedford or otherwise. So who was
this Fletcher?

Blood poured again from the pitcher. The rum was awful strong. Then knew it was not the rum but the wound in his leg that breached him thus. He pushed up from the stool. He was a man in bad shape. Two days of hard use. He considered the candle, burning itself to drown out. Then stumped hard around the counter and back into the kitchen. Up against the fireside were a pair of rifle muskets, his own and a newer one, a gun he did not have to touch to know its quality. Hung above from a peg were sets of pouches for both guns. At least he was not unarmed.

He managed to spread the fire and heaved a couple logs atop the coals. Then discovered in the kettle a single potato so overcooked it was split and fell apart in his hands but he ate it down. Looked for bread but found none. The potato primed his stomach. Found the rind end of a bacon, skewered it on the poker and charred and ate it, burning his mouth. Then for the second night in a row vomited his supper, this time into the coals. As if his stomach craved what it could not hold. He leaned, weaving, a sick ox unwilling but with no choice but to go on.

There was no water in the bucket so he drank some from the tepid kettle and then, with no possibility of climbing the loft ladder made his way into Sally's room, sat on the bed and slowly wormed onto it. He had to use both hands to pull his right leg up to lie flat. Then, heaving and beaded with sweat stretched hard to pull some coverings over him. Guessing he'd fever by morning. So wide awake his very pulse thrummed off the walls and pounded back upon his eardrums. Hoping against the fever he already had. Wondering if he'd sleep, and if he did, if he'd wake from it.

In the morning he would recall waking sometime during the night wondering where Luther was, if the dog had left him also. In the morning he would not recall that between this thought and his next abrupt descent to sleep he'd lain on his back and sobbed.

They made their way up the brook path under the feeble starlight obscured by vast hemlock and spruce, the path a pitched trough in the darkness, boulders and stones only known by their sudden upheavals underfoot. The course best marked by the mild tumult of the brook to their right, the sound and the sparse available light caught riding the silvered back of the water. Fletcher hitching along best he could, not letting either of them assist or guide him, claiming any touch at all brought fresh pain to his shoulder. Twice he slipped and fell and both times he would not let them help him up, saying, "Don't touch me, it idn't going to do naught but make it worse."

Otherwise he trudged dogged and silent but for the whistle of his breath between his clenched teeth. When they finally came into the opening of the marsh with the meadow hummock grass lit white he stopped, his head tilted at an queer angle to his neck as he studied the studded water of the bog pools. The other two stopped with him and waited a time and then Cooper said, "Are you all right?"

"I'm better," Fletcher said. "A time or two there I thought I was going to faint old-ladylike. I just can't seem to catch my breath back."

After a moment Cooper said, "Can you move that arm?"

"It hurts something wicked when I do."

"But you can move it."

Fletcher was silent. He'd answered the question.

Cooper said, "Likely it's your collarbone got busted then. That don't mean it hurts any less than if it was your shoulder. But it'll heal easier. It'll be sore but it won't cripple you. There's a way to bind it up will help some."

Fletcher said, "I left my rifle down there."

Cooper was quiet. Then he said, "Well, he can't shoot but one at a time. And he idn't in such good shape himself." Then he said, "I'm going ahead, get a fire up. You stand here till the dizziness passes but don't get chilled."

Sally said, "I'll wait with him."

Cooper swung his head to her. In the starlight she could see the white spread of his teeth. "I know you will." Then he walked forward toward the dark bunch of gloom that was the trees under which their tent was pitched. Even in starlight it couldn't be seen under the big trees. In a moment his figure was gone into it and they might have been the only people on earth. They stood there, both of them tender and alarmed, both shocked.

She said, "He shot him. Just like that. Cooper said it weren't a bad wound. You figger that's true?"

Fletcher turned his face dark to her—framed by his hair the best she could see was his eyes, something shining. After a moment he said, "I wasn't in no condition to see."

Sally wondered if all she could do was keep hurting this boy. She spoke carefully. "You recall I didn't pause a beat coming to help you. And still am." She then did pause a beat, not expecting response but wanting that clear. She went on. "When the Canadian troopers come took him was the closest I ever seen him overcome by another man. And he did that defiant and proud. And you got to recall he's back— whatever trouble it was he worked his way out, without me even showing up. That's the man I know. So maybe I didn't hesitate but still it was something to see—Blood knocked down like that. So easy it seemed."

"Easy to you."

She waited, wishing he'd not do this. Then recalled he was hurt bad, that it wasn't simple petulance or jealousy. She said, "I'd guess, whatever ways you imagined meeting him, having him try to brain you was likely the last. All I can say, cepting I'm sorry you're hurt, is I don't guess it's what he'd of wanted neither. It was all a mistake. You got to recall, he's got no idea who you are."

"They were British."

"What?"

"The ones come after him. The Canadians don't have regular troops like that."

She was quiet a moment, almost angry. Then understood. She said, "Fletcher, it idn't going to do any of us any good you keep like this. What you told me this afternoon, I don't exactly know how I feel about it. The truth, even without everything else, is you're like nobody I ever met before. I need time with that, time to see how it feels, time to see how much is you and how much me. You consider it, you'd resent it if I was just swept along. Wouldn't you now?"

"No." He was abrupt, adamant. "It's passion. You either got that or not. It's not something you mull." He turned as he spoke so he was looking away from her, off ahead where the trace of fire could be seen.

She waited. When she spoke she was even, calm. "Fletcher," she said. "You need to know this about me. You put me in a corner, any corner, even if it be a corner I might want, even crave. And I'd make Blood look like a maiden aunt coming out of there. I been in one corner or another all my life. If I ever was to get in another it'd be because I was stupid. Not for no other reason. Not one. You understand that?"

He was shivering, a small tremble as the cold cut through the pain, his state of mind. Still not looking at her but she saw him nod, a curious motion that was checked by a suppressed groan. She wanted to touch him, to offer comfort. Suddenly in doubt if her words were too harsh, then catching herself, thinking That's how it happens. Don't do anything from sympathy you'd regret two minutes from now.

As she was thinking this he turned, slowly, one experimental step at a time. He was closer now and again she could see his eyes. More of his face also. Ahead of them the fire leaped and grew, as if Cooper was bent upon informing any who might care where they were.

Fletcher said, "Cooper told him I was his son. Nothing more but that. I heard him. So Blood knows that much."

Sally said, "Likely Cooper felt it was yours to tell the rest. However you chose. Or not at all."

Fletcher nodded. He said, "It's why I'm here. To tell him. But it idn't going to be tonight."

"No. I'd guess not." She felt better. They were both serious yet there was some humor back in his voice. What she liked about him. One of the things.

He said, "I got to wonder how he feels. Lying down there, wounded by one son after doing his best to murder another. Even if he only did learn that after."

"Knowing Blood, I'd venture he don't feel good about it at all. Wound aside."

"You think he's curious about me?" Sally realized he was crying, tears running down his face as if his eyes opened and required no effort otherwise from his tilted body.

She wavered, looking at him, his eyes dark pods flecked by starlight as if somewhere far within were the reflections of white birds.

"Why of course he is," she said. "Most likely more about you than all the rest of this. All Cooper did was let Blood get started. You can bet he's wicked curious." Then she reached and touched his face softly and said, "Let's get to camp before you fall down."

* * *

Cooper sat waiting them, a shirt from the packbaskets cut in strips across his knees. He stood as they came in and said, "I've been studying this. I think I got it worked out. A way to bind you up to help it heal and so it won't hurt so bad."

Fletcher said, "All right."

"You got to get out of your shirt. Can you get it over your head or need I cut it off you?"

Fletcher said, "I'm not feeling so good. Cut the bastard off."

So Cooper and Sally worked together, silent, the job simple but the teamwork coordinated. Sally stretching tight the fabric while Cooper cut from the neck opening down to the hem, then again, each tender and intent, sawing the length away from the hurt arm. Then they shucked the shirt off the other arm. All throughout Fletcher with his eyes shut tight and cursing, the words breaking out through his teeth and when the shirt was finally gone his breath gave way in a gasp. He stood naked-chested, his eyes dry and blinking, shining, his lips compressed.

He said, "What's next?"

Cooper took one of two long strips and wrapped the forearm with it, starting at the middle of the strip and overlapping so when he was done the arm was shrouded tight from wrist to elbow with two strips still dangling. The other long strip he wrapped three times tight around Fletcher's chest high on his ribcage and crossed the strips up over the opposing shoulders and crossed them again in the back and repeated this twice, so that Fletcher seemed to be wearing flimsy tight bandoleers and these he finally tied off in a smooth knot at the back of the neck.

Then Cooper said, "Here comes the hurting part."

"I been waiting for that." Fletcher was sweating and his skin had gone white except for his face which was mottled pink and white like the inside of a flayed hide.

Cooper took the bound forearm and held it up tight to his brother's chest and Fletcher heaved a little to one side. Cooper ran the dangling strips from the forearm beneath the shoulder straps and pulled them tight so the forearm was pinned to his chest and ran the ends of the strips down his back to the chest wrapping and tied the forearm strips behind. When he was done, Fletcher could not only not move his hurt arm but his shoulders were pulled back tight and down, so the bone might heal as natural as possible and not humped up in the hunch such pain would beg. Cooper explained all this while he was working, on through to when he tied the last knot he explained this theory of healing.

Fletcher said, "How'd you come to figure this?"

"I seen sailors come off ships rigged the same way. Most healed right up well. Some'd have a little lump to their collarbone but that's about it."

"You done?"

"I guess. How's it feel? It feel tight, even all around?"

"I think," Fletcher said. "I'd like to lay down." And before brother or girl could grasp him he sank to his knees and swayed there as both crouched and held him from toppling. His face was down at the ground and they held him, looking at each other over the top of his bowed head, neither sure what to do next. Then Fletcher lifted his head and looked at Sally and said, "I'm feeling a little green. I don't want to try my feet again but if you two was to help I believe I could get to the blankets." And without waiting he moved one knee forward and they heard his teeth grind and they steadied him as he brought the other knee forward. In this fashion they got him the five feet onto the blankets and then eased him down and over onto his back. He was groaning and cursing again and his chest was slick with sweat. The two ineffectual nurses crouched either side of him on their knees.

He said, "Just cover me up good and I'll do my best to swoon to sleep."

They slept that night all three together, Cooper and Sally each along-side of Fletcher, pressed close as they could without touching him. In all their outerclothes now as the fire died and the bulk of blankets over Fletcher. He lay mostly still, his mouth open and his chest rising and falling in slow breathing that, to Sally at least, sounded as if there was a measure of peace there. She lay on her side watching him and reached one hand slow under the blankets to rest it on his naked belly. Think-ing he might feel the light touch of her in his sleep and that it might soothe him. And her fingers came onto a hand already there and she thought it must be Fletcher's and then realized it could not be. She stopped her motion and her hand lay up against the other. She looked across Fletcher and saw Cooper on his side also facing her, his eyes open

upon her. She looked at him a long time and he met her look, giving
nothing, asking nothing. After a time she slipped her hand so it was half
up on top of Cooper's hand, half down on Fletcher's belly. After another
time Cooper moved his hand up and rolled his fingers open and took
her hand in his and they lay like that, looking at each other, linked over
the boy between them. When she closed her eyes she felt a faint pressure on her fingers. She let that happen as if she had not noticed it. Then,
just as she was sliding to sleep, she understood at a different level than
she'd ever before guessed at. She pressed his fingers back.

At the first tint of dawn coming over frost-drooped land, the fog freezing a ghostcoat onto the trees, the banty trapper Gandy came silent
through the ruined settlement and passed on down to the tavern where
he studied the cold chimneytop before circling the building close, listening. With ginger touch he tried the door and felt the stop of the bar.
He came to a stop outside the whore's room. There was sound through
the log walls. A rhythmic gasp of breath. His first thought was that she
was with someone and then regarded the evidence and determined she
must be doing herself. He pressed closer against the frost-burred logs
and let his ear melt a circle there as he swelled in his breeches and then
listening tried to fit what he heard to what he imagined he should be
hearing and the two did not meet at all. He had no great experience in
such things but what he heard resembled more a cut-throat hog than even
his worst estimation of a woman and his breeches relaxed again, a sor-
rowful thing. It would've been some sport to have had her this way, both
alone but together as well, her not knowing but that mattered not to
Gandy. He'd had a hen once and it had been a bloody awkward thing, a
great hot handful of feathers he'd pumped up and down clutched tight
and he came away smeared with blood and yolk from a soft-shelled egg.
But the wretched rasp came again through the wall and whoever was in
there was not the girl. He circled again to the front and paused a moment,
studying the barn and hogpen-turned-chickencoop and considered the
hens there but the urgency was passed. With another in its place.

He tapped on the door. Thinking to rouse the dog that was a white
terror in Gandy's dreams and so bring out whoever lay moaning in the
whore-crib. But there was only silence. The maniac cackle of an unseen

loon far out on the lake, the sound like a spike of ice sent through the air. He tried the door again, this time a firm rap. Three hard pikes of his knuckles. He waited. Nothing.

He studied the door, the jamb and sill. It was stout all right but not as well-made as it appeared. Gandy recalled the builder, the youth Sam Potter. And his young wife who alone among the territory women had been kind to him, had seemed to appreciate he was not threat but possible companion. Who, as she grew round in all possible ways with the baby that would kill her seemed to become even easier with Gandy, as if she understood his absorption with women was a consumption that men would have scoffed at. As if knowing that the larger she grew the more he lusted her, as if he alone knew what women were not only made for but the delight they took in being that. At least he thought so. He thought The power of a prick to make her breasts and legs and arms and belly and ass expand like that. Thinking if she was his he'd keep her pregnant all the time. Wondered at men who stood apart from their women swollen with get, as if they did not know them. He recalled the Potter girl's smile that she spread over him, as if she knew how he cavorted with her in his mind. And her killed like that, trying to birth that boy's child. A waste but no bringing her back either. Except the odd times when she flooded over him. And she falling apart underground. It was a mighty effort, those times.

But the matter at hand. He got his belt knife out. Long and slender-bladed, honed fine. He could run one hand down a sunken trap chain and follow it with the other gripping the knife until the first came upon the caught but burrowed muskrat, feel the brush of snapping jaws just over his knuckles and slip the other hand blade-first up over his first hand and kill with one sharp thrust. Which tool he now slid into the gap between jamb and door and worked slow and quiet, patient, seeking to lever through the gap and come up under the bar. It took some time. He didn't even look at where the blade slid between the wood but tipped his head off to watch the road in a general way and the shifting slips of fog more particular. To see if they revealed themselves to be in any way more than fog shapes. And so did not turn his head back to his work until he felt the blade catch against the bar. When the bar fell he pulled the knife free and studied the edge and he turned the knife over in his hand and by doing this transformed it from tool to weapon and then let his shoulder jog the door. All this quick and deliberate. He stuck his foot in the opening and kicked hard against the bar and heard it clatter out from the other guard and the door went in and he with it.

It was Blood he found in the whore's bed. Lying in twisted fevered bedding with one leg outside, wrapped in crude bandage, the wrapping soaked through with dried and fresh blood and a clear fluid, enough so the blanket under his leg was daubed and stuck to his leg. Blood was hot but not sweating although the skin of his face was gummy, the texture of mush cooked too long. Gandy went immediately back and rebarred the door. Considered digging through the cold fireplace ash for coals and pokering a fire up but did not; there was no knowing if Blood would want their occupancy advertised. He went instead to the tavern side and poured and drank off a dram of rum and poured another larger one, took up the pitcher of water and carried both back to bedside. Where Blood now lay with his eyes open.

Gandy said, "I knew something weren't right so I let myself in. I got water and rum both here. You got a preference?"

Blood's voice was scabbed, thrown by force through a wad of phlegm. "Water." He made effort to raise his trunk and head.

"Here," Gandy said. He bent to set the rum on the floor and held the back of Blood's head and brought the pitcher to his lips and let him drink. When he was done Gandy said, "Was it the militia or the local boys shot you?"

Blood said, "This leg is a mess. I heaved all the night with it. It needs the dressing changed on it."

Gandy studied him. Then said, "You'll want hot water for that. I paused over building a fire, not sure you'd care for any to know you was here."

Blood said, "Damn the man that cares if I'm here or not."

Gandy thought He just idn't going to answer me. He said, "You want this dram of rum while I go build a fire up, get water to heat?"

"No," Blood said.

Gandy paused.

Blood said, "Go on, take it with you. Just not so hard you're useless to me."

"I was just thinking of the least drop."

"You get a fire going, come back and help me out so I can set and warm while the water heats. Then you might gather some eggs and eat with me. I ain't been able to keep food down but I got to try."

"I could happy eat an egg."

"Could you move along? I don't care to have this leg rot on me."

Gandy bent and took up the rum, held it delicate between his thumb and first finger. Turned for the door.

Behind him Blood said, "You seen the dog?"

"He's not about, that I seen."

Blood said, "It's strange. Of all this plight, his being missing some-how worries me most."

"Good god man," Gandy said. "This whole country's burned and gone to hell and you lie there shot fretting over a dog."

"I know it." Blood said.

Moments later from the other room Gandy called, "I see you got yourself a fancy new rifle."

Blood pushed himself up, used both hands to lever his bad leg off the bed and dragged the other after it and sat on the edge, rippling with fresh pain. "Yes," he said. "I did. Come in here and help me stand. I'm chilled through. I'd set in a chair and feed the fire while you went for eggs."

Trying to determine if he should get rid of Gandy or enlist him some way without informing more than was needed. And decided the only way he could know this was to get up and move himself. Use Gandy for what he could until he knew best, one way or the other.

Sally was up before the brothers, squatting over the remains of the fire, cautiously raking the coals with a hemlock stub and adding wood to mound a small blaze. Fletcher was warm enough when she woke and she guessed he'd lie right where he was most of the day. Or let Cooper build the fire high. Sheets of cold fog drifted through the woods, mixing with streams of mist lifted from the pools. She had her shawl over her shoulders while she waited for water to boil for tea. After the pecu-liarity of the night before she was uncomfortable rummaging their food supply—the strange intimacy with Cooper had delivered her to a new, greater distance. She dropped a handful of tea into the seething pot and set it on a fireside rock to steep. After a time she poured out a cup and sat sideways to the fire to drink it, looking at the two boys, the one rigid with his mouth agape as if to draw all available air into his lungs, the other curled under slight covers, the one blanket pulled up as a cowl over his head so only his mouth and nose protruded. There was a thick rim of frost at the blanket edge where his breath settled moist coming out of him and froze.

She couldn't organize her mind. It was all in pieces, bits that wouldn't line up. At sixes and sevens. Something Blood would say. Calamities and opportunities all jumbled up together and no sure way to distinguish one from the other. There'd been a woman in the house in Portland who'd mastered the mystic qualities of numbers. Sally wished she'd paid more attention. Even though she doubted it could help her much now. This was more than numbers. Herself, Cooper, Fletcher, Blood. The four of them, what was that? A sum she could not do, she knew that. She drank her tea and considered the sleeping boys. Even as she considered Blood. What was clear by night less so by day. And she finished her tea, knowing she was the last person he might welcome to see. Whatever grace his doubts might have allowed her, she'd wiped clear the evening before. Abandoning him. Still, she would not leave it thus.

She stood. Bent and added some stout limbs to the fire and turned the pot of tea on its stone to keep warm. If she could write and there were supplies to do so she would leave a note she would be back. But she could not and there were no such supplies, at least in sight. So despite the chill fog she took up the boots and woolen stockings from the night before and squared them neat on the rock beside the tea. If they failed to read that it was not her fault. Boys, she thought. How could it be they were capable of missing so much and knowing so much besides? She looked again to them and recalled once more the coupling of hands over the belly of the one boy the night before and thought There is nothing simple in this life. Then turned and walked slow along the edge between the woods and marsh toward the brook trail. On one of the bog ponds was a single drake duck, drifting in a broad slow circle of its own making on the water. If it saw her pass it did not care. She was barefooted and the cold hard ground was a strange comfort against her feet. Driving her forward.

* * *

There was a healthy fullness of smoke from the tavern chimney, reassuring but a little frightening too. Perhaps his wound less than it appeared. If so she could guess at his temper. But her feet were cold stubs now, all she needed for boldness—that and the resolve to be the one to seek and not the other way around. She found the door barred and hammered blue knuckles upon it, calling out Let me in. As if she had the right. Which at least to her lights she did. There were any number of accounts to settle and she bet Blood thought so as well.

The door cracked open in such a way that the bar might be used to lever it closed. The rodent face of the lecher Gandy appeared in the opening, one eye peering at her. Behind him she heard Blood cry out to ask if she was alone.

"Best I can see," Gandy said, keeping that one eye on her.

"Open the door," she said. "Quit eyeballing me."

"Let her in," said Blood.

He was at the table, naked from the waist down, a blanket wrapped about him, his wounded leg stretched toward the fire, clean bandages wrapped around the thigh. A wad of stained and bloody rags lay on the hearth. On the table was a much-diminished basin of water run red with blood alongside a pitcher of water and two tin plates stained with egg yolk. She was sorry to see the plates; the odds were against Blood offering her food. She was hungry from the uneasy night and the cold hike down.

"If you came back to get that sockful of money you missed your chance, leaving it like you did last night," Blood said. "Although it seems a bit light anyhow. You bring my keys back?"

"I got three gold pieces stuck aside. I meant to buy horses with em but never made it even halfway to Van Landt's. There was soldiers all over this country yesterday. But I bet you know that." She reached into her blouse and took out the pouch of keys and dropped them on the table. "The lockbox is in the storeroom."

He studied her, as if smelling for honesty. Then he said to Gandy, "Leave us be some time. Don't drift off, just leave us be. Go milk that cow."

"I can't milk a cow."

"Don't be a goddamn fool. Of course you can milk a cow. I need to talk to this girl private. Get yourself another dram of that rum and go sit beside the cow and drink the rum and think about it. You'll figure out how to get it done."

"I ain't sure I should leave you with her. Why wadn't she here in the first place, tending you?"

"You're considerate," Blood said. "But you don't want to know too much of my business, idn't that right?" And held his eyes on the little trapper.

Gandy looked back at him and then took up the dram cup and went into the tavern and came out again and said, "You need me, holler. I'll come quick."

Sally stepped toward the pair of rifles against the fireplace. She said, "Get. Or I'll shoot you too."

He drop-jawed. "It wadn't you shot Blood, was it?"

"No," she said. "But I shot a wolf once. Next to that, you'd be nothing."

When he was gone Sally walked close and studied Blood's leg. She said, "That don't appear too bad. It went right through?"

"It did," Blood said. "I'm touched you came to check on me. What is it you want?"

"Don't be nasty. What happened wasn't nobody's fault but your own. You'd knocked and called out instead of trying to brain that boy you might not be happy this morning but most likely you wouldn't have a hole in you. All those boys wanted was to talk to you. Nobody planned to shoot you, not as far as I know."

He studied her. "You know more about it than I do."

"That's not my fault."

"You might tell me what you know. That one boy in particular, he's a mystery to me."

She said, "Is there eggs left?"

"Not unless Gandy missed some in the coop. We ate what he brought in. Are you trying to make a trade with me?"

"No," she said. "I'm hungry is all. I got nothing to trade. Those boys, that's business between the three of you."

Blood studied her. After a time he said, "I know the one. It's the other has no place in my mind. You know the one I mean. I only had two sons and one's long dead. As you know." He paused, perhaps meaning to remind her of other, bolder intimacies. Secrets shared. He said, "There's meal if you care to turn out some quick bread."

"I come to make sure you was all right. And to get some of my things. I ain't got time to make bread."

"You're abandoning me when there's little I can do about it. Perhaps when I need you most."

"Blood," she said. "I ain't sure what I'm doing. But I can't be two places at once. I can't be setting here tending you cause I've thrown my lot in otherwise. I made a choice. Could be it's strange the way it happened but I always knew someway I'd leave even if you didn't. You think about it, it idn't that strange how I went to them. I learned something from you Blood. Maybe you have ideas about what that might be but I don't want to hear em." She paused, tightened her face with thought and said, "Opportunity. Not to miss when it comes. I never seen it much before. All I know, those boys are like nobody I met before. The one, that Fletcher, he's tender to me, a way no man has been. Not even you." She made a small grin. Not altogether without regret. "I don't forget the ways you been kind to me. But neither do I forget all the rest either." Before he could respond at all she looked away from his face, not wanting to see him and said, "Excuse me."

She went into her room, leaving the door open. She was hiding nothing. Saw the mess where Blood had slept the night before. She took down from pegs her winter clothes and her best summer skirt and bodice and blouse and made them all up into a bundle on the bed. Then took the cleanest of the blankets and wrapped it around her clothing and tied the corners in a rough knot together to make a handle of sorts. Dug under the tick mattress and pulled out her neckerchief knotted over her own money and hefted it and took the bundle up in the other hand and went back into the room. Blood was right where she left him, had been watching her through the door. He ran his eyes quick over her burdens.

"Sally," he said.

She said, "Those gold pieces of yours is up to the camp. You hadn't shown up last night we was going to buy horses and come searching you this morning. I bet Gandy told you but yesterday this country was filled with soldiers that left it near a shambles. Still is, best I can see. Just so you know. I can bring em back to you or we can set and you can count through this," and she lifted her own money, "and see if it adds up to that much or more. I'd trust you."

"Why?" he asked, his voice extraordinarily simple.

"Because I got no reason not to." And then added, "And I druther not have one." Then she looked away from him and back. "Blood?"

"What is it?"

"With everything I seen and heard, this whole country was burned or torn up. A load of men was killed, more arrested. With all that, how come nobody bothered this place here?"

Blood rubbed his face with his hand. Sat silent. After a time he said, "It's complicated. Most simply there was a deal made that wasn't kept. A deal I knew nothing of. More than that you shouldn't know. It's safer you don't know."

"Safer for me? Or your boys?"

He didn't hesitate. "Even if you weren't with em. Safer for you all."

She considered this. Then her face softened and her voice was low. "It's true that when the boys and I made our way down here last dusk, the place weren't touched. The front door was open but nobody'd been inside. But they killed Luther. He was dead in the yard. He died fighting em. There was a torn shred of coattail in his jaws."

Blood just looked at her. His face somehow the best reflection of her own feelings. She simplified, not wanting to name anyone. "He's buried. Up behind near the stream. Where there's a little birch."

Blood only nodded. His face gathered back, near a sneer. As if he assigned private blame. She didn't want to know if that involved her but guessed not.

She looked away, at the fire coiling in the fireplace. And saw the new rifle leaned beside Blood's own. The double set of pouches on the wall peg. She set down her bundle of clothes and took down the new set of pouches and slung them. Then picked up the strange rifle and said, "This don't belong to you. I'll just carry it along with me."

"You're a hard girl, Sally."

Her mouth twisted. "You know better. You want to settle the money now or wait on the gold brought back?"

Blood shrugged. He said, "It idn't nothing to me, either way."

"You mean to tempt me? Or bribe me someway?"

"I speak the God's truth. It just doesn't matter. Do what you will."

"Blood," she said. "I never thought you this sort of man."

"Long ago I gave up on whatever sort of man I was."

She said, "I already heard that story twice. One time from you, another version more recent."

He said, "The one shot me. That's my son, Cooper. I can't believe I didn't see it before. That wet night they both first come in. But it's the other's the puzzle. Last night, when I was laid out on the floor, Cooper called him his brother."

"I can't help you, Blood." She shifted her load around to accommodate the long gun and then went close to him, standing right up against his chair. Then she said, "Both of you, Fletcher and yourself, you'll be laid up a span. You wanted, time to time I could slip down here, see if you was all right. I ain't much to nurse but I seen my share of bad things. You want to keep that wound dressed clean."

"No." Adamant, almost angry. "Gandy told me where you're pitched. It'll be a hard job just to keep him quiet. I got no idea what faces me. But you three keep tucked tight, you hear me?"

She was quiet then. Her face pinched tight with new knowledge. She said, "Oh Blood. God damn." A sad voice.

He made an effort of a smile. He said, "You was to wait a minute more that useless Gandy would at least have some fresh warm milk to fill you up."

"I ain't so hungry anymore. I got to get on." She leaned then and touched his forehead and stood away, looking down at him. A long look. Then went with her load toward the door.

Once more he called to her. "Sally."

She said, "I ain't quit the country, not yet. You'll see me again. I'll bring that gold back to you, the time comes."

She opened the door. Gandy was bent low, leaning up against it. A bucket a third full of milk was behind him and he jumped back, knocking over the milk. It spread a white sheet over the frost, then pooled in the furrows of the hard ground. She turned back and looked at Blood. His torso was twisted in the chair to watch her, his face blemished with the effort.

She said, "I was you, I'd get other help. This one's near useless." She stepped down onto the grass.

Again his voice came. Even stepping away she knew it would. Her name as a plea: something she'd not heard before from Blood, not once, not at their most joined. Plaintive, it stung her. Old debt raw and true.

She paused. The air was hard, thickened, drawn close and shivery with cold. She turned once more. "Fletcher's mother. Her name was Molly," she said. "There. You got it out of me. Maybe I was just born to betray. I certain hope not."

Then she turned away and walked. Past Gandy and the milk spill. On toward the fog and then into it. By the time she reached the road it was as if the tavern was altogether gone. She went down the road over the bridge and turned up the trail along the stream. Her bare feet making no sound in the drawn-down morning. The only noise, harsh as a sailor's Jew's harp, was her own breathing.

When she came into the marsh and the camp the fog had thickened to the point where she thought it could start to snow and there would be no way to know. Cooper was up, squatting by a low fire with a couple of long alder switches strung with young trout stretched over the fire. He looked at her as she came in, watched her place the rifle against one of the tent-poles and hang the pouches but did not speak. She went under the fly and set down her bundle, bent to look at Fletcher. He was sleeping, flat on his back, his face composed but through his open mouth the passage of his breathing had the faint hiss of pain to it.

She went to the fire and took up her boots and stockings undisturbed from the rock and sat across from Cooper. She hiked her skirts to her knees and began rolling the stockings up first one leg then the other. She felt him watching her.

She said, "I brought that other rifle back. It got left last night. If I'd thought I'd of asked Blood for a pitcher of rum to help ease Fletcher but I didn't." Then she pushed her skirts down and while working her boots on and hooking the lacings, she looked up at Cooper.

Cooper looked away from her out at the trout and fiddled a bit with the sticks and then looked back at her. "He's better off without it anyway I think. He'll sleep through the first part of it, the hardest part. Then we'll just have to see. It was a smart thing, getting that gun back. We're all going to need food but that boy's going to need meat the most of all.

But I'd of hated traipsing off on a hunt and leaving you two without a weapon to speak of. This country's quiet now but it idn't going to stay that way long."

"I'd be nervous, you going off shooting, after yesterday. People'll be edgy to the sound of a gun."

He said, "That boy needs fat meat. It's cold enough, if I was to get a deer or young bear, the meat'd keep. I'll be way up in the woods anyway and fog like this a gunshot don't travel far. Just hope I get that shot, that's what you should be thinking. How's he doing anyhow?"

She glanced back. Fletcher still slept. "He looks peaceful enough."

"I meant the other one."

"Blood? He's a little worn. But he's all right. Took some of the vinegar out of him, at least for the time being."

Cooper nodded. Then uprooted the alder switches and brought the trout over and with his belt knife shucked them like so many ears of corn into the tin pot they used to boil water. He laid aside two on a stone and covered the pot with its lid and settled it into the ashes where it would keep warm.

He said, "These two is for you and me. The rest make him eat when he wakes. Even if he says he doesn't want em. And get plenty of water into him. Can you shoot?"

"I can."

"I'm not looking for anyone to bother us three today. But you never know who'll come along." Cooper stood. Got into his blanket coat and took up his rifle and pouches and then leaned and handed her one of the trout. Stood over the fire eating the other. She ate slowly, watching him. When he was finished he went to the other gun and checked the priming and set it in under the fly.

He said, "It's dry." He turned to look in after his brother and then came back out and stepped around the fire close to her.

"Cooper," she said.

"I just want to say," he said in a rush, "I'm sorry to've mistrusted you. You stuck clean with us last night. And that other business, when we was all going to sleep, I don't want you to think the wrong thing of me over that." He held her gaze, his face flourishing blood under his skin.

Her lips were suddenly dry. She wet them with her tongue.

Abruptly he turned away. "I'll be back," he said.

Her voice low, just loud enough for him to hear, she said, "Luck."

She sat watching him slip soundless into the fog, the blanket coat bright and then muted and then gone. Still she sat watching after the last spot she'd seen him. Sat until the fire was low enough that she grew cold and then looked to the small heap of firewood and stood up so quick she almost lost her balance.

Seven

∽≈

Much of the following week passed quiet and cold, the oppression of fog stiff and unmoving over the land, roiling slightly over the rivers and lakes. Broken by the occasional rifle shot of a hunter and the weary repetition of axes as the remaining men threw up the roughest of shelters before winter came upon them—these crude camps little better than squat log bunkers built around the chimneys still standing from the burnt-out homes. Men working alone when it was their own homes to rebuild and in groups when providing for the wives and children of the men taken by the militia to the jail in Lancaster—those men not yet heard from or word of their fate. Some people had left altogether, sometimes just the forsaken women and children, other times whole families whose men had been untouched but still elected to depart the enshrouded bereft land.

The few remaining empty structures were occupied by the members or partial members of two or more families, with no talk of who should profit from the place come spring and who would return to their original pitches to begin again; it was enough to be in tandem against the winter. The people, even the men hard awork, moved through those days with the shambling gait of survivors, struggling to parse what had occurred and what might be done about it but most narrowly bound to necessity. A group of people foundered as sure as a ship with blown canvas, snapped masts, strewn rudders, stove both fore and aft. What men remained were rowers not navigators.

So Blood and Fletcher convalesced undisturbed, each assisted and tended but also spending much time sleeping or abed and so passed abundant time considering their situations. Fletcher was comfortable as long as he didn't move and so quietly enjoyed the care of his brother but most clearly Sally, who if not romantic was at least tender and attentive and there was unavoidable intimacy that he was cautious to reciprocate but not exploit, thinking he showed himself in a strong fashion and, watching, believed she was responding to this. He wished nothing more than for her to comprehend him as a gentle man. As for his father and his broken collarbone he allowed only that the man had made a mistake, determined to wait for their next meeting without judgment. For his part, Blood was more agitated. That Gandy was an ineffectual nurse meant spit to him—of true concerns he was divided. The past and future seemed colliding and his damaged leg at times was merely practical—get the damn thing healed—and at other, stranger more fevered times, night-hours mostly, the wound took on mystic qualities. Thoughts he would not revisit during the days, most of which he spent fireside, the leg stretched for warmth, the wound either freshly dressed by himself and other times open to the heat and air. An instinctual combination. He forced himself to hobble around and daily looked for improvement. Sometimes he saw it, other times he thought himself delusional. He was short of patience.

Twice Sally visited him and both times he sent her away. Brusquely and with unkind remarks that accomplished the job. The opposite of what he wanted but determined she would never know that. Not the only reason being that if she were there he would probe after his sons. That job he was saving for himself. Also, he missed her.

At noontime on the fifth day a horseman came up the road from the south and passed unchallenged for there was no sentry. The horse a gaunted gray speckled with dried mud and manure-stained from poor stabling, the rider in black from hat to boots and all points in between but for a boiled white shirt gone yellow at the neck and cuffs, the black of his overcoat and vest and trousers a shabby dull tone, a plumage of neglect and age. A minister of the Congregational denomination from Lancaster who once or twice a year traveled unannounced into the territory to hold a service for the general endowment of the inhabitants and to sanction what unions had occurred through need or desire since his last appearance. A man respected not so much for his calling or ability as for his simple unambiguous vinculum to the greater world.

The minister tied his horse to the tavern hitching post. Blood was alone, Gandy hunting or as likely sleeping away the increasing quantities of rum he pilfered while Blood slept. As if Blood did not know this.

While Blood had not yet met the minister he knew immediately who he was, even something of the sort of man he was. Luckless in life, lean of faith, dependent more upon his office than it upon him.

Blood inclined his head in greeting. He said, "Reverend."

"You are the man Blood?"

"I am."

"I bear a message from Emil Chase."

Blood nodded as if this was expected. Without mockery he said, "This portion of the building is my domestic quarters. Come take a seat with me. It pains me to stand."

"You have taken a wound."

"I have."

"Mister Chase did not mention that."

"He would not have known of it."

"I have no use for public houses such as this. But my reputation suffers nothing from my entering one."

I expect not, Blood thought. But only hobbled back from the door and swept a hand to indicate the table. Which was clear of all but a pitcher of water and his horse pistol.

The minister stepped inside. "Are your needs being met? Have you care?"

"I want for nothing. Let us be seated. I can offer you water still bright from the stream or tea if you would prefer."

The minister said, "You're not the sort I expected."

Blood said nothing.

The minister went on. "I mean no disrespect."

Blood sat at the table. He said, "Sit with me or stand as you're comfortable. I take no offense. Men are the agents of their own fate, Reverend. And that should end our theological discussion. You have a request from Chase?" He suspected he knew already what the request would be and was trying to decide if he should be amused or offended.

The minister removed his hat and held it before him. His hair was surprising to Blood, a rich chestnut brush on a man otherwise devoid of notice.

He said, "The number of men arrested in the insurrection here are too great to be housed within the jail at Lancaster. The majority have no capital warrants beyond simple resistance. Chase is charged with inciting insurrection but it appears he and the Sheriff are coming to agreement. The man Watkin, who was the instigator of this sad event, died in transport from wounds suffered through his own hindering to lawful arrest."

Blood spoke, not so much in interruption as one clarifying. "The problem is one of population, as well as sufficient grounds for holding such a number of men, is that correct?"

The minister said, "In a manner of speaking."

"I fail to see what use I may be. I'm no jailer, nor wish to be one."

"No," said the minister. Then, as if confused he went on. "Yes. I have not made myself clear. I was merely attempting to offer a broad view of the situation."

Blood said, "Can you speak plainly and to the point?"

The minister looked upon Blood with a spark of caution. Either more intelligent than he appeared or had been forewarned by Chase. Blood suspected the first. The minister said, "The High Sheriff of Coos County has accepted the pledging of a bond and the sworn word of the men detained in order to secure their release pending further decisions to their fate. Mister Chase has offered to put up the deed of his mill to secure that bond. The men in question, down to the last one, have agreed to be so sworn."

"A happy and equitable solution," Blood noted.

"Yes," the minister enthused. "But between Mister Chase and the Sheriff there remains dispute over the value of the mill deed. The sheriff requires a sum somewhat greater than the two concur upon."

"And Chase suggests I might provide that sum?" Blood was intrigued.

The minister lifted his face and studied the ceiling beams for a brief time. Then he looked back at Blood. "That is his hope, sir. He believes you might consider such generosity beneficial to yourself, as well."

"Is that so?" said Blood. His tone mild.

The minister nodded.

"You have a precise figure?"

"I do."

"No doubt that would include a minor surcharge for your services in this matter."

The minister purpled. "I seek only to aid men in distress. To assist in what appears to be largely a matter of misunderstanding."

Blood got the ox goad from where it leaned against the table and brought it between his legs and levered himself upright. He said, "I'm glad to hear that Reverend. It will make it all the easier for you to return to Mister Chase with my answer. Which is this, and a simple one at that— please recall these words: Let Hutchinson hold the deed and the swearing of the men as bond. When those men walk up this road Emil Chase may stop here. Whatever money he lacks to satisfy Hutchinson, we can discuss at that time, as well as the Canadian agreement. Mister Chase will understand that reference."

The minister said, "I fail to comprehend you sir."

Blood dug in his breeches and removed a ten dollar gold piece. He said, "Please deliver this to the Sheriff. The issue of money is not the only one that lies between Chase and myself. Today no other money shall travel southward with you. None beyond that ten dollars will go direct from my purse to that of your High Sheriff. I'd as soon fuck a pig. Do you comprehend that?"

The minister replaced his hat. His face the color of raw liver. He said, "I understand you all too well. Would you trifle with the lives of men in such a way?"

Blood said, "If you recall my words exactly, and repeat them to Chase and not to Hutchinson, then I trifle with no one. I believe the burden of trifling lies upon you. Would you have a drink of water before you depart? You look dry."

That same day a wind roused out of the south and the clammy weather began to disintegrate, the light weak but the warming air enough to melt the hoarfrost and soon the world was wet and emitting a low glisten that rose as much from the muted colors of the wetted brush and limbs as from the blanched sun.

Late in the afternoon Blood gimped outside. Gandy had been gone since morning. Blood made his way in a long tortured circuit about the house and came upon the still-fresh grave of the dog. The heaped soil was thawing and when, at great effort, he bent to touch his finger to the mound it came away wet and brown. He rubbed it off against his pant leg, the one split all the way up his side and tied together at the bottom above his boot. So the cloth flapped open. His leg was chilled but he figured fresh air was good for the wound.

He made his way to the barn. He got an armful of hay over the bars into the pen for the oxen. The milk cow was in distress. There was nothing he could do for her. Even if he were able to lower himself to a milking stool with his leg stretched flat under her he doubted he might ever rise. And in her torment there was no telling how she might react to such a sight as he.

He sighed. To be able to load the oxcart, yoke the steers and go. But this was no longer a choice, no longer a simple practicality.

He made his way to the hog stockade and with great effort turned around to sit on the entryway of the chicken coop and reached behind him to scrabble his hand among the flustering peckish chickens and so one at a time scooped out a half-dozen eggs. These he carried to the house and set in a bowl on the mantel.

He returned to the barn for the halter and lead of braided leather and beat the half-wild milk cow with the goad until she stood quivering, motionless as he haltered her. Then in slow awkward procession he made his way up the road, the cow trailing behind, Blood jouncing rough each step of the way, sweating and tight-chested with the exertion. At the mill the door was open and a group of young boys stood hostile and silent, watching him come, all of them armed, some with rifles or old flintlocks and others with simple weapons such as sickles or froes. He stood in the road and with great unwavering authority ordered one amongst them to obtain Mistress Chase.

She came to the door and stood looking at him, silent.

He said, "Send these children away and shut the door. I've news for you."

She studied him a moment more and then stepped down into the yard and without her speaking the gang of youth drifted up the road, still in sight but out of earshot. She pulled the big door to behind her.

Blood watched her and waited. She was a handsome woman close to his own age with her life marked clearly upon her. As if her misfortunes were not a product of her choice but the nature of life itself. Perhaps, he considered, she was correct.

She said, "I had thought you were out of the country. But you secured a wound as well."

Blood said, "I was an unwitting and unwilling puppet. But I'll not plead my case to you. The circumstance of opinion lies against me, I know. But I wished you to know that I've reason to believe your men will be released soon. Perhaps tomorrow."

She was silent a pause and then said, "You engineered this as well?"

Blood held his sigh. He said, "I was approached this forenoon by an agent of Mose Hutchinson. I was offered the opportunity to ransom your husband and the rest of the men. I refused this, being unwilling to have Hutchinson benefit from this sham. But I made clear your husband is welcome to discuss his needs with me in person. It was not the answer hoped for but one I presume will in the end suffice. My belief is that the Hampshire men do not truly know what to do with the men they took from this country."

"My husband would not appeal to you directly, himself. We are not without means."

"The proposal put forth to me did not strike me as being to the benefit of either your husband or myself. I simply wish to ease your mind as best I can, informing you of the situation and how I expect it will be resolved."

She paused again. Then she said, "Others speak of the coincidence of your arrival here this spring with the beginning of our misfortunes. Contrary to what you might think, I myself take no such simple view. Still, I regret that a man of your wit and ambition cannot serve the territory in a manner more uplifting than the one you chose."

Now Blood sighed. "My girl has gone off. I've no real use for the cow, even if I could tend her. Which I can't. But with the number of children and people housed here you might find use for her. Her milking's been irregular the past few days but once she's at ease she'll let down well again, I would think."

The Chase wife looked at the cow as if for the first time. Which Blood knew was not the case. Then she looked back to Blood. "How was your wound obtained?"

"The same as all such. Through altercation."

She cocked an eye. Then said, "Is it clean?"

"It seems to be fine. Draining somewhat but in a healthy fashion."

"You have experience with such things?"

He said nothing.

After a bit she said, "For the moment at least, the use of your cow would be a great help here."

"I had thought as much."

"When things return to some form of normalcy she could be returned to you."

Blood shook his head. "I don't want her back."

The Chase woman scrutinized him openly. Then said, "It will be a harsh winter for many. A cow could be of great benefit to one of the families that stick it out."

"I would leave that discretion to you. You'd be in the best position to choose."

Again she paused. Then cast her eyes strongly upon him and said, "It would be a kind thing to do, Mister Blood. But, you must know, there can be no question of payment at such a time as this."

Blood said, "The cow is useless to me. A scant few days more of the treatment she's been receiving she'll be useless to all. It's her fortune I'm looking out for, no one else's."

"You care more for the fate of the cow than those she's to serve?"

"Beasts," said Blood. "Do not manufacture malice. They hold it only when it's earned." And he dropped the leather lead on the ground and turned away, wobbling damnably on the goad as he got himself in motion once more. His leg has stiffened.

The Chase woman called after him. "Mister Blood."

He stopped but did not turn.

She said, "Once she settles, I'd send down a bit of milk and butter."

He turned his head over his shoulder. "No," he said. "I've lost my taste for it."

He resumed his march. There was a solitary raven beating against the stained glazed sky. From the lake beyond the mill came the throaty gabble of rafted geese. He heard her call to one of the boys to come catch up the cow. Then all he heard was the suck of his boots in the dissolving mud of the road. His head down to watch his way.

* * *

That same afternoon the three encamped in the marsh sat out on a granite ledge in the ashen sunlight, warming themselves and watching three horses in leather hobbles grazing the rough grass of the hummocks. A bay and two chestnut geldings of indeterminate age but fair soundness that an hour before Cooper had appeared leading strung together, all three geared in shoddy bridles and saddles, the horses knotted together with bridle reins run back from the headstall of the first horse on to the second and then again the third. Coming up the narrow trail behind Cooper along the brook snorting and one or another pausing and jerking its head as if to throw off the whole affair but falling into line again as the others went along. Once they came into the open land they quieted as Cooper unsaddled them and used the reins to fashion loose hobbles, removed the headstalls and stood back and said, "Well. You were so lathered up coming through the woods. Now what're you going to do?"

They stood watching him, ears pricked, heads alert. The bay horse walked to one of the pools, lowered its head and drank, came alert dribbling water looking around. The chestnuts followed. Then settled to cropping grass, each working its own route careless of the others but in the practice of herd animals never moving in such a way they couldn't see their fellows. Also watching the three humans sitting on the long whaleback ledge of granite.

When Cooper approached Sally about the gold to go after horses she backed away, walking without speaking from the camp out into the marsh where she turned and waited for him. When he did she already had the pieces clenched in her hand but she did not offer them. She said, "What do we want with horses now? Blood's right down the trail."

He frowned at her as if disappointed. "We're not done with this country yet. But close. Old Fletcher is healing better than he knows. And the day comes we choose to leave, we might care to do it quick."

She nodded. She wanted him to know she understood this. She wet her lips and said, "I already told you I can't ride."

He shrugged. "All the better reason to get em now, before they're needed. Give you a chance to get used to em."

She considered the implications of this. She handed him the gold and said, "You want I should go with you? To Van Landt's? He knows me, he's not laid eyes on you."

Cooper said, "I believe it's better it's just me. If he has the horses they'll be high, with all that's been going on. But this idn't paper money or a note of promise. It should do."

She said, "I could at least show you the way."

He looked at her a time. Then reached and laid the fingertips of one hand on her forearm. He said, "You best stay to look after Fletcher. I can find my way." He took his hand away. But kept his stare upon her a brief beat of time. Then shook his head and walked away.

Cooper made a leisurely circuit of the horses, gradually making his way to each and running his hands over the animal, starting at the head where he worked slowly with his hands until one lay along the jawline and the other up rubbing as if at a knot behind the near ear until the horse dropped its head low, putting the ear even with Cooper's chest. As if the horse would lay its head against his chest. After a time of this he made his way along the horse, running his hands over the neck and withers and back and if the horse stood well for this, down underneath the belly and legs. Then back to the head where he'd started for a few minutes, before moving along toward the next horse. Often the one just finished would follow him some few steps.

Sally and Fletcher sat on the ledge. Sally watching Cooper and Fletcher watching Sally. But when she turned to him he looked out at the horses, at his brother, at some imprecise point of the marsh.

"How's he know to do that?"

"He grew up with horses."

"But you grew up together. Don't you know em too?"

"I can ride," he said. "But I never was handy with em like he is."

She looked back at the boy working the horses. With some nugget of pleasure, some satisfaction unnamed lodged within her.

Cooper came up and said to Fletcher, "You had to do it, could you ride?"

Fletcher worked his lower lip with his teeth. Then said, "I could. It'd throb some I spect but nothing I couldn't live through."

Cooper turned to Sally. "That bay horse, he's the one for you. We need to get you started."

She said, "He's god-awful big. Why him?"

He shrugged. "He's big enough I guess. But he's got the most sense. Of the three, he's the calmest."

She thought about that. Then said, "How calm does that make him?"

He grinned at her. "Calm enough."

For want of a curry or brush Cooper cut a section from a burlap bean sack and with this wadded in one hand one at a time went over the tethered horses, not so much a cleaning as a pretense of such, gestures familiar and soothing to them.

He rode each horse around the marsh, circuiting the old beaver ponds and the trickle-streams that flowed from them, turning the horses at odd and sharp angles, making them stop and back, then moving them forward again. Once with each horse making them wade through the deepest of the pools.

The last Cooper rode was the bay he'd singled out for Sally. She sat watching and couldn't see much difference in the bay from the others; they all seemed to behave more or less well for Cooper. The bay was skittish about entering the water. Cooper turned the horse several times to face once again the water, pausing before trying to urge the horse on until, by some decision Sally couldn't detect, Cooper would turn the horse again. And sit waiting. Until that final revolution when the horse stepped forward and walked through the pond as if it weren't there at all.

When they came out the other side Cooper rode the horse in a smooth trot three times around the widest opening of the marsh before cutting straight across and drawing up before where Fletcher and Sally sat on the ledge. He stepped down from the horse and stood a moment by its head, kneading the skin behind the horse's ear. The horse dropped its head down level with Cooper's chest.

His face serious but bright with pleasure he said to Sally, "You ready?"

"You mean now?"

As if he hadn't heard her he said, "This is all you really got to know: Keep the reins tight from your hands to the bit. Not so as to pull his head down but tight enough so he knows you're the one in charge. And don't set on the saddle but down in it. So your behind and your thighs feel like they're part of the saddle. You hold him that way, and sit him that way, then all you got to do is use a little pressure with the hand and leg to tell him which way to turn. You want him to go forward bring your hands up a little and tighten both legs. Other than just getting used to him and letting him get used to you, that's all there is to it."

"That sounds like a lot. How do I make him stop?"

"Like starting. Except draw your hands back a little. You don't have to saw, just a light touch. He'll know what you want."

"You going to walk around with me?"

"No. He'd be following me then. Instead of paying attention to you."

"Seems to me, it wouldn't hurt you was to take at least one turn around with me."

He glanced hard at her. "If he's going to dump you off he will. You ain't ridden until you been throwed. Now, you going to set talking all day or are you going to ride this horse?"

"Well." She was nervous. The talk about being thrown hadn't helped. She made a final feeble plea. "I guess I don't have a choice."

He was swiftly serious. "This horse, in the days that come, might be the best thing ever happened to you. You understand?"

She looked at him. His eyes were hot on her and she felt her own flare to meet him. All nervousness was gone. She slid off the ledge. "All right," she said. "But you hold him while I get on. I got to figure out my skirts."

Once she was settled, with her skirts under her but pulled back so her legs were bare from midthigh down to her boots, Cooper let go of the headstall and the horse began to wander among the ponds, Sally slipping in the saddle, dropping first one rein and then the other, having to stretch forward along the horse's neck to retrieve them, her rear lifted high as she slid her hand down toward the bit for the rein. The bay walked at leisure, in no particular pattern and without visible agitation, as if awaiting this strange human to locate itself and send some directions his way. Meanwhile he was content to amble.

The brothers sat on the ledge, not talking, both watching the vision of the girl riding. She was beginning to guide the horse.

Cooper said, "I knew that was the one for her. That bay horse, as long's she can stay on him, give him some idea what she wants, he can do the rest."

Sally was moving the bay slow along and between the pools of water. Around a clump of thick young alders. The horse working well. Cooper said, "Look at that. That horse is just waiting for her to learn what he needs her to learn. That's a good horse."

Fletcher reached back with his good hand and pushed off from where he leaned against the ledge. "Alright," he said. "Which of those sorrels do you figure for me?"

Cooper grinned at him. "I ain't sure. Let's go look em over."

When Blood returned from giving away the cow it was without satisfaction of any kind. Even being done with the animal gave no pleasure. His leg was hurting badly and it looked to be an evil night before him. Already the brief warmth of the day was gone and the wind was lifting off the lake. He was cold and sore and came up to the tavern to find Gandy waiting with a skinned and gutted young bear, the carcass hanging from the meat-hook by the tavern door. An old trapper's hand-sled with fresh bloodstain in the yard.

"Meat," Blood bleated. His body washed with the colors of pain. He wanted hot water and to change his dressings. A big fire and a cup of rum. He would've been happy with potatoes for his supper. Let Gandy come tomorrow, was what he wished.

Gandy said, "This should keep you some time, the weather stays cool. If it don't freeze up like a rock. Then you can hack at it with a axe. But I need to settle. I need powder and lead for the winter. I expect some rum as well. If you ain't been keeping a tab I have. The bearmeat is just the tip-end of it."

Blood said, "I'm sorely worn. Leave the bear hang. We'll settle on the morrow."

Gandy said, "No I don't believe we will. I want to be done with it tonight. I hauled the bear with my sled and plan to leave before nightfall with my winter provision."

Blood shook his head. "It will have to wait. One more night sleeping on the tavern floor won't be the death of you."

Gandy studied Blood a moment and then easy as a cat swung the rifle up and covered Blood. He said, "Things've turned against you Blood. I can't say I'm sorry but wouldn't say I'm glad neither. I just don't plan to get caught in the midst of any of it. So I'll load my sled and head for the Dead Diamond country tonight. I can do it with you approving what I take in trade or I can do it otherwise. But, unless the Lord smiles such that you're here come springtime this is the last you'll see of me. You clear on that or do you need another hole in you to sharpen your senses?"

Blood leaned on the goad. He said, "I hadn't expected this of you."

Gandy said, "I ain't survived so long in this hellhole land by being as much a fool as you think me Blood." He stepped up and kicked open the tavern door, still holding his weapon upon Blood. "You go on first. Go slow."

Blood looked at him, heaved his head back on his neck and said, "Slow's all I've got right now Gandy. But you'll have to load your sled yourself. You're not such a man as to heft a powder keg one-handed. The pig lead idn't light neither. So why don't you calm down with the long gun. I got no desire at all to be blown again. This time, it might go lucky and be the end of me."

Gandy grinned. He said, "I'll tell you what. We get things moved out of your storeroom, agree on quantities and such. Then I'll determine how to get it loaded."

"Rifle or none, I'll be no man's slave."

Gandy said, "More what I had in mind, is when you see what I intend as mine by rights, you'll see I'm not greedy but fair. Then we might close this deal more civil than we opened it. I ain't such a hard one. I'm just determined to quit this settlement by this evening."

Blood studied him a moment, straightened a little so the goad was a better prop and said, "Is there news you own I ought to as well?"

"No," said Gandy. "Not beyond what ripples in my bones."

Blood studied him a long moment. Gandy held the rifle steady, looking right back. Blood sighed and stepped up into the darkened tavern. He said, "I need to make a light."

"Do it then."

Blood lighted a stub taper and they passed into the tavern side. Blood went around the counter and set the saucer with the stub on the counter and drew the pouch of keys from under his shirt very slow, even though

Gandy knew what he was about. He took the larger key and opened the padlock from the hasp of the storeroom door. The chain bolted to the floor fell away. He swung the door open. Then stepped back, leaned on the counter and said, "Let's see your accounts. Roll it on out here."

Gandy rocked one-handed three kegs of powder out and then a matching weight of pig-lead that he stacked atop the kegs, his rifle bobbing up and down and around. Blood thought if he were to die from Gandy's weapon it would most likely be by accident.

Gandy now surveyed the interior of the storeroom. He said, "Them empty powder kegs, they been rinsed?"

"No."

"Did you stove the tops or they still of use?"

"They're stacked right behind the empties. Down behind."

Gandy said, "If I was to fill a couple from the hogsheads, they wouldn't leak, don't you think?"

Blood shrugged. "Those powder kegs're lined with sailcloth soaked in beeswax. It keeps the powder dry. I'd think, if they keep wet out, they'd hold it in pretty well."

He stood watching Gandy. Who said, "I'd like four of em. You think I been that much use to you, on top of the powder and lead?"

Blood did not. He nodded and said, "Take four. When you come hauling furs through the muck next spring we can argue about whether you was worth that much or not."

Gandy grinned at him. Then set to filling the kegs with rum. When he had sealed he moved them out alongside the powder and lead. It was an impressive load. Blood himself, had he been healthy, would not have coveted the long haul by hand-sled.

Blood said, "Is that it?"

Gandy paused. "That girl, when she run off, did she leave behind any of her skirts or underthings?"

"No," Blood said. "She took em all."

Gandy said, "That's a shame. Some one little piece or another would've been pleasant to have as a memory."

Blood said, "There's bolts of cloth for dresses and skirts and the like folded atop the hogsheads."

Gandy said, "You ain't been able to sell the first cut of that, have you?"

Blood was silent.

Gandy said, "I don't believe I'd care for it myself." Gandy still held the rifle, butted under one arm, that hand holding the stock up by the trigger guard. "Now," he said, "I'm going to move this bit by bit to the door. You follow on, but not too close." And he half-crouched by the first powder keg and began to tip it on edge back and forth so that it rocked toward the counter opening. It was hard work and the rifle clenched under one arm made it all the harder.

Blood moved slowly along with him. When they reached the end of the counter Gandy had to crab sideways to get through the opening. When he was partway through Blood took one last step and said, "Wait."

Gandy tipped his face up from where he was bent over the keg. The rifle was sideways in the opening. "What is it," he asked.

"You forgot one thing," Blood said. And caught up the little leather and lead sap from the shelf behind the counter and split Gandy's head open with it, such a soft puff of sound but the lead crushed right through the bone. Gandy fell across the keg and briefly his arms and legs worked as if he might swim someway off the keg and away. His rifle clattered to the floor.

As Blood stood looking at him Gandy slipped from the keg and fell. The keg turned sideways and lay pinned in the narrow opening with the dead trapper. Blood wiped the sap on his breeches and surveyed the scene.

As if asking Gandy he said, "Now how in hell am I going to climb out over you. You goddamn fool."

He turned and went back and relocked the storeroom, disregarding the chain and the items out on the floor. There was nothing to do with them this night. Then, moving slow, he trod carefully up over the little trapper's body. Turned back and took up the candle and went into the other side of the house. He shut the door and barred it. He needed to get the fire up and water heating. His wound was in fearsome ache, a blister of pain the size of a man's head. Seeing to that was his first job. He staggered to the fireplace, then, just before he began to lower himself down to the floor to blow up the fire, he spotted on the mantel the eggs gathered earlier. At least, he thought, I get through this, I'll have something to eat. A bit of drink after that. He was cautious but drinking some no longer bothered him in the least. If nothing else he'd earned back that right.

* * *

Dusk into nightfall. Fletcher was already sleeping. Sally sat out by the fire with Cooper, both drinking tea, not talking. She watched him as he gripped the tin cup, gazing blank into the fire, one foot tapping up and down, the knee jogging with his preoccupation. She knew before he stood that he was about to. And also what then.

He still did not look at her but upward where the flame tips bled into the night. He said, "I'm going to walk on down there. Take a look around. Maybe have a little talk."

She said, "You don't want to do that alone."

Then he looked at her. "Why ever not," he said. "What's he going to do, shoot me?"

There was nothing funny in his grin and she knew it. She paused a moment, then revealed herself. "I been down twice on my own. He's in a foul humor, drove me off and all I wanted was to offer help. Blood's still struggling to get around—you think about why that is, and unless you got less sense than I know you do you'll see it idn't the time. At least not alone and neither one of us is about to leave Fletcher here solitary in the state he's in. Anybody that wanted could come in and he'd never even wake to see their mischief. No." She raised a hand to hush Cooper. And went on. "Also, there's no way to know if Blood's alone. The last thing you or him wants is anybody incidental to connect you two. It idn't just that useless little bastard Gandy neither, but men slipping up private in the night to buy drink from him. They don't stay but carry it away. Cooper, trust me, this idn't the time for it. Not yet. We got to get Fletcher stronger. And it may strike you strange but Blood himself, the more he heals the best it will be. For both of you. Can't you see that?"

There was a long pause while he again studied the firetip or the stars, she could not tell. Then not looking at her, he lifted his blanket coat from the tent pole and finally turned. He kept his eyes full upon her as he put it on and when he was wrapped against the night he said, "I got to. I'm beginning to feel at loose ends here." And did not wait for her reply but walked from the circle of light into the dark. This time she did not watch him go but took a stick and jabbed apart the settled fire and then stick by stick built it high. To build a beacon for him? She wasn't sure what he'd meant—that last remark.

* * *

Sometime after this she went back into the tent and stood over Fletcher. Even with the fire it was cool enough to see her breath. She knelt to one side of him and removed her boots and woolen stockings, folded her shawl atop the neat pile and still wearing her skirt and bodice slowly peeled back one corner of the covers and slipped in beside him. He was on his back, his arm strapped to his chest, his breathing even and a little moist. He did not stir as she came in and settled herself, on her side facing him so she could study his profile. Small bubbles of saliva broke against the corner of his mouth, catching the firelight, bright beads rising up and then gone.

Throughout the cold days of healing she'd sat long hours on the blankets beside Fletcher with her feet curled under her, chatting with him, lifting his head to bring the tin cup of water to his lips. He'd asked about her life with Blood and she refused to talk of it. He asked of her life before that and she refused him there as well.

"It's not so much I'm shamed of it," she told him. "As I'm just done with it. I got no idear what comes next but I know I'm not going backward. There's nothing to be gained by hashing it over. Past is past."

"I'd not judge you by any of it.

"It's not your judgment that I care for," she said, not certain this was true. "It's myself. I can't make a bit of it go away but that don't mean I intend to carry it forward with me. Don't mistake me—I don't expect a thing of you."

"I wish you wouldn't talk that way."

She went on, "I don't expect a thing of anybody. For the first time ever I don't owe nothing to nobody. I like that."

As if this was enough, he relented. She knew his great patience was rare and understood this was a gift bestowed upon her.

Other times he talked of his ideas for the future. But these were vague, near to awkward and he would stop of a sudden, as if come against a barrier he held no idea how to penetrate. She knew this barrier to be herself. But was content to let him come to that stop. If he would hesitate to pursue her in that sketched future he should expect no encouragement from her. Let's see what happens, was what she thought.

* * *

Sometime later she woke, wrapped in blankets, warm and her breath gasping as if drinking the cold air of the night, lying carefully bundled beside where Fletcher slept. Then slowly came more awake. The fire was up, just barely and there came a sound she could not place. She sat up as she woke further.

Cooper sat before the fire on a stone, his back to the tent, a black hump obscuring the dart of flame. He was leaned over, not looking at the fire, his head in his hands. He was crying. The sort of silent hard contorted cry she knew so well, the soul-crying of privacy. She came out from the covers and went to him. Up beside him and knelt there, reached and touched him. Just touched his shoulder, his arm. He turned to her. Eyes and cheeks wet and swollen. He looked at her as at a stranger: his face distorted, wild torn and damaged.

"Cooper," she said.

He came down off the rock to kneel before her. His arms dropped at his sides as if broken.

Again she said his name. And reached to touch his upper arms with both hands. He lifted his face and looked upon her again. He touched her arms, ran his hands up and down them. She gripped him. His arms went around her, his hands hard upon her back, working at the muscles there. And held her clenched and rose up so he was standing and she with him, against him. Once up he did not stand gentle with her but ran his hands once more hard over her back and then bent against her and picked her up and carried her out into the dark, into the marsh, into the hummocks of harsh frozen grass. Not at all anything she wanted until it was happening and then all she wanted even as it changed everything, all notions of time right or wrong gone from her. She looked back over his shoulder at the camp behind and then looked away, up into the night sky. At a point that was not marsh and not hummock but some place in between he stopped and dropped to his knees and settled her onto the ground, a placing not rough but determined. All she landed on was the earth. She fit against it as if it had been waiting for her. Her legs spread wide as she went down, her skirt pulled up, her own hands doing that job. The sky a maniac of lights. He on his knees struggling with his breeches. Hurry. Hurry she thought. Then his graceful obliterating weight. All of it. All throughout her. She got her heels up, the soles of her feet pointed toward the stars, the moon, her moon. As if her feet would lead her there.

The world gone red and black, blood-pods bursting over and again.

Later they lay clenched to each other. She began to shiver, shaking against him. He tried to wrap her in his arms, to hold her against him, to turn her away from the cold ground as if that was what caused her chill. She pushed against him.

"Goddamn it," he said.

She shuddered, pushed harder. "Let go of me." Her voice grim.

He heard this. Rose up and gathered his breeches to his waist and reached to help her stand. She rolled away, going around his hand, pushing herself off the ground, feeling as if her body carried all the marks it possibly could, the stains of earth and mud and grass and blown dead leaves in her hair and blood coarsening the skin of her breast and face. She pushed with her hands at her clothing and then went around him some half dozen steps toward the camp. And stopped. It was no place to go.

Behind her he said her name.

She stood where she was. Her arms wrapped tight over her breasts, her thighs pressed tight against the convulsing. He came up beside her. She kept her eyes ahead of her, looking at the fire, the faint orange glow backlighting the canvas. Her voice flat as pond ice. "Get me a blanket. If he's awake don't say nothing."

When he came back he opened the blanket as if to wrap her. She snatched forward and took it from him. Pulled it tight around her, over her head, up hard against her throat.

He said, "Sally."

She thrust her free hand from under the folds and slapped his face as hard as she could.

He stood against the impact. "Christ," he said, a small voice of despair.

"What do you think I am?" she said. Then, "Shut up. I don't want to hear anything from you. I already know."

He stood rocking a moment before her. Then, his voice with the lisp of anger said, "Don't tell me what I think." And turned and walked toward the fire. She watched him go, his feet flat and steady over the uneven ground. When he reached the ring of light she saw him stand a moment looking into the tent and then he turned and in one swift sagging motion settled crosslegged on the ground before the fire, his hands loose in his lap. He watched into the flames. His head did not move. He did not look out into the dark where she stood.

Her sex was swollen but the ache was sweet. She thought I ain't no better than a animal. Then realized that was somebody else thinking, not her. She walked forward into the fire circle and sat on the stone Cooper had been on when she first awakened. She was looking at him but also without turning her head could see into the tent where Fletcher lay sleeping. On his back, breathing through just-parted lips as if he had no more pain. She looked back at Cooper.

He was still looking into the fire. Without turning his head he said, "I'd be lying I was to tell you I hadn't wanted to do that. But it idn't what you thought it was."

She said nothing.

He shook his head. "No. You're wrong."

She said nothing.

He said, "But still there's a part I don't like. I hate it. To do such a thing to my brother."

She said, "It wasn't your brother you done it to."

He looked at her then, his eyes terrible. "I swear I never meant to hurt you. When you come from the bed I was in a bad state. You seemed everything I needed. It wasn't a accident you were there then. Tell me you think it was."

She said nothing.

He said, "When Fletcher and I come up here we only had one thing on our minds. Then when he first met you and talked about you I thought it was a simple thing. Some boy thing. When I met you I thought he had good reason but you weren't a girl to get tangled with. For plenty of reasons. That's what I thought. But what happened wasn't a gradual thing at all. It was that morning we were trying to get to Van Landt's and the militia rode up. We was hid up that hillside and I turned to see you lift your head and crane after the men riding by. I can't tell you what it was. It was the way the cords of your neck stood out. It was the look on your face. It was something delicate and fearless all at once in you. I'd never seen that before, just like that. Not a woman I'd ever met. Come to think of it, not a man either. It was something rare, was what it was."

She was silent still. She recalled the time he spoke of but not the moment he'd seen her that way. She knew when it had been such with her for him but would not speak of it, not to him. Not yet.

He went on. "Fletcher is the last person I'd ever want to hurt this way. Any way. He is." A pause. "And you. You too."

Very quiet she said, "You already have."

"I know it."

She said, "Cooper."

He looked at her.

She said, "What happened tonight—"

He interrupted her. "I won't speak of it. I won't say a word. Nothing good would come of telling him. And more than that—I swear to God I'll leave you be. I won't moon around after you. I won't give you reason not to trust me. I won't do a thing not proper. I won't be bold, even, as best I can do it, in my head. I'll do everything I can do to see this works out. It idn't just him I'm doing that for, you know, it idn't just that at all—"

Now she interrupted him. "It's a mess, idn't it?"

He looked at her.

She said, "Cooper."

"I told you," he said. "I'll leave you be."

"Cooper," she said. Her voice changed, upthrust.

He was silent now.

She said, "When I first came out tonight. And found you setting here by the fire, so full of sorrow. That was something I know. I seen you then, something like you seen me." Now she paused and determined, went on. "Not that it was the first. But tonight, all I wanted was to take that sadness from you. I didn't want to make it more."

His eyes bright upon her but he did not speak.

"What was it, Cooper? What happened down to Blood's tonight?"

Now he faltered, looked away, then back. "I druther not talk about it."

"Cooper you got no choice."

He gazed into the fire. She thought He's a man, once he lets you, you can read his face.

"I'm warm enough," she said. "We can walk out and set up on one of those humps in the grass."

"I'm not sure that's a good idea."

"Cooper," she said. "It don't make a difference anymore. Don't you know that?" She stood and waited. One of the horses blew when she stood. The night sky spread broad, the moon was down. The fire was low, a mound of red and black large enough to cover the three of them sleeping.

He looked up at her. And she saw it in his face and felt it within her at the same time and she thought There is not a solitary thing wrong with any of this.

And so walked out barefoot through the frosted raw-edged grass with the blanket drawn close about her but pushed back off her head so she could see clearly all around and above her. Hearing him coming behind her. She loosed the blanket a little in the front. So when she turned to him she would want all the warmth he carried. So when she turned to him she would feel every bit of his life come against her. Right or wrong, she wanted that.

He had not seen his father. Had halted in the copse of spruce across the stream from the tavern thinking he would just sit and study things a bit. See if there were other men about, inside the tavern or out. Recalling her warning. Once the door opened and meek light spilled into the yard as his father held the jamb and swung stiff-legged to the bottom of the two steps and stood and peed, Cooper able to see the great head swing about as he took measure with his relief. His father turned slow and clambered back inside. Still Cooper sat, his father most likely alone. Sat long enough to grow very cold. Watching the slender vapor of chimney smoke rise straight as a mast. But did not understand, did not know, until he rose and went not down to the road and across to the tavern but rather retreated up the trail toward the marsh, that he was frightened. That he did not have the courage to stride across and strike the door and demand or simply ask admittance. The courage to face what he did not know. The courage to apologize and attempt to begin again. Or simply offer his aid. That he was simply a badly frightened boy. And understood that he had lost not gained in

wounding his father. The reflex had been one born of fear not boldness. And stumbled his way back to the camp knowing something of
himself he had not known before and did not like and was helpless
before.

They sat quiet some while after his telling of this. Wrapped amply
against the cold, the blanket around them, clinging entwined, their
bodies a furnace interim. So quiet their breath steamed audible into the
night and the stars seemed to emit a faint crackle.

Finally Sally spoke, her voice low and warm, close against him. "I
didn't ever know my own father," she said. "But I couldn't imagine such
a one as Blood."

"When I came looking I didn't know it," Cooper said. "But all I
needed was to meet him face to face and see what he would have to say.
And then banish him from the rest of my life. But it idn't going to be
like that. However it ends here, he's going to be somewhere inside of
me all my days. And not in a single way I want or admire."

Sally was quiet, then picked her way carefully through a handful of
words. "Could be, some of those ways might serve you good some day.
Even if it's not more than knowing they're in you."

After a moment Cooper said, "I don't like it but I got to ask you
this."

Sally said, "You'd be stupid not to. The first thing you need to know is
that Blood brought me into this country tied like a beast to the back of his
cart. And that remains most important of what's true between him and
me. But there's been times, small things to most anybody but me I suppose, when he's shown kindness. Never so much that it cost him great
effort. But still they was there, those things. I think," she said. "I think
when he done those things it allowed him some measure of comfort also.
As if he'd long since come to believe he wasn't capable of kindness to
another human being. There were times, times when he was tender to
me. And I'll not lie to you Cooper. I was tender with him as well."

Cooper was quiet.

She waited and when he still said nothing she said, "Don't get me
wrong. Even so, I never doubted that if it was in his favor he'd not think

twice before selling me to whoever wanted me or cut my throat if I was more nuisance than worth."

She took a breath and went on. "So. Do we trust? Do we choose to trust a bit more than ever before?" And thought if she'd gone too far better to know now.

"Sally," Cooper said. "I am surely, sorely, lost."

She pulled her head away enough to tilt her face up to see his. He was holding the blanket around both of them and she ran a hand up between them to cup over his head, her fingers in his hair. She said, "No. You idn't lost. All that's lost is some idea you had of yourself. You're right here, same as me."

"And Fletcher. He's here too."

"So who's the guilty one? Me?"

"No," he said. "Not you."

"Is it you then?"

"I guess it is."

"I should just walk out of here," she said. "I should just wrap my things and go. Leave you two to your business with Blood. Just leave simple like that. Clean as I can. "

"No," he said. Then, "Is that what you want?"

"No."

"You sure?"

"Cooper," she said. "Everybody lies, but there's big ways to lie and small ways. The small ones are just a kindness and don't count. My offering to leave is one of those. It's the last thing I want. But, you'd said yes, or even hesitated, I'd been gone. Now that, I learned from all the lying I ever saw people do. But from your father, I learned the big lies idn't worth it. It's a lesson he never knowed he was teaching me." She stopped like she was out of breath.

Cooper was quiet so long she thought he might never speak again. That she might have pressed hard against a hurt too fresh to bear up under. She wished that wasn't so, wished she could take it away. But there was nothing she could say, nothing she would say. So she let her fingers work the slightest touch to his hair.

Finally she said, "It's a strangeness, idn't it?"

"Oh yes," he said. "It is, Sally. It certainly is."

They lay curled on their sides, Sally wrapped within him. Her back to his chest, his arms around her with heads so close that sleeping they inhaled the other's breath. Their legs wrapped in unbroken chain. The blanket over them caught by frost in a crude heap of angles. In the pre-dawn a single planet made a modest beacon in the west.

An owl called the night with it deep into the hemlocks.

Fletcher woke under the canvas flat on his back and tested the arm in the sling strapped tight to his chest. The bite of pain in his shoulder was dulled, a shade less each day. It was early and he was alone. He pushed the blankets off him and dragged his breeches close and one awkward leg at a time got them on. The hardest part was arching his hips up so his weight fell onto his shoulders as he got the breeches over his waist. Then getting them buttoned one-handed. He got to his feet and took down his blanket coat that was stiff with cold and worked it over his shoulders for a crude cape.

Then went out to the fire. He stood a time looking out at the marsh where the small prominence of frosted blanket seemed too small to contain all it did. After a time he took up a long stick with his free hand and stirred the mound of fire until he turned up black and smoking lumps of charred wood that steamed in the cold air and began to glow red and flicker edges into flame. There was a heap of firewood and he worked slowly to add one stick at a time until the fire was a bright living angry creature. With great effort he filled the iron pot with water from the tin bucket and put the pot on a stone close to the fire to heat for tea. Only then did he walk slow out over the rough ground, the frost breaking under his bare feet so there was a trail of dark prints behind him as he went. When he came up to the blanket he studied it some time, then shuffled his position and kicked hard at what he thought was the small of his brother's back. And kicked again. Wishing he had his boots on. Suddenly almost crying because he wasn't able yet to lace his boots.

The two on the ground came up together, a rough lurch to something close to sitting and the blanket fell partly away and the girl grabbed for it. To cover herself from his eyes, he thought. As if she'd forgotten she had clothes on. Her eyes blinking.

"Oh Jesus," his brother said.

"I got water on for tea," Fletcher said. "God damn you both." And turned back to the camp.

Blood was out of bed some short hours before first light. Cursing his night-stiffened leg. He left the fire cold and lit the taper stub left from the night before and carried it into the tavern and surveyed the mess before him. He went blind in the dark to the barn and cut a length from the coil of hempen rope, then back into the tavern where he bound Gandy's arms to his sides so they would not impede movement, bound the ankles together and ran the other end of the rope in a harsh tight loop around his own waist. Harnessed so, he took up the goad and fought his way out of the tavern into the dark, straining at the dead-weight load. On the frosted land the body moved more easily. He went struggling and panting, leaning into the job with both hands gripped to the goad that he moved before him and planted to draw them both along. At the edge of the stream he untied himself, went back to the tavern and several times returned to the streamside, carrying one-handed a partial quantity of lead Gandy had selected. When there was a plenty of it, he eased himself down and finished wrapping the remaining rope around Gandy. Drew it snug tight and knotted it hard. Then wedged the pigs of lead under the ropes, adjusting so they were secure. He stood once more and put his weight onto his good leg, bent as much as he was able and used the goad as a lever to roll the body over the bank. Where it caught on a rock and turned sideways, headfirst toward the water, stuck. Blood used the goad to pry and finally the little trapper slipped down into the water with barely a sound, turning some few moments in the current and then, as if the water sighed, the stream opened and Gandy was gone.

By first light not only was the wound dressed but he was washed and shaved, in the cleanest shirt he could find, his belly full of tea. His leg throbbed from the early exercise, as if a raven were snared within the flesh. So gingerly he made his way along the stream to the narrow path that branched off following the brook toward the marsh. He paused here, taking air in great gulps, and bent to study the ground. On the path, compressed between the rocks brookside and the woods growth, it was difficult to make out much except the obvious recent passage of a number of horses. Going up only, not returning. He'd seen no such sign coming along the wider road by Perry Stream. He went on, laboring over the rocks wrapped in moss, the moss here and there sliced in a crescent opening from the sidewall strike of a horse hoof. After a while he determined it was three horses. He recalled Sally relating she'd held back gold to buy horses with and their aborted effort to do so. He guessed they'd proceeded. These tracks were fresh, not more than a day old. He wasn't sure this was a good thing but guessed it could be, he played his few cards right. At least the three up ahead could leave swiftly, the time came. If they would. Blood smart enough to know already he could be the impediment to that quick departure. He'd cut that impulse, whatever the cost. If his cards were few he still had the advantage of knowing the full range of the game.

The boys were standing either side of the fire, apart but facing each other. Cooper saw him coming and shifted to watch, Blood gimping proud as he could. Then Fletcher did the same. Blood couldn't see Sally but as he came closer he saw Cooper's mouth was bloodied, his lower lip bloated, seeping a red stain into his thin beard. Fletcher stood hunched to one side, his right arm in a sling that was muddied, mud on his breeches and a daub on one cheek. His eyes red, swollen. There had been a tussle of some sort, grappling over Sally, Blood guessed. And suspected the whole struggle useless—the matter already settled, she had made her choice. The boys eyed his approach silently. He was an interruption they hadn't expected. He liked that. Now he saw Sally seated on a heap of blankets in the back of the tent.

The group was mute, awaiting him. He settled himself on a rock fireside and stretched his hands to warm. He looked at the boys, Fletcher and Cooper. Then he spoke, reasoned and calm, a job with his heart and leg yet hammering from the hike. He was gentle, determined to be that. He spoke to Cooper. "Let me be clear. If you own any regret over shooting me discard it. What you did was right—protecting your brother, Sally, yourself. The three of you. Taking care of your own. It hurts me"—he let amusement slide over his eyes and was serious again— "but I've pride in you."

Cooper said, "I don't care for your pride. But you're right, shooting you was never my intent. I'm not short on anger toward you, but not that sort. There's accounting due but I can't compel you. All I'm after is some answers and giving you the chance. And Sally reports your leg appears to be healing well and I'm glad of that."

Blood thought he might regret it later but wanted the boy down a notch. So he said, "Was it you lurking in the spruce last night?"

Cooper colored. He said, "I wasn't spying you."

Blood nodded, as if this were reasonable. He said, "No."

Cooper said, "I come down determined to talk. But wanted to see if you were alone. It idn't simply a matter of walking in to visit. This whole country is fearsome, and we've pretty much squatted tight. Nobody much knows us and we can't be certain if that's a good thing or not."

Blood nodded again. He was content to give the boy time. "You must've seen Van Landt at least. Are those my horses back there?"

"No," Fletcher spoke up. "They belong to us."

Blood looked at him. The long austere gaze most men broke from. Fletcher did not. Blood said, "Are you going to be the difficult one?"

"No," Fletcher said again. "Not so long as you talk to me as well."

"It was a hard job getting up here. I'm in no hurry to leave. It doesn't appear I chose the best of times but that's no reason to be testy."

Cooper said, "It was your money bought the horses." He shrugged. "I'll give you a note for it—we didn't bring that kind of amount with us. You know I'm good for it."

"Ah yes," said Blood. "I'm sure you are. But let them be my gift. A note'd be useless to me I expect."

Before any could question this he went on. "It was as well you avoided the tavern last evening. I had some troubles. It weren't a great thing but nothing you needed to see."

Cooper nodded, understanding his father would have the confession. "My nerve failed me."

"Is that so?" Blood cocked his head, his tone flat.

"Yes sir." Cooper was angry at being pushed.

Blood sat silent looking off. Then looked at Fletcher and Cooper both, his eyes traveling between them as he spoke. "Time to time, nerves fail a man. That can be a good thing, you recognize it's a gift, to trust that instinct. I'm not talking about lack of courage, but something more rare, almost elegant. You learn to trust your mind, something doesn't feel right, you believe that." Now he looked only at Cooper. "Like I said, I had my own little spot of trouble last evening. Somehow, some part of you knew that. And you did the right thing." And then could not help himself. "Then again, times you're in one place when you ought to be in another."

Fletcher spoke up. "That's clever. I'll keep it in mind. But sometimes, a man runs. And that's all he's doing. It don't even have to be a case of nerves. Just plain failure to face hisself, what he's done. A coward. Those times, running is just running. Although I expect a man of that sort, he'd find a way to dress it up in his mind. He'd have to, to live with hisself. There idn't nobody can run that far."

Blood had been sitting with a hand on each knee, his bad leg stretched flat before the fading fire. The day was warming, the last of the mist lifting from the trees. He'd be happy anyone added wood to the fire but would not ask. Now he let go his grip of his knees and turned his hands over, so they lay open, palms up.

He nodded and still mild-voiced said, "Yes. This is why we're here." He was quiet a moment, aware all three were watching him. He had a bad moment when he wanted to look at Sally. Then he said, "And it may be as far as we go. I'd not blame you, either of you, if you were to be done with me after. Because it's my account you want, isn't it? It's what you came for."

It was quiet. Blood sat in that mute verification. Then said, "There's one question I'd like to ask first. Because I might not get the chance after." He looked from boy to boy.

It was Cooper, as Blood guessed it would be, who answered. He said, "You can ask whatever you want. Just recall that asking doesn't mean you get an answer. There's too many years free of your curiosity to guarantee you courtesy. It depends on the question." And looked at his brother.

Fletcher studied his father. Then nodded. As much as he would give.

Blood thought We'll see how long that lasts. He spoke to Cooper. "We'll address those years you seem to know so much of in a moment. But right now, what I'd like to know is, what's your story?" And was looking at Fletcher. Who opened his mouth but no sound came forth. Then his face closed to clear menace.

Sally came off the blankets then, sudden, moving out to the fire, hands working at her stained clothes. "Wait," she said. "All of you wait just one minute."

All looked at her. A little stunned. Not one had forgotten her, each for his own reason but still she came upon them unexpected. A tension was broken—a pattern of communication barely established abruptly lost and Blood knew she had done this with purpose and was angry. Until that moment he'd felt to be in control of the situation. He was confident he could steer the boys, right down to the very end which he expected to be rightfully hostile, bitter, a finality of all night-dreams and the broken wheel of his soul. He was a man expecting to die within days, although he had not, and would not, simply give over to it. These were his boys and they had come with a purpose and he intended to see that extracted and fulfilled. Intent on maintaining that he was Blood not Bolles because they were his sons and must know what they came from. To cleanse forever what altered version they might have carried north. Not to destroy—he was done with destruction, had in fact made the choice that dreadful summer morning seventeen years before when he quit New Bedford. So to ensure they lived with the full light of knowledge and had that to fashion the rest of their days. Since they sought him, whatever papered or varnished past they believed in would be the cost of truth. Let them become men. Perhaps, he thought, better men.

And now this girl. Knowing enough to guess something of what was being constructed. And not willing to let that happen. Blood knew she had someway already succeeded—the angle was tilted. Sally, thought Blood—angry yes but admiring as well. For this was her advantage: All three held her dear, regardless of the wounds imposed by the simple fact of her existence.

She was out now, a little breathless, still trying to smooth her mostly ruined clothes. Blood spoke up as she was coming but without hope of averting her. He said,

"Sally, join us. You've heard something I imagine of both sides. Now watch them converge and see if truth is born."

She peered at him, pursed and angry. As if she knew his intent. Even if not fully her own, he thought. She said, "You're in fine fettle, Blood. That leg must be healing pretty. But I'm not of a mind to chatter with you." She turned to face the boys, both still holding their original posi-

tions. She said, "I got two things to say. The first is this: You two stop
fretting over who did what to who or why or none of that. Just stop.
You got the rest of time for that but right now you're being more boys
than men. Set down. You come all this way to talk to this man here.
Your father. Who came now to talk to you. So just goddamn stop. Set
down where you're close, all three. Where you can talk. Stop jabbing at
each other." She shot her eyes to Blood and back to the brothers. "You
got to recall all three of you been suffering and I don't mean just this
past week. So set yourselves like decent men. I'm going to get a bucket
from the stream and make a pot of fresh tea. Then I'll stay or go as I
please. But I ain't going to leave you to murder one another. So set
down." And stopped, a halt. As if she'd overstepped. But the brothers
had already turned their heads from her and were looking across at each
other.

Blood cocked his head a little—he'd heard the chime of doubt layered within her seriousness.

"Come set," she said. "Alongside him. So you can all not only see and
hear me, but when I'm done all three can stop peering around one to
the other. It drives me crazy. What I got to say next is simple but not
easy for me. Fletcher."

He looked at her. Cooper had already sat on the fireside log next to
where Blood was on his rock. Fletcher was halfway across to join him
but stopped. Sally just saying his name tightened his mouth to a firm
clamp. He waited, as if he might change his mind about anything or
everything when he heard whatever she was to tell.

"Fletcher," she said. She was struggling, reaching for gentleness without sympathy. "Fletcher. Early on, right after both you and Blood got
hurt, I was down there. To the tavern to collect my things. Blood," she
paused, started again. "Your father wanted to know who you was—"

Blood interrupted. He said, "Go get the water girl. We all could enjoy
some tea." Without pause he turned to Fletcher and said, "All she told
me was your mother's name. It explained things a little but wasn't the
huge betrayal she thinks it is. Come set. I recall your mother well. And
am curious about her certainly. But most curious about you."

Fletcher came and sat, not next to his brother though there was room
on the log. But on a fire-ring stone beyond the log. So the three made a
crescent with Blood at one end.

"Damn you Blood," Sally said but didn't wait or want response. She made for the brook out of sight in the hemlocks.

The three sat silent and watched her go.

Blood said, "Now, could one of you toss some sticks on the fire. I find myself chilled easy these days. I got overheated tramping up here." Without pausing he went right on. "Yes I recall your mother well. Molly. Now one thing, before we go further, I've things to say will surely hurt one or the other of you, sometimes maybe both. There's plenty of pain to go around. But I'll stick as close as I can to simple truth. Remember that."

Fletcher said, "So you recall her."

Blood said, "I been silent with it all so many years. It's a deep hole I've held close and now we get the stories pulled out of it. The last time for me. Which is one more time than I ever expected. Her name was Molly. I'm shamed to admit I never knew her last name but such was the nature of those relations." He paused, his eyes briefly on Cooper, back to Fletcher. "Although she was unlike other girls. My attachment to her itself was unconventional. And that became part of the entire affair for me, a part of my despair, a part of why I removed myself from my family. From all of you. There was of course the greater, final reason, but it was only one of many."

Cooper interrupted, his voice low. "What greater reason?"

"No." said Blood. "I won't talk of her yet. You must understand that. Or I'll never get through the rest of it."

There was question rising in Cooper's eyes but Fletcher spoke. "You're going a little in circles. But you asked who I am and I'll tell you, you stop sidetracking."

"Yes," Blood said. "Circles. But go on."

Fletcher said, "My mother's name was Barrett, Molly Barrett. This is who she was and what happened. As you likely guessed, like many girls end up working in taverns, she was in off a farm from far out near Wareham, determined to put as many miles between them sheep and herself. She never was a common whore—"

Blood said, "I never thought she was, then or now. I knew it well."

Fletcher looked at his father, something between patience and anger. Sally was back, working unobtrusively to set up the tea. Fletcher said, "When you disappeared she heard the story like most all the town. I've got no idea what she first thought but it wasn't long and she realized she wasn't as done with you as she believed. So she turned it over in her mind and went direct to the warehouse office and asked to speak with old Eben Bolles hisself. Perhaps you recall this of her or perhaps you don't but despite her appearance there was a peculiar force about her. People believed her. Not just over me, though I was the big issue at that moment, but all her life, from what I recall and what others more recent have told me."

"Stop," said Blood. "Is she dead? You speak as if she is."

Fletcher studied him a little more. Blood was becoming curious about those silences. What was going on in there. Then realized the girl Molly had been the same. The boy's mother, in the boy. Blood felt a tug, some bit of lost endearment.

Fletcher said, "She spent most of the afternoon alone in his office. It was only recent I learned what took place there, what discussion was had, what agreements made. When she left she was housed with a midwife the next six months until I was born. From there I was taken direct to the home of your brother, Uncle Proctor, who already was caring for Sarah Alice and Cooper along with his own five. It was a household, I can tell you. Cooper and I was the little ones. Sarah Alice babied both of us, without as far as I ever knew, being partial to Cooper or at least not letting us see if she felt that way. She was so much older, we was both barely ready for school when she was gone and married. She tried to keep close but we were boys and like I said, though Uncle Proctor and Aunt Peg were every way kind and loving, Cooper and me, we were our own little tribe in that big group. Although now I think on it, Great-grandfather was part of that tribe too, wouldn't you say Cooper?"

Cooper had sat through all this watching his father. Without looking at his brother he said, "Yes. He's never made a secret of spoiling the both of us a little more than the others. I guess he feels some obligation apart from them. Also, I do believe he takes pleasure in it. In the two of us. He'd cuff me he heard that."

"Wait," said Blood. "Now wait. This is all too much."

Sally was pouring tea. The three sat with Blood's cry left out, mingling down unanswered to reveal the simple bones of anguish beneath. Sally came round, three separate trips with scalding tin cups. Settled herself some way apart, where she could tend the fire and fuss with the tea and hear everything.

Blood put the cup on the stone beside him. Too hot to drink, so many names and faces. He studied both boys a moment and they let him. It was altogether possible they were innocent, had been left purposely uninformed—in fact given their youth, the disparity in ages, it made sense.

So he retreated and began again. "Tell me. Grandfather is still living?"

Cooper said, "Ninety-six this November. Blind as stone and pretends he's deaf but he idn't. Employs a free nigger to lead him from the house—he lives with Proctor and Peg now as well—every day to and from the office. His legs are feeble. Although last winter that boy was sick two weeks and Great-grandfather made the trip each day just fine." Cooper drank tea and set the cup down and said, "He sent you a message but charged me only to deliver it when we was done. Done with you."

Blood had a pretty good idea of what that would be. He remained silent now, waiting. He felt Sally's eyes upon him, guessed she knew what he was up to. Fine with him as long as she only listened. He'd been a fool with her. She felt no debt, no gratitude for him.

Fletcher spoke up. "Unless you've lost interest, I'd tell you the rest of what happened. Not so much to me as my mother."

"Why yes," said Blood. "We got distracted. Please."

Fletcher sat silent, worked a little at his tea. Not so much preparing anything, just not hurried: Molly again. Blood wondered if he should speak of this, if it would please the boy, and decided to wait. See how it turns out. Fletcher said, "I never knew, couldn't find a way to ask without sounding rude, if money was paid her. Although I'm inclined to think Great-grandfather made sure she did not want for anything. Not that she required much. After I was born she returned to Wareham, to her people, the Barretts. Now that I consider, she at least had some help; she had a little house, not much more than a cottage but it was all hers. A couple acres that she planted to garden and kept a cow and chickens. Summertimes she was an oddity, a woman working with the men on the common crops, hay and such. Someone told me she was a fine hand to mow. She never did marry, nor have other children. Though she was approached. But she kept to herself. Again, mostly this is just what I been told."

Blood said, "So he did buy her off. Grandfather Bolles, I mean. Took you in to raise and sent her up back where she'd tried to get away from. That sounds like a clear trade-off to me."

Fletcher shook his head. "No. I mean maybe there was a little but I think mostly it was what both wanted."

Blood glanced at Sally, then back to Fletcher. "Most women want to raise their children. Of course she saw advantage for you but still, the rest sounds like what she most likely had to accept, to get better for you."

Fletcher took time, finished his tea. His tone now dropped a little he said, "No. It wasn't like that. She had the right, anytime she was to New Bedford to come see me. Now that didn't happen often, New Bedford was a fair tramp for her to make. Most often when she did come it was in the fall, when her family brought cartloads of apples, springtime too, after shearing. But mostly I think she had her fill of the place. I think she was uncomfortable, coming to the house."

"Your Aunt Peg could be a formidable woman."

Fletcher looked at him as if he didn't know what Blood was talking about. As if he'd been interrupted. He went on, "The other part was summers. Summers she had me for a month. From after my first birthday until the summer I was nine. When, before I was supposed to go that year I talked to Uncle Proctor. Who talked to Great-grandfather. Who talked to me. It was the only time he ever was angry with me, something terrible. He wanted me to know all my people, not just the Bolleses. But I would not go. I stood there in the little sitting room he had off his bedroom and told him however many times he had me carted out there I'd turn around and walk back. If it was every day all summer long."

Fletcher stopped, as if the story was over. Looking into the mound of coals, the sun striking his shoulders and the back of his head. His tea, cold and forgotten on the stone beside him. With his free hand he rubbed at the bindings over his right forearm as if trying to get to the skin beneath. Blood knew the feeling.

Finally, his own voice lowered, as if meant for Fletcher alone, the best he could do, he said, "She mistreated you?"

His own voice near the same as Blood's, Fletcher said, "No. I was shamed of her. It wasn't a life I wanted any part of. I was too young to understand how strong she was to've done what she did. I was just shamed by her. She knew it, which was why she stopped coming to see me in town. I was a little boy and she was the one part of my life I hated. There was times I was envious of Cooper, envious his mother was dead."

Cooper said, "You never told me that."

Fletcher said, "I knew it was wrong. But I couldn't help myself. So I stopped going. Time to time she'd send me a sweater or socks she'd made me. But they was either too big or too small. Or I just pretended they was. I don't know. I just didn't want em. And then the winter I was twelve she did die. Took to bed sick and only came out to go in the ground. I didn't even go to the funeral."

Then was quiet. After a bit Blood said, "I'm awful sorry."

Cooper stood and said, "Excuse me a minute." And walked off behind the tent, past the horses and into the woods. Sally looked after him but stayed where she was.

Fletcher looked directly now at his father, his eyes hardened. He didn't get that from his mother, thought Blood. Fletcher said, "It's peculiar strange. The last few years, as I've learned the truth about you, how and what you did, I determined never to be anything like that. To be careful, thoughtful. Gentle with whoever I love or come to love." He paused, looked off toward the woods. Then turned back, fiercely went on. "But now, sitting here listening to myself tell you of my mother, it occurs to me I already failed. I see I've got that same ability in me: to turn away cold from someone dear. It's a sad thing. And I can go on, knowing it's there. And try to live my life different. I came thinking I wanted you to know I was in the world. It seemed real important to me. Now I don't know. There's no pride in meeting you."

Grimly, swiftly he stood, teetered for balance and said, "I'm filled with tea myself. Excuse me." And walked off, steps hard and certain, taking a route toward the woods somewhat different than his brother had. To be alone.

Blood did not watch until he was gone from sight but dropped his eyes to the fire and then, feeling Sally watching him, he raised his head and gazed off into some unknown distance. Hoping she would not speak, hoping she would have the grace to leave him alone.

Eventually she said, "How you doing, Blood?" Her tone not the harsh scald he expected—not altogether kindhearted but even: a tone he could respond to or ignore. He was grateful for that.

After a bit, he turned and said, "Mostly strange. I come expecting anger. They've much to be angry over. But it feels all turned around."

She said, "Well. They idn't you, Blood."

"Don't you be so certain," Blood said. "It's likely there's much they don't know, is what I'm thinking."

She said, "But that's why you're here, after all. You can set em right."

Blood gazed upon her, near envious of her understanding of his sons. And then over her shoulder and out past the horses, he saw both boys together. They spoke a short time and came forward. Toward him. There was something in the way they walked—perhaps it was only seeing them together and comprehending the bond and force of the two— but Blood was chilled. He reached down to check his leg but it was cool. He knew he should rise and walk around, that the leg was stiffening. But he only sat and waited. Drew his jacket together. Sally observed him through this and finally glanced over her shoulder.

She said, "Here they come."

And just like that, Blood was ready for them. Of most importance was the growing certainty that whatever they did know of him was arranged, somewhat cleansed, diminished to the role of Man Who Simply Disappeared. Blood felt the hand of his grandfather in this, seeing old Eben from that first morning, keeping the family tight, the story controlled. As the boys grew other questions would certainly have come up but Eben and Proctor and Peg were certainly able to expand the original versions meant for small boys so they seemed reasonable for young men. Of his own father, there was no question—Matthew Bolles had always been in thrall to Eben. Blood in swift clarity determined There are only four things that matter now. To have the full story out, for the boys to make sense of as they would. To learn what he could of Sarah Alice. To receive from Cooper old Eben's message, surely the condemnation Blood had deprived his grandfather of all those years ago by slipping away. And finally, regardless of what it took, whatever anger must be stirred, whatever ruse employed, to compel the boys to leave, the sooner the better, this very day if possible. Even if it meant driving them to a final and unbreakable loathing of him. Whatever that took, even fresh lies, wounds imposed. He would see them leave. He had some tricks left, old dog. Guessing Sally would go with them, at least someways. He couldn't picture her in New Bedford and doubted, when it came down to it that either Cooper or Fletcher would either. But no matter. Let him save her as well.

The country was teeming with gathering madness and it would be senseless to have these three caught in it. As for himself, if he could drive off the children, he still held hope he might slip off as well.

The boys were before the fire now, come to a halt and for the moment drifting. Blood saw this and knew Fletcher had confessed his breaking down. Blood took a breath to launch himself but as he did saw the drift flee Cooper as the boy stepped forward, squatting on his haunches so he was just inches from his father, his face even with the beard something frightening. His mother's eyes. Betsey there furious before Blood. And so it was Blood drifting instead, his thinking broken, fragmented for a frightening moment.

Then Cooper said, "Just so you know, you wasn't ever hidden. Not so much as you might've thought. Every few months, at most a year some feller would come in asking for Great-grandfather. I was probably about twelve when he began to tell me of these reports." In astonishing imitation that seemed to contain portents of what else was to come, Cooper said, "He'd say 'It appears your father has taken to driving swine. Doubtless believing he has found kindred fellowship. Not a thing you should bother your schoolmates with. But one you should know. These bastards, they take delight in delivering such news. And more delight in that I buy their silence. They think it needles me. But your father is intent upon his own mission—a thing I care not to attempt to understand. Take heart, boy. Madness does not run in the family.' That sort of thing. But I got to ask, you were so resolute to forsake us all, why stay where such word was bound to trickle in. Why did you not go off to the western prairies or such? It's a puzzle to me. What thinking was behind it? Was it not enough to forsake us?"

Blood tipped a little. Such misunderstanding. His son, his wife's eyes; did not move; no hand reached to steady him. Just waiting.

Blood said, "Could I trouble one of you for a cup of water? This leg flashes me hot and cold." Immediately regretting mention of the leg, as if for sympathy.

Wordless Fletcher dipped a cup from the bucket and brought it. While Blood drank Fletcher took Cooper's old seat on the log. Cooper had not moved.

Blood said, "There is so much. You boys know a fair bit. But there are pieces more than you've been told. And perhaps others that you know but haven't thought all the way through. I mean no disrespect to either of you but you're young men—the way of things may yet appear clear to you. It seems you're beginning to learn all those shades between simple and complicated on this adventure you set yourselves upon. And there is more to come."

"Father," said Cooper. "Obvious, there's more sides to a story. We came after yours. What we make of it is our business. But you obfuscate. Can you not speak plain? Why did you stay so close?"

Blood said, "Now it seems mean-spirited. The way you phrase it. But I meant no harm. Only to myself."

"How could that be?"

"Think upon it. As you said, I could have gone west. Or south. I could have taken ship to Europe, South America. I had access to such funds. As far as I know that money still lies in my accounts. But I remained in New England. I would not allow myself the luxury of any life but one that reminded me. No. That word lacks sufficient strength for what I was about. Each day I was determined to face myself as I was, as I am. A man capable of the most heinous of actions. Who expected no forgiveness. Not from you or any of the others or even that incredible old silent Lord. But forgiveness from myself. For what is unforgivable, all of it. And there was plenty. Have you considered it from that position, that possibility?"

Cooper was no longer angry but the eyes were still Betsey's. When she was confused and perturbed. Cooper took time, mulling this, then said, "I suppose a man might feel he had no choice but for such self-abuse, and consider it not choice but duty. A man of terrible crimes he somehow escaped but who nevertheless was stricken by them. Is that the sort of thing you mean?"

"Yes."

Cooper nodded, still troubled by this vision. As if a comprehension was opening ever wider to him but could not fit it to the man before him. Finally Cooper went on, "And after you left word came out bit by bit of the other business you were up to. And surely you felt a terrible guilt when Mother and Hazen died. And there's not the least triteness intended when I say you idn't the first man to find himself in such a mess. But few choose to flog themselves naked in the wilderness over it. And there was the other thing, you so easy leaving the children that remained. As if your guilt was more important than Sarah Alice and me. I was just a baby missing my mother. Who my sister did her best to substitute for. But Sarah Alice. She was a young girl, only what—twelve, thirteen. Such a horrible thing to do to her."

Here it is, thought Blood.

Cooper went on. "To leave her at such a time. I can still barely comprehend it. What possessed you to care so little for her? I'll make you angry but I don't care. It was selfishness, pure and simple. From all I heard, all I learned, the most I can figure is flat-out selfish. Nothing grand or noble about it. That's what I see."

Blood was quiet some time. Clearly the truth had been kept from them. How now to proceed, to reveal that monstrosity of himself. He realized at this point they had found him, revealed themselves, and remained mostly untouched. Fletcher had learned an unpleasant aspect of himself but the years would reduce the pain of it, be it a part of him or overcome. But they had won, was what he was thinking. Young men intent on facing the dragon and returning home. And perhaps he should allow that. Rid himself of his perverse pride and let them vanquish him. If nothing else it might serve to get them moving, although again he expected he would need anger for that. And like that the anger was there.

He was on his feet then, hitching himself back a couple of paces to face easily them both. Already with some satisfaction because his coming up near toppled Cooper who caught himself with one hand, remained crouched but guarded now. Good, thought Blood.

Blood said, "Listen now. I'll tell you some truths. Hear me and consider carefully and you'll see there are gaps in what you know—some only I can fill. I will be simple and plain, as you asked. I have no expectation for any form of forgiving. It will be years and families of your own before you may understand. And even then, pray to God, your grasp will only be partial. For some actions can only be fully comprehended by the man who commits them. To know truly their aftermath. Meditate upon that a moment."

His eyes away from both boys he went round to the bucket, filled his cup and drank it down. As he drank he looked at Sally. Her face was composed and she nodded. As if she understood all he was about to undertake. He filled the cup and carried it back, thinking she knew more of him than his sons did.

The short walk was good for his leg. He felt strong.

Cooper had moved to the log so he and Fletcher were side by side. A reflexive defensive reorganization. It suited Blood. He stopped before them. Everything was tactical at this time. Blood had the swift understanding that this was the day of his life. Nudged behind that was the lesser understanding that he might die soon, perhaps this very day. This did nothing but enforce him.

He said, "We begin with the day Cooper's mother and your elder brother died. It was an accident. So I appear free of blame. Except for this—Betsey Marsh was a superb sailor, the storm was standing well off the horizon. So what happened? Something unsettled her, was troubling her, something of sufficient torment to divert her from her usual keen engagement. There was only one thing sufficient to cause that distress. She had lost the affection and attentions of her husband. Of myself. How she learned this was simple—she was a woman of great inner strength and as you pointed out I was hardly the first man with a happy wife and family to take the occasional tumble with a tavern girl. So it was more than that. It was this, a terrible thing: I had grown cold to her. My affection was withheld, at most perfunctory. The simple kindness within a marriage had gone out of me. I believed myself in great crisis of the soul— I could not order things in perspective, attach moral value to my actions— but in fact I was merely selfish. I continued my ways and rebuffed my wife. She never reproached me in even the most cunning of ways. All she did in response was to continue her affection—on the rare occasion requested she always undertook gladly her wifely obligation. She placed my needs and concerns above her own. Which I not only disregarded but became short and ill-tempered with. To the point of shrewd abuse. So ask yourselves, what so distracted her the day she died? It was an accident but I might as well have stove the boat.

"So where was I that afternoon my wife died? You believe it's simple. I was with this boy's mother. With Molly. But I was intoxicated with her. I could not get enough of her and had ceased the usual precautions—let us give them their true name—I no longer skulked as most men do. She overwhelmed my mind, my thinking, as if I had been a boy, one closer to her own age. She was young, younger I believe than either of you be. Consider that. What did she make of this man, old I'm sure in her eyes and married as well? I do not know. For smitten as I was I would know nothing of her, I cared nothing for her thoughts, her hopes, what she wanted in life. In short I treated her as a puppet, a toy for my own use and pleasure. Take that behavior and add it to the damage I was inflicting upon my wife, join the results of my absolute selfishness and you begin to see the monstrosity of myself emerging. One woman to satisfy my lust, the other to keep home and table, but of both I would have nothing beyond. For only thus could I stand apart and not be bothered by the cares and hearts of others.

"Now we come to the final part I suspect you know nothing of. That has been withheld, perhaps not only from you but all others as well. For there is only one other that I can be certain knows and she was not mere sole witness but victim.

"That afternoon when I left Molly the final time I returned to the house in a passing shower, the timid end of a summer storm. And learned that the dinghy was lost, that Betsey and Hazen were missing. By nightfall it was clear they were drowned. Then we had to wait, to see if the tides would deliver them or not. It was three days I believe—it could have been four. I sat mute and motionless throughout that time, not sleeping, nor taking food. I was allowed this because it was believed to be grief. And it was but of a sort peculiar and without honor. I sat in great silent self-pity, that I had brought this to pass, that I had brought this upon myself. I could barely conjure their faces for fear of a wild raving, which I could not allow. For that would have revealed what it was I mourned. Not the death of my wife, the mother of my children, my helpmate and partner in life. And not the boy, his laughter and pleasure and future all lost. But only myself, my life a ruin of my own making.

"And then they were found. A morning tide left them on the stones. I shall be brief to come to the final part. Urged by your sister, I viewed their horrible remains and then deserted the house, unable to assume the duty and responsibility that might have restored me in the eyes of others, perhaps even allowed me a measure toward restoring my own life. Instead I quit. I deliberately took myself into the mean streets of the town and indulged in a gruesome drunkenness, a gin-haze of some days that I descended until all was lost—I was in a blackness that to this day I have no recall of. Except for how and where I returned.

Blood paused. Fletcher was very still, for the moment at least over-whelmed by this version. Cooper was somewhat otherwise, as Blood expected. There was an agitation growing in his eyes, an awareness slowly peaking toward outburst, anger. Blood thought You wait boy—not yet.

So he went on, his tone unchanged, strident, demanding. "Somehow through that blackness of the lost I made my way back to the house. Where I woke to a bright morning. But even as I woke bits of my entrance into the house the night before came back to me, fragments of a wretched lucidity, fragments confirmed by my location. I looked about the room and all was destruction, a final verification. It was then I left.

"When I entered the house that night I discovered your sister. Sarah Alice, who no doubt, on top of all the other duties thrust upon her tender years, had been worrying over my absence, perhaps fearful that I had taken my life in grief or been set upon by the gangs of boys that reigned over most of the port streets at night. But who heard me come in, fumbling, staggering, falling. And crept down in her nightgown to assist me, to offer me help, perhaps even to weep that I was home and safe. And I looked up and saw her on the stairs. At first I thought she was her mother—the resemblance of the two was strong. But by the time I fell upon her, I knew who it was. And still I proceeded. I carried her as she began to fight me, as she realized my intent. Her fists against me as effective as butterflies. I carried her not to my own bed but to hers. She fought me, then, there, hard but briefly. I tore the gown from her and while she whimpered and pleaded, trying to cover herself with a sheet, I destroyed the room. Chairs, her writing desk, chests of drawers, all of it I smashed to kindling. So she would know my capacity for devastation before I visited it upon her. Which I then did. What greater violation can take place between man and woman than it be between father and daughter? There is none. To have outright murdered her would have been less."

Blood said, "That's my account." He was done. All in. But for their response. He drank the last of the water and tossed the cup down.

He took his eyes from the boys, lifted his head. It was late morning, gaining noon. The day had warmed. He was hungry—a thing almost barbarous. The body urges onward, he thought.

Cooper and Fletcher glanced at each other, a silent consultation. Then Cooper spoke, his tone strange, mild. He said, "It's passing strange. I suspect you're right—it will be years before I understand all you just told. However much is truth or not, it's truth to you. I feel a pity. But still, it's passing strange. In the spring, a man came through, one of those I mentioned earlier, to inform you was headed far north, up to the Connecticut Lakes country, the wild country, with a cartload of trade goods. Fletcher and I talked about it. Not only did we know where you was bound, but the sound of it suggested you'd be here some time, most likely long enough to catch up with you. As you can imagine, and it doesn't dispute your account, everyone in the family counseled against it. Some quite strong. There was tears shed in the attempt to dissuade us, even threat of losing positions in the House, being disinherited. But those were from Uncle Proctor and while he meant it in his anger he also knew he didn't have that power. The paperwork's secure and you know who engineered that. So there was considerable opposition to the plan. But for two. Do you care to guess who those two might be?"

Blood was breathless, his chest hammered. He wished he could sit but knew he must remain standing. He would learn what he might and then there was his final job. Blood recognized the easy tone of Cooper's voice. It was his own—the one he would employ to lead a man on. Blood suffered. He said, "No." Shit he sounded feeble. He roused. "I've spoke plain to you. Do the same."

Cooper said, "The first was Great-grandfather. Who encouraged us to go. Who said it was well past time someone hunted you down. Who, I realize just now, is probably the only one knows enough, not just the details but knows life, enough to do the sums and understands, much as can be, how you think. Do you agree?"

Blood was quiet, his teeth set so his jaw ached. He dreaded what was coming. He simply nodded.

Cooper stretched his arms before him, then swung one leg over the other knee and crossed his arms over his chest. Blood watched this transformation as if watching himself. Understanding the boy had concluded the situation was in his hands. Blood waited.

Cooper said, "The other who urged us along was Sarah Alice."

"No," said Blood, his voice drained from him.

"Why yes. When we visited her and told her our plans she was pleased. She wanted us to find you."

"How can that be?" His voice stronger, cautious of the trap.

"Well," Cooper said. "She's well settled. Married to the son of Samuel Phelps. You may recall him—he owns the forges and now a foundry that we do business with. She has children, two little girls. Elizabeth and Susan. You're a grandfather, Father."

"She denies my actions." It was not a question.

"Ah," Cooper considered this. "I could not use those words. She told us another story."

"What other?"

"Of how you went missing. No one could find you. She told how all the relatives tried to console her, both sides of the family, Marshes and Bolleses all but how she could look at them and see their own sorrow and what was worse, pity for her. The pity that she might well be an orphan. All she had was me and I guess that gave her something to cling to, an obligation she could take as her own."

Cooper paused, as if to allow Blood to ponder these events missing from his own account. Blood would not have it. He said, "She has chosen to forget. She has chosen to deny and so to live. Well enough."

"Father."

"What? There is no point disputing with me. Certainly, she would not have revealed the truth to you. Her little brother." He corrected himself. "Her brothers. Setting off to find me."

"Father."

"What?" Blood was recovering, growing angry.

Cooper said, "She invited you to visit. She fears the toll your hard life has taken on you. She hoped to restore you. Even to offer you a home as you grew older."

Blood cried, "No. How could she? To look upon me, even once."

Fletcher said, "I was there, too." His voice almost genial.

Blood could only shake his head.

Cooper said, "Father."

Blood looked at him.

Cooper said, "When word came that you were alive, that you'd taken passage to New York, Great-grandfather thought to check the house. And found it in shambles. Each room disturbed and objects destroyed throughout. But that was all."

Blood stepped forward, closer to his sons.

He said, "What are you telling me? What game are you playing?"

His voice quiet, Cooper said, "None. But that afternoon, after you saw their bodies and ran from the house, when you disappeared before the services, before the burials, when, according to you, you went off on a bad drunk, that very day Aunt Peg and Uncle Proctor took both Sarah Alice and myself to their home. Father, do you hear me?"

Blood gazed upon him.

After a time, not so long perhaps, Cooper gently said, "There was nobody there. The night you went to the house. It was empty. We were already gone."

Blood stood blinking down upon his sons. A strange blurred focus. Cooper dropped his head and took it in his hands. Fletcher continued to study Blood, then looked away as if he could not witness this moment.

Of Blood. Unpinned. A stillness of mind so complete he heard his own heart beat. Then—for the briefest of instants he understood—there was grace bountiful in the world. An illumination golden as the day and more solid than any nightmare, destroying all possible conjures of his mind. He was . . . he was . . . he did not know—soaring? Stretched clean before God—hope purity mercy glimpsed.

Reach?

Then the vertigo—his shell threatened collapse. The temptation to sag to the ground immense. The lost years the idiot stain the wrack of himself—the fragile wheel of his life nothing but waste. A spin of frenzy, drain, loss. Lost, all lost . . .

But. He was quit. Not done. He commanded his body to compose, to settle. End this trembling. He was not done. Work, he commanded again.

He would go on, because he must. And to do this he needed movement. So he did what he always did, which was to address base needs. He turned smoothly from the boys and forced the leg to swing along. He made his way to the cup just tossed down and bent for it, the index finger in the loop of handle all the victory needed, proceeding to the bucket where he drank cups of water, still cool. He realized not that great a time had passed since Sally had brought it from the brook. For once, slowed time was what he needed. Grace?

He moved a few steps away from the fire, away from Sally, closer to the boys. Almost under the hemlocks, the faint shade chosen for the great hump of boulder he could lean against, not sitting but not standing.

Almost at rest. His mind was clearing, there was much before him, with little promise of rest. All he'd learned he'd mull in the days ahead. If there were days ahead.

Perhaps it was his movement, but both Cooper and Fletcher had come to their feet, all three suspended. Blood scrutinized the others: Cooper's face a perfect mask; Fletcher's strained, leaping with passion. While he would not deviate from his path, Blood resolved to offer the boy something, some kind words before this was done. Which in his mind was imminent.

He said, "This country is rupturing. The invasion, the burnings, the arrests of men was only the beginning. For reasons that don't concern you, I feel confident to be an object of retaliation. So. I will leave you presently, return to the tavern and sometime this night, before dawn, I will slip through the backtrails and be gone. I'll take nothing to hinder me and will go afoot. I can go off trails altogether if I feel the need. My travel will be slow but any looking for me will be hindered by absolutely no key as to which way I go.

"As for you three, decamp now. Loosen your horses so they may graze and water while you organize. Travel light. Leave behind the fine gear; take weapons, simple blankets. Do not go south along the river—it's the first place any would look. You'll do as you choose I know but let the old man betray a whisker of wisdom. Go west into Vermont or better northwest into Canada and travel one day farther than you think you need before coming back into the States. Then go south. If you're intent on New Bedford ride in New York until you can cross into Massachusetts. Go now. Riding in daylight, rough and fast, you'll be near safe by nightfall. And you're young. Ride on through the night."

He was done. But for one question and farewell. He paused, knowing he had to.

He'd expected Cooper but it was Fletcher. He was direct. "Ride with us. There is nothing at the tavern you need. We have arms enough. The girl can double-up."

"No." Blood said. "You have horses so you can go swift. But horses require roads. The three of you, if you were to be questioned, could make the argument you were saving the girl from me. Make up a story—you've done it before. But even if I wanted, my leg would not stand the pounding horses deliver. I'm best alone in the woods."

Swiftly he stepped to Fletcher. He reached and touched the boy's cheek. He said, "I'm proud to have met you. Perhaps, some years from now, you'll see me again. I'm well pleased that, to use your words, you are in this world, Fletcher Bolles." And before the boy could respond, Blood stepped back a little and reached again, this time the boy's good shoulder and gave a small shove. "Get out there now. Loosen those horses. Go."

Blood turned from him to Cooper. Blood went close but did not touch him. He said, "You had a message for me, you said. From Great-grandfather. I'd know it now."

Cooper stood a moment, then shook his head. "I won't leave you with that."

Blood said, "Recall. I know the man well. I expect no words of sympathy or affection. In fact would not believe them. But you return to New Bedford and he asks, you won't be able to lie."

Cooper pondered this. Blood waited. The horses were out free and Blood scanned them. Horses well up to the job. It was time to leave these boys. With the girl. He looked back to Cooper and saw his son was ready.

Cooper said, "He said to tell you, were you to return to New Bedford, he'd strangle you with his own hands. If it was his last act." He dropped his gaze.

Blood was silent. No matter the statement was close to what he expected—the old man had long since comprehended the waste of Blood's life, an unforgivable transgression.

So Blood said the only thing he could. "When you see him tell him perhaps I'll visit his grave."

Blood was swift. He took the boy's hand, clasped hard with his own, then set him free. Blood swung away, caught up his goad where it rested and struck for the trail.

Behind him he heard Cooper call out. "Father."

Blood went on.

"Micajah Bolles."

Blood turned. Cooper silent, raised one hand palm out. A salute and farewell at once.

Blood returned the gesture. As he did he saw Sally looking after him, her face hurt that he had nothing for her. But he could not. So Blood

trudged hard away from them, not looking back. Engrossed now with
the moist dangerous rock-and-moss descent.

The three at the camp engaged in brief dispute over departing, with no
conclusion beyond Sally threatening to saddle her horse and ride out
then and there. Cooper damped her fast; the decision did not rest with
her. So she walked away from them out into the marsh to one of the far
pools where in the pure afternoon light she undressed and swiftly waded
into the water to wash herself. Both boys watched as she sank into the
water, out of sight as the marsh grass hid her. After a long moment of
silence Fletcher finally turned to his brother and said, "He made it clear
he didn't want us in it. That he wants us gone."

Cooper said, "What he wants is not what matters. What matters is
what we do."

Fletcher said, "I suppose." He paused, glanced toward the invisible
pool and looked back at his bother. "Goddamn it, Cooper," he said.

Cooper said. "It was your own heart that hurt you. Not me."

Fletcher looked at him and said, "Well. Easy for you to see it that
way." He said, "But Cooper. What he thought all these years. What a
thing to live inside a man."

Cooper nodded silent agreement. Then he said, "Sarah Alice must
never know."

"We can tell the story such that it won't be a lie."

"Yes. It's what we leave out." Cooper paused and went on. "It's the
same with Father now—it's not what he wants that's important. How
we proceed, is what we'll live with."

Fletcher was quiet a long time. Then he said, "To never wonder if
he got out as he planned."

"That's right. To know one way or another."

They stood like that, each sagged with the exhaustive night and day
fallen fully upon them. For all their differences, both stood together. As
they always had.

After a time Fletcher looked again to the marsh, Cooper following
his gaze. Sally was lying on the bank of the pool, drying in the warmth.
Distance the only discretion she appeared to need or desire.

Fletcher said, "We best have a plan before she gets here."

Cooper said, "Sally won't like it. But we get ourselves ready and set tight for the night, first light we can scout quiet to see if he got off. Or if we got to help. Nothing would please me more than finding that tavern empty. But I got to see it with my own eyes."

Fletcher nodded. All the agreement needed.

Blood was in a bad way. At the moment his wounded leg had the upper hand. Several times going down the trail he had to stop and sit perched on a boulder or fallen log, his leg stretched straight before him and his upper body slumped forward over it, his hands tight to the goad to keep himself upright. When he walked the leg felt mushy and when he sat the pain was liquid throughout him, as a radius general and indistinct from the leg. As if it had held up long enough and now was demanding his attention. Blood not altogether unhappy with this—it concentrated his mind. That stumblebum brain. Straight ahead he told himself.

When he finally left the torture of the brook trail he moved easier, the track beside Perry Stream more traveled, broader. The sun was overhead and the air even through the overgrowth of boughs and limbs was becoming softer to presage a mellow early autumn afternoon. This combination bolstered him sufficient so when next he stopped he waited until the worst of the spasms passed, then working slowly got his boots and breeches off and crept down the stream bank to sit waist-deep in the water. There were frills of ice along the edge and capping river rocks but the water was a soothing shock. Cold enough to stiffen his muscles if he stayed too long, it neatly and effectively took the pain away, swirling it off downstream. Where it might coil some moments around the unlucky greedy Gandy. A river of the dead, Blood thought. But I won't be one of them. He scrabbled up the bank and got his breeches on. Cold and numb from the waist down, he chose to walk barefoot, carrying the boots.

Once out on the main road before the tavern he paused. In the damp-packed surface of the road ran a set of tracks, the broad furrows of heavy wagon wheels, the matched steps of heavy horses, the shod hooves leaving depressions twice the size of his spread hand. For the second time in as many days he worked his way in the roadside brush until he could spy the stout freight wagon with bare hoops pulled up before the mill. Men were moving about, around the wagon. He recognized them as the ones taken by the New Hampshire militia. They began to drift off, in pairs and groups, some assisting others, most upright but moving with the slowed gait of men sore and used. Blood retreated down the road.

At the tavern he cut an entire haunch from Gandy's bear and, inside with the door barred, worked some time to get a fire built up, the haunch seeping blood onto the table. He needed a strong bank of coals to roast the meat properly and he intended to do that, thinking he would eat from it for a couple of days. He needed to eat, and he'd need to carry food with him. He set a pot of potatoes to boil over the high fire. Also the kettle as he removed the cloth from his wound and cut strips for new bandage. It might be the last clean dressing for several days.

All this activity undertaken with the blurred erratic energy of a man imitating one going neatly about the business of survival. His mind overcome with the great truth just learned. He was unclear what it meant—save for the vast mess of waste behind him. That contemplation was for another day. Time to time the temptation to sit slumped or lie down was almost overpowering and the man that worked to save himself was a man unsure just who that self was—this a deadly stupor and he knew it. So on he trudged. He craved rum and would not allow it.

By late afternoon he was turning the spitted bear haunch every half hour over the coals and the grease from the meat each time he turned it bathed the meat in a caul of sheen that ran down and spatted angry bursts in the coals. The smell of the roasting meat reassurance of strengthening to come.

He stood in the open door while Emil Chase drove the freight wagon past, loaded mostly with family and what few household items they had been able to rescue. The wagon now with a canvas cover stretched over the bowed uprights. Chase and his wife and eldest girl sat on the open seat and not one of them so much as glanced over to where he stood. Blood watched them go down the road. Headed he did not know where nor care. Most likely the western prairies. Blood guessed the deed to the mill had been signed over to Hutchinson, not as bond but as outright purchase of freedom. At the back of the wagon a young girl of five or six leaned peering over the backboard and she waved at him. Blood lifted his hand. Behind the wagon a milk cow trotted at the end of her tether, her udder swinging side to side. Not his cow—not that he cared.

There was a fresh load of angry men in the country. And he knew Mose Hutchinson was not done with him. From the look of the men off the wagon it seemed probable it would be a few days before they grouped enough. And Blood did not care for that slender margin—those same men might be tired and worn and have great cares and undertakings ahead of them. But they had spent a week confined as well as the long rough ride home. Plenty of time for plans and schemes. Blood thought I'm weary of all this. Indeed. The hour was upon him.

There she was. The grime and anger all washed away in her slow floating paddling around the clear-tea water of the pool—she could not swim but the water wasn't deep and she had no panic of it—using her hands to scrub herself in slow motions, the motions softened by the water and exactly what she thought a lover's hands should feel like although none had yet, but in that time it seemed her body was in a place it belonged. Her anger had frothed high and then worked itself off into the water as if her hands pushed it clear. Now she lay out in the sun with only mild regret and a sensation of near sadness.

Regret that she'd been so swift to leave the camp as to not think to bring clean clothing for after bathing—those she lay atop she was done with. It wasn't even a question of washing out the grass and mud stains. They would be left here. And so her return to the camp and the boys would be brazenly naked.

Anger, she thought was like so many things. Once spent, the hollowness was revealed. Let them ride out in the morning. One more night in the camp might not be such a bad thing. A chance, before they left, to make clear she was no prize. That she belonged to no one. If they—if Cooper did not like that, better he know now than a day out on the road. She'd be honest. And let them see Blood was safely gone. If by chance she and Cooper stuck, she'd not have that between them.

Thinking of Blood. The terrible mistake of his years of misbelief. His choice to run, to not stay and face his deeds, real or not. And so the relentless punishment of himself. It was some mystery that led a person from one fate to another. How easy it would've been for Blood to have chosen some other girl to bring north. How easy for her to still be in Portland. She owed Blood, always would.

Then came a thought. Cunning in its simplicity. It had been more than a week since she'd fucked for money. She couldn't recall who it had been and made no effort, wanted no face to be the last. But she was done. She didn't know what would happen next in life, couldn't and wouldn't predict. But she knew this. She was done whoring. If it came to it she could work honest in a public house. She'd learned to garden; there were worse things than being a hired girl on a farm somewhere. But even these things she considered remote—she could go where she would and three things were true—she was not destitute and she was a little more than pretty. And she had wits. Yes. Blood had taught her some of this but most she learned on her own. Because of those wits, she could thrive and she knew it. And she was not a whore.

So. Blood's tale was sad but not horrible.

Sally sat up now. The early autumn sun was dropping behind the trees and the air was cooling. She was determined to remain alone as long as she could. She did not want to hear whatever Cooper and Fletcher were discussing. She did not want to talk over the events of the day. And if all three chose silence, she preferred to take hers here, alone.

She wondered how Blood was proceeding. What he had made of the day. She truly hoped he was underway. She wondered over his mind.

She wondered if he realized he was only a coward. Nothing more. The coward who ran.

Sometime later she plucked her way through the marsh back to the fire. The brothers were cleaning weapons. Both looked up as she came in and wordless watched her dress in her best clothes. The fire was dying.

Cooper spoke briefly. They would leave before dawn. But once certain Blood was gone, they would backtrack up Perry Stream—where best they knew Van Landt had the only remaining farm, the others burned—and from there over the crude untraveled trails to Canada. No one there would question their leaving such a place behind. Following Sally, the boys dressed in their fine clothes to travel, to appear distinct from the inhabitants of the territory. Unfortunate travelers making their way from an ugly place.

The horses stood saddled. The gear and arms in three separate piles.

Sally said, "We need sleep." And went for the last time into the tent and still dressed knelt and smoothed out the layers of blankets, then turned back a corner and slid in. Waiting for no one she closed her eyes.

Eight

෴

Sometime after midnight Isaac Cole came at a tired trot down the road along Perry Stream. Only baleful starlight through the trees but the road was clear and firmed again with the night cold and the footing was good. This roundtrip for nothing—Van Landt not only refused to join with him but didn't even have a horse to sell. Or so he claimed. That was all right. Cole saw opportunity a-plenty.

When he came out on the road by the river he turned north and went on, past the dark tavern that he watched for his full passage and here his heat increased slightly and his pace also as if the sight fueled him. Then came abreast of the mill, dark with the doors shut tight. The miller had purchased freedom for the men but at great cost to himself. Cole was grateful but did not regret Emil Chase's leaving. Isaac Cole and the miller's brother Peter now the senior men. Whoever was sent to operate the mill would soon learn that. For by the time that man arrived, whoever Mose Hutchinson found willing to take on the hazards of the mill and the people, there would be a lesson and example in place. One that no newcomer would take lightly.

He passed the frost-burnt garden piece beside the heap of charred timbers that had once been his home, bits of rail fence still standing, black bars against the frost-whitened ground lit pale in the night. Each rail of which he'd split himself on some other innocent day. Even after ten days and the alternating wet and dry weather there still came the faint smell of burnt home, of clothing, of goods, of livestock slaughtered in the barn and their carcasses left to burn with the barn and the remains rot slow with the freeze and thaw. Then he was beyond it and running harder now. He'd been traveling three hours this night but despite the failure with the Dutchman he was not tired but exhilarated. He was going toward a group of men waiting his leadership. He swung north with the curve of road along the lake and saw a light burning in a window, the light dim, a single candle-lantern with the shutter closed upon it. He already anticipated the heat of the room, the cloister of men.

Isaac Cole slowed to a walk and opened his blouse buttons to the night air. He wanted to go in cool. Not drenched in sudden sweat. For the measure of ten paces he allowed himself to smile. Somewhere on the high country beyond the lake a fox barked. Cole slowed even more and by the time he paused before his single rap on the door he was ferocious.

In the firelight Blood dressed the wound a final time. There was still an ooze but the fluid was clear and the rind around the wound seemed less bright, less angry. Once done he discarded the split-leg breeches and slowly worked his legs into his one pair of loose-legged trousers. Sagging on him. He'd lost weight since he last wore them. He sliced from the bear haunch and ate his fill. Seared and pink at the bone. He cut the remaining meat in great slices and piled them on a scrap of paper and tied it up with string. That meat and the money—the paper money of greatest value—that he would carry with him, he wrapped tight in a blanket that he made into a slender roll to sling over a shoulder and bind with a thong from that shoulder to the opposite hip. The least encumbrance on his back. From the storeroom he loaded pouches with powder and balls; the rifle and horse pistols took the same caliber. He filled a third pouch with wadding and caps. That pouch did not sling but was looped to fit his belt so it would be tight against his side. When he was done he locked the storeroom but left the money chest on the table and laid the two keys atop it. He sat at the table and whetted his belt knife until he could slice hair from his arm with the edge. Late in the evening he pulled close to the fire and fed the lesser banknotes into it. Left the stack of promissory notes on the table for whoever might find them. A pale reminder of what was owed him, of what he'd provided.

Around midnight he let himself slowly out into the yard. The door left ajar. With a pistol shoved in his belt he carried the chest of remaining coins. His teeth gripped the set of keys. When he was satisfied he was alone he stumped to the road and onto the bridge. He opened the chest and poured forth the stream of coin. They dropped invisible into the night, dull nuggets signifying nothing. A spatter against the current. One coin turned falling and caught the briefest slash of starlight. He locked the empty chest and dropped it also. It was heavy but had a tight seal and so would float. He watched it twist away downstream out of sight. When it was gone from sight he spat out the two keys. They so slight he didn't even hear them strike the water.

Back in the tavern he barred the door. Emptied the pistols and rifle and swabbed the bores clean and reloaded and charged all three pieces. Then he stood in the faint light from the dying fire and equipped himself: blanket roll, pouches, pistols stuck through his belt, rifle in one hand and goad in the other. It was a load but not so much he couldn't manage. And he saw himself, two three days out, toughening, walking, his legs learned their pace. In a sense, he was already gone. It was an old feeling. Twelve hours—four sleeping, eight walking—and he could trust his luck.

He piled his equipage on the table in neat order but remained fully clothed. Even down to his boots. He took off only his coat, folded and laid alongside the rest on the table. Then went into the girl's room. He had no regret she was gone. Better she was where she was. He thought briefly of the three hundred dollars in gold she'd taken from him and in a way was proud of her. And the children had the horses.

The room was warm from being shut tight through the day and he eased himself to the far wall and quietly let down the narrow shutter from the opening. The thickness of one log, too high and narrow to admit anyone but a child. He needed the cool air. He was warm and feared it might be fever but felt too sharp, too quick for that. It was just hot air captured in a tight building.

He sat on the edge of the bed, atop the bearskin covering. And for the first time all day he felt of a piece. His leg felt sturdy, his mind clear. It had been a day of inflicted trauma—he'd known that starting out. And then the blow of revelation. Looking back he now thought it a wonder he'd made it through the rest of the day to reach this point. Not a matter of pride but simple fact. He began to consider how his life could have been and stopped himself. He was changed, and in the weeks and months and years to come he'd have ample opportunity to examine the past. Or not. There was no repair to be done.

The brief revelatory moment at the marsh returned. Detailed. His burden was gone. If the golden glow of redemption was more faint, less blinding, it was replaced with something more lasting. His future was open to him. There was a stirring, some faint notion and for a moment he held his breath, half expecting it to shrivel away. But instead it came full-blown as a series of scenes—a plan. He would retreat the very way he'd come, back the rough trail to the Dead Diamond River and on then to Maine. Where he would take ship to Boston. From there he would write his bank in New Bedford for a letter of credit upon his accounts. And then somewhere away. Someplace warm, he thought. Where a man would not suffer the damp cold, rain or snow. Perhaps Savannah, which he'd heard was a city of refinement and comfort. Or perhaps even further, warmer. New Orleans. He had the means to set himself up well. Modestly, to begin, as a newcomer ought. But with a level of comfort new to a man of his age and hard years. He would rejuvenate. He imagined himself in a white suit of some fine light cloth, a small knobbed walking stick. He would learn the dialect of French spoken there. He would slowly visit the churches of the city and see which denomination struck him as right—a process he contemplated with satisfaction. He would read newspapers, obtain books. And in time, he would write letters. To Cooper. To Fletcher. But first to Sarah Alice. A long letter he already knew. Pages, a packet of pages on good paper. The letter of his life.

And he would reclaim his name. Not yet. Not this night. But when he reached Portland. He would leave Blood there. He would be simply Bolles. Micajah Bolles.

He paused then. And there came again the lambent grace and glory of redemption and he saw that it would be so.

He swung himself onto the bearskin and stretched out, not sure he would or should sleep. His brain felt hot with motion. He saw himself out in the autumn woods, moving. He needed some brief rest. It had been the longest day. But he was restless, ready and eager and considered rising, hiking into the night a few hours and halting for a catnap then. It was the right thing to do. He lay a moment loath to leave the softness, the comfort. Then he slept hard.

*   *   *

Sally woke to a cramp in her leg, that ran from balled toes up into a knot in her thigh. She jerked upward and saw Fletcher sitting out by the fire, Cooper sleeping against her side. She worked her hands hard on her thigh and crimped and loosened her toes until the spasm passed. When she lay back again, Cooper, his mouth close against her shoulder, said, "You all right?"

For answer she reached and touched him, her hand falling against his bare stomach. She felt his shiver under her touch and she held her hand there a moment longer and took it away. She whispered, "No."

"What can I do?"

"Nothing."

He sighed and lifted the arm that was next to her and did not touch her face but let his hand cup lightly over her hair, his fingers just resting there. Then took the hand away.

They lay silent side by side.

Out on the rock Fletcher sat, barechested against the frost, the straps of bandage over and around his chest and shoulders. His free hand held their single pistol, a gift from their Great-grandfather that until this night had been wrapped in oiled cloth in a pack-basket, a beautiful thing of polished walnut and brass fittings. Not truly a tool of the woods. He had his legs crossed at the knee, the pistol loose atop the knee, his hand easy but for a slight motion of the barrel indicating he covered the hemisphere of darkness before him. Behind the tent the horses shifted and settled one against the other, sleeping upright. They the best measure of peace available.

Cooper turned to Sally and rose up silent on his elbow and leaned to look down at her. Their eyes open to each other. He said nothing. Just looking. Then sagged enough to kiss her forehead. Her eyes lost him a moment as he did this and then found him again as he lifted away from her. Then without speaking he slipped from the blanket covers and walked out to his brother.

"Fletcher," he warned low.

Fletcher didn't move at all, still peering into the dark beyond the near-dead fire. He said, "I heard you coming."

"It's time to trade."

"I heard you wake up."

Cooper stood behind his brother. He said, "I knew you did." He moved forward and lifted the pistol and said, "You got to sleep some."

"I can't."

"I slept a little," Cooper admitted. "It idn't easy. But, even if you just lay down, rest yourself some, you'll be happy for it come morning."

They were quiet a time. The one still seated, the other standing. Finally Cooper said, "What I'm going to do. Is walk out and pee. I come back, I want to see you stretched out under the blankets. You hear me."

Fletcher gazed into the fire.

Cooper stepped past his brother into the dark. Then he turned back and was facing into the tent. Sally could see his face. He wasn't looking at her. He reached his free hand and placed it on his brother's good shoulder. He stood silent like that. Sally lay watching, privileged. It was a passage of time all three took part in, each connected and each alone. Then Cooper took his hand away and went out into the night. Fletcher sat a time and then swung around on the stone to face into the tent. He saw she was awake and turned away to study the dark night briefly before looking back at her.

"You want me in there?"

She nodded. And then was unsure if he could see or read such a trifling gesture in the dark. "Yes," she said. "I surely do."

He looked away again into the night and then in a rough hard hitch came up from his rock and paused for balance. Stretching his legs on tiptoe and shifting his lower back side to side. Then came in toward her. He was barefoot, just in breeches and bandages. As he came she reached and opened the blankets for him.

Men, alone or in small groups, melted along the trails. Oft going tree-shadow to tree-shadow. Watching the moon caught in the eastern tree-tops. Those with horses walked ahead, leading their mounts, a single hand draped behind to clutch tight the reins below the bit to keep the horse from surging. In such silence as the slippery wet frost-thickened land would allow. All in convergence.

*   *   *

It was still full dark when Blood awoke. Sudden. From deep sleep to blunt swift clarity. He lay alert not moving for a moment. Impossible to know if he'd been asleep for hours or twenty minutes. Then from the woods beyond the back of the tavern came a single note of a thrush, warning the night. He rose slow, stiff, and groped for the goad left against the wall, found it and supported himself. The day loomed, less a promise than the night before and he told himself this was just waking—some movement to limber him and some tea and he'd be in as fine a mettle as could be hoped. Just thinking this improved him so he made his way to the hearth, stirred the fire for hot coals and tipped split wood onto the mound. He pulled the crane out and peered at the kettle where only a skim of water rested on the bottom. He turned to the table and took up the bucket and it too was empty. So skip the tea or haul water? It wasn't even a question—the fire was up and a stomach of hot tea would carry him farther than one empty.

He took up the bucket and goad and at the door had his hand on the bar when he paused and set the bucket on the floor, returned to the table and slid one of the horse pistols through the belt of his trousers. Back to the bucket and door. He took the bar away and stepped out.

It was lightening, a rare morning, cool but clear and lacking the usual fog from the lake. It would be a fine day. He went across the hard ridges of mud-frozen yard to the stream and let himself down the bank to kneel with his bad leg stretched and filled the bucket. Back up the bank to level ground and paused to steady himself, the weight of the bucket pulling at his left side. The oxen in the barn heard him and crooned for him and he reminded himself to go cut them free before he left. Again, almost a portent, he missed the dog.

A half-dozen men came like wraiths from the clump of sumac and alder and fanned before him, all armed, gray in the dawn. He did not pause to learn faces or consider speech but underhanded threw the bucket which sent an arch of river water over two of the men, a silver thing almost solid in the dim light, the bucket striking hard the stomach of a third as Blood drew out the pistol and shot one of the men closest. The impact broke open his chest and brilliant crimson blood spattered the air as the man went down. Blood already moving forward, his legs both working as he gripped the goad a third of the way down and jabbed hard a face, then swung it sideways to crack ribs and jabbed up again, knocking away a rifle. There was one man dead and two down and others scrambling. A rifle was fired and he heard the peculiar extraordinary suck of air as the ball passed his head. He ducked and came up with the goad and struck again and again, holding it now by the end and swinging it as a flail. He was frenzied and the oxen in their stalls were bellowing. Then he realized it was himself bellowing. The men remaining before him fell away, feinting toward the goad but backing away. He lunged and struck once more and saw a split open across a man's face and then Blood turned and ran. Ran still bellowing across the yard and made the door and did not shut it but on hard for the table, grabbed up the other pistol and turned to face the door behind him. It was empty.

He advanced slowly, going around the table along the wall toward the door by degrees and the yard revealed itself. He could see two men down, the one shot and one of the others he'd struck. A couple of men leaned over them. When he appeared in the doorway a rifle went off and he dodged back but heard the bullet strike the log wall outside the door. He stepped back into the door and sighted the horse pistol at the two men over their comrades. He fired and heard a yelp and again a rifle fired. He stepped back and kicked the door shut and got the bar up.

He was panting and his lungs ached and there was powder burn under one eye but his leg didn't hurt at all. He went to the table and recharged both pistols. Then stood thinking. That last rifle fired, that had not been either of the men still standing. Or the shot before that. It could be the other two or three but them he imagined back in the bushes. He'd caused some harm with the goad. What it was, he decided, was more than what he saw. More men beyond that initial handful. And clear as sight he saw more on the way.

His first thought was he'd missed it. That yesterday he should've loaded himself before going up the trail to the marsh to warn the children. And gone from there in the last golden light of day off into the woods where all he needed was the sun or stars to lead him.

Aloud he said, "Fuck these bastards. Let em come." There was not a man among them equal to him on his worst day. Blood was far from his worst day. He left his loaded weapons on the table and went to the tavern and cursed the locked storeroom and the lost-forever keys but worked the fullest of the hogsheads from the counter and rolled it across the floor and through the doorway where he bent and heaved to push it upright and press against the door—a barricade of weight against the bar already in place.

He pulled the ladder to his loft away from the wall and went up to push back the trap door and back down for his long rifle and the horse pistols and the pouches of powder and shot. Working without hurry but steady, focused. He wanted everything laid out beside him. He built up the fire so the heat would rise and warm the loft. Last thing he took the kettle and filled it with coals so he would have fire to light the match-fuses for the small cannon. If he needed it. He doubted he would. It was the only way to think.

In the loft he stretched on the floor and listened. His leg throbbing now, a bright cry of his body to keep him fully alert. He wouldn't open the gunport until he had to. Until he did, no one outside would know where he was. So he sat listening to the wrinkle of the stream and the fluting birdsong of morning. Beyond that, under it, he heard the lilt and tilt of voices. Once the bristled cry of a horse greeting another and the curse and slap of a man stilling the horse. Blood grinned. He thought You out there. You're already out of surprise.

At the marsh they were up and moving about to break camp and load the horses when they heard the gunfire, clear as if it were at the edge of the marsh in the unmoving morning air. A smattering of barrage, then silence then three final shots, spaced evenly each a breath apart. All three looked to the others, halted in their tasks.

"That was right down to the stream," Fletcher said.

"No," Cooper said. "That was to the tavern."

Sally said, "Oh. No."

Both boys looked at her, not speaking what each thought.

Cooper said, "All right. What we got to do. Is keep right on. Make sure everything is packed tight just how we want it. The last thing we need is to tear off down there and have something come loose or forget where something is."

"I'm ready," said Fletcher.

Cooper turned to him. "Well good for you. Now you can just double-check yourself and we'll all be set."

Sally said, "I'm most ready also."

Fletcher said, "I'm riding down there." He turned and caught up the reins of his horse and turned his back to mount when Cooper took him by the shoulder. Fletcher turned.

Cooper said, "You given any thoughts to how a one-armed boy'll ride in to whatever it is and be much good?"

Fletcher stood silent.

Cooper nodded. He said, "Just check your rigging one last time. Make sure your knots is tight. Let that horse get the wind from his belly and I'll cinch that saddle one more notch. All right?"

"All right."

Cooper turned so he addressed Fletcher and Sally at once. "We got three guns between us. I figure we ride down close by, then Fletcher and I'll ride ahead and scout it. We got no idear however many men there is. If Father's dead they'll all be congregated at the tavern I expect. But if he idn't, men could be strung out a ways. So each one of us gets a gun. I'll take a long rifle since I can ride and shoot and load at the same time. That fancy pistol will do Fletcher more good than a long gun." He looked at Sally. "You can handle a rifle?"

"Blood showed me. But I ain't about to set back hiding while you fellers ride in."

Cooper said, "You're looking at it wrong. We ain't planning to hide you out. Just you set up the road a piece and let us see what's there. If Fletcher and me run into trouble, we're heading right back up that road. Where you'll be waiting. "

She turned and finished tightening her bundle on the cantle. Then without looking swung up onto the bay. She reined the horse in a sharp circle to calm it and brought it up short. "I don't like it," she said. "But there idn't time to argue it." Cooper studied her a pause as if she complied too easily. She met that gaze. He handed up the rifle and the pouches.

Fletcher mounted also. Once up he said, "Pass me the pistol."

Cooper took up the pistol, checked the charge and handed it to Fletcher. Who said, "Pass me up the axe too. I want it."

Cooper looked at him. "How do you expect to carry it?"

"That's my business."

Cooper took the axe from where it leaned against a young beech and handed it up. Fletcher took the pistol for a moment between his teeth and used his free hand to rein tight the horse and transferred the reins to his bound-up hand, wrapping them hard and knotting them onto his wrist. So he could guide the horse no-handed. He took the axe by the heft under the head and gripped it in the same hand as held the reins. So the long handle rode down along his right leg and the bit of the axe was riding on the knuckles of his right hand. Where he could get it easy with his left hand. He reached up and took the pistol from his mouth and said, "I got every intention of being a warrior if it's called for." His face grim.

Cooper then mounted his own horse and took a last look about the camp. He held the long rifle across his chest, crooked in the elbow of his reining hand. He turned to the others and said, "We ride down slow and look sharp all the way. Nobody hurries. All right?"

Sally said, "Let's go."

Fletcher said, "You lead us brother. Set the pace."

It was quiet in the loft. Less quiet outside. Blood straining hard to hear. From time to time he heard a murmur of exchange, once the splash and curse of a man misstepping a rock in the stream, the ring of metal as a rifle barrel struck another, even the slithery wet swipe of a ramrod driving home a charge. The muffled snorts of horses and the creak of leather as a man stepped either off or onto a horse. He was far from alone but the men outside, impossible to number, had at least one dead and some wounded to consider. However many there were of them, Blood imagined they considered the tavern a considerable daunt. Briefly he worried they'd consider fire and then ruled it out—they were men after all and their grudge against him would be measured hard against greed for his stores. So far he considered himself in the superior position.

After a time he heard bootsteps breaking in the softening mud of the warming day as they crossed the yard: one man. Blood lay without moving.

Below he heard the man heave against the door.

Knock, Blood thought, and smiled.

The man pounded on the door.

Again in his head Blood said I'll be right there. You fucking idiot.

The man called out. Blood's name, twice. Blood thought he knew the voice.

More silence.

Blood thought Pick your words.

After a bit the man cried, a tone both defiant and solicitous, "All we're after is talk, Blood. There idn't a one of us that don't mistrust you but you know us all. Blood, we want to hear your side of things. We come first thing in the morning because we was afeard of just this sort of misunderstanding. Now you killed one man already and grievous wounded two more. It all adds against you but we been talking and we can see how from your view it looked like mischief of the worst sort. But all we're after right this moment is talk. Talk. Blood? You hear me? Blood?"

It was Isaac Cole. Damn it thought Blood. If it'd been him I blew open this morning all the rest of those peckerheads would've scampered. Cole hiding back in the bushes to see if they could take me. Some fearsome leader. Blood grinned again. And remained silent.

Below he could hear Cole stamping back and forth by the door. Someone across the yard called something he couldn't make out and Cole answered only with a grunt. Then it was quiet. A short time passed that was near peaceful. If only Isaac Cole would get the hell off his doorstep it would be so.

Then Cole pounded again on the door. "Blood," he called. "Blood? You wounded? You need help? Make the least noise and I'll call up men and we'll axe-in the door and tend you. Blood? You hear me?"

Well, he didn't want that. Blood took up his belt knife laid on the floorboards before him. Above were strung a pair of stout leather thongs that ran to the gunport-shutter that opened at the front of the tavern. Lifting the knife he brought the edge against the tethers that held the shutter closed. The leather was taut and dried from the summer heat. The blade went through and the shutter collapsed down in a brilliant clap of report. Blood could see a group of men gathered out at the stream-edge, more than he'd hoped for but less then he'd feared. All recoiled against the sound from the house. He liked that moment, when all ducked or cowed and one even broke for the meager cover of the streambank. From here he could see it all. But for the man before his door.

He called out, "Cole!"

Nothing.

He cried again. "Cole. If you stand where you are you're safe. If you walk away I swear to God I'll put a hole through you could pass a fist. You hear me?"

Blood saw the group of men coming together now, swiveling one and all to watch. Some brought their rifles up against their chests. They didn't worry him. Shooting from where they were at the narrow opening their shots would angle high over where he lay and pass through the shingles. If it rained he'd be uncomfortable and that was about it.

He waited. He couldn't hear but could sense the man below him, suddenly pinned against the side of the tavern. Likely worrying that Blood could work his way forward and reach to touch the top of his skull with the muzzle end of a weapon.

Cole said, "You're bringing bad to worst, Blood. All we wanted was to talk."

Blood said, "Step back so I can see your face and talk then."

Quiet again. Then Cole said, "I don't trust you for that Blood."

"Why a course you don't. Recall that it was me assembled this army of men to put you in jeopardy. Recall it was me arranged this meeting at daybreak. It was me that brought the militia down on you, not just the second time but the first one too. Think on it hard Cole and you'll recall it was me not only advised but led the group of you to Lancaster to break that poor bastard from the jail there. As if it did him any good. How it strikes me, Isaac Cole, is that you're the last to speak of trust to me."

Another long silence. During which Blood thought Well nobody likes to hear the truth but goddamn I've done it now. There idn't any good way he can respond to that, not with all his fellows watching.

Cole rabbited. A hopeless helpless awkward zigzag toward his men. Blood took in a breath and raised his rifle halfway, let his eye settle on the scooting man, then brought the rifle the rest of the way to come to rest aimed at a blank point in the yard. Blood breathed out and at the edge of his vision saw Cole flounder into the space allotted him and Blood pulled the trigger and the hammer went down. In the moment before the loft filled with smoke Blood saw Cole stretch both hands over his head and drop the rifle he was carrying, his arms stretched as if to carry him away, a rending of his shirtback occurring also that lifted him for a moment as if his body would follow his arms and then he folded like a thing discarded and draped over the earth.

Blood already had the rifle down and was stretched low and flat himself when the men across the yard brought their weapons up and fired back. Many shot too fast and struck the outer logs of the building but a half-dozen shots came through the opening and as Blood had guessed busted holes in the shingle roof. A rain of froe-riven cedar-shingle splinters fell over him. He lay with his eyes shut. The chips fell against him soft as needles from the shingle-memory of the trees they came from. Even while they fell his hands were moving over the rifle, from pouches and back to the gun, reloading, still lying pressed flat. Lay right there and see what happens next. He opened his eyes.

The horses picked their way single file along the steep brook-trail, slick with a light freeze on the mossed boulders and hardpack mud of the trail. As they came down the final incline into the broad confluence with Perry Stream they heard again a single shot, muffled by the stream and the trees alongside the road but clear enough coming from downstream. The tavern. They heard also the return of fire, a volley of ragged firing. Then silence. Cooper was in the lead and he pulled his horse up and sat listening. When there were no more shots he turned in the saddle and said, "I guess we know who the one shot come from."

Sally said, "Let's ride down there." She kneed the bay around them. Cooper stretched and caught up the bridle of her horse. "Slow down girl," he said. "Let's consider a moment. What do you think, Fletcher? It sounded like a bunch, that last volley."

Fletcher said, "It did."

Sally swung her horse around out onto the road down along the stream. Fletcher kicked his chestnut up and Cooper came after. Then all three rode silent side by side. Quiet with their thoughts, private plans. But a party joined.

They went down the road. It was a pretty morning. The sun was up enough to raise a light steam from the stream and dapple in through the leaves, splashing bold color and cutting thin slantwise shafts across the road. Time to time they rode through one of those beams and were blinded a moment, blind and warmed at once. All three felt pitched, keen, and the horses read this through the rider's bodies and anticipation trembled and filled the horses as well.

They came upon the oxbow just above the tavern. It wasn't yet visible but the open land on the other side of the stream ran all the way down to the tavern and Sally could see the backside of the barn and somewhat closer the ruined garden plot. She reined in her horse and said, "This is a good spot to pause. Any farther and we'll be seen. But it's close enough I can tell what's going on. I been up and down this path all summer."

Fletcher said, "I hate the idear of leaving her here alone. We don't have the least notion of who's where. Or who might be coming along."

Sally said, "I'll be fine. I got the rifle and this horse can get me away from most anything I need to be saved from. But one thing you got to know, going in."

Fletcher said, "What's that?"

"Blood's tougher than all those fellers mobbed up, is my guess. But there's this also. There idn't nothing I seen makes me think that when Blood's in a corner he thinks about any skin but his own. Not anyone. You hear me?"

Fletcher said, "I already know that." He looked at her a long moment and then turned his horse from her and kneed it forward. He looked back once. She couldn't tell if he was looking at her or his brother.

Cooper said, "I got to go."

"Get along," she said.

"Sally," Cooper said.

"Go," she said. "I'll see you soon."

Two reports. One, then perhaps fifteen seconds later, another. The brothers were still in sight and Cooper turned in the saddle and looked once again at her. She raised her hand. A flat gesture, saying nothing. Signaling only she'd heard the rifle fire as well. She sat her horse in the middle of the trail and watched the brothers as they went slowly around the bend. At that point she guessed they had another minute, perhaps two before they came into view of the tavern—and the view of the men there. She turned the bay horse back up the trail to the head of the oxbow where the bank was steep on this side but the water was shallow enough for a ford over stippled rocks. She had to sit the horse at the bank-edge as it considered the descent and the water beyond. She was patient. She knew the horse would go. After a thought about it, he did.

*   *   *

The body of Cole lay slumped out in the brown wreck of the yard midway between the tavern and the streambank. The remaining men had retreated down for the shelter of the bank and the screen of brush. It was Peter Chase who first grasped the ineffectual angle from which they fired at the narrow gunport in the second story of the tavern. All they were doing was shooting holes in the roof. Proud of his thinking. He waded the stream to the far bank and found there a stout hemlock with good limbs for climbing and cover. He checked the charge of his long gun and set to climbing the tree, to bring himself level with the slit-opening of the tavern.

Blood lay where he was, watching the man climb the hemlock. Even though the climber kept as much as possible to the far side of the bole Blood was able to identify him. It didn't matter in that all were adversary now but Blood thought It's the right man for the job. It was a complicated bit of thought—admiration for the one who understood the mechanics of elevation along with a sense of rightness that it was the brother of the one Blood held most responsible for all this, more so even than Sheriff Hutchinson. Hutchinson was clever; Emil Chase had proved not to be. Blood considered it likely that with Cole dead and Peter Chase now climbing to what Blood already knew was his death, there was a good chance the others would just plain quit. If not, he guessed that a load of balls from the cannon might be all that was needed for their final conversion. He could imagine the havoc of terror the blast would bring to those crouched in the brush and bank-cover. Young trees would be stripped, chopped through, clods of earth would blister up and blind and smear the men hiding. It was all timing. And patience. Perhaps a half an hour at most, altogether. Then another hour of waiting and watching to make sure none remained for ambuscade. Which he doubted.

He admired Peter Chase as he climbed. The man was doing a good job, working his way up slow, keeping hid as well as he could. Blood wondered if Chase regretted his white blouse or if he'd even given it thought.

As Chase came near level Blood studied what lay directly in front of him. The sun was striking the front of the tavern now. So there was

a slender long bar of light just inside the gun port. Which meant Chase
would not be able to actually see him. Chase would be shooting blind.
So would select the middle of the port as the best bet. Blood wormed
slow to one side so he was lodged up tight against the swivel gun on
its crude carriage. He guessed where Chase would stop and raised his
rifle so there would be no last-moment flash of metal to alert the sharp-
shooter. It was hard to hold the rifle in place so he rested it, still up,
only awaiting final adjustment when Chase selected his spot. Then
he waited.

Chase found his site. A little high, Blood judged it. Blood took his
rifle firm against his shoulder. Chase had his own rifle rested over a
bough of the hemlock. But had to lean out to sight along it. He took a
long time doing this. Long enough so Blood wondered why he was
waiting to let the climber shoot first. And realized it was not only because he knew Chase had misjudged. But also to allow Chase that one
small moment to recognize his mistake.

The report. Splinters were torn up from floorboards near five feet
from where Blood lay. A puff of smoke drifted away from the hemlock.
When it was gone Blood sighted on the white shirt. He could see Chase's
face over the bough, peering toward the building. Then Blood let out
his breath and like laying his hand on a child's cheek pulled the trigger.
There was the flash in the pan and then the concussion. And smoke
around him as well. So he couldn't see Chase fall. But heard him. Blood
wondered if from within the dim recess of his redoubt that flash had
been visible to Peter Chase. He hoped so.

After she forded the stream she rode the bay at a hard trot in an angled
line to the back of the barn, keeping the barn between her and the yard
before the tavern, riding out away from the stream as well, riding quick
but watching all around her. As she went she heard the shot come from
the trees beyond the tavern, heard the return and saw briefly something
crashing from the big hemlock, a tumbling white weight that she realized was a man. Then was hidden by the barn. She pulled up and turned
the horse so she was looking not only at where she'd come but also the
streamside, where if any had seen her coming she guessed they would
appear. She doubted anyone was watching much of anything but the

tavern itself. It had been a considerable amount of shooting and that last shot assured her Blood was alive. Her as well as the swarm of men.

She tied the horse to a lone post behind the barn. Inside, the oxen were heaving and moaning in their stall. She took a moment she felt she didn't have and talked to the horse, running a hand over his neck up to his ears as she'd learned from Cooper, telling him to set tight, it would be all right, there wasn't anybody after him. Told him to wait right there for her. Then with the rifle held crossways against her breast she eased around the side of the barn. From here she could see the backside of the tavern and a slice of the yard before it. She could see a couple of horses tied and thrashing down in the shelter of the streambank and after peering a bit could make out a few men, white faces in the underbrush, all gazing away from her, all focused on the tavern. What she also saw was that the little window-shutter on the backroom that had been hers was open.

Then came the sharp clatter of hooves as Fletcher and Cooper came fast down the road across the stream. She guessed since the last shooting they'd been holding back, looking things over. Now they raced their horses down the road, both pressed low. The men along the stream swung around to watch them pass behind. One man raised his rifle to shoot but did not. Perhaps because the riders were moving too quickly, perhaps because the man recalled the position Blood held behind him. More likely, Sally guessed, none of the attackers knew the boys, might even assume they were help arriving. In any event the man lost his boldness and sank against the bank again.

The riders swung onto the river road, crossed the bridge and still at a hard gallop came into the tavern yard and pulled their horses to a churning stop. The horses moving back and forth as the riders swept the streambank now before them with their weapons, the boys both silent and grim and quick. The men remained crouched by the stream. It was all a development none could quickly grasp.

Cooper swung his horse so he half faced the tavern. Loud, his voice without waver, he cried, "Blood?"

There was no response.

Fletcher was reining his horse back and forth, the pistol up level with his chest, the short weapon held in such a way he could aim any direction quick.

Cooper cried, "Father?"

Then Blood spoke. From where she was Sally heard him plainly yet it seemed his voice was low, calm and intimate. He said, "You boys ride on. This idn't your affair."

"That idn't how we see it," Cooper called back.

Cooper turned his horse back toward the stream and rode forward. He spoke to the men crouched there. "You've denned the wrong fox, boys. He idn't the one you're after. He don't care. But he'll sting you bad. It looks like he already has."

One spoke. "How come you to know so much about it?"

Cooper said, "I know all I need. Of him. And of the rest of you too. That man Blood idn't the rot among you. Look to yourselves and leave him be."

"Is that right?" the one crouched asked. "He someone special to you, you know him so well?"

"You're goddamn right he is." Fletcher moving forward toward his brother.

Blood called, "Cooper. Fletcher. Both of you. Get back up in the yard. Get back toward the house." The boys were directly between Blood and the stream, their horses and the boys themselves obstacles, obstructions, leaving Blood ineffective.

This comprehension seemed to spring from the ground rather that emit solely from Blood. Fletcher jerked his horse back as men came out from the brush. But a group were along both sides of Cooper's horse before he could move. A half-dozen men either side. Grimed streaked faces, some bloodied or powder-blackened or both, turned up at him. Hands reaching up over him to hold him in place, hands over the bridle, hands taking the long rifle from him as if it were a gift he bestowed, the men keeping the horse aligned straight so any attempt by Blood would risk more the boy or the horse than any of them.

Fletcher was back twenty feet from his brother, out in the open, near the body of Cole. His horse fought to gain ground away from the dead man, either forward or back or sideways. Fletcher had the pistol swinging slow over the group of men. One of them grinned at him. He looked quick over his shoulder and saw he blocked his father still. Jerking steady with his bound hand, each jerk a painful cable to his shoulder, the axe swinging and the bit-edge raking his knuckles, he backed the horse some few feet away from his brother. Looked again and guessed his father now had clear range to the group.

It was quiet in the yard. The only sound the blowing of Fletcher's horse.

Sally crowded against the side of the barn, her fingers tight white gripping the rifle. Thinking if she rode in right then it could work for or against Cooper. Thinking she wasn't any good where she was. Trying for the nerve to run for the backside of the tavern, where she could work around the corner and be close enough to shoot. There would be ten, at most a dozen feet where men could see her run. She wasn't afraid of them shooting. She was afraid of losing her surprise. She was afraid of pressing the men who held Cooper. Her legs were trembling and aching with wanted action.

Fletcher feinted sideways with his horse, leveled the pistol at the man closest to him. "Let him go," he said. "Let him go."

From above Blood spoke. "Be quiet boy." Then in the same mild tone he said, "Let the boys go. Let them ride off. Once they're gone from sight I'll come walk out there."

One of the men said, "No."

Blood waited.

Fletcher moved his horse back another step. As if aware he was more danger to Cooper the closer he was.

The man spoke up again. "You walk out, Blood. With your hands empty and we'll let these boys ride as fast as they can. That's the best we'll give you Blood. There idn't another choice. It's not haggling we're after here. Not no more."

Cooper booted his horse hard. It had been shivering and sidestepping back and forth against the men holding it and the boots were all it needed. It lunged cruelly forward and Cooper jerked the reins free and harsh-turned the horse so men spilled away against its surge. Cooper called out his brother's name as his horse broke free of the men.

Fletcher brought the pistol to bear upon a man and fired. At the same time Blood fired from above, once with the rifle and then again with both pistols, firing and feeding the loaded pistol into his right hand and firing again. Two men were down unmoving and a third was crawling improbably toward the body of Cole, a dark smear of blood and urine staining the ground.

Cooper was partway to the road when he wheeled his horse. "Fletcher," he called. His brother was on the far side of the yard, away from the road. The attackers were retreating back into the streambank but were still between Fletcher and the road. Cooper called his brother again.

There came a shot from the retreating men and Cooper bent in the saddle, his torso flat against the crest of his horse's neck.

Sally broke then and ran, not even thinking of cover. Partway toward the tavern a man saw her coming, turned and fired at her and she veered for the back of the tavern.

Blood was reloading his rifle when he saw Cooper fall forward. The horse stopped, as if suddenly empty of command. Blood watched Fletcher kick his horse forward and ride toward his brother. The remaining men had formed into a tight group. Blood saw one raise a rifle toward the boys. He dropped his own half-charged rifle and dragged the pot of coals toward him and took up a fuse match, pressing the strip of twisted rope into the live coals, pushing hard for the sudden flare and dense smoke that would show the fuse was lighted. His hand was burning.

Cooper sat upright. He said, "Fletcher get Sally." The front of his blouse was a great ragged rose. He went off the horse sideways. When he fell the horse stood a moment and then turned and lowered its head to study the boy.

Blood roared. "No!" The fuse was beginning to faintly smoke and he took it from the pot and jammed it into the touch-hole of the swivel gun.

Fletcher jerked his horse around and charged upon the group of men, the axe up in his left hand.

Sally stepped from the corner and fired at the entire group, wanting to kill them all even as one raised his rifle and shot the charging boy out of the saddle. Fletcher driven back right off the horse that never paused but surged on. The axe swinging up a lazy slow arc in the air before dropping flat-bladed against the earth a scant useless dozen feet from where Fletcher lay. Again from the tavern the roar of Blood. This time not a denial or beseechment or whatever that first No had been but this time a simple awful anguish pure as the sound a soul might make forced from a body.

Then the cannon went off.

* * *

Sally stood a moment. The noise was unlike anything she'd ever heard. It struck the hills around and came back and back and back again. But saw only first Cooper and then Fletcher, over and over. She couldn't see where they lay in the mire of the yard. Just each going down from their horses. As if forever they would be struck from those horses. The cannon pulping the men across the yard was something she would only recall later, never clear enough for her satisfaction. Then she turned and ran for the back of the tavern.

There were still men moving. Some thrashing and others working their way toward the safety of the stream. The boys lay, one face up, the other down. And the ones uncountable, the ones Blood had not been able to see escape altogether as he fought to work in the bitter smoke filling the loft. His eyes ran water. Then he was up, draped over the hot gun, fighting it in its carriage to raise the angle a little so he could destroy the streamside and whoever hid there. Even as he did this he saw one man in midstream struggle onto a crazed horse and whip the horse across the stream and up the road. One getting away. His boys God-damnit. He jerked and prodded at the gun, forcing it loose in its carriage. Doing what the discharge could not. Moving it by a scant third of an inch. All he needed or wanted in this world. Or any other. His mouth was on fire and he spat out the burned-up match and set another in the pot of coals to light. Those boys rode in, boys coming for their death. And began to recharge the gun. Ripping open the seal on the powder cask, tearing the beeswaxed linen with his fingers. Dead trying to forestall his own dying. Breaking nails against the wood staves of the keg, his fingers bleeding. God damn those boys. A great charge this one would be, double the powder and double the load of musket balls. If it split the gun so be it. Dead in the yard below. He wanted to destroy everything he could see.

Not crying, her face dry and hard-set, she did not pause to reload the rifle but left it leaning against the logwall. Then reached and jumped and her fingers scraped the bottom of the shutter. Jumped again, this time as if it were the last thing she might ever do and caught the edge of the opening with first one hand and then the other. Lay hanging against the side of the building while she secured her grip. Working one hand at a time until she would tear the wall down before letting go. Then kicked with her legs against the walls until one foot found purchase against a log and she lifted and the other foot pressed sideways into a space between two other logs. Up once more and just like that she was peering into her old room. She got her arms through and then her head and shoulders. It was a tight fit. There was only one way and that was face-first and down. Eight feet to the rough floor. She wished the bed was under the window. And saw again the brothers going off their horses and cursed silent her own fear and squirmed her way in. There was a moment where her waist held her balance, exactly half in and half out. She reached for the floor below and gave a last squirm and went down.

It took her breath. Her left hand was in great pain and she'd struck her head hard enough so her vision jogged and floated a moment where she lay on the floor. But she was up, still unsteady but up. Her wrist was all right. It hurt but she could use it. For a moment she looked at the bed. The bearskin cover. Blood had been sleeping there. The room stank of dirt, the dirt of man, a sourness of decay.

She went into the kitchen and saw the hogshead against the door. Good. She had no thought of opening the house to the scum outside. This work was hers.

She stood quiet a moment. Above she could hear Blood moving, a hard rough sound as if he pushed himself about. The loft ladder was in place. She heard Blood talking to himself, a steady flow of bile and hatred, not words but some keening beyond language.

There was a fire in the hearth. A stack of firewood. She spread the fire with the poker, spread it so it came out onto the hearth. Then piled the firewood, all of it, evenly over the coals, each log set so there was space for air to draw through and build the flames and draft for the chimney. So the firewood trailed off the hearth and up against the walls either side. It began to catch but was too slow. She turned back to the room.

She took the stool and added it to the fire. Then the ladderback chair. The fire was gaining but still too slow. She turned to the table. There was a blanket roll, some weapon pouches, on the table. Blood had intended to leave. She reached and with one hard push cleared the table. It made a noise as everything struck the floor. She stood still.

Upstairs the crooning continued. She upended the table and let it down slowly so it rested against the fire. That was better. She studied it a moment. She thought This idn't going to be fast enough.

And saw Cooper again. The awful rose-smear of his blouse. His words Fletcher Get Sally. And saw Fletcher and the axe again, both somehow joined in her mind, a loathsome beauteous pinwheel in the air.

Upstairs the cannon went off again. Dirt sifted from the rafters and stung her eyes and she couldn't hear a thing. The sound so great it went through her as a wave. It seemed to her the walls trembled but it could have been her eyes. The fire collapsed a bit. It was all too slow. She thought He'll do it first, himself by accident, madness.

Overhead the keening rose to a moan, a curious sound—a jubilation— as if at last Blood had identified and extinguished all enemies. Each and every one. Almost, she thought, as if he were happy.

Without thinking she went forward and took up a stick of firewood, one burning well. She lifted it high over her shoulder and went to the ladder and using her free hand went up. Her head and shoulders followed the burning stick through the opening. Blood was lying over the top of the swivel gun as a man lies spent on a woman. His head turned away from her, turned to the narrow slit view outside. His head was nodding up and down in a crisp slapping motion, someway in time to the sound that came from him.

She spoke his name.

If he heard her there was no indication.

Her raised hand was burning. Just beyond Blood were the kegs of powder and shot he'd hauled up. She had spied this place before. She calculated her throw.

Her hand was burning.

She cried his name. This time loud, a harsh indictment of him. All of her condensed into the single word. Even as it came out of her she recognized it to be some uneven twin to his own song.

This time he heard. He turned slow and saw her. His face twisted and burned. An awful smile for her.

She threw the burning stick. It went away from her, turning over and over in the air, rising to strike the rafters where it angled down hard, away from the kegs, toward Blood himself. She did not wait to see it strike. She lifted her feet from the rung and held the sides of the ladder and went down fast. Now she was crying and her hand still burned, was only beginning to burn.

In the kitchen the wall behind the chimney was on fire. The smoke so thick she wrapped her head down into the crook of her arm. The smell there fear. And the death of all the place, all those who ever had entered, had even so much as passed by.

She went into her room, pausing to look at her hand—the pain so great she expected to see flame in the flesh. And then was floating. That room also a murk of smoke but she looked to the narrow high slit of fresh blue sky and lifted herself and floated toward it.

She was sprawled on the grass behind the tavern. Then she was up and running for the barn, reaching as she ran, snatching up the leaning empty rifle. Useless at the moment but she knew not to leave it. And the pain had left her. As if it would remain behind. A mystery and a wonder. Don't even think about it she told herself. Running.

Then the tavern exploded. The roof and loft and the fire was blown open to the richness of unimpeded air which the fire ate and towered and she was running toward a pair of shadows peeling away before her in the grass. Then the fire broke through into the storeroom and the entire building blew apart. Pieces of logs spinning through the air easy as swallows. Great splinters, white as flesh.

She was struck and went down. The grass back here frost burned but still green at the roots. Life itself. The smell and taste of the earth. Noontime of a fall day.

Postlude

The Year of Our Lord Eighteen Hundred & Ninety-Six

He was an early riser. He always had been but the women slept late and so what had been pleasant habit became compulsion: the desire for those few hours when he was alone in the world and might fashion it any way he liked. It didn't matter that he only had to suffer his way through breakfast and could escape to his office and then his rounds. Her silence, her implacable silence offered up as judgment upon him followed him throughout his days. Each day, each the same. As if she read through him, through the three-piece suit and the light phaeton and the matched pair of fancy gray driving horses, through the leather grip so respected by everyone else, respected and feared, which was an attitude he liked. It was not just his profession but a calling, a thing near holy. Other people saw it, others accorded respect to him. How she could deflate him with her silence was something of a mystery. There had never been the first unkind word between them. None even passed along from his wife, her daughter. And yet before the old woman he felt stripped, as if he were a boy dressed up in a man's suit. Not an impersonator so much as a thing not yet mature. A man with gray at his temples, a veteran of the Civil War.

A lovely morning in July. The house and gardens on the hillside above the lake outside of Geneva, high enough so he could stand on the broad front lawn and see the rooftops and steeples of the town. Or could turn to look straight before him to the broad width of Seneca Lake, this early a silver flashing surface of light waves with a broad swath of the rising sun reflected over the water, too bright to look at. From the town the lake stretched south twenty miles, widening only slightly. A finger of a lake, one of half a dozen that ran north to south across the ripe fertile band of western New York State. People spoke of the Finger Lakes as if they were simply lovely bodies of water there for the people to live around, to enjoy, to fish from or boat upon, to have summer cottages against their shores, to enjoy the moderation the water provided throughout all the seasons of the year, but every day after his morning office hours when he drove his team out on his rounds through the surrounding farm country—farms of richness and wealth, dairy and grain and orchards of all manner of fruit and the great vineyards that were strung on the temperate clay hillsides overlooking the lakes—every day of this he recalled exactly whose fingers these lakes represented. The hand of God laid down upon this land, a hand blessing all that lay around it, as if God had seen this land and loved it and wanted to impress upon it His love. No matter that Jonathon Astor knew the lakes were glaciated striations. For who can say how the hand of God moves?

Surely not he. Who had been a student of medicine when the war emptied the college and he ended up spending four years sawing limbs standing it seemed either in cold mud or under a canvas that accelerated the summer heat, his apron and arms stained with blood, the cauterizing iron held waiting by one young slightly wounded orderly after another, the iron an extension of his hand as were the saws. For the most part the men he did not disfigure were the ones he saw die, eaten slowly up from their wounds as their flesh turned yellow then green then brown then black as the gangrene ate past all efforts to check or halt it, so much so he could smell a man stretcher-borne and know if he would live one day or five. The other, lesser wounds, the ones he repaired, he did not praise himself for. For all but a fortunate few of those men were sent back into the campaigns that all gained names that seemed someway burnished but to him were only a long trough of blood and limbs and death and more than once, more times than he could count, some face peering up at him as he brought the saw down for that first awful rip, that face was a face he'd repaired someway the week before, the month before. Until he stopped looking at faces, no matter if the wounds were slight or mortal. All the faces of boys. Even the ones older than himself. Mere boys.

After the war he returned to the village of his youth. Two days after he returned he presented himself at the home of the doctor that had birthed him. Doctor Warren was a man in his sixties, with a wife a decade and a half younger and of so many tales told. And the late-born daughter, the single child. All Jonathon Astor wanted at that time was the remembered quietude of his youth. Which he knew he would never regain. But the old doctor was the place to start. Jonathon was not the sort of man to come back into his town and become a rival to anyone, even one gaining in age and with a reputation for silent work and little attention to late bills or any payment made at all. Especially such a man. At that time Jonathon cared nothing for the stories of the doctor's wife. He'd seen all that man can pitch against other men and rightly thought that every town needs something to talk about. And it was simple partnership he sought—there was no thought or intention or reason to expect any greater union. What both men understood was that each was vital to the other. Vital to the town and the outlying people. What the doctor saw was what the young man expected—a link, a succession. Not for himself so much as the people he served. And the young man, who was not so young as he liked to think and certainly not how others saw him, he also wanted that sense of continuity. That there were places and times where the world made sense. Where he might birth children and then later birth their own. Where he might even bring some calm to those same people he once birthed as they lay dying. He had no great notions of the measure of any one person's days. Old age and slow death were aberration and not the other way around. As the old man knew. So they made good partners.

What he hadn't counted on was the doctor's daughter. The daughter of their September, a child born to the doctor and his wife when they'd given up on children. So much younger than he that he hadn't considered her at all—a ragged child wearing out good clothes in rough play when he left for the war was how he recalled her. So was unprepared for the day just less than a month after he began working with her father when at the end of the day they had driven up to the house in the doctor's buggy, still discussing the farmwife who had gone mad and was speaking in tongues and eating earth and they sat in the yard before the cobblestone house as they determined to return to the remote farm again first thing in the morning. Then the younger man climbed down from the buggy to walk the mile into town where he stayed not at his parents' home but in a boardinghouse where he might stay awake as long as he liked reading journals and medical books, some even imported from Europe. He stepped from the buggy and bade the doctor a good evening and in the swift early autumn dusk turned to see her coming around the house, through the white painted gate that led to the back of the house where he'd never been but where he'd stretched his neck more than once to admire the flower gardens. And there she was.

Seventeen years old in an indigo dress with her red-blond hair worn loose and thick onto her shoulders and carrying a nosegay of cultivated deep purple asters and with rose-waxen light over her she stopped and looked at him and boldly said, "It's one thing to be serious and another to be gloomy. Put these in water and they'll cheer your room." And thrust the flowers at him and before he could respond beyond reddening she turned and went up the three stone steps and across the porch with its narrow columns and into the house. Without looking back.

Estelle Warren. Twice that fall he sent notes inviting her to attend social events and twice she responded, denying him without dismissing him. But also both times filling additional pages with her thoughts, a scattering of thoughts upon books she'd read or things she'd observed, notes of the everyday. As if some part of her turned to him even as she hesitated. Both times he went alone to the events and neither time was she there with someone else. He did not speak to her father of her and the doctor never mentioned his daughter and neither did his manner or treatment of the younger man change—toward favor or not—but remained constant, professional, occasionally ruminative over some diagnosis and always solicitous of the younger man's opinion. He'd not met the doctor's wife, had only twice glimpsed her from a distance and both times she was hurrying away, as on some errand of sudden and terrible urgency.

The following spring he opened his small hoard of savings and purchased a lapstrake catboat, a thing of great beauty and a craft of ways all unknown to him. He felt he'd taken a deep breath that would never be released again. But had spent portions of those long winter evenings regarding the long-since dried flowers and her brief message to him and concluded she was right. Was it a coincidence of the season that she gave him flowers that matched his name? He decided it could be but he could rightly guess Doctor Warren had at some time mentioned in passing the name of his new associate. What he pondered with greater gravity was her message to him. Even in doing so he guessed that he was failing her in some vital way. What he arrived at was that it lay only within his own hands and will to effect his future. So he bought the boat.

He paid for half a dozen lessons and then spent another month of evenings and weekends out alone on the water until he could handle the boat in all but the worst of weather. He had no desire or intention of being a foul-weather sailor. To sail, for him, meant relief from sullied things, past and present. He was not after testing himself but rather mastering a pleasure. It seemed enough.

In late June he sent a third note. He invited her nowhere but simply stated that he would call for her on Saturday afternoon at one-thirty and suggested she attire suitably for the water.

He rented a gig and was sweated through his shirt under his white suit when the horse trotted up the drive of the cobblestone house. He feared himself a fool but she was waiting on the porch, dressed also in white, with a broad-brimmed hat that tied under her chin. She did not smile but greeted him gravely and stepped up into the gig even as he was hurrying around the horse to assist her. When he came up beside her she looked down at him from the seat and smiled at him.

Estelle walked back and forth on the marina dock looking at the catboat and then turned to him and said, "She's beautiful."

Jonathon stepped down into the cockpit and reached a hand and this time she let him assist her onto the decking. Then she turned and said, "The word is, that you sail with a passion. Most every evening."

He said, "I guess I'm the talk of the town then."

"Oh no," she said. "I had to ask to find out what you were up to. What's her name?"

His throat was thick. Stowed earlier was a basket of lunch and bottles of fresh spring water and one daring bottle of wine hidden under the napkin lining of the basket. He wanted a swallow of the water. He said, "*Violet.*"

"Violet?"

"After the flowers. The color." He was shaking and half turned and bent to cast free the mooring lines, thinking if he could only get the boat underway, wondering if he would be able to sail at all or if they would wobble helpless and stranded.

"Of course," Estelle said. "Violet. People would've misunderstood Aster. Thinking yourself grand is what they'd have thought." She seated herself on the decking and lifted first one foot to her knee and then the other and removed her shoes. He was loosening the sheets and eyeing the pulleys to make sure all ran clear and the sail flapped loose against the mast. He took up the single paddle to push off from the dock. All the time seeing the undersides of her thighs as she snapped the lacings through the eyelets of her shoes. She dropped one shoe into the cockpit and went to work on the other and then looked up at him just as he was looking at her.

She said, "Do you care if I go barefoot?"

He reached for the tiller and begin to pull the sheet to tauten the mainsail and said, "I like to go barefoot myself, once I'm under way. It feels right, my feet against the boat, against the decking. And, if there's much breeze at all, water sprays in. So your shoes get wet anyway."

They were out away from the other docked and moored boats and he was letting the sail fill more and more. They began to move cross-wise to the wind toward the open water of the lake.

She said, "I don't care a thing about my shoes getting wet." And reached down and plucked them both up from the cockpit and held them in one hand, ankle-high white calfskin shoes. Her eyes on him, her eyes laughing but her face serious, as if she expected him to know her intentions, she swung the arm holding her shoes out over the catboat and dropped them into the water.

Now he smiled at her and pushed the tiller hard and brought the sheet in so the sail snapped tight as the boat came around into the wind. There was the brief lovely moment when the boat shuddered and then it leaped forward. Water began to sheer up both sides of the bow and all that lay ahead was the long expanse of lake water and both sides the gentle even-rising hills speeding by.

She reached and caught a side rail and with her other hand tore free the knot under her chin and her hat flew lost behind them. Her hair flailed her face. She called, "Oh my. Jonathon Astor. What're we doing?"

"Sailing," he called. "We're sailing."

Five years later they married, little more than a month after they buried her father on a cold but lovely spring day. Clouds in high fleets fleeing the sky. It was the day he first met her mother. A woman wrapped in a thick black shawl over somber old dark clothing. The woman would not take his offered hand and stood with dipped head through his brief burst of condolence and testimony. When he was done, Estelle beside him, he stood a long awkward moment in the silence that lay over all of them, off to the side the huge clump of townspeople and farmers come to bury their doctor. While waiting in the silence that fell after his outburst he had the strange thought that it was a true act of faith for so many to come, so many that trusted the man now dead and buried to keep them from the same fate. Then the woman raised her head and looked upon him. Her face lined and wet and shriven. She studied him, a gaze that ran into and through him. At the time he thought it was the circumstances. He felt Estelle beside him. He felt he was capable of anything. He even believed that was what the woman looking at him saw. So he bent and kissed her cheek. His lips had hardly swept her skin when she turned her face back down, away from him, denying him.

She did not attend the wedding. Which was not a wedding but a civil ceremony of official brevity and then followed by another ceremony also sparse in the church of his parents. Some measure of respect for the so recently dead father of the bride. He did not mind—he'd had his fill of spectacle. But wished it were otherwise for Estelle. Not that she indicated desire for anything otherwise. And by that time he knew her so well as to know that even if her father still lived this was how she'd have wanted it.

Should he have questioned their going from the church and quiet supper afterward to the cobblestone house? Could he have questioned it? Could he have asked his wife to leave her mother alone at such a time? It certainly wasn't about sex—they long since knew each fold and twist the other was capable of. It wasn't about privacy—the cobblestone was three stories of rooms of which they might take their choice—the mother slept alone now in the groundfloor bedroom—the room where she and her husband had always slept and since his death unchanged. But there was this as well—he wanted to live there. From most any point in Geneva a person might look out at the western ridge above the lake and see the house. It was the house of the doctor. So he happily drove his bride back to her house. Where he moved in with her.

Jonathon and Estelle failed also to produce children, the romping merry band of children that had filled his mind. It was not for want of trying. It was a mystery. She struck him as an exceptionally healthy young female in every respect and after several years he surreptitiously examined his own seed on a glass slide and there certainly was an amplitude of life striving beneath the eye he pressed to the eyepiece of the microscope. So they went along. It was not a question of failed pregnancies, of miscarriage. There just were none at all. And so over some years they determined without ever speaking directly of it that theirs would be lives twinned and nothing more, and oddly or not neither seemed sad over this, at least not to the other. In a way they both seemed to hold their youth. Although he would ponder sometimes, out riding the dusty roads of summer, the phaeton gliding behind the team, the story Estelle had told him, once and only once, of how her mother and father came together, and he would turn this over in his mind and wonder if it somehow fell through the woman, this lack of conception. And Jonathon Astor came to believe that this barrenness was a thing passed from mother to daughter, something of the blood, some fragility of constitution. As if his mother-in-law had exhausted in her one late bout the ability of the women of her line to produce children. An anomaly of biology but he'd seen his share of these. And it fit somehow with the tight caustic woman who unfailingly referred to him as Mister Astor as if she would not admit more than one doctor in her life. A woman who could not read nor write but managed her finances with no help and in secrecy. Not so much as if she were hoarding but as if she trusted no one. Although he carried the financial burden for everything that he could see, everything that the household and grounds consumed. The very house and grounds that were not even his but owned wholly by the old woman. Estelle would inherit these upon the woman's death and he knew Estelle was not the way her mother was. Still, he had as much pride as any man, and it was a bitter spot held deep within that while the people of the town might see him as a man outstanding and respected, under the roof that was not his own roof he felt always as if he were a vague nuisance.

And then, just as it had for Doctor Warren and his wife, what came was a single miracle child when he was forty-eight and Estelle five years younger—both well past the point of even the remotest hope. When in fact both were in the flush of having brought peace to their union and were not only content but sometimes watching parents struggling with their children and he so well acquainted with the frights, the terrors that children produced for parents, both somewhat relieved to be freed from all that. And then one evening in the quiet of their own room she turned to him and told him and even as she spoke all the chips and cogs of misstep and hesitation and oddity of the past weeks fell into place for him and he stood silent watching his wife until she laughed and told him his mouth was a flytrap.

Alexandra they named her. And that July morning when he wandered the grounds in his silent opening of the day he heard her piped five-year-old voice chasing after him, coming up from the gardens, calling him because she alone among the women rose early like himself. He turned his eyes from the splendor of the lake below and walked to the gate that led into the garden and waited. He did not open the gate but watched her, running up through the dew-wet grass, holding something, her hands cupped out before her, her legs long and feet bare and her hair light blond loose about her face as she ran to him, carrying some treasure, some discovery, some new bit or piece of the world that she was learning and still believed or behaved as if it had been fresh-made, as if the world had sprung into being for her alone. She'd seen him at the gate and cried, "Papa!"

Jonathon stood with his hands loose upon the picket tops of the gate watching her come and he could almost believe that she was correct; this ancient earth had been waiting all along for this creature to inhabit it. Now he could smell bacon and coffee and knew it would not be long, ten minutes perhaps before through a window Estelle would spy them and call for breakfast and he would sit once more across from the old woman and chat with his wife and wipe jam from his daughter's face. So he swung open the gate and went down on one knee, slowly, feeling the grit of his age in his joints and was swept with sadness—the almost certain knowledge that while he might live to see his child's children all odds were against it. He held himself steady with one hand on the gatepost until she was close and then flexed the muscles in his legs and opened both his arms toward her pell-mell run and said, "What is it, Xandra? What've you found?"

What she loved about the house were the windows. Great broad tall double hung windows that lined each room, each floor, that could be flung open to the summer air so that the house seemed nearly to float or, in cold or wet weather could be closed and she could stand and watch the weather just beyond the glass, often sliding down against that glass. The windows to her were the heart of the house and so seemed to her an ample and unchanging extension of her husband—the same lightness and security he took her into that first wet-soaked night years before when she opened her eyes and saw him leaning over her and knew she could entrust herself to him entirely. She did not consider herself fortunate or that it was luck; neither did she feel she'd earned it but simply that it came to her as a simple and extraordinary gift. As if the world had opened an otherwise closed hand and revealed itself to her. It was some time before she fully understood that her husband felt the same way—a solitary man eighteen years older than she whom the ladies of the town had given up for bachelorhood.

Perhaps it was the afternoon that he drove her out from their rented lodging in the town up onto the hillside where for an entire spring and summer men had been working to build this house, a house she knew nothing of until she first saw it that early autumn day. Just two years after meeting him. Married twenty-one of the months of those years. And through that spring and summer he'd kept the building of the house secret from her. So they rode up in his doctor's buggy and she saw the house rising out of the raw ground and what she saw first was not the view or the size of the house or the rudely laid-out gardens and raw plantings but the windows. She had a moment while the buggy was still moving where she wondered if she'd complained too much of the darkness of their rented lodging and then knew it was not so—that he simply knew she needed windows the same way he seemed to know everything else she needed. Not a bit of this did he feel obligated to provide. But rather offered to her because each knew that the accident that brought them together was too precious to ever be ignored. That both sought each in their own way, always, to honor. Life, they both knew, was accidental and fragile and delicate as breath. So he gave her windows. The house just a place to hold them. Before her feet were even on the ground she knew this. When she turned and met his gaze and the droopy smile that was his for her alone she had said, "Don't let them put shutters on."

And he had said, "There are none planned."

Years later after her daughter was born and she watched the child grow she made a determination, when Estelle was three, perhaps four, to allow her girl to grow up with as much freedom as possible, to abandon the notions of the times—of constraint and overbearing supervision—children as household creatures almost—and allow her the independence of her own mind. She insisted only on two things—education and manners. And even these she allowed the child to discover on her own as much as possible. Largely she was pleased with the results. It did not hurt, and she admitted this to herself, that Estelle was curious and cautious at once, that the girl's own nature seemed to preclude fashion or any overt fascination with decorum but was a proud bold girl of independent but not flaunting mind. She watched her daughter and wondered how much of this was her method of raising and how much just the nature of the girl. Oftentimes, watching her daughter grow to a woman, she could not help but wonder how different they truly were. If her own circumstances had allowed would she have been as wise as her child. She liked to think so. She believed her child was in a way a lovely second chance for her own life.

She knew Estelle would marry the young surgeon returned from the war before her daughter knew this. It was not, as she knew he believed, that she disliked him. It was that she distrusted other people and was honest enough to admit to herself that it was from fear of being found out—of being unearthed as the uneducated backward woman she believed herself to be. That at the pit of her soul she knew herself to be. She had entrusted herself to her husband and only to him. She could not do it again with another man, ever, in any way. It wasn't scorn she feared so much as having that pit opened wide within herself and taking her over. Which she always, each day of her life, feared might happen. She knew her will—and knew that will was not always enough safeguard against the mysterious workings of the world.

And yet the rot seemed to work within her anyway. She knew Jonathon Astor to be a good man and yet could not but keep him at a distance and within that distance she saw she diminished him. But she could not explain herself to him. She wished he understood her silence. But it was not something once in place to breach. Not some idle summer afternoon, not ever. If I could write, she thought, I'd leave him a letter for after my death. But it was not a letter she could dictate to anyone. Not even perhaps thoughts that could be arranged beyond the stream of emotional flow. So, she thought, he will never know. A thought largely free of distress. Most of life consists of not-knowing.

And then finally there came her granddaughter. So late as to be given up for by all as her own daughter had been. And who was the very image of her own mother. As she'd never seen or even guessed that her mother might've once been. But was unmistakable in the child. And again she thought I've been given something here. Something I never even thought I wanted and nothing that can be shared. For there was no one to share it with and no reason to do so. But still a gift. As if life would not quit but insisted on informing her over and again that whatever form she thought was settled upon was only one quivering instance, true and intact but merely a moment before another truth asserted itself. A blond-haired child with those wide and deep pale blue eyes, lashes so fine as to not exist at all. The past then was not passed and life not a line but a circle, one far wider and deeper than the simple round of birth to death. She loved this child and the child was also a torment to her memory.

And because of all this she recalled that man who allowed torment to eat all but the final hard stone of his soul. She held no regret for his death. But after so many years forgave him for the deaths of the others, his own children. She slept little these late days and often times in the small hours would let herself quiet from the house to go into the gardens under starlight and gaze down at the breadth of lake and allow herself those few tears that remained to her. She was not embarrassed by their scarcity—they were an abundance to her, each one rolling slow

seeping from her eyes was a bound-up fullness of all of her. It was a lovely
thing. And at that hour nothing she had to fear explaining to any other
person. Tears for the dead. Tears for the long-gone.

July afternoon, late day with the sun still high. Seated in the deep shade
of the porch that ran across the back of the house looking out over the
flowerbeds and rose gardens and arbors and terraces, the hammock
strung between sturdy English walnuts, the croquet course laid in a
flat area of close trimmed lawn, the hoops and flags slight wavering
beckonings for the temporarily suspended game. Below there, out of
sight was the vegetable garden. There were a pair of men who came
weekly to tend the yards and flowers, another who daily not only took
care of the carriage barn and horses and equipment but who just in the
last two years had been assigned the vegetable garden. When she could
no longer do the work, even the simplest of weeding and harvesting.
She was dependent now completely on others. Who did not do things
quite as she liked but close enough so she held back her sighs. The cost
of age. Seventy-four years old. But she was not helpless.

On her lap a wide shallow basket. On the porch floor a deeper basket. Nested in the basket on her lap was a bowl. She was shucking peas.
Lifting the fat pods one at a time from the lap basket and splitting the
pod with her thumbnail and raking out the peas into the bowl and then
with a slight lift that twitched in her lower back each time dropping
the empty pod into the basket on the floor. English peas although no
one called them that anymore. They had varietal names she could never
keep track of. It didn't matter. The world changed. She still feared the
gas lamps that burned clean and radiant at night. She missed her chamber pot. Thought it unnatural to walk in light from her bedroom in her
nightgown to the bathroom down the hall. The world was new. She was
shucking peas. It was the same old world. Her granddaughter sat in the
porch swing watching her.

"Nonnie?" The voice the hope of girlhood.

"Alexandra?" Looking up from the peas, letting her hands rest on
the sides of the basket.

"Sammie in the barn had kittens."

"Did she?"

"She did. Five." The girl paused and then rushed into it. "I was thinking I'd like one for my own. My very own."

"Well now. I'd think you'd have to ask your mother." Knowing
where this was going.

"I already did."

"And?"

"She said barn cats are for the barn. They keep the mice down. She
said a kitten in the house would just want to keep going back to the barn
and that I should just play with them out there."

The old woman nodded. She said, "Wouldn't that be enough?"

"Oh Nonnie. I want one all for my own. It wouldn't want to go back
to the barn. Not if it lived with me. And I'd take care of it, I would."

"You told your mother that?"

"I did. But she said she wasn't sure I was old enough. But I am. I am."

"Umm." The old woman was silent and the little girl was also, waiting, knowing what hung in the balance of that silence. After a bit the
woman prodded her hand in the remaining peas and studied them.
Then she looked up at the girl.

She said, "Do you have one picked out special?"

The girl squirmed on the swing and it rocked gently. "I think so.
There's two I like for sure."

"Well now. It has to be a special one. One that you take into your
heart. Maybe you should go play with them and see if either one strikes
you that way."

The girl came off the swing and stood before her grandmother. "And
Mama?"

The woman nodded. "She has the last say. But I'll talk to her."

The little girl turned and ran down the steps onto the lawn, cutting to run around the side of the house to the gate that opened onto
the drive and the barn beyond. Floating back came her voice. "Thank
you, Nonnie."

Out loud, but far from the girl's hearing the woman said, "A little
girl should have a kitten."

She sat a time still resting. Such labor, those peas. Take me quick was
what she thought. Not to linger. Another year at most if she kept failing like this. Her desire such a puny thing before whatever design was
assigned to her. She wished she had more courage. The courage to face

boldly whatever it was came her way. To not fear it if it happened to be long slow years of enfeeblement. And then realized she did have that courage. Just because it wasn't what she wanted didn't mean she couldn't turn her face directly into it if that's what was called for.

She'd ridden five days and nights without stopping except to water the horse and drink herself although it was a terrible job getting off and on the horse and times she'd pause to let the horse crop late-season grass but she refused to stop, to talk with people, to buy food. Something in her back was wrong from when she'd been knocked flat and breathless. It hurt to ride but the idea of stopping was worse and so she did not halt but let the big bay horse find the way and when she did stop for water the horse seemed to know she was his charge and so would stand easy while she fought to remount. At night working their way slowly along roads through the dark with dogs coming from farmyards to howl their passing and days also they went slow as she felt the horse slowly failing beneath her but he'd stopped eating as if his own memory prodded him on. South and westward across Vermont and then crossing into New York State near Whitehall and through the rough farmland little better than where she'd come from and then out into the broad wide valley of the Mohawk, following that river and then south and west again onto the turnpike running alongside the Canal. At dusk on the fifth day in a rainstorm she came into the streets of Geneva with her vision fluttering and the horse also fluttering each step forward and she recalled people stepping away from her as she came on, recalled watching them and wondering what was the matter with them and then she went down. Or the horse went down. Or both together. Later, she liked to think it was both together, that they crumbled at the same time.

Later, when she was awake again, under the care of the man she would marry sooner than she would've believed at the time, she asked about the horse and was told it had died. It was with this news that she pushed up in the bed against the pain that encased her as a sheath and told this quiet kind man everything about herself she would ever tell another soul. Which was not all, not quite, but all she would give of herself to another. And he stood listening to her, not insisting she lie back, or rest, or wait, or any of the platitudes he might've offered but instead listened to her telling as if he knew it was the only time he would hear even this much. When she was done she slept three days and when she woke recalled her telling and watched him as he tended her to see if he would raise the questions he might have, that he must have. But he did not. She knew it had not been a fever-dream. And so came the first understanding of the trust that would absorb her as certainly as the pain had so recently. That she would give herself over to. Because it was either that or keep riding and she'd ridden one horse to death and would not do the same to another. At the time she thought There's an abundance of ways that life settles itself. She had never changed her mind about that.

So. A girl would have a kitten. She could do that much. She rocked in her porch chair a bit; her gaze soft off into the July afternoon. Just late enough so the shadows from the house and trees were beginning to spread out. Still hot but there was a breeze and she was comfortable. She thought I will not flinch, not before anything. She regarded the basket of peas. Half-done. Half to be shelled. Sweet new peas for dinner. She could smell a chicken roasting, the smell lifting from her lovely windows. She held plentitude. But the work before her. She lifted her hands from the basket-edge and studied them. Old spotted hands worn thin like winter stems. The one with the hard purple scar across the palm and insides of its fingers. The other just an old hand. She buried them back into the peas and let them rest there a moment. A job to be done. She took up a pod and split it and raked out the peas into the bowl, discarded the casing and then dipped her hands again for another pod. Her hands found the rhythm. She lifted her eyes from the job. A soft gaze far out beyond the gardens. Her hands did not need her eyes. Her eyes could see anything they wanted to. Her hands knew the work. They went on.